Disclaimer

This book is a work of fiction. Names, characters, organizations, places and events other than those clearly in the public domain, are the product of the author's imagination. Any resemblances to actual persons are purely coincidental.

No part of this publication may be reproduced, stored in any retrieval system, or transmitted in any form, or by any means, electronic, photocopying, recording or otherwise without the prior written consent of the author.

Acknowledgement

I would like to thank Mary Brewer for her encouragement and helping with the editing of this book.

The front and rear covers were provided by the extraordinary artist Quyen Lee, a resident of Ho Chi Minh City in Vietnam. To view additional work by Mr. Lee or to contact him please view his Face book page.

Table of Contents

Disclaimer iii

Acknowledgement v

Introduction...ix

Chapter 1   Cash Monkey 1

Chapter 2   Seven Months Earlier 11

Chapter 3   Recondo School 21

Chapter 4   You Bet Your Life 31

Chapter 5   This Should Have Been Easy 39

Chapter 6   The Final Exam 51

Chapter 7   Jump School 61

Chapter 8   Forms And Shots 71

Chapter 9   Camp Kaboom 79

Chapter 10   Better Than Us 89

Chapter 11   First Blood...99

Chapter 12   People Are Strange 109

Chapter 13   Into The Dark Kingdom 121

Chapter 14   Hurry Up And Wait 133

Chapter 15   Rescue And Reward 143

Chapter 16   A Question Of Value 153

Chapter 17   Vung Tau 165

Chapter 18   A Chance Encounter...175

Chapter 19   The Second Day 187

Chapter 20   The Natives Are Restless 197

Chapter 21   Run Through The Jungle 205

Chapter 22   A Long Scary Night 215

Chapter 23   Lights And Whistles 227

Chapter 24   Hoc Minh 239

Chapter 25   The Dog Bone 249

Chapter 26   Bombs And Boredom 259

Chapter 27   The Nick Name 269

Chapter 28   It Couldn't Get Any Worse....................................277

Chapter 29   But It Did Get Worse..287

Chapter 30   One If By Land..299

Chapter 31   The Bug Out...309

Chapter 32   Thunder And Foster's..321

Chapter 33   Meet Mr. Black 333

Chapter 34   Shambala 343

Chapter 35   The Kingdom Of Laos 355

Chapter 36   Skull People 365

Chapter 37   The Lost Village 377

Introduction

This is my third Vietnam war novel and my most ambitious. It continues where The Hobo Woods ended. It is meant to be a standalone novel but you will gain additional character insight if you read my first two books.

It is set in early 1970 after the election of President Nixon. His political survival depends on his promise to end the war in Vietnam. He has begun the withdrawal of American troops from Vietnam and the policy of Vietnamization. The number of United States soldiers has gone from a high of 536,100 in 1968 to 234,600 in 1970, a fifty-six percent reduction. The United States no longer wants to commit to large scale military operations. The South Vietnam army is required to take the lead role in combat operations.

Not since the Civil War has the country been so divided. College campus' are wracked by protests against the war and large cities across the country are besieged by civil rights demonstrations. Racial strife appears in the enlisted ranks and drug use increases amongst the troops. The United States continues to support the largely unpopular, corrupt, Catholic government in Saigon. The majority Buddhist population begins to demonstrate against the government. Saigon becomes a city of intrigue with rumors of coups. The Paris peace talks are stalled and Nixon grows increasingly impatient with the North Vietnamese.

In Cambodia, the Ho Chi Minh trail had largely been replaced by the Sihanouk trail as Prince Sihanouk allows the North Vietnamese to use the deep water port of Sihanoukville to bring weaponry and supplies in from ships sailing out of China. The North Vietnamese then transported the weapons the short distance to the border of South Vietnam without fear of U.S. interference. With clandestine American backing General Lon Nol disposed Prince Sihanouk early in 1970 and installed a anti-communist government friendly to the United States, Lon Nol attempted to dislodge the North Vietnamese from their sanctuaries along the eastern Cambodian border with South Vietnam. His inexperienced army was no match for the battle-hardened North Vietnamese troops. It was then the South Vietnamese made several large military incursions into the eastern border regions of Cambodia. Led by Lieutenant General Do Cao Tri, with American air support and advisers, the South Vietnamese were quite successful. The North Vietnamese soldiers abandoned tons of supplies and fled deeper into Cambodia. Even with their initial success, it is obvious to anyone with combat experience that the South Vietnamese would never be able to defeat The North Vietnamese Army without continued American support.

Under this backdrop the story begins. One thing is certain, no American soldier wants to be the last man to die in Vietnam.

CHAPTER 1

Cash Monkey

Holt was twenty two years old. He was sitting in a ramshackle bar several miles east of the Cambodian border just outside of base camp. He sat at the end of the bar occupying himself by making concentric circles with his bottle of beer in the condensation pooled on the bar. His face was wreathed in smoke from his Marlboro cigarette.

Behind him were several tables filled with Chinese Nung mercenaries playing Mahjong. They were slapping ivory carved tiles onto a table top crowded with beer bottles and overflowing ashtrays. They were loud, and Holt couldn't tell if they were arguing or just having fun.

"Hey Devil, you come play with us. Bring your money over here," said a mercenary he knew as Sergeant Kang.

Holt stared at their reflection in the clouded, smoky mirror behind the bar. He turned to face them. "Hey, do you assholes understand English?"

Kang held up his hand with his index finger and thumb close together. "Just Ti Ti, very little."

"You understand when it's time to eat, and you certainly understand when it's payday."

Kang said something to his companions Holt couldn't understand. Their faces clouded and they stared back at Holt.

"Tell me why I should play a game I don't understand. It would be easier if I just gave you my money."

"Yes. That good. You give us your money."

"How about you just go fuck yourself instead. You understand that?"

1

Kang started to stand but his friends pulled him back into his seat. "You bad man, Devil. You number ten."

Holt caught the attention of the slim Vietnamese girl who waited tables.

"Baby San, get a round of beers for my Chinese friends."

As the girl busied herself at the cooler, the owner of the bar came through the swinging saloon doors from the kitchen. Her long, shining black hair was pulled into a pony tail on top of her head. A small Rhesus Macaque monkey rode atop her shoulder. As she neared the bar, she extended her arm and the monkey scurried down. The monkey wore green fatigue pants and a small green beret. He began tugging at her apron. She pushed him away but finally relented and took an eye patch from her pocket and gave it to him. He expertly fitted the eye patch over his right eye. Throughout the day he moved the patch from one eye to the other.

"Why does he wear an eye patch?" Holt asked.

"I never ask him. He's monkey." she said without further explanation. She took out a cigarette and Holt leaned across the bar to light it. The monkey extended its hand for a cigarette and she slapped it away.

"I'm trying to get him to quit. He's too small. He coughs when he smokes." She said something in Vietnamese and he sulked away to his chair, a small, intricately carved, teak throne.

Behind him, Kang thanked him for the beers. Holt extended his middle finger without turning around. The Chinese laughed.

"Why do you bother with them? They don't like you."

"I come and bother you and you don't like me either. Just trying to make friends."

"I like you okay, maybe. They fear you. They think you a demon. A devil man."

"Fear might be better than like. I'm okay if they fear me. Why do they fear me?"

"Your face. They say you can't be killed although many have tried. You've killed beau coup VC. VC put a bounty on you."

Holt lifted his finger to touch the scars on his face. "The VC have bounties on all soldiers."

"You different. Five thousand dollars for your head."

"You mean they want to cut off my head?"

"That way they know for sure you dead."

"I've been told the scars make me look sexy."

"They make you look like a devil man."

Two more Americans walked into the bar. They were dressed like Holt, wearing tiger striped fatigues and green berets. They removed their hats and greeted Mama San. The monkey, whose name was Cash, got two beers from the waitress and walked the bar to the waiting soldiers. He set the beers in front of them and held out his hand. The soldiers laughed and paid him with Military Payment Certificates, MPC's, the colorful Monopoly-like money the soldiers used in Vietnam. Cash hurried back to Mama San and handed her the bills. She rewarded him with a small, green banana.

"Does he get a banana every time he brings a beer?"

"No. Too many banana's and he shits himself. The girl doesn't like changing his diaper."

"He wears a diaper?"

"He does. He's embarrassed by it. That's why he wears pants."

The Chinese were getting loud so Mama San yelled at them. "Chinese are disgusting. They're nothing but flat faced dogs." With that she barked at them and they started barking back until she shouted something which silenced them.

Some South Vietnamese Rangers entered the bar and took tables away from the mercenaries. They too were dressed in the ubiquitous tiger striped fatigues, although their fatigues were tailored tight to their slender bodies. Cash ran down the bar, he hissed at the Vietnamese, and spat on the floor. The Rangers hollered at him until Mama San silenced them by slapping down on the bar and glaring at them. As Cash walked back to his chair, he picked up a bill from the American soldiers and stuffed it into his pocket.

Holt tipped back his beer and finished it. Cash brought him a new one and waited. Holt handed him a bill and said, "I need change with that."

"No change. He not that smart. He just monkey."

"Mama San, what's your name?"

"Why?"

"Calling you Mama San is awkward."

"My name not important."

"Mama San, you take me back to your room and love me long time." "You getting drunk. You just boy. Mama San needs man, a big man,"
she said as she held her hands apart lewdly.

"No, for real. I stay in Vietnam with you. Give you many Baby San. We'll be happy."

"Vietnam not happy. We're a small, tired country that everyone wants. First China comes and fight. Then the French. Next we fight Japanese and then the French again. Now you Americans come and want to fight so we be free. Vietnam always free. We always fight to stay free. That's all we do is fight. You should leave us alone, then we'll be free."

Holt picked up his cigarettes, but the pack was empty. He searched his pockets for another pack. "Mama San, do you have Marlboro?

She went to a counter behind the bar and opened a drawer. "Five dollar."

"You must be crazy. I can buy a whole carton for two dollars."

"Then go buy them. Five dollar."

Holt leaned back in his chair.

"Alright, 'cause I like you, two dollar."

Okay. Two dollars. You're robbing me."

She said something to Cash and held up two fingers. Cash sifted through Holt's money. He selected two bills and handed them to Mama San. He took an extra bill and put it in his pocket. Holt started to object.

"You tip him. He work hard. If girl brought you cigarettes, you'd tip her, right?"

"That's cause she's cute."

"She just baby. She my daughter. No boom boom girl. You behave. You want boom boom, you go to massage parlor. Here, you act nice," she said, banging the bar.

Holt was chastened and apologized.

"Americans think all Vietnamese women prostitutes. Men are all pigs."

Cash came over to Holt and picked up a cigarette. Mama San said something and he put it back. He went to his chair sulking. "Stupid monkey," she said.

"Mama San, how do you know the VC have a bounty on me? Do you talk to the VC."

She just shrugged her shoulders. "You have curfew. Soon, you all go back to your camp for the night. VC have no curfew."

"Does the Major know this?"

"Everybody talks to everybody. We all friends here. Mama's bar is neutral, like Sweden. Everyone comes to Mama's bar."

"Remind to watch what I say from now on."

"You just sergeant. You know nothing," she quickly changed the subject. "You have girl back home."

"No. Vietnam is my home. You be my girl. How old are you?"

"How old you think I am?"

Holt studied her smooth face. "You could be anywhere from twenty to fifty. I have no idea. It's like you Vietnamese women don't age."

"I'm too old for you. You need young girl. Stay in Vietnam and in two years you marry my daughter. She good girl, no boom boom."

Holt looked at the girl. She had long black hair tied back in a pony tail and wore a white blouse and loose fitting black, pajama pants.

"She's very pretty. You must be proud of her."

"She's a good girl. Works hard and doesn't complain."

"She has nice little titties."

Mama San reached and pinched Holt's ear until he squealed, "You be nice."

"Where's your husband?"

"Dead. He was ARVN captain. Stupid man, go fight with Marines up at Dak To. I tell him stay here. I told him, I could buy him an exemption. But he want to fight and now he dead and now I all alone."

Cash sat next to Holt and started picking at the hairs on his arm.

"He like you. He no like anyone. Chinese want to eat him. Vietnamese want to eat him. He knows that you his friend."

When he was done grooming Holt's arm he looked down at Holt's money expectantly. Holt gave him a single and Cash left happily.

"What does he do with all his money. Does he have a girlfriend?"

"If he wants to eat he has to pay. What do you Americans say? No free ride."

Holt stretched and got up from chair. "I have to go back. Maybe I see you tomorrow?"

"Maybe. Maybe you go out in jungle and die. Don't forget, VC want your head. If I see you again, I'll be glad. If you die, I'll be sad."

"Shit. At least someone will be sad. See you later, Mama."

"Wait, do me favor." Mama San dug through the pockets of her apron and extracted a envelope. "Please, you give this to your big man."

"Big man?"

"Yes, your big man, man in charge."

"The Major?"

"Yes, him."

Holt examined the envelope. "Sure, as soon as I can. I'll have to find him. I don't usually hang out with officers."

As Holt walked towards the door he stopped at the two Americans. "I heard you two bozos were dead; killed on your last recon?" "We'll still be here long after they find your bones picked clean by the vultures in the A Shau valley."

"That's why I believed them when they said you were killed. Neither one of you assholes know how to read a map. The A Shau is five hundred miles north."

"Give or take," slurred the one soldier, obviously drunk.

"Hey, Mama San, buy these two a beer and put it on my tab. They're going to die tomorrow," Holt said.

"Hey man, don't even kid around like that."

"You're right, I apologize. You're both to pretty to die here."

"That's what your mother said last night while we were tag teaming her."

Mama San hollered after Holt, "Come back! You have no tab. If you die, who pay your bill?"

Holt left the bar and turned left past the tailor shop. He turned left again onto the main camp road. He passed through the first ring of barbed wire and through the camp gates which were guarded by two sleepy Chinese Nung soldiers. The outer ring of the camp housed the Montagnard mercenaries. They lived in a combination of bunkers and tents. Past them was a second series of barbed wire pits and fences and another entrance gate. The second ring was

6

home to the South Vietnamese Rangers and their families and their American advisers. Cooking smells hung in the humid air. The third ring was German razor wire and designated the American compound. Here, housed in deep concrete bunkers and sand bagged tents, lived a odd assortment of mismatched units.

There was a section for Army engineers responsible for various construction projects. Another area, marked off limits, housed a unit of civilians believed to be CIA employees. Next to it was a deep cement bunker, bristling with various antenna's that was manned by Air force personal. The Air force guys were seldom seen and rotated assignments on a four week schedule. Next, in the center of camp was the Special Forces compound. There was a large medical tent and mess hall area on either side of a large concrete bunker dug into the ground. This was the tactical operations command, TOC, where the recon patrols were run from. It too had a wide array of antennas on top of it. The whole American compound was ringed with bunkers built out on the Conex shipping containers and layered with sandbags. Over eighty five containers were used in the construction of the camp. The containers were interconnected by four foot deep trenches. In fact, trenches ran throughout the camp in a bewildering maze and connected each location. Four large mortar pits housed the large 81 millimeter mortars at each point of the compass. To the north was the helipad and to the south were the barracks tents for a company of American Infantry that rotated on a thirty-day basis. Currently, the infantry was from the twenty fifth infantry division. The infantry manned the perimeter bunkers and the twelve foot high guard towers at each corner of the camp. There were latrines and piss tubes scattered throughout the camp. The stench of burning shit hung over the camp.

Holt walked to the TOC bunker and down the wide wooden stairs to a four inch thick metal door which was open. The interior of the bunker was a single large room with a pitted cement floor and cider block walls. Overhead were large six-by-six timbers topped with perforated metal plate. On top of the metal plate were four feet of concrete and an additional four feet of sandbags. The room was divided by eight-by-eight posts supporting the roof.

The left wall housed tables and shelves holding an assortment of radios and was manned twenty four hours a day. Against the back wall, large scale maps covered the surface. In front of the wall was a plywood table covered by assorted maps and ringed binders. There were tables and chairs scattered about the room. The bunker was lit by strings of bare sixty watt bulbs powered by an enormous generator maintained by the engineers. At some point, someone had strung Christmas lights in the bunker and they were never taken down. It gave the bunker a strange, festive appearance. The entire room smelled of sweat, coffee, and cigarettes.

Holt stood at the entrance letting his eyes adjust to the interior gloom. He finally saw First Sergeant Banter. "Hey, Top. I was down at Mama San's bar—"

"Why do you go to that rat hole? We have a perfectly good club here on base."

"I like hanging out with the natives. Soak in the local color and all that shit. Anyway, as I was leaving Mama San gave me this, said I should give it to the big man," he said, as he handed over the envelope.

As the First Sergeant started to rip open the envelope Holt said, "She said it was for the big man. I assumed she meant the Major."

"The Major ain't here. Holt, who runs this camp?"

"You do, Top," he said sensing he had made a mistake.

"God damn, I do. If I ain't the big man, who the fuck is?"

"My mistake, Top. Sorry."

The First Sergeant extracted a piece of folded paper and spread it out on the table.

Holt looked down at it. "It's a map. Right?" he stared at it some more. "Holy shit, it's a map of our camp."

"Be quiet. Red, get over here," he said calling to Sergeant First Class. Brown, Holt's Team Leader. "Take a look at this."

Sergeant Brown was a tall, Texan with a sunburned face and a shaved head. He stood two inches taller than Top who was six foot one.

Sergeant Brown studied the map as he stroked his big, bushy mustache. He turned the map and oriented it to the compass. "This is good. It's damn near perfect. Where did you get it?"

"Duyen gave it to Holt."

"Who's Duyen," asked Holt.

"Mama San, that's her given name."

"How did she get it?"

Banter looked at Brown who shrugged.

"Sergeant Holt, what I'm about to tell you doesn't leave this room. Duyen provides us with information from time to time. We give her some harmless stuff that she passes on to the gooks."

"Is she a spy?"

"No. More like a conduit of information. This map is another level of info. Did she say where she got it?"

"No."

"Maybe the fucking gooks are planning an attack against the base.

They got just about every detail down right."

"I thought we never got attacked," said Holt.

"Every once in awhile, they probe the outer perimeter. We get mortared and rocketed every night, but nothing very serious. But this map," he said tapping the drawing, "is something else. You say nothing to Duyen about this. Not one fucking word. You keep this to yourself or you could get her killed."

"Not a word, Top. But who could have drawn it?"

"Fuck, every shit burner, hooch maid, and KP who works here probably doubles as a VC or NVA informant. They're ours during the day but at night, well, that's another story. Alright Holt, you're dismissed. And remember, don't say anything about this to anybody."

Top folded the map and walked over to the radios, leaving Holt alone with Sergeant Brown.

"Red, can I ask you a question? Mama San, I mean, Duyen, told me the NVA has a bounty on my head."

"The Green Berets all have bounty's on them, not just you."

"But she said they want my fucking head on a pike."

"Yeah, I heard about that. It's your face. They think you're a demon. They say you walked into the valley of death and came back as death itself." he paused and lit a cigarette. "I was going to tell you but I didn't want to spook you. It's no big deal. These gooks are superstitious. They believe all sorts of crazy shit. I mean, you do look pretty fucking grim. Take it as a compliment."

"It's my fucking head. I'm kind of attached to it."

"That's why we never allow ourselves to be captured. You save the last bullet for yourself. Right? Get captured and they will fuck you up. Hell, that way if they cut off your head, you'll already be dead."

Holt sighed. "Thanks for the advice. It's comforting."

CHAPTER 2

Seven Months Earlier

A pimply face clerk entered the sergeant's room uneasily. He looked around and saw Holt. "Are you Sergeant Holt?"

"Who's asking?"

"The CO wants to see Holt ASAP."

"I'm Holt. Tell him I'm getting dressed and I'll be there in ten minutes."

"He said ASAP."

"I just took my first shower in two months. Do you think he wants me to come to his office in the nude? Ten minutes, asshole."

Holt rubbed a towel across his head and worked some Brylcreem into his hair and tried to tame his hair into a semblance of flatness. Satisfied he had done the best he could, he pulled on a set of clean fatigues and slipped into some Ho Chi Minh sandals. He put on his shoulder holster containing a Colt 1911 forty five automatic pistol and found a clean boonie hat.

As he started out the room one of the other sergeant whistled at him. "Look all you want but I'm saving myself for true love."

"True love costs five dollars at the steam baths. And that's only for a short time. There is no love in Vietnam."

Holt pushed through the screen door and walked down the boardwalk to the Captain's office. He held his breath as he walked past the piss tubes.

He entered the orderly room and was pointed to a chair. "I'll let the Captain know you're here," said a clerk.

After a few minutes he was told the Captain would see him.

Holt walked past the clerks, knocked on the Captain's open door, and entered his office. Sitting behind his desk was the company commander of

Delta Company, Captain Robert Jung. Sitting across from him was Special Forces Master Sergeant Soujac. He had met the sergeant once before when he visited him in the hospital where Holt was recovering from multiple wounds.

"Have a seat Sergeant. You can smoke if you want. Give me a minute to examine your 201 file."

Holt pulled a cigarette from his pocket and Sergeant Soujac leaned towards him with a battered Zippo to light it. Holt nodded his thanks. Captain Jung closed Holt's file, looked at sergeant Soujac and said, "Paul, do you want to start."

"Do you remember our conversation at the hospital?" Holt nodded. "Good. You have about thirty days left on your enlistment. Is that correct?" Again, Holt nodded. "From time to time, the Special Forces have found themselves in a position where we need more men then can provided through the normal recruitment process. It started in 1957 and a few times since then. We identify certain experienced individuals, such as yourself, who would be suitable candidates for entry into the Special Forces on a accelerated training schedule. Right now, in mid 1968, we find ourselves in dire straits. Only about twenty percent of our group has combat experience. About twenty five percent are not even Special Forces qualified. Ten percent are not parachute qualified. You've been in Vietnam almost two years and have extensive combat and leadership experience. You've proven yourself time and time again under fire in some of most horrific combat imaginable. You've repeatedly demonstrated your courage, endurance, and leadership abilities. That's something we can't train you for. You either have that or you don't. You are a proven commodity. Your combat experience far exceeds anything we do in training. On your last mission, you became separated from your unit and evaded the enemy for three days before you found your way back. We could never train you for something like that. You just need your skills honed a bit. What I'm proposing is a once-in-a- lifetime chance to join the most elite organization in the Army. Are you interested?"

Holt sat chewing on his thumb nail. His heart was beating hard. He scratched his head. "What would I have to do?"

"My understanding is that you are considering re-enlisting."

"I was thinking about it, but only if I could remain in Vietnam."

"That's no problem, that's where you're needed. You would re-enlist and from here you would proceed up to Nha Trang. In April, we established the Recondo school. It's a condensed three week course to establish, or, in your case, to certify the skills necessary for the Special Forces. Upon graduation from Recondo school, you'll go through jump training either at Nha Trang or at Udorn Air Force base in Thailand. Once you have your wings, you'll get a final evaluation, and once accepted you'll be assigned to a Long Range Reconnaissance Ranger unit for thirty days of additional training and that's it. You'll be done and become a fully fledged member of the Green Berets."

"It seems there's a lot of potential for failure and if I do, I'll be stuck in the Army as a line dog for three more years."

Soujac tapped his finger on the arm of his chair. He got a cigarette and offered one to Holt. "You're not going to fail. It's not in you to fail. I'll be with you every step of the way. I'll go one farther, if you do fail or if you want to quit, your enlistment will be null and void. You can return to civilian life. I can't do better than that."

Holt looked at Jung. "What's your opinion Captain?"

The Captain opened up Holt's file and ran his finger down a page. "Let's see. You've been wounded five times and have five Purple Hearts, you been awarded four Bronze Stars, three for Valor. You have a Silver Star and finally a Distinguished Service Medal. What can you possibly do in your life that will match that? Are you willing to waste all this to return to a job you'll end up hating? You have a high school education. What type of work are you even qualified for? You aren't meant for a life of mediocrity back in the states. The Army is my career. I have two more months to do here and then I'll return to the Special Forces myself. You'll join a brotherhood that will last your whole life."

"What Distinguished Service Medal?"

"The one you were awarded for you actions at the French Fort."

"I don't know anything about that. Never got it."

"What do you mean, you never got it."

"Just that. This is the first I'm hearing about it."

"This is outrageous. The DSM is the nation's second highest award for bravery. There wasn't any ceremony? Let me ask you something, how did you get promoted?"

"I woke up and my stripes were pinned to my pillow. The nurse found the orders on the nightstand."

"That's the extent of it?" "Yes."

"I'll look into this. This is bullshit! There has to be a awards ceremony. An award of this caliber shouldn't go unnoticed."

"I don't want any ceremony."

"Just the same. I'm going to find out what happened."

"If we could get back to the offer," said Sergeant Soujac.

"Is there a re-enlistment bonus?"

"Soujac smiled. "I was wondering if you were going to ask. Of course there is. The bonus is eight thousand dollars, and that increases each year you're in and with rank. In your case, it will be payable upon completion of all training since you have the option to leave. Well, what will it be? Do you need time to think about it?"

Holt exhaled a long, heavy breath. "No, I'm good. Let's do it."

"You're sure? I don't want to pressure you."

"Yes, I'm sure."

"Good. Why don't you go back to your barracks, pack up your things, and go out and get drunk with your friends tonight. Report here at 1000 hours and I'll have your paper work ready to go. Everything we discussed will be in writing."

Holt stood and shook hands with Soujac and then with Captain Jung. He left the office in a daze and made his way back to his barracks.

Before going to the barracks, he stopped in the supply room to see what he had to do. As he entered the door, Sergeant Grimes came around the counter and wrapped him in a bear hug. "Congratulations, Sergeant Holt."

"How the hell did you hear about this? I just left the Captain's office."

"The Captain called me and told me all about it and requested that I expedite your processing. If you're going to stay in, you're making the right decision. You wouldn't last in the regular Army."

"Thanks, Sarge. I appreciate it.

"Let's see what we can do." He shuffled through some papers running his fingers down the forms. "Empty your locker and foot locker. Leave your bedding. I'll need your rucksack and canteens. Keep your fatigues and boots, and whatever miscellaneous clothing you have. Return your rifle; you can keep your forty five and your web gear. Just check the pistol in at your new assignment. If you're missing any small stuff, I'll just write it up as a combat loss. Stop by in the morning and I'll have you out of here in five minutes."

"Thanks Sarge, you've been a good friend to me. Do you think I'm doing the right thing?"

"I can only speak from my experience. As a black man, life in the Army has been better for me than life would have been in Louisiana. For you, your life might be short, but one thing it won't be, is boring. You have a life of adventure ahead of you."

"Not crazy about the short-life part."

"Five Purple Hearts in two years. You always seem to be where the action is. Who knows, you may get lucky and actually retire. You'll be at the EM club tonight?"

"Sure, gotta say my goodbyes."

"I'll bring Sergeant Yolks and we'll have a great sendoff."

Holt sighed and look down at his cot. Three years in the Army and all his possessions could just about fit in a pillow case. His fatigues were clean when he put them on and would be good for another few days. He only had one other decent set of fatigues, and those he had folded and stuffed into his duffel bag. He had some socks, a couple of pair of cutoff shorts, and two t-shirts. A pair of boots and a pair of gook sandals and that was it; that was all his clothing. He folded up his web gear and his shoulder holster and placed them in his duffle bag. He went through his locker and sorted through some books. He saw a bundle of letters from Janet and looked at them. He thought of burning them but decided to keep them along with the pictures she sent. He held the envelopes to his nose and took a deep breath. They had long ago lost their scent of perfume and now just smelled damp and musty like everything else in Vietnam. He felt sad.

He caught a ride to the 12th Evac Hospital and stopped at administration. He was given the number of the ward he was looking for. Inside the ward he asked for Sergeant Mercado. Outside, he was told. He went through the door and saw Nick. He was sitting in a wheel chair with his left leg elevated. He saw Holt and glared at him.

15

"Get over here, asshole," he said.

As Holt got closer, Mercado reached up, pulled him close, and kissed him on the cheek.

"All's forgiven?" Holt asked.

"You shot me in my leg. Let me shoot you in the leg and then we'll be even."

Holt got his cigarettes and offered the pack to Nick. They sat smoking for a while.

"I know why you did it and I guess I should thank you. You promised you'd get me home and that's where I'm going."

"I'm sorry, Nick. It was just so fucked up on that hill. What with Camp—" Holt trailed off.

Mercado reached and squeezed Holt's hand. "I know, pal. I know."

"I just couldn't lose another friend. I wasn't thinking right." Holt's eyes teared up.

"I was pissed at first, then I figured it out."

"So we're okay?"

"You're my brother. Of course we're okay. I'm going to finish my time working with Yolks in the kitchen. No more fucking jungle for me. It'll be good experience cooking on a large scale. Maybe I can put some Spanish flavor in the Army slop. When I get home, I'll know what I'm doing."

"So, you're going to work at your parents Bodega?"

"Sure am. Find me a beautiful Puerto Rican girl and make babies."

"That's good, Nicky. You deserve it."

They reminisced on the past missions and all the guys they knew. Holt told him about his decision and was surprised when Mercado agreed it was best.

"Shit! You're more gook than American. You'd never make it back home. It's better if you stay."

They talked some more. Holt got Nick's address and promised to write as soon as he got settled.

Holt leaned over Mercado and hugged him. "I'm going to miss you, brother, I really am."

"I'll miss you too. Go on. Get out of here and go get drunk."

As Holt neared the door, Mercado said, "No fear, brother."

Holt looked him and smiled. "Damn straight! No fucking fear on earth."

That night, the first night of their three day stand down, the Enlisted Man's club was packed. Holt sat at a large picnic table with the remaining members of his old squad. Vinnie, Popeye, Fish, and Dickhead. They were joined by Sergeant Kelly from the third squad and Mad Dog and Doc White, the former medics from Delta Company. The Filipino band was setting up on the small stage. The air was clouded with cigarette smoke along with the smell of beer and sweat. Overhead, two large fans turned in lazy circles in a vain attempt to stir the heavy humid air. The table top was crowded with beer cans and red painted tin cans serving as ashtrays.

Sergeants Grimes and Yolks came through the door, their arms loaded with two bottles of Jack Daniels and cokes.

"I hope you youngsters can handle your liquor. Technically, this is breaking all the rules," said Sergeant Grimes as he placed the Cokes and Jack Daniels on the table. He called the waitress over and asked for plastic cups and ice.

As Grimes busied himself with the drinks, Sergeant Yolks proposed a toast. "To our newest career soldier, Staff Sergeant Donald Holt, soon to be Staff Sergeant Holt of the Special Forces."

Holt had to quiet the table and explain the nature of the toast. When he was finished he was barraged by questions.

"Damn, Sarge, you won't be going out with us?" asked Popeye.

"What are we going to do without you?" said Fish.

Holt quieted them down. "You guys don't need me anymore. You're all experienced veterans now. You are the ones the new guys will look up to. You're smart and you're brave, and if you do your job, you'll get through this and go back home. I'll never forget you guys. You were the best squad anyone could ask for." Holt raised his cup. "To the Fourth Squad, no fear."

"No fear," they all shouted in unison.

The band was about to begin but a Sergeant went on stage and said there would be a slight delay. He was greeted with boo's and curses. The door to the club opened and someone shouted, "Attention!"

Everyone turned to the door as Captain Jung and Lieutenant Mason entered, and the room fell silent.

The officers made their way to the stage. "At ease, men," said Captain Jung. "This will only take a minute."

The men quieted and Captain Jung proceeded. "It came to my attention that a grievous injustice has occurred. An injustice that will be corrected right now. Sergeant Holt, will you step forward?"

When Holt joined them on the stage, the Captain continued. "Sergeant Holt was awarded the Distinguished Service Medal, second only to the Congressional Medal of Honor for valor, for his actions, at what is now called, The French Fort. I would like to read the citation." When he was done, the room erupted into shouts and applause. A photographer took several pictures. Holt's face was beet red.

Holt held up his hands for silence. "I want to thank the Captain and Lieutenant for this presentation. A lot of you guys were at the at the fort and this award belongs as much to you, as it does to me. Thank you, Captain."

"One final thing," Captain Jung paused, "from now until the club closes, the drinks are on me. So, enjoy your selves, men."

The cheers roared even louder.

The officers walked with Holt back to the table. They were offered a drink which they declined. "You men enjoy yourselves you don't need officers around. How would you bitch about what jerks we are?" Jung leaned into Holt. "I told Sergeant Soujac to postpone our meeting until after lunch at 1300. Have a good night Sergeant, you deserve it."

With that, the band started up. Two slender girls in miniskirts stepped on stage and did a passable rendition of 'These Boots Were Made for Walking' by Nancy Sinatra. The more the men drank, the better the band sounded. When they played the Vietnam soldiers anthem, 'We got to get out of this place', by the Animals, everyone sang along.

A little after nine, a drunken Sergeant Kelly stood and shouted for quiet. "I want to make a toast to the best damn platoon sergeant we ever had. He's not here tonight but I know he's here in spirit, here's to Sergeant Wendell Camp!"

Everyone raised their drinks and shouted, "To Camp."

Holt stood and swayed a bit. "He was the best damn friend a man could have. To Camp."

They all shouted and cheered. Holt sat and had tears in his eyes. "I miss that mother fucker so much."

"We all do. He was a good guy," said Kelly.

They laughed as they told stories about Camp. As the evening progressed, the stories grew more outrageous, the lies bigger and bolder.

At ten o'clock, the club manager called last call and the men started to filter out back to their barracks.

Holt stayed awake until midnight talking with Fish, Popeye, and Kelly. They drank quietly. Holt got their addresses back in the world and they all promised to stay in touch, knowing full well they wouldn't.

CHAPTER 3

Recondo School

After signing his re-enlistment papers, Holt was driven to the airstrip. It was here that his preferential treatment ended. His orders were examined and he was directed to sit with another group of five men at the side of a building. No other information was provided. It was apparent none of the men knew each other.

An hour later, a three quarter ton truck pulled to the side of the building depositing another six men. There were some casual conversation, but for the most part the men remained silent.

Holt examined the men and saw they all wore the Combat Infantry Badge. Their shoulder patches represented the various infantry units of the 25th Infantry Division. All were deeply tanned with close cropped hair. Three men had Ranger Tabs on their shoulders and they sat together eying the other men suspiciously. Ten of the men were E-5, sergeants. Holt and one other man were E-6, Staff Sergeants.

At 2:30PM, a second lieutenant addressed the group. He read each of their names from a clip board. He said their transportation to Nha Trang would arrive at three PM. The flight to Nha Trang was approximately two hundred and seventy miles and would take about two hours.

A half hour later, the lieutenant returned. He told them to grab their gear and walked with them to the airstrip to a waiting C-7 Caribou. The Caribou was a smaller cargo ship known for its ability for short take offs and landings. He read their names again and told them to board the aircraft. Inside, an Air force technical sergeant told them to take seats, stow the gear underneath the web seats, and buckle their seat belts. The men found seats on either side of the plane. The center of the plane was loaded with wooden cargo boxes. Holt stretched out his legs and pulled his boonie cap over his eyes. He tried to sleep.

The flight took less than two hours. Nha Trang was a sprawling, rectangular complex on the South China Sea. Part of it was a peninsula that jutted out in the ocean that housed a naval installation, the 864th Engineer Battalion, and 5th Special Forces Nung Camp. North of that, was the Special Forces Logistical Center and the Special Forces Headquarters. Next to the headquarters was the MACV Recondo School.

When the plane landed, they were greeted by a Special Forces Staff Sergeant who again checked their names to a clip board and directed them to a two and a half ton truck. They drove a short distance and passed under the archway of the Recondo School. Once again, their names were checked off of a list. They formed up in two groups of six men.

"I am Sergeant First Class Rowlins. I will conduct your orientation. You men on the left are Team A. For the time being, your team leader is Staff Sergeant Holt. You on the right are Team B and Staff Sergeant Jenkins is your team leader. At some point during training you will all assume the role of team leader." He pointed to a small barracks and told the men to stow their gear, Team A on the left and Team B on the right.

"In fifteen minutes I want you outside in team formation. Dismissed."

The men started to walk toward the barracks and were told to stop.

"Within this camp you jog everywhere you go. If you're not jogging, you are running. Do you understand?"

Within the barracks, Holt took the cot nearest the door. It took less than five minutes to stow his meager possessions. He lit a cigarette and walked over to Sergeant Jenkins, a slender black man, around Holt's height. He held out his hand and introduced himself. "Don Holt, from the 2nd of the 27th."

"Joe Jenkins, 1st of the 27th."

They shook hands and Holt asked him, "Were you in the Valley?"

"Yeah, that's where I got promoted. Holt? Are you that crazy fucker from the Fort?"

"Yeah, that's me. That was really a shit show. Nice to meet you Joe."

"Same here. Do you know what goes on here?"

"Same as you, brother. I know nothing. I guess we better get outside."

They stood in front of Sergeant Rowlins. "We'll get you some chow, you got thirty minutes to eat and then we'll process you in and issue you your gear. Enjoy your meal, it's the last decent meal you'll have for the next three weeks."

Holt finished his meal quickly and went outside to smoke a cigarette. He was joined by Sergeant Jenkins.

"I don't mind telling you, I'm more than a little nervous about this. Did you have to re-up to get this assignment?"

"Yeah. You?"

"I was thinking of staying in, but now I wonder if I made the right decision."

"I know what you mean. I guess we'll find out together," said Holt.

At the supply room they were issued camouflaged jungle fatigues, boonie hat, poncho, and poncho liner. They got their web gear, twenty empty magazines, four standard canteens, and two collapsible, two quart canteens, a compass, strobe light, and a combat knife. They also picked up some empty claymore mine bags, a medical kit. and four tubes of camouflage face paint. At the armory, they each signed for a AR 15 Colt Commando rifle and a Browning Hi Power, automatic nine millimeter pistol and holster. It was at the armory that they got two claymore mines and enough ammunition to fill thirty magazines, and six hand grenades. Finally, they received an unusual camouflaged ruck sack. Two of the ruck sacks had the standard PRC 25 radios attached.

"Don't hesitate picking the rucks with the radio. We change each day. You will all carry the radio," Sergeant Rowlins said.

Between the supply room and the armory were two long tables where they assembled their equipment. Rowlins instructed them exactly how he wanted the gear to be packed.

"Gentlemen, when you are done here go over to that sand pile and fill a sand bag. Hand it to the Sergeant and he will weigh it. Your sand bag will weigh exactly forty pounds. Place that sand bag inside your ruck sack, it will simulate the additional equipment you will normally carry on patrols."

The men assembled in two rows according to their teams.

"Before I release you for the evening, we are going for a short two mile jog. We are not going for speed but to build up your endurance. If anyone falls out they will be dismissed from this program immediately. Any questions?"

They began the run at a slow jogging pace and gradually increased to a fast jog.

The sandbag began to rub the small of Holt's back. He ignored the discomfort and just concentrated on the run. He looked to his left and saw Jenkins with a tight grimace on his face.

"How you doing Joe? Smile, this is supposed to be fun."

"Fuck you," he said, breathing hard.

They ran down the west side of the compound and turned north. Holt figured they had gone a mile. They began the final mile on the east of the compound. Jenkins pace slowed.

Holt was breathing hard through his mouth and was covered in sweat. He could smell the ocean.

"Joe, keep up. You're falling back."

"Shit man, I'm hurting."

Holt slowed his pace and two men passed him.

"Keep going, I don't need your help," Jenkins said.

"Just keeping pace with you. I'm surprised, I thought you black boys could run all day."

Jenkins glared at him but said nothing.

"C'mon, we only got a half mile more. Look ahead, there's the barracks."

Jenkins stumbled and Holt reached out and grabbed his web gear.

"God damn it. Wolf Hounds don't drop out. Pick your head up and run."

When they arrived to the barracks, Holt released Jenkins who leaned over and retched. Holt put his hands on his hips and walked in tight circles, trying to slow his breathing.

Jenkins straightened. He mopped his face with his boonie hat, he looked at Holt, and nodded his head. Holt nodded back.

"Sergeant Holt, over here," said Sergeant Rowlins.

Holt started to drop his pack.

"Keep your rucksack on and get over here."

"What's up?" asked Holt.

"Did you help Sergeant Jenkins complete his run?"

"No, I did not. I may have offered him some encouragement but he completed the run by himself."

"If you were in the jungle and you were running for your life and Jenkins fell out, what would you do then?"

"I would stop and offer him encouragement."

"You would, huh?"

"I've never left a man behind and I'm not about to start here."

"And what if your mission depended on leaving someone behind?"

"I haven't seen a mission in Vietnam that was worth a man's life. I wouldn't leave anyone behind."

Sergeant Rowlins held his gaze, staring straight at Holt. "Go on, get back in formation." He addressed the assembled men. "The Post Exchange is going to stay open for another hour. If you need to get anything do it now. This will be your last chance. Lights out at 2100, reveille at 0500. Formation here, at 0530." He turned and walked away.

In the barracks, Jenkins asked Holt what Rowlins said to him.

"He said I should have left your skinny, black ass behind. I told him that's not what Wolfhounds do. We all go back together."

Jenkins started to say something and Holt cut him off. "I'm going to the Post Exchange, are you coming or do you need to be carried?"

Jenkins laughed. "Fuck you. Yeah, I'm coming and I don't need any help from your scrawny white ass."

The Post Exchange was like a mini store. It carried an assortment of goods not provided by the Army. There were magazines and paperbacks, food, cameras, watches, and stereo equipment. Just about anything a soldier could want to make his time in Vietnam more bearable. You could even order a car and have it available upon your return home.

Holt purchased six large packs of beef jerky, a dozen packets of assorted Kool Aid, a dozen packs of chewing gum, and two cartons of Marlboro cigarettes. He also bought a new olive drab towel and a pair a dark tinted aviator sunglasses. He paid for his purchases with MPC, Military Payment Script. The clerk punched his ration card for the cigarettes.

He smoked a cigarette as he waited for Jenkins outside. Together, they walked back to the barracks.

As Holt lay on his cot, an overwhelming wave of sadness came over him. He missed his friends back in Delta Company. He missed Alfie, the company dog. Before he left, he made Sergeant's Yokes and Grimes promise to look after him. Grimes had built him a dog house out of a old ammo crate. He even had some new guys cover it on all sides with three rows of sandbags. Alfie would be fine. Holt assumed he was used to guys coming and going. Holt missed his ex wife, Janet. He knew he had to write and tell her what he was doing. Maybe she would write back. He felt homesick like he did the first days of basic training. Homesick for a home he didn't have.

The lights flickered off at nine PM, he closed his eyes and slept without dreaming.

The next morning they were woken an hour earlier than promised, at 4:00 AM, and started another two-mile run in full gear. Holt kept an eye on Jenkins who smiled back. "I'm good. No problem."

When they were finished, Holt leaned forward hands on his knees. "This fucking sand bag is rubbing my back raw."

"Let me adjust your rucksack for you. Cinch these straps down and the bag will ride higher between your shoulder blades. It gets the weight off the small of your back and won't rub as much."

"Thanks, Joe. Appreciate it."

Jenkins then went around and showed the others how to adjust their packs. A new instructor stood back and smiled. "Alright, ladies. Now that you have your bra straps adjusted, head off to chow and be back here in forty five minutes."

After eating, Holt stood outside smoking a cigarette. The instructor stood a few feet away eyeing Holt with disdain. "You'd better put some meat on those bones; you're too fucking skinny. You look like one of the gooks."

"So I've been told."

The rest of the morning was spent in classroom training. Here, they saw the full training class, with over sixty men divided into six man teams. This is how they would spend their days, in a combination of physical training and classroom work. The classroom work consisted of an intensive course of map reading, land navigation, artillery adjustment, and other essential skills.

The physical training consisted of the normal pushups, sit ups, squats, and pull ups. On day three, a mile was added to their run. On day four they ran five miles, and on day seven they ran seven miles.

On the seventh day they went to the rappelling tower. They had to climb to the top of a fifty foot tower in full gear on a rope ladder. Holt struggled with the ladder. He kept twisting on the ladder and banging his shoulder into the tower. He made it to the top but it was ugly. At the top they were given leather gloves and instructed how to wrap the rope around their bodies and through a D ring. The key to success, they were told, was to hold their left hand high on the rope and your right at your waist. You gauge your descent by looking over your right shoulder at the ground.

The instructor told Holt to step on the wall and hold himself there. This was to prove the ropes ability to hold him suspended in the air. He was cautioned to kick away from the wall so he wouldn't catch his chin on the tower. He kicked out and loosened his hand and slid down several feet. Again he was told to hold. Finally, he pushed from the wall and in several smooth jumps reached the ground. He removed himself from the ropes and got back in line. After four more rappel's down the wooden wall they were given a short break.

Holt sat with Sergeant Jenkins smoking a cigarette. "That was fucking awesome. I really liked it."

"It was scary at first. But once I knew I could hold myself and control the decent, I was able to relax and enjoy it," said Jenkins.

"What's nice is the instructors treat you with a measure of respect. They're not screaming at you and calling you names. But they keep telling me I'm too skinny. How am I supposed to gain weight if we're running seven miles a day?"

"You do look like a chicken that's been picked clean."

After the break they climbed the tower again and repelled from the open side. Standing on the edge of the tower, the floor simulated standing on the skid of a helicopter. They were cautioned to kick out far enough to clear the floor. Once again, they held themselves suspended in air to gain confidence in their ability to control their decent. After five times, they were all able to descend quickly and smoothly. Finally, after everyone completed the tower training, they all repelled from a hovering Huey helicopter at a hundred feet. On the ground, everyone gathered and were talking excitedly about their accomplishments. The instructors gave them a break and let them enjoy the moment.

Next there were classes on advanced first aid training. They learned how to start IV's and administer blood expanders if someone was seriously wounded. The men paired off and practiced on each other. Holt and Jenkins paired off together. Jenkins went first and inserted the IV needle on his first try. Holt barely felt a thing. Jenkins was not so fortunate. Although his veins were prominent, they rolled when Holt started to insert the needle and it took several attempts before Holt had the needle properly inserted. When the instructor came to inspect their progress, he noticed the blood on Jenkins arm and table. Holt had to do it again. To his credit, Jenkins never made a sound or flinched as Holt inserted the needle.

The second week began with a trip to Hon Tre, an island five miles off shore of Nha Trang. It was here they first noticed the class had been reduced; nine men had dropped out. On Hon Tre they practiced day and night patrol techniques. They were introduced to Long Range Reconnaissance rations, or LURP rations. The freeze dried rations came in eight varieties. Although lighter than standard C-rations, they required one and a half pints of water to cook and reconstitute them. Water was a precious commodity in the field and this was a severe draw back. They were told that normal rations on patrol were usually a mixture of LURP and C-rations.

They also became familiar with a variety of American and foreign weapons. Sergeant Rowlins returned to conduct the class on weapons. Holt gravitated to the Swedish K sub machine gun and the Soviet made folding stock AK47. In addition to their weapons training, they continued their physical training with daily runs on the beach. Each day they added distance.

That night the instructors met to compare notes. It was agreed that four men would be dropped from the course.

"I have a problem with two of my guys. Sergeants Holt and Jenkins," Sergeant Rowlins said.

"I thought they were doing okay. I have no problem with them," another instructor said.

"It's nothing they have done. We have the swim test coming up and both of them have said they are not strong swimmers."

"Didn't Soujac pick those two? I don't want to be the one to flunk them."

"It doesn't matter who picked them. If they can't pass the swim test, they're out. That is unless we start making exceptions," said Rowlins.

"As far as I'm concerned the swim test is bullshit," said another sergeant. "What are the chances they'll ever have to swim a hundred yards in a bathing suit. Maybe if they're life guards on an Air Force base but, here, in the jungle, it'll never happen."

Sergeant Rowlins looked worried. "We'll see what happens. Hopefully they can make it."

The morning of the swim test the men assembled on the beach wearing swim trunks. The water was calm and flat with barely a ripple. Four more candidates were missing.

Seeing the instructors in bathing suits dispelled one myth. Rather than being heavily muscled, hulks, most of them weighed between a hundred and forty to a hundred and fifty pounds and had slender, well-muscled bodies.

They each were given an inflatable life vest and were told if they inflated the vest, they failed. They had to swim out a hundred yards to a floating dock, turn around and swim back without touching the dock.

Rowlins spoke to Holt and Jenkins. "Look, I don't care how you do it or how long it takes, just fucking do it. Don't touch the float. Touch it and you fail. Once you make it out there, coming back is easier. The current will help you. Good luck."

Holt was chewing on his thumb nail. "Shit! I swim like a brick. I'm really nervous about this."

"Most brothers ain't known for their swimming ability," said Jenkins.

"Where did you two learn to swim?" asked Rowlins.

"Rivers and lakes," said Holt.

"Same here," said Jenkins.

"You never swam in the ocean?"

"I've never been in the ocean," said Holt.

"Shit! The salt water is going to keep you afloat. All you have to do is use your arms and kick your feet. It's almost impossible not to stay afloat."

"Let's just get through this shit. I really don't want to flunk out now."

Holt punched Jenkins lightly on the arm, "No fear, brother."

"Yeah… no fear."

They watched as the first group of six men dove into the water and swam to the float. One man inadvertently touched the float and was sent back to the beach.

When it was Holt's turn, Holt ran into the ocean and dived under the water. While under, he did a clumsy breast stroke and surfaced in about thirty feet. He then began swimming conventionally arm over arm. He took comfort in the buoyancy of the salt water and concentrated on his arm strokes and kicking his feet. At one point, he looked up and realized he was almost to the float. As he neared the float, someone shouted to turn around. He did an awkward dog paddle to turn himself and started back. He was exhausted and breathing hard. Someone shouted at him to lay forward and do a breast stroke. He regained his strength and looked for the beach. He had another fifty yards to go. He sucked in a giant breath and dove under the water. When he surfaced, he did it again and again. Twenty yards to go. Now he went arm over arm. His swimming was ugly and clumsy but he kept moving forward. Finally, his feet touched the sand, he ran up onto the shore, and collapsed to his knees. He coughed up water. Drool and spittle hung from his mouth. He wiped his mouth and sat at the water's edge looking for Jenkins. He saw him about thirty yards out. His swimming was violent and uncoordinated but he was making progress. Sergeant Rowlins swam by his side offering encouragement. Finally, like some sort of injured seal, he threw himself on the beach and lay there panting.

Holt extended his arm and helped him up.

"God damn it! Black folk don't fucking swim," said Jenkins between gasps for air.

"Brother, it was hard to watch you. You made me look good," said Holt.

Rowlins came out of the water and said, "You ladies tired? Get your asses back there and change into your fatigues. I think we'll go for a little run."

CHAPTER 4

You Bet Your Life

They spent the next few days in physical training, classroom work, and day and night patrol tactics. Their final exercise was an five day combat patrol in the jungle surrounding the base. The patrol would consist of five men and a Special Forces sergeant.

Holt was happy to see that Sergeant Rowlins would be their team leader and he and Jenkins would be in the same group. They spent the morning and going over their patrol area and preparing their equipment. Each man was given a map and a small notebook to write the call signs of the various units supporting them. The five men consisted of Holt and Jenkins both E-6, Staff Sergeants, a E-5 Sergeant, and two Specialists E-4's who they had trained with sporadically during the previous two weeks.

Sergeant Rowlins entered their hooch and they all stood. "Gentlemen, you have all been issued your gear for the upcoming patrol. I am here to tell you exactly how I want it packed and to go over each item. First, you have your combat suspenders and web belt. Sergeant Holt, why are you raising your hand? I just began. What could I have said that merits a question?"

"Sarge, I have my own customized web belt. I was wondering if I could wear it?"

"Put it on, let me see it."

Holt slipped into his combat harness. On each side a Claymore mine bag was sewn connecting the front and rear suspender straps. In the front was a replica of the NVA ammo pouch he bought in Ben Tre. It spanned the suspenders and attached with clips.

"I can hold ten magazines in each side bag and another ten across the front for a total of thirty magazines," Holt said tentatively.

"Let me see that rig."

Rowlins tugged on the straps and turned Holt around and tugged some more.

"I like this setup. I like it a lot. If you make it back from this patrol, I want you to show this to our Quartermaster. This is good. Now, if I may proceed, you will each carry a minimum of twenty magazines. Like Sergeant Holt, we use empty Claymore mine bags. On your web belt you have two traditional ammo pouches. Into each you will place two hand grenades. On your suspenders you will have two more grenades. Sergeant Holt, how many grenades are we carrying?"

Holt hesitated and looked puzzled. "That would be six."

"Correct. Now we know that we both can add. Any math questions you may have, ask Sergeant Holt. On your belt you each have a customized nine millimeter Browning Hi Power, automatic pistol. It has a thirteen round magazine of which you will carry four additional magazines. The pistol has a longer barrel with a threaded end to attach a silencer. The silencer is secured in a special pouch on the holster. You will also carry one canteen on your belt along with a medical compression bandage. We carry the Marine Corps Kabar knife either on your belt or taped to your suspenders. Tie your compass to your body with parachute cord. I keep my compass in my shirt pocket with a string tied through the button hole. You will also secure your strobe survival light to your belt with parachute cord. Now, pick up your ALICE pack and place it on the table. Who can tell me what ALICE stands for?"

Holt raised his hand. "All-purpose Lightweight Individual Carrying Equipment, Sergeant."

Behind him, one the specialists coughed the words "teacher's pet."

Rowlins face reddened. "Who said that?" He stomped over to the man and stood nose to nose. "I have a good mind to drop your sorry ass right now. Sergeant Holt has two years combat experience. He has more combat decorations and commendations than I have. Just look at him, you can tell he's been through the shit and he's still standing. This is no fucking joke.

We are going on a real combat patrol deep in Indian country, just the six of us. You, you dumb son of a bitch, step out of line just once and you're out. DO YOU UNDERSTAND ME?"

"Yes Sergeant," came the stammered reply.

"Alright, continuing. You see we have spray painted the rucksack with black, green, and brown stripes to simulate your camouflaged fatigues. Your Car 15's have been similarly painted and fitted with a suppressor. This is the large pack. In the three pockets on the back, we carry three canteens. Beneath them we strap on two, two-quart collapsible canteens. On the fold down carrying deck we strap our ground cover and poncho liner. We do not carry ponchos. Between the canteen pockets you will carry two smoke grenades placed through the provided loops. I want two of you to take CS gas grenades instead of smoke. We use the gas to break contact—hopefully we won't need them. In the inside compartment you will carry two star clusters and your food. You can select your own rations, a mixture of LRRP's, or C-rations, in any combination you want. Bring enough for five days. Keep in mind you'll be eating them cold. No fires and no cigarettes. We each will carry a Claymore mine and an extra radio battery. In a separate Claymore bag, you'll carry a hundred round belt of M-60 ammunition. We don't drape those over our shoulders Mexican bandit style. The shine on the bullet casing is too noticeable. We also carry an individual medical kit consisting of bandages, tourniquets, blood expander, morphine ampoules, and a pill kit. Those pills will only be issued on my order. You also have four tubes of camouflage, latex, face paint. Finally, here is a bundle of old camouflage netting. Rip it up and wrap it around your rifles and the machine gun. Make sure it doesn't interfere with the action of your weapon. Take strips and place them in the loops of your boonie hats. During the patrol you will alternate roles. Each will walk point, operate the radio, and carry the machine gun. Each will take a turn as team leader. You, dumb ass, do you see anything different about the M-60 machine gun?"

"Yes, Sergeant, the bi-pod has been removed and the barrel looks shorter."

"That's correct. And it's been fitted with a more effective flash suppressor. We use the M-16 bi-pod, it's spring loaded, fits the barrel, and comes in its own canvas carrying case." Sergeant Rowlins studied his list. "I almost forgot, we will carry one M-79 grenade launcher and each man will carry six high explosive rounds. Who wants to carry the M-79?"

One the specialists raised his hand.

"Good. Don't forget your personal gear, toothbrush, insect repellant, and sweat towel. No soap or toothpaste. You'll brush your teeth with water. It is now 1330 hours. Be ready for inspection at 1500 hours. Chow will be served at 1600 hours. We will be at the helipad at 1730 and depart at 1800 promptly." With that Rowlins turned on his heel and left the barracks.

After preparing their gear, Holt sat with Jenkins on a small wooden bench outside the barracks. Holt lit a cigarette and offered the pack to Jenkins who declined.

"Are you nervous, Don?"

"Sure. I don't want to fuck up. When you think of it, it's no different than going on a LP or ambush patrol. Shit Joe, we know what we're doing."

"I guess you're right. It's just that listening posts and ambushes don't last five days."

"We'll do fine. It's those two spec fours I'm worried about. As far as I'm concerned they're FNG's."

"They can't be fucking new guys or they wouldn't be here. They both went to Ranger school. They're probably just here to earn the Recondo tab and go back to their unit."

"Yeah, I'm sure you're right. We'll see."

Holt leaned back against the barracks wall and lit another cigarette. "I guess I am nervous. I'm smoking like a chimney."

"How come you volunteered for this?"

"Who knows. I got nothing back in the States. With my fucked up face everyone is going to stare at me. If I was going to do another three years, I wanted something different. A new challenge. How about you?"

"I'm staying in. Going to be a lifer. I figured this will look good on my 201 file. I heard you can make rank quick in this outfit. Plus, I think I'll look good in a beret."

"That's a good of reason as any in the Army. Fucking war is winding down. I hope we don't get stuck as advisers to some gook outfit. I don't trust those mother fuckers."

"I heard we'll get assigned to some A Team along the border. Maybe if we ask, we can stick together."

"I'd like that. I hate having to make new friends. I always try and stay separate from my squad but it's hard to do when you live with them twenty four hours a day. You make friends even if you don't want to. You make friends and it hurts when something... You know, if someone gets hurt."

"You lose somebody close?"

"Yeah, a really good friend. He died in my arms."

"Shit, it's Vietnam. It don't mean nothing."

"You're right Joe, Not a fucking thing."

At precisely 1500 hours, Sergeant Rowlins returned. He handed each man a roll of green aviation tape.

"I want each of you to tape up every buckle, every swivel, every metal piece that can possibly make noise. This tape is used to patch up bullet holes on the skin of helicopters. Once you put it on, it ain't coming off."

Once they adjusted their straps and buckles, they wrapped them with the green tape. Sergeant Rowlins tugged on their web gear and slapped their packs looking for any noise.

"Good, very good." He turned to one man, "You're Weaver, right? Let me see your rifle." He examined the weapon and the netting tied around it. "This is good. It looks like a stick with leaves. That is what it should look like. All of you, you did a nice job. We've practiced patrol techniques for a week now. You should all know what you're doing. Just keep your wits about you and we'll be fine. Grab your shit and we'll head over to the mess hall. After your chow, put on your camo face paint and we'll ride to the airstrip. Once there, we'll go over everything again. By now it should be second nature."

"I almost forgot, I have a something else for you to carry, it's a survival radio used by the helicopter guys and our pilots. Its range is only about a mile and pretty much has to be in the line of sight. If you get separated, you'll need it. Let's go get some chow."

The meal consisted of roast beef, mashed potatoes, and string beans. Holt finished his quickly and mopped his plate with a piece of white bread. He asked the Sergeant if he could have some extra beef to make a couple of sandwiches, which he did, slavered with mayonnaise. He wrapped the sandwiches in foil and stuffed them in his pack. He filled one canteen with ice tea and returned to the table. He noticed the men were pushing their food around their plates.

"You guys should really eat up. It's the last decent food we'll have for five days," Holt said.

"How can you eat? I got butterflies crawling in my stomach," Weaver said.

"It's just another day at work. Dude, we've trained for this. It'll be fine. This ain't your first patrol so just relax."

Sergeant Rowlins, seeing the men were done, said, "Alright, clean your trays and get back here so you ladies can put on your makeup."

The men came back to the table and took out their small survival mirrors and laid out the tubes of camo face paint.

"This is some new stuff we're trying. It's latex based and hypo allergenic. Don't want you girls getting pimples," said Rowlins. "It is also sweat resistant, but we will have to reapply it. Remember the class, black on all your high points, your forehead, cheekbones, nose, and chin. Green on your cheeks and under your eyes. Use both shades of green and brown. You want to mimic your fatigues. Make sure you get your ears, neck, and hands. When you're done, check each other. Make sure everything's covered."

When they were done the men inspected each other.

"Here's something interesting, where did the tiger stripe camo come from?" asked Rowlins. A couple of the men looked at Holt who just shrugged. Rowlins continued. "They came from the French. They developed it in the fifties and called it the 'Lizard pattern'. We picked it up in the early sixties and now it's commonly used throughout South East Asia. Different variations, but pretty much the same. Alright, let's head out."

They walked towards the main office. "See that Recondo sign? One by one stand in front of it and get your picture taken. We'll then take a group shot."

A clerk with an expensive thirty five millimeter camera took their individual photo's and several of the group together.

"Gentlemen, there's our ride," Rowlins said, pointing to a three quarter ton truck. Five men piled in the back and Sergeant Rowlins sat up front with the driver. They recognized him as one of the instructors. The ride was short and the men avoided looking at each other. Each lost in their own thoughts. At the air strip, they piled out and stood near the helicopter. The chopper was devoid of markings. It was painted a pale blue on the bottom, and the top and sides were painted in a mottled pattern of flat black and green.

For several minutes Rowlins talked with the driver. Finally, they shook hands and Rowlins walked to them.

"You each know where you're sitting. We exit on the left side. Do just as we practiced. Jenkins you are starting on point followed by Lafontaine. Weaver, you're third with the radio. I'm fourth and Baker you're fifth. Holt you are rear security. We switch every day. You assholes know your shit. Just do as we rehearsed."

The air crew, dressed in their Nomex flight suits, inspected the ship. Satisfied with their pre-flight inspection they climbed aboard. The helicopter blades started turning slowly and built up speed. The six men climbed aboard and took their assigned seats.

They rose from the ground in a swirling cloud of red dust. The nose tilted down, they gained speed, and were finally airborne.

Holt sat behind the pilot looking out the open door. He turned and saw Rowlins looking at him and nodded. Baker was next to Rowlins with his head down mouthing a silent prayer. Lafontaine, a tall slender boy sat across from Holt picking at his nails. Jenkins sat by the opposite door looking down. Weaver sat between Jenkins and Holt.

Off to their side Holt could see a small, egg shaped Light Observation Helicopter commonly called a 'LOACH,' and above him were two slender Cobra attack helicopters; their escorts. The Cobra's had shark mouths painted on their noses.

Holt looked down at the rice paddies giving way to the lush green jungle. He leaned his head back and smiled. He felt like he was going home.

CHAPTER 5

This Should Have Been Easy

After thirty minutes of flying Holt felt mesmerized by the featureless terrain below. It appeared to be an unbroken, green carpet of jungle. He took this time to go over their mission in his head. First and foremost they were to avoid any contact with the enemy. This was an evaluation exercise. They headed northwest past Khanh Hoa. They would turn north and go west of Ninh Hoa and land in a small clearing. Once on the ground they would proceed to Highway 21 where they would setup and observe the highway for any night movement. They were looking for any intersecting trails used by the NVA to move troops or material. Enemy activity in the area was reported as light.

This was just a five day exercise to access their patrol techniques and their ability to adapt and function in the jungle.

The observation helicopter directed them to a small, oblong shaped clearing about two miles ahead. Their helicopter skimmed the tree tops and approached the clearing. It flared suddenly and dropped down, hovering about three feet above the ground. The men quickly jumped to the ground and ran for the protective cover of the trees. They moved about twenty feet into the wood line where Jenkins signaled everyone down. They formed a circle with each man looking out. Specialist Weaver called in a sit-rep report, telling the command unit that they had landed at the initial LZ. The situation was normal and the landing zone cold.

Jenkins turned to the patrol members and flashed five fingers four times, indicating they would hold in place twenty minutes for any sign of enemy movement. In the distance, they could hear the helicopter making false landings to disguise their entry point. They sat silently for twenty minutes, each man studying the jungle in front of him. During this time, Jenkins consulted his map and compass and determined their initial route. Weaver and Baker, the two specialists, were looking around nervously. Rowlins bent over Jenkins map. Lafontaine was fiddling with something on the M-60 machine gun.

Holt withdrew the tail of his towel from his shirt and wiped the perspiration on his face. He did it carefully so he would not mess his makeup. He smiled at the thought and would have to tell Janet he was wearing makeup now. Perhaps she could give him some hints on application. The men rose on Jenkins' signal and headed off deeper into the jungle. Holt looked at his watch looped through the button hole on his pocket flap; twenty minutes exactly. As the men started off, Holt dropped back about twenty feet to cover their rear. The men walked slowly and silently through the dense undergrowth. Obstructing branches were gently moved away and held for the next man, who did the same.

It was rapidly getting dark and Jenkins was focused on finding a suitable place for their night lager. He came upon an enormous fallen tree. He halted the patrol and moved forward. After a minute, he signaled the men forward and pointed to a spot between two large limbs of the fallen tree. He looked at Sergeant Rowlins who nodded his head in agreement. Jenkins marked a spot on his map with a grease pencil and showed it to Rowlins who nodded once again. Rowlins handed the map to Weaver who called in their position and informed them that they were stopping for the night. Guard assignments were given with hand signals. Guard would begin at 2300 with two man, two hour, shifts. At 0300 they would begin again with one hour shifts. At 0600 they would rise eat breakfast and resume the patrol at 0700. During training, they were told that the army had determined that guard shifts should be no longer than two hours. Boredom and exhaustion would limit the effectiveness, if any longer.

Holt opened his pack and dug out the roast beef sandwich. He leaned against his rucksack and slowly ate his sandwich, washing it down with ice tea from his canteen. Finished, he now wished he could have a cigarette.

He and Baker had the first shift. The radio sat between them. His watch confirmed it was 9 PM, 2100 hours in military time.

They were surrounded by an orchestra of insects. Mosquitoes fluttered against their face. They could only brush them away with their hands. Slapping then would make too much noise. At one point, Baker leaned on Holt and Holt nudged him sharply with his elbow.

"It's okay, sorry, I'm awake," whispered Baker. Holt whispered back, "It's 2200, call in the sit rep."

The next hour passed slowly as Holt checked his watch frequently. The hands of the watch seemed to barely move. Finally, at 2300, Holt leaned into Baker and whispered into his ear to call in and wake Jenkins for the next shift. Once Holt was assured that Jenkins and Lafontaine were awake and the radio was moved, he settled back and covered his face with his boonie hat. He cradled his rifle across his chest and closed his eyes.

He thought how odd it was to choose to live in the jungle. The jungle, which Joseph Conrad described in 'The Heart of Darkness' as not a fit place for white men to live. Holt smiled and thought Conrad had to be a bit of a racist to make such a comment. But he understood what he was saying. The jungle was such a wild and untamed place, it exerted an irresistible pull on some men. Everything here was designed to cause you harm, if not to outright kill you. To live and thrive here meant you had gained mastery over your life in such a horrible place. At home, back in the 'normal' world, he felt he had no control. He reacted to situations which bounced him from one encounter to the next. He was a good boy and did what was expected of him.

But here in Vietnam, everything was a challenge. The simplest things were challenging. He had read the book by Conrad in the hospital and now carried it with him. He consulted it as some did the Bible. As he fell off to sleep, he wondered if anyone would consider his life to be 'normal.'

Holt woke for his next guard shift. It was 0300, 3AM. He told Baker he could sleep, that he would take the shift by himself.

He sat in the silence of the jungle with only the insects and the perpetual dripping water for company. When the guard shift changed at 0400 Holt went back to what passed for sleep. He felt that even when asleep he was conscious of the noise around him.

At 0600 the men woke. Holt stretched his legs and slowly stood. He moved a few feet away and unbuttoned his pants. The stream of urine steamed in the cool morning air. When he was done, he dug through his pack and pulled out his second sandwich.

The men switched assignments. Today Holt would carry the radio. The second day passed quickly and was uneventful. They walked north parallel to the highway below them.

On the morning of the third day, Holt walked point. A little before noon, Holt stopped and held up a clenched fist. He moved forward about ten feet and stopped. In front was a well used, hard packed trail. He turned and signaled Sergeant Rowlins to come forward.

With Rowlins at his side, Holt pointed. Both could clearly see the footprints of dozens of men. Some of the prints were the canvas sneaker type boots worn by the NVA and some were the tire-tracked prints of Ho Chi Minh sandals. Rowlins dropped to his knees and reached out and felt the ground. He rocked back on his legs and stood next to Holt. He leaned in close and whispered, "Those prints are fresh, no more than a day old. The ground is still damp."

Holt whispered back, "How many?"

"No telling. The prints overlap each other. Maybe twenty or more. They are coming from the north and heading south. The trail looks like it's curving in from the west."

Rowlins squatted and tugged on the small soul patch under his lower lip.

"I have to call this in. They're going to want us to follow it, at least for a while. Shit! It happens that sometimes these training exercises turn into the real thing. You up for this?"

"Sure. No problem."

"I'll get on the horn and call it in, then I'll tell the others."

He walked back toward the group of men. To their credit they were all alert and facing out. Their camouflage was good. Holt could barely see them from only fifteen feet away, they blended into the trees and leaves perfectly. Holt saw Rowlins with the handset pressed to his ear. He was reading off coordinates from his map. When he finished, he addressed the men and told them of the altered assignment. He turned to Holt and motioned him to continue.

Holt walked in the trees, keeping the trail about ten feet to his right. Baker was behind him as his slack man. They walked silently for over an hour. He was comforted by the sounds of the birds high above them in the tree tops.

After another thirty minutes, Rowlins snapped his fingers. Holt stopped and saw Rowlins with his hands together; he mimicked breaking a stick and held up ten fingers. They would break in place for ten minutes.

Holt got his canteen and took a long pull of water. He felt good, alert, and in control. Holt reached into his pant leg pocket and pulled out a strip of jerky. Overhead, the sky began to cloud and he could feel the temperature drop a few degrees. Suddenly, Holt heard something. It sounded like a bird laughing. He turned to the group assembled some five yards behind him. He spread his arms wide and lowered them. The five green men got to their knees and then lay flat on the ground facing out. Holt brought his hand up and cupped his ear and pointed ahead.

Holt slipped out of his pack and crawled forward. He brought his rifle up to his shoulder. He heard them before he saw them. It was a small boy of about eight or ten and a very old man. They walked down the trail holding hands and talking softly. The old man said something and the boy laughed.

Holt was concealed by leaves and tangled vines. The boy was closest to Holt. Holt sighted on the boys head and moved the selector switch on his rifle from safe to semi automatic. The two Vietnamese came abreast of Holt and he placed his finger on the trigger. He took a deep breath and held it. Holt tracked them with the sights until they passed. He crawled forward, scratching his cheek on a thorn. They moved down the trail and finally were out of sight. He turned north and looked up the trail. He stayed this way for ten minutes.

He crawled back off the trail and signaled Rowlins to tell him what he saw.

Rowlins looked down and chewed his lip. "Are you sure?"

"No uniforms. The boy wore a t-shirt and shorts and the old man had on a white shirt and shorts. No weapons. The old guy carried a canvas bag, like a tote bag, over his shoulder." He paused to let this sink in. "Do you think there's a village up this trail?"

Rowlins scratched at his beard. "There's nothing on the map." "Well, they had to be coming from somewhere and going somewhere." "This is fucking nuts. Two gooks out in the middle of nowhere just taking a walk," he scratched his jaw. "Let's move out. Go another two hours and then start looking for a place to spend the night."

Holt started to get into his pack, he placed a hand on Rowlins shoulder. "Just so you know, this trail is curving west. We're nowhere near the highway anymore."

Rowlins unfolded his map and spread it out on the ground. "Where do you think we are?" he asked Holt.

Holt studied the map and pointed at a spot. "Right about here," he said. "You got your grease pencil, I'll draw in the trail."

After Holt was done, Rowlins agreed the drawing was accurate.

Rowlins tapped the map. "We'll follow the trail today and half a day tomorrow. Then we go east and find this small clearing. Unless we're told otherwise, I want to be picked up midday, the day after tomorrow. I'll let the others know. Be ready to move out in ten minutes."

Holt ate some jerky and drank some water. The men took a few minutes to eat a small meal. Holt took the opportunity to touch up his face paint, and then they were on their feet.

Holt walked slowly, watching the placement of each step. He was amazed at how quietly six men could move through the jungle. Even though he knew where the men were he had difficulty seeing them. Their camouflage blended perfectly in the dappled sunlight coming through the leaves. After an hour's walk, he called everyone to a halt and he walked into the trees to his right. He wanted to confirm they were still parallel to the trail. He came back and signaled they continue.

The ground was soft, covered with decaying leaves and thin twisted vines that snaked up the trees. The air was thick with humidity combined with the smell of rotten vegetation. It smelled like a dumpster outside a grocery store in August. He looked at his compass and picked out a gnarled, bent tree fifty feet in the distance. This was the only way to navigate in the dense jungle where visibility was extremely limited. Set your compass on something you could see, remember, and walk to it, then do it all over again. In another hour he would start looking for their NDP, their night defensive position.

He heard a rustling in the branches overhead and looked up. He saw a small group of monkeys swinging branch to branch. Good, he thought. If the monkeys were around the enemy was not. He picked up his pace a little. He stopped for a drink of water and saw land leeches on the leaves next to his arm.

The inch-long little creatures stood up searching for the source of warmth they felt. He shuddered and slapped the leaf away. He would have to remind the men to check themselves tonight before dark.

He checked his watch again. It was getting near time to stop. Up ahead he saw a large, fallen tree entangled in bushes and vines. He halted the men while he went and investigated. The spot looked good. The tree would provide cover to the front and some rocks would conceal them to their rear. He signaled for Rowlins.

"Does this look good or do you want to keep going another hour?"

"No, this is good. We'll get the men settled and hunker down. You did good work today."

Holt nodded. Rowlins signaled the men to the fallen log.

That evening, after placing their trip flares and Claymore mines, they checked each other for leeches. Jenkins had one in his armpit and Baker had one on his right ass cheek. Baker squirmed as Holt squirted it with insect repellent and pinched it off. He showed it to Baker who looked away with disgust on his face. Everyone settled down to eat their evening meal.

Holt got a tin of ham slices and ate them with crackers. He had yet to try the LURP rations. He vowed he would tomorrow. He put his pack against the tree and leaned against it. He chewed slowly, savoring the taste of the salty ham. He ate a cracker and offered one to Baker who sat on his right. He declined. He was fussing with a LURP ration of chicken and rice. He added the water and was squishing the packet between his fingers to mix it. Holt watched as he took a spoonful and made a face. Holt held up a bottle of Tabasco sauce which Baker accepted. He added some to his meal and spooned another mouthful. He looked at Holt and nodded.

Holt chewed another cracker and thought the silence was getting to him. He was used to the casual banter and laughter of the men in his squad as they ate their dinner. Not talking and no cigarettes were getting on his nerves. He remembered how much he enjoyed his coffee and cigarettes at night. He pulled his boonie hat low over his eyes and tried to sleep.

Somewhere after 0200 Baker nudged him. Holt saw that all the men were awake and staring over the log. Rowlins crab walked over to him and said, "Lafontaine heard some noise on the trail."

"You want me to go check?"

"Yeah, be careful though."

"Make sure these yahoos don't shoot me." Holt crawled off into the jungle and got near the trail. He waited and heard nothing. Through the bushes and leaves he saw some shadows moving and counted the silhouettes of five men walking down the trail. They moved silently and were soon gone. He crawled back to the log.

He crawled over to Rowlins and leaned in close.

"I saw five men heading south. I couldn't tell if they had weapons, couldn't really see anything, just five shadows. I thought two were wearing pith helmets but I can't be sure."

"Did you hear them talk?"

"Didn't hear anything. Just saw their shadows move. Five. Of that, I'm certain."

"I'll go call it in." Rowlins looked around. "This is a good spot. It's far enough off the trail that nobody should blunder into us."

"Yeah, I thought so too."

The rest of the night passed without further incidence. In the morning, the men woke. They were antsy and on edge. It was now certain that this area contained NVA activity. The men on the trail confirmed it.

Holt and Baker went into the bushes to urinate. As they were buttoning their pants, Holt whispered, "Don't forget to wash your hands." Baker responded by bringing his hand to his mouth and licking it. Holt gave him a thumbs up and they returned to their position.

Holt dug into his pack and found a Chili Con Carne LURP meal. He ripped open the package and added some water and several large dollops of hot sauce. He folded the edges of the package and kneaded it to mix the water. He set the meal aside and opened a tin of crackers with his P38 can opener. He retrieved his plastic spoon and took a large mouthful. He chewed thoughtfully. He held the meal out to Baker, "You wanna try. It's not bad."

Baker tried a spoonful and nodded, "Chili, right?"

"It would be better hot, but all in all, it's pretty good," Holt whispered.

After everyone finished their meal they gathered around Sergeant Rowlins. "Today is the fourth day, ladies. Tomorrow we go home. Today we'll continue down the trail. Tomorrow we head back east to try and find this clearing," he pointed at the map, "to get picked up. We have a good idea where this trail is. It looks like it continues west straight into Cambodia. Holt you'll walk point until noon, then Baker will take over. Tomorrow, Baker you'll switch with Lafontaine and carry the sixty and Lafontaine will walk point. Any questions? Alright, lets pack up and get moving."

About two hours in Holt found a small stream running with cool, clear water. They all stopped and passed their canteens forward. Holt filled the canteens while Baker watched his back. Once they added their purification tablets, they continued their march. A little after noon, Holt found a secluded spot and the patrol stopped for lunch.

When they finished, Holt got up and walked to his right until he saw the trail. He returned to the patrol and pointed at the trail twenty feet away. He made a walking gesture with his fingers and pointed south. Rowlins understood the foot prints of the men last night were visible and going south.

Holt switched with Baker and now walked slack. They continued on throughout the afternoon. At 1500 hours they stopped for a break. Rowlins studied his map. He sent Baker to confirm their relationship to the trail. Baker returned saying they needed to turn east just a bit to stay twenty feet off the trail.

The men gathered around Rowlins. "I don't see any value in continuing to following this trail. We have it accurately mapped to this point. It continues west. We're going to turn east and proceed to the clearing. If everything goes well, we should reach it sometime around 1400 hours tomorrow."

"That's if the clearing still exists. How old is this map? The clearing could be overgrown by now," whispered Holt.

"The map is current so we'll go on the assumption the clearing is still there." Rowlins took a small, plastic protractor and drew a straight line to the clearing and determined a compass heading of ninety five degrees east. "It's about twelve kilometers to the clearing. We should be able to do three kilometers today and easily do nine more tomorrow. Baker look for a NDP around 1800 hours. Any questions? Good. Drink some water and we'll leave in five minutes."

Rowlins signaled Holt over. "What's your impression of Baker?"

"He's good. He's doing alright. I thought he was a little flaky at first but he's settled down and is solid."

"Just keep an eye on him and check his compass headings. I don't want us drifting off target."

Holt walked up to Baker and looked over his shoulder as he set his compass to a ninety five heading. "You got a plan worked out?"

"Yeah. We have to cross the trail. Once we do, I find something at ninety five degrees and walk toward it and just keep repeating that."

"That'll work. You should know, Rowlins thinks you're doing okay. Don't fuck up and you're in."

"I'm trying not to."

"I'll stay about ten feet behind you. It's too thick in here to go any farther."

At 0615 Holt snapped his fingers. Baker stopped and looked back. Holt pointed to his left at a jumble of fallen logs nearly concealed by bushes and vines. Baker nodded and walked to the logs. He waved to Holt and Holt led the patrol to the location of their night position.

After dinner Holt saw Rowlins on the radio. He saw him put down the handset. Holt crawled over to him. "Problems?" he asked.

Rowlins shook his head. "The school agrees with me that we come into tomorrow. But some fucking Colonel thinks we should continue to follow the trail. I'm waiting to see what happens. Like this fucking trail is any big deal. This jungle is a spider web of trails. We could spend a year out here following trails. I reminded the Colonel that this was a training exercise and not a combat patrol. Fucking REMF officers!"

"So, what happens?"

"We'll go in tomorrow. The school has the final say on what we do."

"You got your mind made up on if we passed. I mean, I didn't take my turn as team leader yet."

"You all passed as far as I'm concerned. If it bothers you, you'll be team leader tomorrow. You know where we're going. Keep everything else to yourself."

"Sure, Sarge. No problem."

The next morning the men were ready at 0600.

Sergeant Rowlins addressed the men. "Holt is team leader today. Baker walk point for awhile and then switch with Lafontaine. Jenkins carry the radio and Weaver walk drag. We leave in fifteen minutes. Sergeant Holt, take us home."

Everyone's energy was renewed knowing that this was their last day. Holt went over the map with Baker and they left promptly at 0615.

CHAPTER 6

The Final Exam

By noon time, 1200 hours, they were all drenched in sweat. Holt's armpits and crotch were soaking wet and sweat ran down his back and settled in his butt crack. Holt's map, even though encased in plastic sheeting, was beginning to show the effects of the humidity. It was beginning to wear at the folds.

Lafontaine came forward to take point. Holt checked his compass setting and went over their line of march.

"We're doing about a kilometer an hour so we should reach the clearing by 1600. Any questions? You okay? Nervous?"

"I'm fine. I would rather have stayed with the sixty but I know we all got to switch up."

At 1400 they took a break. Holt, Lafontaine, and Rowlins studied the map.

"We're right on track. But if we're off fifty feet side to side, we could miss the clearing," Holt said.

"By the time we get there, we'll have somebody above us. They can direct us to the clearing. That's how we do it. They should have over flown the area yesterday. If there was a problem they would have let us know," said Rowlins.

"From your lips to God's ears."

"You religious, Sergeant Holt?"

"Can't see where it hurts to say a prayer now and then."

"Well pray you ain't fucking up and we're close to that clearing."

At 1615, 4:15 p.m. Holt began to get concerned when he saw sunlight through the trees ahead. He stopped Lafontaine and moved forward. He walked about five hundred feet and saw a stack of trees to his left. It was an old, crumbling bunker. Moss had grown all over the logs. Twenty feet more and it was the clearing. Holt determined it could land one helicopter easily. He rushed back to Sergeant Rowlins and reported the news.

Jenkins was on the radio calling in their arrival and requesting an immediate pickup. The aviation unit confirmed birds on the way.

As Lafontaine led them to the bunker, two North Vietnamese soldiers turned in from the jungle ahead of him. They fired first hitting Lafontaine twice in the shoulder. He went down hard. Holt shot the two soldiers before they could see him. The silenced Car 15 barely made a sound. He walked past Lafontaine and shot the NVA soldiers again. He threw their weapons in the jungle. When he returned to Lafontaine he was already striped of his pack and his shirt was open.

He had been shot twice. Once in his upper left shoulder below the collarbone and a second bullet wound to the left of his nipple. To his credit, he didn't make a sound while they worked on him.

Rowlins barked at Jenkins, "Where's that chopper?"

"Inbound, ten miles out."

"Tell them we got one wounded and the LZ may be hot."

"Holt, did you see any more?"

"Nothing Sarge. Maybe they were just left behind to watch the clearing."

"Let's hope so. Weaver grab his rucksack. Me and Jenkins will get him to the ship. Baker you cover us. Holt get to the clearing and pop smoke when you see the chopper."

When Holt saw the helicopter, he threw out a yellow smoke grenade. The pilot confirmed the color and came into the clearing. The five men ran towards Holt.

AK 47's opened up on the ship from the front and from behind the running men. The pilot lifted and turned the helicopter so the door gunner could fire on the bullets coming from their front.

A burst of AK fire caught Sergeant Rowlins across his legs and he went down. "Keep going, I'm alright. Get to that ship. Move it!"

The door gunner had to stop firing to the front as the men ran towards him. He redirected his M-60 to the woods. They slid Lafontaine into the cargo hold and climbed in after him.

"Where's Rowlins?" Holt shouted above the noise.

"He got hit. I thought he was behind us," shouted Jenkins.

Holt grabbed the door gunner and pulled him forward. "You guys take off. We're missing someone. I'm going to get him. Send in another ship. You got that?"

The gunner nodded he understood and Holt ran back in the jungle.

Holt found Rowlins scrunched down behind the bunker. There was sporadic rifle fire coming from the woods and chipping the logs.

"What the fuck are you doing here? I told you to get on that ship."

"No, you did not. You told me to go up and pop smoke and that's what I did."

"God damn it. You know what I meant. You're a fucking asshole! Get out of here."

"I really think you should calm down. What's done is done."

"Fuck you. I ain't never lost a man on a training patrol. Not once."

"I appreciate your concern but you're not losing me," Holt said calmly. "They're sending another chopper for us. Maybe ten or fifteen minutes. There are two Cobra's up there right now. They'll strafe the jungle and that will be it. Let me see your legs."

"My legs are fine."

"Okay. I can't carry you and your pack. I'm going to leave a little surprise for the gooks."

Holt wedged Rowlins rucksack against the logs and placed two hand grenades beneath it with the pins pulled. He took off the CS canister gas grenade from the loops on the back.

"Can you walk?

"I can walk."

Holt peeked over the top of the logs and saw soldiers running through the trees. He fired off several short bursts and saw one shadow fall.

"Come on Sarge, we got to move. We can't stay here."

Holt stood and pulled Rowlins to his feet. They started for the clearing. Rowlins legs collapsed underneath him. Holt reached down and picked him up and ran as best he could for the clearing.

As the Cobra attack helicopters prowled the wood line, Holt threw out a green smoke grenade and waited at the clearings edge.

The small observation helicopter came in firing its front mounted mini gun.

Holt threw the CS tear gas grenade behind them. The down wash from the helicopter blew the gas into the jungle. Holt picked up Rowlins and ran for the ship.

"Damn it, let me walk. I don't want you carrying me."

Holt placed Rowlins on the floor of the little chopper and pushed him in. Holt barely had time to climb aboard before the helicopter lifted.

The co-pilot turned to Holt and shouted, "What's wrong with him?"

"His legs are all shot up."

"I'll call it in."

There was an explosion in the woods and Holt knew the gooks had found Rowlins' rucksack.

Holt got his medical kit out and held up a morphine ampoule to Rowlins. He shook his head. Holt got out his cigarettes and lit two. He held one down to Rowlins who accepted.

Holt sagged back against the canvas seat and drew deeply on the cigarette. He held the smoke for a while and slowly exhaled. Finally, he sat up and shrugged off his pack and leaned back again. He got his canteen and offered it to Rowlins who shook his head.

"Sarge, what's up? You look pissed."

"Those motherfuckers back at the school will never let me live this down. Being carried out by a trainee."

Holt spread his hands and shrugged, pursed his lips and blew him a kiss.

Holt swore he heard Rowlins growl.

When the Loach landed, the helicopter was swarmed with medical personal. They slid Rowlins onto to a gurney and rushed off with him.

The pilot walked over to Holt. "I need his name and your name for the after action report."

"I'm Donald Holt and the other guy is Sergeant First Class Rowlins. His first name is Hank, no wait, I guess it's Henry. I'm not sure."

"I'll find out. I guess those are your people over there," the pilot said, pointing to a small group of Green Berets in camo fatigues. "You can wait with them."

"Shit, I'm just a trainee at the school. I got no people."

"Well go ask them what to do. Nice work out there."

"You too. Really appreciate you coming down to pick us up. It took brass balls to land in this plastic egg."

"It's what we do. No man left behind."

"You mind telling that to the Sergeant Rowlins. He seemed pissed I came back for him."

"Give him some time. I'm sure he'll be grateful."

Holt put his rucksack over one shoulder, lit a cigarette, and walked to the men waiting outside the hospital door.

"Not quite sure what I should be doing right now," he said.

One of the Sergeants turned to him and said, "You the guy that brought our boy home?"

"I guess."

The Sergeant grabbed Holt's hand and shook it vigorously. "Nice work, uh, I don't know your name."

"Sergeant Holt, Sarge."

"Well, Sergeant Holt, nice work. I heard you had to carry him to the chopper."

"You might want to leave that part out. He was pretty angry about that."

"Oh believe me that part will never be left out." The assembled group all laughed. They all shook Holt's hand.

"You good to go? Nothing wrong?"

Holt shook his head.

"Wait over by the Jeep and we'll run you back to camp. There's a Coke machine over there, get you something cold to drink."

"I don't have any money."

"The Sergeant dug out some coins from his pants. "On me."

They drove Holt back to the training facility. "Drop your gear in your barracks and report to the Headquarters They'll want to talk to you. They'll be waiting, so be quick."

At the Headquarters building Holt was directed to wait to speak with the commanding officer.

After a few minutes, a clerk directed Holt into the Major's office. Without introduction, the major slid a small tape recorder across his desk towards Holt.

"You can smoke if you want. The other members of the patrol are being debriefed at the mess hall. I want you tell me what happened out there. Start from this morning."

Holt recounted the day's events in as much detail as he remembered. Midway through he lit a cigarette. When he was done he sat back.

"What made you go back for Sergeant Rowlins?"

"I'm sorry, I don't understand."

"You went back for Rowlins, why?"

"I'm confused. Why wouldn't I go back."

"You were told to get on the chopper and leave, were you not?"

"No. He never told me that. Anyway, it wasn't his decision to make; it was mine. I was the team leader that day and Sergeant Rowlins was just an observer. I've always been told we never leave a man behind so I went back and got him." Holt stared at the major before continuing, "Are you implying I did something wrong?"

The major shuffled some papers on his desk and said, "That will be all for now. Go back and wait at the barracks. Grab a shower and get cleaned up, you're smelling a little ripe. If you want you can see if the mess hall has any food left. I imagine you're hungry."

Holt returned to the empty barracks and stripped off his dirty fatigues. He took a quick shower and put on a clean set of camo's and went to the mess hall.

There was a group of instructors sitting at a table drinking coffee. Holt walked down the serving line and asked the mess Sergeant if he could get a sandwich. The mess Sergeant reached across the steam table to shake Holt's hand.

"Thanks for bringing Sergeant Rowlins back home," he said. "I got some nice, rare roast beef and some fresh baked rye bread. That sound okay?"

"With mayo?"

"Sure thing. Find yourself a seat and I'll have a girl bring it to you."

As Holt was looking for a seat, the instructors waved him over. He sat and had to recount the events once again.

A young Vietnamese girl brought Holt's sandwich to him. As she put his sandwich on the table, she looked at Holt and grimaced and said something under her breath. She quickly turned and walked away. Holt saw her with some of the Vietnamese workers huddled together, stealing glances at him.

"What the fuck was that about?"

"Don't let it bother you. You got a scary face. Probably some dead ancestor, ghost thing. These Viet's are pretty superstitious. Could be anything."

"Maybe she saw a bat fly past her. That's like a black cat thing over here," someone added.

Holt finished his sandwich and asked, "What should I do now?"

"Go to the barracks and wait. We had three other patrols out. The officers are gathered and determining who graduates. You got nothing to worry about unless you really fucked up on patrol. You didn't fuck up, did you?"

Holt shrugged. "Not that I'm aware of."

"Then relax. They'll call you when they're ready. Make sure your team is showered and shaved. Wouldn't hurt to clean up your boots a little."

"I'm a student here, I'm not a team leader."

"Just do it, okay."

Holt entered the barracks and saw the team members in various stages of dress. Jenkins came up to him wrapped in a towel. His body looked like it was chiseled out of a block of ebony, every muscle was clearly defined.

"Man, we were worried about you. They separated us and each of us was grilled about the patrol. They wanted to know every little detail," Jenkins said.

"They barely asked me the time of day. Their big concern was why I returned for Rowlins."

"Same with us. We all told them we thought Rowlins was right behind us. It wasn't until we got to the chopper that we found out he fell behind. We told them you ran back for him and we took off. We were taking heavy fire and couldn't remain on the ground."

Holt sat on his foot locker and rested his elbows on his knees. He took a deep drag off his cigarette.

"You guys did nothing wrong. Fucking shit happens. You got on the chopper like you were told and I went and got Rowlins. I was the one that told the chopper to take off. It's as simple as that."

Jenkins was about to say something when a Sergeant First Class poked his head through the screen door. "Assemble in the mess hall in one hour for graduation ceremonies. Congratulations, you all made it. Look sharp," he said.

The men dressed in their standard jungle fatigues and were assembled outside the mess hall ten minutes in advance of the ceremony. In total, twenty one students were graduating. Two thirds of their original class had been dismissed.

The ceremony was efficient, quick, and without fanfare. A major pinned the subdued Recondo patch on their right pocket and posed for a photograph. After each man received his patch the major gave a short speech and the ceremony was concluded. A captain went to the front of the room and read off a list of names. Sixteen men from the graduating class were going on to Airborne training at the Air force base on the southern end of the Nha Trang compound.

Holt walked over to Weaver and Baker.

"I didn't realize you guys were going to jump school. I thought you were here for Recondo tabs and would be gone," said Holt. "When did you volunteer?"

"Shit, we didn't volunteer. They volunteered us. We just found out about it," said Weaver.

"You're here, you might as well get it over with. Look at it this way, it's an extra sixty five dollars a month."

A sergeant told the men to go over to the supply room and purchase extra tabs and rockers for their fatigues. "I'd buy a bunch. They are not readily available, so get extra. When you sew these on leave room for the Airborne rocker; it goes above the Recondo rocker. That is assuming you mutts pass jump school."

At the supply room, the men were told the patches and rockers were sold as a set for three dollars. Holt purchased a dozen of the subdued patches and a half dozen of the full color version, as did most of the men.

That evening, after food, they were told they could go to the EM club. They were warned not to get drunk as they would start jump school the next day.

At the club, the team sat together. As a graduation present, Holt bought a bottle of Jack Daniels and round of Cokes. They exchanged background stories and told lies about their accomplishments in Vietnam. No one asked Holt about his scars.

At some point a master Sergeant summoned Holt. He was an imposing figure in his tiger stripes and green beret. "I see your team is getting along. What do you think of them?"

"Not my team, Sarge. But yeah, they're a good group. Let me ask a question. When are you going to tell the two spec fours they volunteered for Special Forces?"

The Sergeant laughed. "What makes you think we want them?"

"Just a feeling."

"When the time is right I'll make them an offer they can't refuse. They gotta jump first. Same goes for you. You don't jump, you're out. You'll find your ass shipped back to a line unit."

"How many guys fuck up the school?"

"You guys have done the worst part already. Coming from here you get to skip all the physical conditioning bullshit. Tomorrow you'll start on the towers. In eight days you'll have your wings."

"What if I freeze? I heard some guys do."

"I'll be in charge of your training. I'll be right behind you. Sergeant Major Soujac said if you freeze I am to throw your skinny ass out the plane myself."

"You know Sergeant Soujac?"

"Me and Carl go way back. Did a bunch of mischief together. He spoke highly of you. One way or the other you'll get your wings. Go back to your men. One more hour and then hit the sack. Don't want no one puking tomorrow."

CHAPTER 7

Jump School

After the rigors of Recondo school, Jump school was almost anti climatic.

Once breakfast was finished, the sixteen graduates turned in all the gear they used during Recondo training. They were allowed to purchase one set of Tiger Stripe fatigues, which most of them did. They loaded their meager possessions onto to a deuce and a half truck and were driven across the base to where the jump school was set up. Upon arrival, they stowed their gear in a barracks and assembled outside.

They were greeted by a tall, slender Sergeant First Class wearing a black baseball cap. His fatigue shirt was adorned with a variety of patches including the Special Forces shoulder patch.

"My name is Sergeant Holmes and I will be your instructor for this eight day course. Since you have all come from the Recondo school, we are going to forgo any of the physical training portion of the school. We will do morning calisthenics and you will be required to pass the standard Army physical training test; the same one you passed in basic and AIT training."

The first three days were spent learning how to properly land and how to exit the aircraft. They became familiar with the T-10 parachute. The T-10 was a non-steerable parachute weighing thirty two pounds for the complete assembly. It had an inflated diameter of twenty-five feet and a descent rate of twenty-two to twenty-four feet per second depending on the jumpers weight. Its service life was twelve years and its shelf life was four to five years.

"We don't keep accurate records of the service life so hopefully you'll be issued one of the newer chutes. We haven't been able to determine how the climate over here affects the chute material. We're confident that mold and humidity have minimal effect. Let's hope so."

Jenkins leaned into Holt and whispered, "He's kidding about that stuff. Right?"

"I'm sure it's just Airborne humor. You know, hazing the new guys."

"We're going to start the training with you jumping off various boxes, benches, and tables ranging from two to six feet high. I will first demonstrate the parachute landing fall. The PLF is a technique that will, hopefully, allow you to land safely without injury. It allows you to displace the energy of landing at high speeds. You will land with your feet and knees together. The moment you land, you are going to go from a vertical to horizontal position in such a manner to absorb and minimize the impact. When landing, you will keep your knees slightly bent. Your feet strike the ground first and you will immediately throw yourself sideways to distribute the landing energy. You will go from the balls of your feet, to the side of your calf, to your thigh, and to your hip and finally onto your side or back.

Keep your arms tight to your chest and tuck your chin in. I am now going to demonstrate the fall."

The sergeant climbed up onto the two foot high wooden box which was placed in a saw dust filled pit. He jumped off the box and did a perfect PLF.

"You now will each do one jump in front of me."

He closely watched as each of the men did their PLF landing. "Line up and do it again."

"There are four more boxes over there. For the next hour we will practice the landing." He watched as each man landed, commenting where necessary. When the hour was up, they took a ten minute break.

Holt and Jenkins stood off to the side smoking and quietly talking.

"Damn! I just know my whole side is going to be bruised," said Jenkins, as he stretched out his back.

"I didn't realize you were so delicate," Holt replied. "Quit bitching, we're jumping into a pit filled with saw dust. Anyway, you're black. How will you tell if you're bruised?"

"Because my body will hurt you fucking moron."

"Field strip your cigarettes and put the butts in your pocket. Don't mess up my training area," hollered Sergeant Holmes. "Let's get back to it."

For the remainder of the day, and the next two days, they jumped off boxes and tables of varying heights until they all perfected the PLF. What once was interesting and exciting became mind-numbing boredom. The whole point was to commit the process to muscle memory. On the fourth day, they jumped from the fuselage of a disassembled C-130. They learned the commands required to complete the actual jumps. The learned the ten minute hand command, the five minute hand command, and the five second command. They hooked up their static lines to cables running the length of the ship and shuffled to the door. They stood at the open door waiting until they were tapped on the shoulder, then jumped to ground. They were told the first person in line was to run their hand around the door frame to insure there were no rough edges that could possibly cut their static line. They did this for several hours. Later that afternoon, they toured the rigging room and saw how the parachutes were packed. They were able to examine the chutes and try on actual parachutes. The chutes weighed a little over thirty two pounds and the smaller reserve chutes weighed half that much.

Holt asked how would they carry their rucksacks.

"That's a good question," Holmes said. "They will be strapped to your harness below your reserve chute. Your weapons will be secured on top of your rucksack. Your rucksack will be attached to your harness with a quick release strap. As you near the ground, you pull the strap and release your ruck and it will fall away from you and hit the ground first. With your rucksack attached, you won't be able to walk normally. You just sort of waddle along. Carrying your packs, you will just shuffle along until you get to the door. You'll probably need help getting into the plane. We will make one jump with a simulated combat load."

They got into a loose formation and jogged back to the plane fuselage for several more practice jumps. Everywhere they went within base camp they had to jog or run.

On the way, Sergeant Holmes explained that they would be making most of the jumps without full combat gear. "The chances of you jumping here in Vietnam is slim to none. Helicopter insertion is the preferred method of combat insertion. But it could happen. The French did a massive combat jump to reinforce their base at Dien Bien Phu in the fifties. It could happen again. An identical situation occurred at Khe Sanh. There was some speculation that a jump would be made there. Any jump you would do here in Vietnam would more than likely be a exhibition jump.

The fifth day they moved onto the tower training phase of jump school. Their first obstacle was the swing landing trainer. Here they were strapped into the parachute harness. The jumped from a deck and were held six feet, dangling above the ground. Apparently this simulated the shock of the chute opening. They were held swinging for several minutes and dropped. Not until everyone had once again perfected the PLF did they move on. Next was jumping from a tower hooked onto a cable. The cable was angled at such a degree to mimic the landing speed of an actual jump. Emphasis was placed on getting their harness adjusted properly. The leg straps had to be adjusted to avoid any contact with the jumpers testicles. The hardest part of this training was climbing up the tower steps. By the afternoon their legs felt like jelly.

As they took a break, Sergeant Holmes addressed the men, "Gentlemen, depending on how you look at it, you have either lucked out or you'll be missing an essential part of your training. This is a new facility and we haven't finished construction of our two hundred fifty foot tower. In the past we have sent our candidates to the 101st Airborne Division jump school at Phan Rang. That's about ninety six kilometers down south. Not only do we lose two days in transport, but more importantly we lose control over our candidates. We train a variety of indigenous people here. We have found that when we outsource training of our native candidates they are not given the proper respect and courtesy they deserve, nor are they accommodated as they should be. So we have decided to do all our training in house. The reality is once you learn your PLF, we could jump on your first day. You can only fuck it up once."

At the end of the day they jogged back to their barracks. Their evenings were free and mostly they went to the EM club for cheese burgers and beer. None of the men over indulged. They needed clear, sharp minds for the training ahead. That evening as they sat in the barracks Weaver came over to Holt.

"Hey Sarge, I got a question. Why do they keep referring to us as 'our candidates'? They know Baker and I are going back to our Ranger unit, don't they?"

"Maybe."

"What does that mean?"

"It means you're here now. And if they want you to stay, here's where you stay."

Holt stared at him a minute. "You looked pissed. Why? This is a much better outfit. Special Forces is top tier. You can't get any better. You'll make Sergeant in no time. You'll get to write your girl you are now a Green Beret. That's got to impress her."

"I don't know. I gotta think about this."

"Don't think too hard. It's not your choice, dude. It's the Army, you go where and when they send you."

He watched as Weaver walked over to Baker, both were frowning.

The next morning Holmes greeted them before they went to eat. "I'm suggesting you eat a light breakfast this morning. You are getting your PT test today. Having gone through Recondo school you should not have any problem passing."

Weaver raised his hand and asked to speak to Sergeant Holmes. He expressed his concern about returning to his Ranger unit.

"You will go where you are sent; where you are needed most." He looked at Weaver. "Don't for one minute think you'll fail this PT test. I've seen your previous scores and if you fail, I will hold you over and you will do this school again until you pass. Understood? Now get back in line."

After breakfast, the men assembled for the test. They had to do thirty five pushups in two minutes and forty five sit ups in another two minutes. Finally, they ran two miles in sixteen minutes.

The men easily completed the pushups and sit ups. Before starting the run, Holt was told he was allowed an extra thirty seconds in consideration of his previous wounds. They were to run one mile straight down the road to where a Sergeant stood with a red flag. They were to turn around and return to Sergeant Holmes.

Holt chose to run next to Jenkins. They started off at fast jog and gradually increased their speed. As they neared the second Sergeant, he hollered at them to pick up their pace. "Seven minutes thirty seconds. Move your ass!"

Jenkins looked at Holt who was breathing hard. "Can you do it?"

"I got this, no problem. You can go on ahead."

Jenkins lengthened his stride and was soon fifty yards ahead of Holt. Holt pushed himself faster and soon reduced it to thirty yards where he held himself. Holt finished the run in fifteen minutes forty five seconds. He was the last one in.

As Holt passed in front of Sergeant Holmes he said, "Good Lord that was pitiful. It was like watching a duck run."

"Did I pass?" Holt asked.

"You passed."

While gasping for air Holt said, "I'm built for endurance, not speed."

"We'll see about that after you've climbed the tower a few more times."

They spent the rest of the day practicing on the landing trainer and the cable slide. At the barracks Sergeant Holmes said tomorrow would be a jump day. They would complete three jumps and the remaining two the day after. One of the three jumps would be at night. He released them for dinner and told them to get a good night's rest.

The next morning, two men were missing from formation. One had a sprained ankle and the other had a swollen knee. They had requested to be recycled and would do the course again. The remaining men were loaded onto a truck and driven to the airbase where they stood before a battered C-47 airplane. On tables outside the plane were their parachutes and a standard issue M-1 helmet fitted with a paratrooper chin strap. They spent the next hour going over their parachutes and adjusting the straps until everything fit perfectly.

"I got good news and I got bad news," said Sergeant Homes. "Today you'll be jumping with a dozen South Vietnamese Rangers on their qualifying jumps. They'll be on one side of the plane and we'll be on the other side. We won't interact with them in any manner. That's the bad news. The good news is since we are jumping with them, we also qualify as paratroopers of South Vietnam. You'll be issued a set of their jump wings upon successful completion of your five jumps. You wear them over your left shirt pocket."

One of the men in the back of the line raised his hand. "Sarge, I've heard all sorts of stories about guys freezing up and refusing to jump. What if that happens?"

"No one is authorized to freeze up in my fucking airplane. Is that understood? You will all jump!" Sergeant Holmes eyed the men. "Seriously, if you repelled from a helicopter you'll have no problem here. You'll be crammed together so tight, ass to elbow, you'll waddle to the door and step off. I'll hear no more talk of freezing up. You won't embarrass me in front of our little Asian allies."

Next they took pictures of each man and a group photograph. "This is in case your chute doesn't open. We at least know what you looked like," the photographer said.

"He's kidding, right?" someone said from the back.

They entered the airplane with some difficulty on the steps. They walked down the left side and took a seat on the webbed seats. The South Vietnamese Rangers entered through the right cargo door. They were all smiling nervously. The engines started and the interior became one big vibration of deafening noise.

Holt was fourth in line right behind Jenkins. He leaned in close and said, "I hope and pray I don't piss my pants."

"You and me both."

"I wish that asshole didn't mention that shit about freezing at the door. Now, that's all I'm thinking about."

Jenkins swallowed hard and looked at the floor.

After about twenty minutes of flight time Sergeant Holmes raised both arms. They all stood. "Clip on!" he shouted. The men all clipped their static lines onto the cable. Holmes walked down the line and checked each connection. He returned to the front and flashed ten fingers, "Ten minutes! Move towards the door."

The men shuffled forward tight to the man in front.

Holt leaned into Jenkins. "I wish we had time to check these chutes again. Yours looks all fucked up. There's all sort of shit hanging out of it. I'm sure it'll be okay."

Jenkins turned his head and mouthed the words, "Fuck you."

Holmes held up five fingers, "Five minutes!" he shouted.

The men inched together tighter. "First man move to the door."

The first man checked the door frame and nodded at Sergeant Holmes.

Holt moved tighter to Jenkins pushed along by the man behind him.

"Ten Seconds!" Holmes shouted.

Above the door the red light went out and a second light turned green.

"Go! Go! Go!" shouted Holmes.

Before he had time to think, Holt was moved along and was at the door. He crossed his arms on his chest, closed his eyes, and stepped out.

He felt a sickening feeling in his stomach reminiscent of being on a roller coaster. In no time at all he felt the jolt of the chute deploying and he opened his eyes and looked up at the blossoming canopy. He grabbed the chutes risers with each hand and held them in a death grip. He felt like he was holding his breath. Finally he looked down to the ground below. There was no sound except the air rushing past his ears. The plane was a distant spec in the sky. He saw the other men dangling like marionettes from their chutes. They jumped at six hundred feet but it felt like thousands. He saw the ground coming up and bent his legs. Without a conscious thought, he did an acceptable PLF. The whole jump lasted about thirty seconds. All around him men were falling to the ground.

He got to feet and started to gather his chute. He walked over to Jenkins on wobbly legs.

"God damn, we did it, brother. We fucking did it!"

Jenkins looked at his crotch. "Shit, I swear I gave a squirt when we jumped."

Holt checked him over. "If you did the wind dried it."

Two hours later they did it again. They were driven back to the barracks, ate, and returned to the airfield for their night jump.

That night in the EM club they discussed how scared they were and how great the jump was.

The next morning, they were at the airfield by eight AM and they had completed their two final qualifying jumps by two PM. Their fourth jump was completed with rucksacks and weapons. The rucksacks were loaded with sandbags to simulate a full combat load.

The men gathered on the ground with their parachutes and congratulated each other. They began the long walk to the truck that would take them to their barracks. Sergeant Holmes was waiting by the truck.

"Congratulations men. You have successfully completed your jump certification. Clean yourselves up, put on some fresh fatigues and assemble at the mess hall at 1600 hours for the formal graduation ceremony."

At 1545 hours the men milled about the mess hall door. The exhilaration of their completed jumps were still fresh in their minds. At exactly 1600 hours they were called inside and assembled in two rows of seven. One by one they were called forward and presented with their wings by a major in immaculate starched fatigues. They were directed to a table where they given their jump certification orders, log books in which their jumps were recorded, and two, eight-by-ten pictures taken the previous day. They were also given cloth badges for both the American and South Vietnamese jump wings to be worn on their fatigues. Finally, they were issued a pair of highly polished jump boots.

"Gentlemen, one final announcement before you head over to the club to celebrate. Report back here tomorrow with all your gear at 1000 hours for your unit assignments and transportation authorizations."

As soon as the major left Baker started in with questions. "You don't think they can just keep us, do you?"

Jenkins shrugged. "The Army can do whatever it wants with you."

"Why are you so hot to get back to the Rangers? How long were you with them?" asked Holt.

"Just over two months. I got friends there. All my stuff is there."

"You don't have any stuff," Jenkins said. "It's the Army's stuff. They gave it to you."

"What about you, Weaver? You want to return to the Rangers?" Holt asked.

"I don't really care one way or the other. Special Forces might be cool."

"See. Weaver got the right attitude. Just go with the flow."

In the morning, they all stood before the Major.

"I'm pleased to inform you, you have all been accepted into the Special Forces. Here are your assignments." The first five men were assigned to Command and Control North at Da Nang. The next were four were going to

C and C Central at Kontum. Holt and his group were assigned Command and Control South at Ban Me Thout.

"You have your travel orders. There's a truck outside that will take you to the airfield. You'll catch your flight there. If you left any gear at your old unit it will be forwarded to you. Any questions? Good! I wish you good luck. It was a pleasure having you here. Dismissed."

As they left the mess hall, Baker mumbled under his breath, "Fuck me."

CHAPTER 8

Forms And Shots

When they arrived at Ban Me Thout, they stood in front of another Major. Apparently the one thing the Special Forces wasn't lacking were officers.

"I know some of you may feel you have been drafted into the Special Forces. Let me assure you that nothing could be further from the truth. Some of you volunteered, some were recruited but all of you were carefully accessed during your time at Recondo and jump school. You have each been given a opportunity to join an elite fighting unit that may not have been available to you under normal circumstances. You might be fearful having heard we suffer an abnormally high rate of casualties. Technically, that's true. But we have a very high rate of survival because we have dedicated aviation units available to us twenty four hours, round the clock. Your field operations will be constantly monitored and supporting fire is available at a moment's notice." The Major paused. "I'm not going to lie to you. You all can expect to be wounded at least once. Not all of you will be but those that are have a better chance of survival with us than in most line units. Our medics are the most highly trained combat medical personal in the Army. For those who have not volunteered to be here you will be given an opportunity to resign and return to your old unit. But we ask you wait a few days and see what we are all about. You'll see that we're very informal here. Normal military courtesy still applies but you will not be subjected to make work assignments. The more distasteful tasks of camp life are farmed out to native employees. You'll spend your down time resting and recuperating or in training to enhance your skills." Again he paused and looked at each man. "Let's take a short break and we will continue in twenty minutes."

Besides Holt and his group, there were three other men at the briefing. They all introduced each other. One of the three men was a qualified Ranger and Baker and Weaver went over to talk to him.

Lafontaine, still recuperating from his wounds, asked Holt, "You think we'll stay together?"

"I doubt it. Me and Jenkins will get split up for sure. Can't have two Staff Sergeants in the same squad."

"What do you think Baker will do? He's been whining about getting shanghaied into this outfit."

Holt lit a cigarette and exhaled loudly. "Who knows? You think this would be a step up for a Ranger. Hell, it's step up for all of us. I gotta ask, you missed jump school, why are you here?"

"They gave me a pass for now based on my performance at Recondo school. I'll have to do the jump training later."

The Major and a Captain entered the room. "Alright. Grab some coffee or a soft drink and let's settle down. Captain Parson will continue the briefing and I will return for any follow up questions."

The men sat in a semi circle around the Captain.

"To begin, I imagine you all have questions about what you will be doing. In Command and Control South, we conduct patrols along the Cambodian border or across the border into Cambodia. All our missions are highly classified and cannot be discussed outside of our organization. The whole purpose of the missions are to observe enemy troop movements and to avoid enemy contact. Occasionally we will conduct ambush patrols and prisoner grabs. We also assist in rescuing downed pilots. The missions normally last from five to seven days. Sometimes longer under special circumstances. Missions into Cambodia are conducted sterile, that is to say, you have nothing on you to indicate you are an American soldier. All your clothing and gear will be of foreign origin. This gives us plausible deniability in the event you are captured or killed. Believe me when I say we will move heaven and earth ensure this doesn't happen. But in the event it does, you will be listed as killed in action or missing in action, presumed dead. This is the main difference of what you do in a line unit or for you Rangers, on your Long Range Reconnaissance Patrols. You might be asking what are the advantages of being here. For one thing, we try to insulate you from all the normal Army chicken shit. We treat you as professionals and expect you to act accordingly. You'll make rank faster here than anywhere else. You can expect to have interesting and valuable assignments all over the world. I can't think of a better place to serve your country. Any questions?" After a moment he continued. "Okay get situated in your barracks and take the night to think about it. Tomorrow, after food, report back at 1000 hours and let us know your decision. Someone can point you in the direction of the EM and NCO clubs. Have a good evening."

The next morning, after breakfast, they assembled in the briefing room.

Before the officers arrived, they got coffee from a large silver urn and stood around talking and smoking.

Baker came up to Holt and Jenkins. "Last night I talked to a few Rangers and they convinced me this was a natural progression and that I was fortunate to be offered this position. I gave it a lot of thought and I'm going to stay."

"Good for you. I think you made the right decision," said Holt. "I guess we should take our seats, I see the officers coming."

The Major and the Captain were accompanied by a Specialist Fourth Class who carried a large brown envelope stuffed with paper. He sat a table stacked with clipboards.

Without preamble the Major began, "So, are we all going to stay?" He looked around the room and preceded. "Good. We have some paperwork to be completed. It wouldn't be the Army without forms to be completed. Once you've completed your forms, you'll go to supply room and draw your gear. Welcome to the Special Forces. Captain Parson will remain to assist."

Completing the paper work took almost two hours. It was getting near noon and the men were told to take a break, have lunch, and meet at the supply room at 1330.

They met at supply and went inside. A Sergeant First Class stood behind a long wooden counter supported by large wooden cabinets. Behind him were floor to ceiling racks of folded clothing with a clerk specialist in attendance. One by one the men were called forward.

Holt moved forward when it was his turn. He was first issued a standard Army ruck sack attached to an aluminum frame. Next came four sets of standard jungle fatigues and four sets of Tiger Stripe fatigues.

"Around base camp you wear your jungle fatigues with full badging. Your Tiger Stripes get no badging and are for field use only," said the sergeant. "Mr. Lao is next door at the tailor shop he'll sew up your badging at a reasonable price."

"Does anyone need an extra set of jungle boots?"

Everyone raised their hand.

"I don't know why I even bother to ask."

Along with the jungle boots, they received a pair of Bata Boots, a mesh-like high top sneaker. "You wear these at night in the jungle to give your feet a chance to dry. They're similar to the boots the NVA wear."

Next came seven pair of socks, four olive drab t-shirts, and four green drawers. Two medium-sized olive drab towels were next along with two boonies hats, one olive drab, the other in tiger stripe. "Mr. Lao will cut down the brim of camo boonie hat. We all wear them trimmed. How many canteens?" the Sergeant asked Holt.

"Four plastic and two collapsible if you got them. I only need one canteen pouch and one cup."

"We got them. How many magazines?"

"Thirty," answered Holt

"Thirty? You sure?"

"That's what I carry."

"Thirty it is."

Finally came web gear, a jungle hammock, ammo pouches, a combat knife, a compass, a strobe light, wrist watch with webbed strap, a mess kit, entrenching tool, a machete, poncho and poncho liner, a ground cloth, a roll of green aviation tape, and a bundle of parachute cord. "Your medic will issue you your medical pouch separately." The last items issued were four tubes of camouflage face paint and two combination locks clipped together with a wired cardboard tag with the combination written on it.

The Sergeant slid a form across the counter. "Review this form and sign and date it. Pack up your gear and wait outside. Next."

Holt stood outside with Jenkins smoking.

"That was efficient," Jenkins said.

"Short and sweet. These guys have it down to a science," Holt responded.

"What's next do you think?"

"Weapons?"

When everyone was done, they walked next door to the Armory, a squat, cinder block building surrounded by sand bags with heavy steel doors.

The same Sergeant opened the locked door and flicked on the lights. "One by one come in."

When Holt entered he was asked which he preferred a M-16 or a Colt AR-15. He chose the AR-15.

"Do you want a side arm? Browning Hi Power or Colt 1911 45?"

"The Browning will be fine."

Holt signed and dated a separate form for each weapon.

The Sergeant reviewed the forms matching the serial numbers of the weapons. "I had a chance to glance at your 201 file. I think you'll like it here. You made a good choice."

"Thanks Top. I think so too."

"Head over to Mr. Lao and get your fatigues badged. Good luck to you." Holt waited at the tailor's on a bench outside until he was called in.

Several others were waiting and they chatted quietly, waiting their turn.

Inside were Mr. Lao, a stooped Vietnamese man with close cropped grey hair, and a small boy sitting on a stool.

Without introduction, Mr. Lao said boonie hat which Holt handed over. The hat was passed to the boy who quickly trimmed two inches off the brim with scissors which looked much too big for his small hands. With the hat given back, the brim was sewed on an old Singer sewing machine and the edge sealed with some sort of glue.

The boy looked at Holt with fear in his eyes.

Holt gave him his four fatigue shirts. Over his left pocket, the United States Army patch was sewn, over his right pocket was his name tag. Beneath his name tag were his South Vietnamese jump wings and on the pocket itself was the Recondo patch. Above the Army patch was his Combat Infantry Badge and beneath that were his United States jump wings. On his right shoulder was the insignia for the twenty fifth infantry division and on his left shoulder was the Special Forces Badge topped by three rockers, the first said Special Forces, the second said Airborne and finally a tab that read Recondo. All four shirts were done expertly in less than ten minutes.

"Is your boy afraid of me?"

"Not my boy. Orphan. He scared of everything."

"He looks terrified."

"He stupid boy." He reached over and slapped the boy across his head. "All done. Eight dollar for me, one dollar to the boy," said Mr. Lao holding out his hand. "You go now and boy not be scared."

Holt counted the military script and went outside and retrieved his gear. He thanked the soldier who watched his weapons. Holt sat with Jenkins while he waited his turn. When finished, they shouldered their rucksacks and walked back to the barracks.

Jenkins looked at his watch. "It's almost three thirty, what's next?"

Holt shrugged as he lit a cigarette. "There's that clerk from this morning, we could ask him."

The clerk said, "Go stow your gear and relax. Tomorrow, you go to medical and get your shots updated. Don't forget to bring your shot card. We should have everyone's assignments by then."

As they walked to the barracks Holt asked Jenkins if the tailor's boy was afraid of him.

"No. Why do you ask?"

"The kid took one look at me and was shitting his pants."

"Do you blame him? You're a walking nightmare."

"Thanks, you always know what to say. That makes me feel better."

The next morning, Holt sat in the medical bunker as the medic read his shot card.

"Let's see what you got here. You got your smallpox, yellow fever, cholera, typhoid, tetanus, typhus, plague, and flu vaccines. You're up to date on all of them. You're good to go. Anything else you need?'

"The supply Sergeant said something about getting a medical kit? Do we get that from you?"

"No. Your team medic will issue that later. It has enough pills so that you could open your own pharmacy. It has to be tightly controlled."

"Thanks. What's up next?"

"Go hang around your barracks. They'll come get you when they're ready. Word of advice, swing by the Post Exchange and pickup anything you need. You might not have time later."

Jenkins was up next. As he passed, Holt told him he would wait outside for him.

Before returning to the barracks, they stopped at the Post Exchange. Holt bought two cartons of Marlboro cigarettes, several large packages of beef jerky, tooth paste and a new tooth brush, some razor blades, and shampoo. At the mess hall they got coffee and sat outside drinking it.

"Do you think they'll keep us together?" asked Holt

"If they know that's what we want then I'm certain that's what they won't do. The Army never misses a chance to fuck you over."

"Will they accept us as real Special Forces?"

"I think we're just fresh meat to be thrown into the grinder. They need replacements quick and they found us."

"Shake and bake Green Berets?"

"Something like that."

"Didn't they say we'd be going to some Ranger outfit for additional training," Holt said while lighting another cigarette.

"I heard them talking the other day. They said they didn't want to lose control of us. The Rangers need guys just as bad as they do. They're afraid once the Rangers got hold of us they would keep us."

At 1100 hours they were called into the briefing room adjacent to the command post. In an informal ceremony they were given their Green Berets by a Major. They took two pictures, one, the presentation of the beret and a second, a beauty shot against a blue screen back drop.

"Your pictures will be ready shortly. Men, be proud to wear the beret and make us all proud of you." And the major left. Captain Parson remained and sat behind a desk stacked with manila envelopes. One by one he called each man forward and gave him orders for their new assignment. Holt and Jenkins were last to be assigned. He called them both up front together.

"I pulled a few strings and kept you two together. You'll both be going to Katum Special Forces Camp." He stood and they all went to a large map pinned to the wall. "Let's see," he said as he ran his finger over the map.

"Here it is, about twenty five miles northeast of Tay Ninh and about five miles south of the Cambodian border. We share the base with the 1st Brigade of the 25th Infantry Division." He turned to look at them. "That's your old outfit, correct? This should be a good fit because it's terrain you're familiar with. It's all jungle, forest, and rubber plantations. You boys won't be climbing any mountains… at least for now.'

"It'll be like going home again," said Jenkins.

"There's a flight out at 0900 hours tomorrow morning. You can take the rest of the day off. Get your gear squared away and relax. Check back in about an hour and your photos will be ready." He extended his hand. "Gentlemen, it was a pleasure to meet you. I'm looking forward to hearing good things about you both."

Before they left Holt began to say, "Captain, our mail—"

"Yes, I know. Once you're settled at Katum we'll get your mail and pay squared away. You'll also get your leave situation arranged."

As they headed over to the NCO club, they saw the clerk from before. Holt stopped him and asked what he knew about Katum.

"Is that where they're sending you? Shit! It's the ass end of the world. Gets hit every night with rockets and mortars. It's one step up from the Flintstones. But hell, they got a club and an airstrip, so it can't be all that bad."

With that ominous warning, he walked off.

CHAPTER 9

Camp Kaboom

They had been at Katum for almost three months.

When they first arrived Jenkins applied for and was granted a thirty day leave for re-enlistment. He returned to the states to see his wife. Holt chose to go to Thailand for ten days and saved the remainder of his leave. Since his return from Thailand, Holt had been on five long distance patrols. He served as a replacement on Sergeant Brown's team. While Sergeant Brown was on R & R, Holt went on his sixth patrol with another team as a straphanger.

The team's landing zone was a small clearing north of Tay Ninh. Almost immediately they came under fire from a large unit of NVA. With their back to the LZ they were surrounded on three sides. They called in helicopter support but the gunship's did little to dislodge the enemy. The volume of fire was so heavy that a helicopter extraction was impossible. Six Americans and sixty Montagnards were inserted in a large clearing six miles away to rescue the patrol. Joe Jenkins was one of the Americans. It took them four hours to arrive. By then, all six surrounded team members had been wounded at least once, two severely. Their ammunition was so low they were reduced to using AK-47's captured from the North Vietnamese. They were out of grenades and exploded all their Claymore mines. They were on the verge of being overrun and declared a Prairie Fire emergency.

A Prairie Fire declaration obligated any available aircraft to come to their aid. They threw out strobe lights to mark the edge of their small, pitiful perimeter and helicopter gunships strafed the NVA as close as ten yards. Between helicopter runs Air force A 1 Sky raiders strafed the enemy with 20 MM cannon fire, rockets and 250 pound bombs. The low, slow flying airplanes came in time and time again under heavy enemy fire. Finally, the support column arrived and the Montagnards savagely attacked the remaining North Vietnamese. The Montagnards set about mutilating the bodies of the NVA. They cut the ears off the NVA to prove their kill to their Special Forces paymaster and receive a bonus for every dead NVA soldier. The final count was one hundred sixty two North Vietnamese killed. Only the six American patrol members were wounded.

The Montagnards claimed credit for all the enemy dead, even those killed before their arrival. The likelihood was that the helicopters and Sky raiders did the most damage.

While Holt waited for the medi-vacs helicopter he thanked Jenkins for their arrival. "You got here just in time. We were all out of ammo and using the gooks AK's. I saved my pistol in case. For a while it didn't look good. Thanks brother."

They both watched as the Montagnards picked up enemy weapons and scavenged through the dead soldiers possessions.

"Once you let those motherfuckers go, there's no holding them back," Holt said.

"They fight like wild animals. You just let them loose and stand back. I swear, they have no fear." Jenkins offered Holt a cigarette. "You hit bad?"

"A bullet bounced off my rib, came out my side and into my arm. Two, three weeks, and I'll be as good as new."

As Jenkins lit their cigarettes he said, "You might want to reconsider your occupation."

"Hell, the way it is I spend half my time in the hospital. Getting wounded is a scam I've perfected."

"Yeah, that's a good plan. I'd stick with it. Your rides here. Take it easy and I'll see you back at the base."

The medic helped Holt to his feet. He picked up his gear and walked to the Medi-vacs helicopter.

Twenty days later he was released from the hospital and was given light duty working with the medics providing medical assistance to the camp's Montagnards. During this time he met many of the camps mercenary contingent and learned enough words to have a passable conversion. Unlike the South

Vietnamese and Chinese Hmong, the Montagnards accepted his facial scars as a badge of honor and courage.

After two weeks, he was called to meet with First Sergeant Banter. "I think it's about time you had your own team. Do you think you're ready?"

"I am. I'm ready."

"I understand you've developed quite a rapport with our Montagnards."

"I've tried to learn about them, their culture and stuff. Like the Indians back in the States, they've been fucked over by their government. I kind of sympathize with them. I've seen them in action; they're good fighters." "That's good. What I'm thinking is that your team will be six Americans and twelve Montagnards. You'll start off doing patrols between Tai Ninh and here. We have a team whose leader rotated home. They're over in barracks twelve. I told them to stand by. Go over and introduce yourself and get settled in. Once you're done there, head over to the Montagnards and find a sergeant named Sangh. He'll be your Montagnard sergeant, together you'll select your team. Sangh is a good guy; been with us a long time. You can trust his judgment. When you're all set, come back here."

Holt found the barracks. He stood outside and adjusted his beret, knocked on the door, and went in.

The room consisted of six bunks separated by wooden partitions. In the middle of the room was a picnic table and benches. Three men sat at the table playing cards and two sat in chairs reading. They looked up as he entered. Holt sat down and lit a cigarette and introduced himself. They all remained quiet.

"How about we all go around the room and introduce yourselves."

"I'm Sergeant Evans, Richard. You can call me Rick, not Dick. I'm the assistant team leader."

Holt waved his hand. "A little more, where you from?"

"California. The northern part. I enlisted. Figured I was going to be drafted anyway so why not get it over with."

Evans was of average height, slender build, and deeply tanned.

"I'm Michael Smith. Sergeant. Also from California. The southern part. Dropped out of college and was drafted. Once I was in I decided to volunteer for Airborne. I also completed Ranger training. Then did the Special Forces training. I figured the longer I kept volunteering for shit the longer I'd stay in the States. And now I'm here."

"You kind of got the surfer vibe going on. Your hair is almost bleached white."

"I did some surfing."

"How long in country?"

"Four months. Me and Rick came over together."

Holt took a drag of the cigarette before continuing. "And you two?"

"I'm Ryan Davis and this is my cousin John Davis. We signed up on the buddy system. Both from Athens, Arkansas. It's a little town outside of Blytheville. We did jump school and got talked into Special Forces training and here we are."

"Never met anyone from Arkansas, or at least admitted they were from Arkansas. John, how long you guys been in country?"

"Eight weeks. I carry the sixty and Ryan is your RTO if you got no complaints."

"No complaints so far. And finally…" Holt said, directing his question to a tall sunburned blond.

"Specialist Five Andy Blaze. I'm the team medic. I volunteered for the works, Airborne, Ranger and Green Berets. Did an extra three months medical training. I can do just about everything except major surgery. Got two years in, including six months in Nam. Been wounded once." He paused and lit his own cigarette. "How about you? You look like you've seen some shit."

Holt gave a brief rundown of military career.

Andy looked at him with a look of wonder. "You've been wounded six times? What are you, a fucking magnet?"

"Sometimes I feel like one. I just got the sixth wound a few weeks ago. Some of the wounds were serious, some weren't." Holt indicated his face. "This, obviously, was a serious wound."

"Shit anytime you're wounded it's serious. I can see I'm going to earn my money with you around. I keep a journal of every patrol. If you got the shits, I write it down. You run a fever, it goes in the book. I write down every pill and every scratch you get. You bleed on a patrol, you get a Purple Heart. Shit these mother fuckers back here want a Purple Heart if they get a paper cut.

You think it would be different with the Green Berets, but it isn't. We got our REMF's like any other unit. We have officers that have never set foot outside the wire and never will. So let me ask, are you a lifer?"

"I just re-upped, but I'm not sure. I'm not a very good garrison soldier. So we'll see how it works out."

"How long you been in country?"

"This is beginning my third year. And before you ask, I'm no gung ho John Wayne. I see my primary job as getting the whole team out of here in one piece. Your safety and my safety come before any mission. I will never volunteer for anything without discussing it with you guys first."

Holt went on to explain their assignment to work with the Montagnards. "Believe me these guys are good. They are savage fighters and hate the VC and the South Vietnamese equally. I've seen them work and I have full confidence in them. I have to go from here to meet their sergeant and pick out the team. Andy, why don't you come along? You can check them out and make sure they're healthy. Bring your medical kit, whatever you need to give them a quick once over."

Holt and Blaze started for the door when Holt stopped and asked, "Hey, do we have a name, a call sign?"

"Yeah, it's Viking. Ain't that cool. Team Viking," said Ryan.

"I like it. I'll see you guys later after I pick up my gear."

Ryan said, "Hey, Sarge, give me the keys to your lockers and me and John will get your gear and get you all squared away."

Holt didn't hesitate. He dug out his keys. "I got some liquor in my locker. Just make sure it's all there when I get back."

Holt and Blaze caught a ride to the outer defensive ring where the Montagnards were stationed. They saw a tall American soldier dressed in tiger stripes. Holt asked where they could find Sergeant Sangh. He directed him to a small wooden cabin three doors down. The sergeant was sitting outside cleaning his M-16 on a table. He stood as they approached.

Holt introduced himself and Specialist Blaze and asked to meet the team.

"Eight here. Three gone." He spoke to a small boy and the boy scurried off.

"Three gone?" said Holt.

"In town. Buy food. You meet later."

Shortly the boy returned and said something to Sangh. He then stared at Holt's face.

Holt offered them a cigarette. The boy held out his hand. Holt gave him one.

"Men come soon. They are best men. Kill beaucoup VC. All brave, loyal men."

"I'm sure they are. You speak very good English."

"Merci," he said and smiled. "I work with French man and now I work with American long time. I Trung Si like you."

"'Trung Si'?" asked Blaze.

"Means Sergeant in Vietnamese."

"You speak gook?"

"Enough to get by."

Holt saw eight men approach and assemble in a loose formation. They all were between five four and five seven with lean, muscled bodies. Their skin was as dark as mahogany. One man stood out. He had a deep scar running along the side of his face.

"That Trung Si Phang. He my second in charge and he point man. He same same you. VC cannot kill. He kill many VC."

"Trung Si Sangh let us talk while Bac Si Blaze check men." Holt explained that over the next few days they would run day patrols around the base to get used to how they would work together. Sangh said he understood and would be ready tomorrow morning. "We stay out for seven hours then come home," Holt said holding up seven fingers.

"Seven," said Sangh pointing at his watch. He held it up for Holt to admire. It was an Army issued watch with a web band. "Old Sergeant, he give me," he said proudly.

"That's very nice. Number one. Do you have everything you need? Equipment, ammunition, weapons?"

"Yes. We all good."

"You have tiger stripe fatigues and face paint?"

"Yes. No need face paint. Face dark now," Sangh said, pointing at his own face.

"Tomorrow we go and shoot weapons. Next day we patrol. Okay?"

Sangh agreed. "Tomorrow we shoot."

Holt nodded. "Doc, how you doing?"

"Just about done. They're all good except this one. He got a slight wheeze in his chest. He's good for tomorrow but I want to check him out more."

"Alright then. Tomorrow you have your men ready at ten o'clock. We go shoot at targets. We see how good your men are. Okay?"

Sangh nodded in agreement.

"Your men, all have M-16's?"

"Five have these," he said holding up an old M-1 carbine. "Others have M-16"

"Okay. Tomorrow at ten."

Holt and Doc Blaze had to walk back to the barracks.

"I have to see Sergeant Banter then I'll come back and brief the men."

Holt met with Banter and briefed him on the afternoons activities.

"I want to outfit them all with M-16's. Can I have permission to draw weapons from the armory? I might need some additional stuff once I inspect their gear."

Banter wrote a short note and passed it to Holt. "This should do it. So tomorrow shooting practice. How much ammo will you need?"

Holt did some quick calculations. "Say four thousand rounds, maybe five?"

"Is it four or five? Tell me what you need and I'll decide what you get."

"Four thousand would be good."

"Alright. Tomorrow, I'll have a truck waiting outside with the ammo and a pass to get the Yards into the camp and onto the shooting range. After shooting, what then?"

"If it goes good tomorrow then we'll go out on a few day patrols. After that we should be good to go. Say, five days from today?"

"Alright, I'll work something up for you. Write up a brief report on how it goes tomorrow. Keep it short."

At the barracks Holt was pleased to see all his gear was put into his new locker and his bed made up. He gathered the men and explained tomorrows assignment.

"You'll each work with two Montagnards on shooting skills. Don't disrespect them. Don't call them gooks. They are from the Bru tribe and came here to work for the Special Forces. They are brave and skilled fighters and have been fighting the Vietnamese longer then we've been here. They fought with the French. We can all learn some jungle skills from them. You treat them as equals. They have good, well-defined leadership. They have their own system of education and justice based on respect for individual rights and dignity. And that's how we will treat them; with respect and dignity. Any questions? Good. Do you have any Cokes in that ice chest? Ryan grab a couple and some glasses."

Holt went to his locker and got a bottle of Jack Daniels. He poured them each a generous shot. "We'll have a couple of drinks before chow and get to know each other."

That night the camp was mortared. The men ran to the bunker next to their barracks. Together, with the team that occupied the back half of the barracks, they huddled in the darkness.

Holt stood in the doorway with a cigarette. "Does this happen often?" he asked Doc Blaze who stood behind him.

"Every fucking night. They fire off twenty to thirty rounds and are gone. Tonight it's just mortars. Sometimes they fire off those big gook rockets. Those things scare the shit out of me."

"Any ground attacks?"

"Before I got here, at Tet, they attacked in force. Broke through the wire in a couple of places. I heard it was pretty hairy. Every once in awhile they probe our lines."

Holt thought of the map he had given Sergeant Brown but didn't say anything.

"You know what? That will be our day patrol. We'll try and find the spot their mortar crews use. Maybe we can follow their trail and see where they're coming from."

"That sounds like a good idea. Make it more than just a training exercise."

"How do you feel about working with the Bru?"

"I got no problem. The enemy of my enemy is my friend."

"I feel sorry for them," Holt said. "When we leave they'll be on their own. They'll be fucked."

CHAPTER 10

Better Than Us

After breakfast the squad dressed in tiger stripe fatigues walked to the Tactical Operations Center. Waiting outside the TOC was a battered deuce and a half truck. Lounging inside was a clerk. When he saw Holt he jumped out.

"Top went ahead and got the weapons you requested and two thousand rounds of ammunition," the clerk said. He handed Holt a clipboard. "You have to sign for them. Make sure they return their carbines and the ammo for them."

Holt took the clipboard and looked at it. "Ricky, jump up there and read the serial numbers to me."

After confirming the numbers, Holt had to sign for each rifle. The form said they were issued to unknown indigenous personal.

"Which one of you bozo's can drive this?" Holt asked.

Ryan raised his hand and got into the cab. Holt sat next to him.

"I can drive anything. If it got wheels, I can drive it. I was driving a tractor when I was eight years old. Learned to drive a car when I was ten," Ryan said. "I got laid when I was thirteen."

"What the fuck kind of hillbilly town are you from?"

Ryan started the truck and fiddled with the choke. He ran through the gears. "We ready?"

"Let's go."

"It was a widow women, lived down the road from us. Husband got killed in Korea. She was real pretty. I used to cut her lawn and do odd jobs around her place."

"And she felt obligated to fuck you?"

"Naw. I guess she was lonely, that's all. She taught me a lot. Taught me how to eat pussy."

"That's a good skill to have."

"My daddy always wondered why I was spending so much time hanging around her place. I guess he kind of knew. Her lawn was always perfect." Ryan looked at Holt and winked.

Holt laughed. "I imagine it was."

"She ended up marrying the Chief of Police. A nasty drunk. Everyone was afraid of him; especially the black folk. Used to slap her around. One night he came home, all liquored up, and I guess she just had enough. Took his own pistol and shot him in the head. The jury let her off. She moved away after that. I would have married her if I was old enough."

Ryan was quiet after that. Holt smoked a cigarette and stared out the window.

"Stop up here. I'll get the Bru. I shouldn't be more than ten minutes."

When Holt returned with the Bru, the squad was milling about talking with some Vietnamese coke kids. The Bru were dressed in full combat gear and wore their tiger stripes. When the children saw the Montagnards they ran off.

When everyone was settled, Holt got in the truck.

"Where's the firing range?"

"On the north side of the camp in front of the helipad."

They were greeted by two bored Army specialists sitting in a jeep. The firing range was a simple setup. Wooden bleachers splintered from mortar shrapnel faced two long tables placed end to end. Two hundred yards away was a trench where the targets were located.

"We'll go set up the targets. Coordinate with us using that radio. Don't shoot the jeep or us," said one of the specialists. "Give us about fifteen minutes."

Holt made a little ceremony about issuing the M-16's. He collected the M-1 carbines and handed each of the five Bru a M-16. When he was done, he told Sangh to have them load up ten magazines, putting no more than eighteen rounds in each magazine.

"I want each squad member to work with two Bru. Instruct them if they have any problems," Holt said. On the radio he told the specialists he was ready. Cardboard man-sized figures were raised from the trench and the all clear was given.

Holt stood with Trung Si Sangh and Phang. The men commenced firing. Holt watched through binoculars as the men fired. They fired in single shot and three round bursts. After two full magazines, they stopped. Down range, Holt watched as the Army specialists raised wooden sticks with a bright red circle stapled to the end. They placed the circle over the cardboard cutout to show where all the bullets had impacted. They showed the majority of the bullets hit center mass.

Holt looked at Sangh who looked back with a deadpan face. Holt scratched his chin and got a cigarette.

"Did anyone miss the target?" he asked.

"Not that I can tell," was the reply.

"How do you score them?"

"Without counting each hole, I'd rate them all as marksmen and about seven or eight as expert."

"Are you sure?"

"Yeah, I'm sure. Come down and look yourself."

"Can you bring the targets back?"

"Sure."

Sangh was smiling broadly. Holt held up one finger telling him to wait.

The specialists gathered up the targets and drove back. Holt laid them on the table and examined each one. He was joined by the squad.

Andy Blaze held a target up and studied the holes. "Shit, these boys can shoot."

Holt turned to Sangh. "How come you didn't tell me you all knew how to shoot this good?"

"Would you have believed me?"

Holt shrugged. "Probably not."

"Your men shoot now?"

Holt looked at the squad and laughed. "No. My men no shoot now. Your men are too good." He turned to the two Army men. "You guys can clean up here and head back."

"Geez, Sarge, we thought we'd be down here the whole day. If we go back now they'll have us filling sandbags."

"Here's ten bucks. Go down to the village and have a few beers on me."

Holt stood with Sangh and watched the Bru expertly break and clean their rifles.

"Can your men shoot AK-47's?"

"Even better."

"I'm very impressed."

"Bru boys learn to shoot when they ten years old. They go and fight with men when they fourteen. All men fight VC. Before American come, the French pay us and we fight with French. Kill many VC."

"How long you've been fighting?"

"Since I was boy. Me thirty six years old. I fight my whole life. I know only war. Never a time of peace. Our fathers, they tell us of fighting Japanese. When American leave we still fight."

"You think the American's will leave?"

"Sure they leave. No foreigner stay in Vietnam too long. The north people will win and you go home just like the French. Maybe then they leave Bru people live in peace but I don't think so. Vietnamese think we animals. They call us mountain animals. Always want our land. So we fight. Someday maybe no more Bru people."

Holt offered Sangh a cigarette and lit one for himself. They both stood and smoked in silence.

"Maybe you're right. Americans don't like us fighting in Vietnam. Someday, we go home."

"You leave us guns and we still fight. I see you and I see man like to fight. You stay with Bru and fight with us."

"Army tells me where to go. They say to go home, and I go home."

"But you like Vietnam better. You stay in Vietnam."

"Let's get the men back in the truck and get back to base."

Before he left the Bru, Holt told Sangh they would be going out tomorrow on a training mission and would stay out overnight.

"Have your men ready at 0600, full gear and rations. Your men did good today. Very Good. They're good soldiers. I apologize if I doubted them."

Sangh gave a soft laugh. "Okay, no problem. Me and you, together kill beaucoup VC."

Holt walked back to the truck and got in. "Let's go, Ryan. Bring the truck back to where we got it. I'll talk to Top about tomorrow."

Holt lit a cigarette and looked out the window. "You ever try and look up that women?"

"Naw, I never did. I mean she was fourteen or fifteen years older than me. I was just a dumb kid. I got a girl at home that writes me. She's real pretty and says she likes me."

"That's good. You need somebody to write to."

"How about you Sarge, you got somebody at home?"

"Sort of, no, not really. I was married but we got divorced. She writes once in a while. Still waiting for mail to catch up to me. Been on the move for about a month. Fucking Army takes forever."

When they got to the TOC, Holt left Ryan and walked inside.

Holt stopped at the clerk. "Top available?"

"Let me check," he said. He put down the phone and said, "Go right back."

"You know this place smells like a locker room, dirty laundry, and farts."

"That's why I got a scented candle burning all the time."

When Holt entered Top's office he was signing some reports.

"Fucking paperwork, it never ends. Fucking Army runs on paper. So, how did you and the Yards work out?"

"Waste of ammo. They're all top shots. Everyone of them fired marksman. A lot would be classified as experts."

"You have a good team."

"About that, I want to take them out tomorrow and stay overnight. A training operation but I thought we might accomplish something too. How about if we find where the gooks are mortaring us from and try and track them back? Maybe set up an ambush and catch them coming in."

Top rubbed his chin. "That's not a bad idea. Maybe you could grab a prisoner? Let's get a map and plan it out."

Top spread a map across his desk and they both studied it.

"They fire from somewhere in this area." He swept his hand across a wide swath of jungle west of the camp. "They fire and then take off west, probably back to Cambodia. I don't want you guys crossing the border. But if you could find their trail, you could catch them anywhere from here to the border."

"That's what I was thinking. We'll leave camp around 0600, cross the road here and get into the jungle as soon as possible."

"Sounds good. Assemble out front at 0530 and I'll have somebody drive you to the front gate. I'll have your maps and call signs ready. I'll let the mess hall know you'll be coming in early."

"Air cover and artillery?"

"Both will be alerted."

"Thanks Top. I'll see you tomorrow," Holt said as he walked out the door. "One other thing, when are they going to get my mail squared away?"

"You'll know when you get your first letter."

Holt went over the mission with the squad. "Full load tomorrow and bring an extra days rations just in case. Any questions?"

"So this ain't a snoop and poop? We're looking to make contact?"

"That's correct, Mike. Maybe we can snatch a prisoner; Top would like that. After food, we'll go over our gear. Let's make it an early night tonight. We got beer in the cooler, right. Why don't we just hang out here tonight?"

Everyone agreed.

"Whose Door's tape is that?" Holt asked.

Sergeant Evans raised his hand.

"I love the Doors. I got a chance to see them when I was home," Holt said. "Who else you got?"

Ricky went to his locker and sorted through some tapes. "I got some Steppenwolf, Creedence, The Animals, and a new group, Iron Butterfly, you really have to be wasted to get into them. My girl sends me the tapes. The Post Exchange has shit. All shit kicking country stuff."

"Whoa now," John Davis said. "Ain't nothing wrong with country music."

"Yeah you're right, if you like songs about pickup trucks and dogs."

Holt walked outside and lit a cigarette. Doc Blaze followed him.

"I miss that shit. Bullshitting with the guys," Holt said. "I had a good squad back in the Wolfhounds. We were tight."

"It'll happen here too. Give it some time. How come you left them?"

"I was short. Had to choose something to do and this came along. The Army has all this shit fucked up. Back in World War Two, you came over with your unit and you went home with your unit. You had time to talk, to decompress. You had time on the boat ride to get ready for the civilian world. Here in Nam you fly over here alone and go home alone. One day you're fighting in the jungle, and two days later you're sitting at your mother's dinner table asking her to pass the fucking butter."

"You did that?'

"Sure I did. This is the way you talk now. You think you're going to change when you get home? It ain't easy being home. You drink too much and get into fights. You can't sleep at night, have nightmares and wake up screaming. Everyone tries to pretend you're okay but you've changed. Killing people don't go away. It's always there hanging in the back of your mind. In some ways, it's a lot better being here."

"People stare at your scars?"

"Haven't been home since I got them. I'm sure they will. I took some leave in Thailand. Girls there didn't care. They get paid not to care."

They stood in silence for a moment.

"You have to go home sometime. You can't stay here forever."

"Yeah, you're right. Let's get the guys and grab some chow."

That night Holt wrote a long letter to Janet and mailed it. Before lights out they all took a shot of Jack Daniels.

Holt raised his glass and said, "To us. Nobody gets left behind. We all come home."

The next morning they assembled at the TOC. The clerk came out with a camera. "Alright guys, line up by the truck. Look ferocious."

When he finished, he said, "You guys want a copy?" All said yes.

Holt said to Blaze, "What's up with all the pictures?"

"Death photos. They have to know who went out and who didn't come back. A picture goes into each mission folder. They create a folder for each mission regardless of what it is."

"Shit. That's pretty grim."

"Save your pictures and at the end of your tour you'll look like you've aged ten years. Let me ask you something, you think we'll be okay with the Yards?"

"Don't call them Yards, that's disrespectful. Call them The Bru. And yes we'll be fine. Their lives depend on us and we depend on them. They know we got the radio. We're the ones who call the helicopters and the artillery. They know they need us as much as we need them. I trust them more than I would trust the South Vietnamese. The South Vietnamese will cut and run at the first sign of trouble."

They met Sangh and his team at the entrance to the Bru compound.

"We are staying out tonight. Do your people have enough rations?"

"We good. Bring food and plenty water."

"Good. Trung Si, do you know how to read a compass?"

He shook his head.

"I will teach you, later."

One of Sangh's men came up to him and pointed at Holt and said something.

"He wants to know if you have face paint for them?"

"I do. I brought extra for your men." Holt dug through his ruck and found the tubes of face paint. He gave the tubes to Sangh who gave it to the waiting man. The Bru applied the camouflage makeup. They took turns putting it on each other. It wasn't so much camouflage pattern as it was war paint. They applied it in broad strokes on their cheeks and forehead alternating colors. Holt nodded his approval. The men looked frightening.

"Okay. We go now." Holt indicated the direction. The men quickly went through the west gate and crossed the road and the cleared area and entered the forest.

Immediately Holt was impressed with their noise discipline. The Bru moved silently and effortlessly through the forest.

Phang led as point man, followed by two of his men to either side of him. Then came Sergeant Evans followed by more Bru. John Davis carrying the modified M-60 was next with more Bru. Holt was in the middle with Sangh and Ryan Davis, his RTO. Ryan was never more than a few feet from Holt. Next was Andy Blaze, the team medic and the remaining Bru. Sergeant Michael Smith was the last man in line walking drag, a position almost as important as the point man. He insured no one was following them.

After about ten minutes Holt whispered to Sangh that they were walking fast.

"Fast now. No VC here. Safe. Phang know when safe."

"How?"

Sangh wrinkled his nose. "Phang smell them, no VC here."

"Phang can smell the VC?"

"Yes," said Sangh, as if stating the obvious.

After about forty five minutes, Phang turned north. They walked another thirty minutes and Phang halted the patrol and indicated they should spread out. Without being told, the Bru formed a circular perimeter leaving the Americans in the middle. Holt and Sangh, followed closely by Ryan, walked to where Phang stood. Phang pointed to a small clearing where the grass had been stamped down and some bushes cut away.

"VC fire mortar here," said Sangh.

Holt looked up and saw a clearing in the branches overhead.

Phang brought over a three foot long stick with a two branches forming a 'Y' at the top. Six inches from the bottom was a small piece of vine tied around it. He shoved it into the moist earth till it met the tied vine.

Sangh held up two fingers. "VC use stick to aim." He put another finger between the two he held up. "You see?"

Holt nodded he understood. Phang was about to break the stick when Holt asked for it. Holt slid the knotted vine six inches higher and cut off the bottom six inches. He scuffed the fresh cut on the ground and handed the stick back to Phang. Phang smiled and returned the stick to where he found it.

"Now, when VC shoot the miss camp," Holt said. "Let's take a twenty minute break. Can Phang follow the VC?" Sangh said he could. "Good we follow. When we find a good spot we'll set up ambush. Maybe the VC come tonight and we kill. Ryan call this in, here's the coordinates. Tell them plus or minus twenty five meters. Then tell them what we are going to do."

CHAPTER 11

First Blood

They set off after their break with Phang following the trail.

It was a little after noon and the sun was directly overhead. Golden shafts of light pierced the forest canopy giving the leaves a silvery, mint color. They traveled silently through shadows. Sometimes Holt was stunned at the beauty of Vietnam. But the beauty concealed the ever present danger. Danger from the terrain itself, the insects and snakes and the stifling, overpowering heat.

It was different on these long range patrols than humping as a ordinary grunt. As a grunt you were expected to cover ten or twenty kilometers a day. Here, the main concern was silence and stealth. Holt marveled at the abilities of the Bru to travel in complete silence barely leaving a trace on the ground. It came to them naturally after a life time of jungle living. The Americans had to be taught patrol tactics and noise discipline. The Montagnards learned at an early age accompanying their fathers on hunts. Here the hunting wasn't for food, but for men. Here your prey could shoot back.

Holt called another break and spoke to Sangh. "We're going to set up for a night ambush. Tell Phang to find a good place to set up. Tonight, we wait for VC and kill them. We have gone maybe, three miles from camp. In two more miles we hit Cambodia. We can't go Cambodia."

"Cambodia same jungle as Vietnam. No difference. VC in Cambodia."

"We can't go into Cambodia unless we're told to go. This is just a training exercise. Maybe next time we go Cambodia."

"Training? I no understand. Who we training?"

"Us. We train how we work together." Holt meshed his fingers together. "You see how Americans work and we see how Bru work."

"We work long time with Americans."

"It's for us. We are new to the Bru. We need to learn how to work with you. You teach us."

Sangh looked puzzled. "I go and tell Phang to look for ambush place."

As Sangh walked to the head of the column Ryan moved closer to Holt. "Hope you didn't piss him off. He looked a little offended."

"I'll speak to him. It certainly wasn't my intention. Out here, in the jungle, we can learn from them."

"But when the time comes, will they fight? I've heard horror stories of working with the South Vietnamese. They drop their weapons and run." "Agreed. The ARVN is useless. It's so fucking obvious that they'll never beat the NVA. And now they're pulling Americans out. When we leave the North Vietnamese Army will just roll through this country. Top to bottom."

Ryan sighed and swatted at the cloud of mosquitoes that had gathered around them. "Beautiful day to day. What would you say, about a hundred and two degrees?"

"There was this guy in my old squad that found a old garage thermometer. He took great pleasure in announcing the temperature all day long. I wanted to shoot him sometimes."

"Hey, Sarge, is my makeup running?"

"No, sweetie, you look fine."

"This new shit is pretty good. It doesn't run off, even when you're sweating."

"God knows what type of chemical shit they put in it to make it sweat proof. Have you ever been in any of the defoliated zones? Now that's a trip worth taking. Every living plant, every blade of grass, every tree is dead. It's as if they have been melted. And they claim it's safe for humans to walk through. When we went there, we were coughing up phlegm and our skin looked like burnt meat. Guys were getting blisters and boils on their chest and arms. Me, I got pimples all over my chest. That fucking Agent Orange can't be safe. Fuck the Army. They will lie right to your face."

"Here comes Sangh."

"Now watch this. He's been up there talking to Phang for ten minutes. He'll come back here and give a one or two word answer."

"Phang says he'll find ambush place."

"That's all he said?"

"Yes."

Holt looked at Ryan and smiled.

After two hours of walking, Holt called a break.

"Ryan, can you call Bird Dog?" Holt said, referring to the single engine Cessna O 1 spotter plane that maintained a discreet presence above the long range patrols. "Tell him I'm going to signal him with my strobe light. See if he can tell us where we are. I'm concerned we're too close to the border."

Holt walked about twenty feet until he came to a break in the overhead foliage. He turned his strobe light on and pointed it up.

Ryan who had followed Holt gave him the handset. "Here, he wants to talk with you."

"Bird Dog this is Viking Six, over."

"Viking Six, take two steps forward. You're in Cambodia. What the fuck, dude?"

"That's why I'm checking. We're turning back now. I'll mark my position on my map. Thanks. Viking Six, out."

Holt called Sangh over. "We're heading back now. We're in Cambodia. We need to Di Di back. That gully we passed, that's where we ambush. Okay?"

Sangh sighed. "Okay, I tell Phang we go back."

Holt stood to the side as Phang and his two men passed. As Phang passed he said, "Tonight VC come and we kill."

"How many VC come?"

Phang held up his hand. "Five, maybe six. Two carry mortar, three or four carry bombs and rifles."

"I'm surprised he didn't tell us what they had for dinner," Holt said to Ryan.

"Rice and fish," said Sangh. "Phang find place VC shit. They eat rice and fish."

"You ever wonder why we're even here?" Holt whispered to Ryan.

They walked for over two hours to where Holt had seen the gully next to the trail. About ten feet off the trail, the ground sloped down about three feet. Phang examined the area and nodded his approval. Sangh and Phang placed their men spaced out about thirty feet along the trail. The Bru dug into the slope with their entrenching tools creating one man fighting positions. Sangh came to Holt.

"You men stay back here, watch back and sides. Okay?"

"Okay," Holt said.

Sangh pointed at John Davis, "Him and big gun," indicating the M-60, "go up front and shoot down trail when VC come."

"Jack, take the M-60 and go where Sangh says. Mike you go with him, take the extra ammo." Sergeant Michael Smith gathered up all the spare M-60 belts and followed John Davis.

Holt asked Ryan what time the gooks usually fired at the base. "Anywhere from eight at night till two in the morning," Ryan said.

"It's 1700 now we got some time to wait. We should eat and then try and catch some sleep."

Ryan passed the message down to Sergeant Evans and the medic, Andy Blaze.

Holt looked back to where the Bru had positioned themselves against the side of the gully. It was only ten feet away, yet the men were invisible tucked into the bushes. The forest started to shadow as the day wore on. Holt dug through his pack and got a can of ham slices. A second can contained crackers. He silently opened the cans with his P38 can opener and took a ham slice and put in on a cracker. He leaned back against his ruck sack and took a bite of the ham. As he chewed he looked up at the tree tops. The sky above was a soft, dove gray color. There was a slight breeze. Mosquitoes fluttered about their faces.

Holt had his eyes closed when Sangh crawled up to him. "Phang hear VC come."

Holt looked at his watch and nudged Ryan. "Tell the others we got movement."

Sangh leaned in close to Holt and whispered in his ear, "Phang fire claymore mines first and then shoot."

Holt nodded his agreement. Holt felt useless. Everything was setup and arranged by the Bru without his involvement.

They waited in silence. They heard some muffled noises and suddenly the night erupted in four violent explosions. The flash of light robbed them of their night vision. The explosions were followed by rifle fire. Holt saw Jack take his M-60 and slide onto the path. He fired controlled bursts down the length of the trail. The muzzle flashes lit up his face. He had a wild look in his eyes.

It was over as suddenly as it began. Phang and the Bru moved onto the trail and began to search the bodies.

Holt told Ryan to call it in. "Tell them six enemy KIA and the mortar tube destroyed." Holt looked at Sangh, "There were six VC killed?"

"Maybe six. Sure, six VC dead."

Holt and Sangh walked up to the trail. "We send two men back. Make sure no one follow," Sangh said.

"What are they doing?" Holt asked Sangh.

"Search bodies. Take souvenir. We sell to GI for beaucoup money. Take ears off for bonus money."

"Tell them don't do that."

"Your big man want proof we kill VC. We give him ears. He pay us extra."

"Shit," murmured Holt.

One of the Bru walked to Sangh and gave him a Tokarev 9MM automatic pistol in a leather holster emblazoned with a red enameled star.

Sangh looked at and handed it to Holt. "You give your big man. He'll be happy."

Sergeant Smith came over to Holt. "Did you see that shit? Text book fucking ambush. They never had a chance. Those fuckers cut those gooks to pieces."

"Did they have a mortar with them?"

"Sure did. A big ass Chinese 82MM."

"Take a thermite grenade and drop in down the tube and put another on the base plate. Then carry both into the woods and bury it under some leaves."

"What thermite?" asked Sangh.

"Go with Trung si Smith and watch."

Holt walked back to Ryan. "What did they say?"

"Nothing. They just took down the information."

"Call them again. Tell them we're starting back and to hold all artillery fire in this area. Tell them we'll come in at sunrise."

"Anything else?"

"No, that should be it." Holt scratched at his neck, "Fucking mosquitoes never quit. Did you know the Bru cut off the ears of the NVA? They get paid a bonus for each kill and have to provide proof."

Ryan wriggled his hand. "I heard rumors about that but I thought it was just bullshit."

"Well it's not bullshit. They just did it now."

"Ain't there some gook belief that you can't get into heaven unless you're in one piece?"

"Who the fuck knows what they believe. We all heard stories of Green Berets wearing necklaces of ears. Maybe the stories are true."

"Maybe in the old days but not now. The officers wouldn't put up with it."

"Tell the guys to get their shit together. We'll be moving out in a few minutes."

It took several hours to walk back to the base. They stopped about twenty yards inside the forest. The base was visible across the road. They waited until sunrise.

"Ryan tell them we're here and we'll pop smoke to identify us. Tell those idiots not to shoot us. Get confirmation on that."

The guards at the gate confirmed yellow smoke and they started across the cleared area. Holt and most of the Americans lit up cigarettes.

"Hey GI, you souvenir me one Salem?" said Sangh and smiled.

"Keep the pack. You and your men did good. Number one VC fighters."

Sangh stopped and passed out cigarettes to each of the Bru as they walked by.

Holt and Ryan stopped at the gate and waited as the Bru passed through.

Phang held up a bloody cloth bag and said something to the Chinese Nung guard in Vietnamese.

The guard spat on the ground and said, "Dong Vat."

Phang said, "Toi du ma may," and walked by. The Bru all laughed.

"What was that all about?" asked Ryan.

"Phang showed him the bag of ears and the Hmong called him an animal. Phang told him he had fucked his mother."

"Nice to see our allies getting along," Ryan said.

"We're all just one big happy family," Holt said.

Phang handed Holt the bag containing the ears and said, "You give Big man for Bru bonus money. Okay?"

They left the Bru at their compound and headed for the TOC.

"You guys head to the barracks and get cleaned up. I'll check in with Top and I'll meet you. Then we'll head to chow."

In the TOC. He shrugged off his pack and leaned his rifle against it, "Top around?"

The clerk looked up from some papers and pointed to his office. "He's waiting for you."

Holt walked into the office carrying the bloody bag.

"Nice job , Sergeant. One mortar crew down."

"They'll replace them."

"Still, it was good work. How do you like working with the Yards?"

"They're better than most Americans. Tight discipline, follow orders without bitching and get the job done. Oh, here, I almost forgot. These are for you."

"What the fuck is in there?"

"A bunch of ears. They said you need them for their bonus pay."

"God damn it. Robbie, get in here."

The clerk appeared at the door.

"Take this shit and throw it in the burn pit."

Top knew Robbie had a side business selling souvenirs to the rear echelon personal at Nha Trang but he didn't think the ears were a sale item. Robbie would dry these ears in the sun and tell the horrible story of how they came into his possession. He'd sell anything: pith helmets, belts and belt buckles, NVA insignia, and NVA flags whether real or fake. The REMF's couldn't get enough and paid good cash money.

"How many Yards did you have?"

"Twelve," said Holt.

Top swiveled in his chair and opened up a locked file cabinet. Inside was a small safe. Holt craned his neck to see inside the safe. Besides various colored folders there was stacks of banded cash. Top pulled out three bundles of Vietnamese notes and handed them to Holt.

"Do I have to sign for this?"

"Just mention it in your report. Don't mention any crap about the ears. Robbie will show you how I want it done." Top waved his hand. "Once again, good job."

"Oh, I almost forgot. The Bru collected these documents." "Leave them on the desk."

Holt stood before Robbie. "Top said you might be able to help me out on the report?"

Robbie handed him a sheet of paper. "Use this as an example. I'll correct your spelling. I'll type it up and you come in and sign it. Sarge, on your patrol did you get any trade items?"

"The Bru striped the NVA; they took anything of value."

"Who did you work with?"

"Sergeant Sangh."

"I know him. He's a good guy. I'll see him later."

On the way to the barracks Holt stopped in the supply room. Sergeant First Class Simmons sat behind his desk.

"I got something for you," Holt said, handing him the Tokarev pistol.

Simmons examined the pistol and the leather holster. "Where did you get this?"

"I went hunting with the Bru. You like it?"

"Very much so." He looked Holt over. "What's the price?"

"Future goodwill. I've learned in the past the supply Sergeant is a good friend to have."

"This is worth quite a bit of goodwill."

"For me and my squad?"

"Sounds good."

"I see you got some cartons of cigarettes there. Anyway you can let loose two cartons. I need to give something to the Bru sergeant who found the pistol."

Simmons slid a carton of Marlboro and a carton of Salem's across the counter. "You could have gotten these yourself."

"It'll save me a trip to the Post Exchange. So future goodwill. Right?"

"Like having money in the bank." As Holt walked towards the door Simmons said to him, "I appreciate this Sergeant Holt, I want you to know that. I'll make good on my word."

After Holt took a quick shower, he dressed in jungle fatigues and the squad went to breakfast. They sat together and ate plates of real scrambled eggs, bacon, and fried potatoes. When they were finished Ryan asked him what they were doing today.

"Clean your gear and restock your supplies. Then make yourself scarce. Tomorrow I'd like to work on our bunker. Bulk it up a bit. But today relax. The patrol was good. Top congratulated us on our success. I have a feeling we'll be going out again in a few days so enjoy yourselves while we can."

Holt and Doc Blaze stayed behind and lingered over coffee.

"When I was in Top's office, I saw he had a safe. There was a lot of cash inside. Do you know about that?"

"We're very enterprising. You know the tailor shop in the village? The tailor makes fake VC flags and Robbie the clerk sells them to the REMF's. Mama san's bar pays us for her beer and soda and cigarettes. The massage parlor, we own it. Everyone gets a fair share. Top uses the money to benefit us. How do you think we have fresh eggs all the time? Top has the villagers raise laying hens and buys the eggs with the money from everything else. The cookouts we have once a month, where do you think the steaks come from? The universal Army barter system. Let's say you have problems at home and need an emergency leave but you ain't got no money. Top will slip you a few hundred with no questions asked. The special forces here in Vietnam, we're in our little world here. The brass know our missions are dangerous and they try and look out for us as best they can. We get our share of bad officers. Top try's and weed them out. Officers may give us our orders but they know sergeants run this outfit."

"It makes sense," Holt agreed.

"We get the best equipment and the best support. That doesn't just happen. Wheels got to be greased. Understand?"

"Yeah, I figured out how the Army works at my old unit." Holt offered Blaze a cigarette and they sat smoking. "That Tokarev pistol, I gave it to Sergeant Simmons for future goodwill."

"That's what I mean. He'll either sell it or keep it. In any event, we benefit from it. Shit, if the officers knew you had it, they would find some way to take it off your hands. You'd never get it home. That's good, what you did. I'll make sure the squad knows about it. We're still sizing you up, you know."

"I figured that. How am I doing?"

"So far so good."

"I have to go down to the Bru. I have a couple of cartons of cigarettes for Sangh and Phang for the pistol and I have their cash bonus payment. You wanna come with me?"

"Sure thing. I have a bag of Tootsie Roll Pops for the kids."

"Sounds good give me about an hour. I have to write up the report on the patrol. I'll meet you back at the barracks, say around ten thirty."

CHAPTER 12

People Are Strange

In the TOC, the senior Sergeants gathered around a table studying a spread out map.

"I heard a rumor we might be getting an officer to run things here," one of the Sergeants said.

"Yeah. It's not a rumor," said Top.

"What happened to the Major?"

"He got himself a cushy job at Nha Trang. He's done with this bullshit. No more of this primitive living. He wants hot showers and clean sheets every night."

"This new guy is supposed to be a hard charger. He just got done commanding a line company of grunts. Got a promotion and now wants back in with us."

Top lit a cigarette. "Whatever. Officers come and go. Sergeants stay. We run things. Hope he knows that."

They went back to studying the map.

"Who's going on this one?"

"Who hasn't been across?" asked Top.

"Viking. But they just got back in."

"It won't be for another few days. They'll get their stand down." Top ground out his cigarette in the ashtray made from a cut down 105 MM shell casing. "Catch Holt at lunch and tell him to assemble his team at 1400 in the briefing room."

At precisely 1400 hours Holt and the five members of team sat in front of a large easel covered by a white sheet. First Sergeant Banter entered the room followed by Sergeant First Class Brown.

"Alright, Red, let's get started," said Banter.

With a dramatic flourish, Sergeant Brown removed the sheet. "Gentlemen, your next assignment is going to be an excursion over the fence into Cambodia."

The team remained silent, filled with both excitement and dread.

Sergeant Brown continued. "You and six Montagnards will be inserted approximately ten klick's across the border into this general area," he said pointing to the map. "You'll patrol this area looking for NVA activity. You will go no farther than fourteen klick's into Cambodia. That is the limit of incursion we have to operate under. We're interested in mapping any existing trails. We especially want to see if there are any improved roads suitable for heavy vehicle traffic. Any truck parks or rest areas. You'll each be given highly detailed maps showing known enemy locations. These areas have been heavily bombed. We want your assessment of damage and the repairs done to those areas. You are not to engage with the enemy. You're there for reconnaissance only. You will have air assets of fixed wing aircraft and helicopters for extraction and ground support. Artillery will be available in the form of 155MM howitzers that have an effective range of 24.7 kilometers. Sergeant Holt, you and I will do a fly over the area to pick out a suitable LZ."

At this point, Robby the clerk, ran into the room and went to Sergeant Banter. After a huddled conversation, Sergeant Banter excused himself. Ten minutes later he returned accompanied by a stocky Asian Major.

"This is our new camp commander Major Robert Jung. He wants to observe the briefing. Sergeant Brown please continue."

Holt looked at Major Jung with genuine surprise and delight on his face. The Major saw Holt and tipped his hand to his beret in a mock salute.

Sergeant Brown coughed quietly and shuffled some papers before continuing. "You'll be going in sterile. Blank tiger stripes, no dog tags; nothing to identify you as Americans soldiers. Supply will issue you a Belgian military paratrooper rucksack. It's an excellent piece of gear in what they call a 'jigsaw' camouflage pattern. You'll also be issued a McGuire rig for helicopter extraction. My understanding is that you are all familiar with it. It's similar to a parachute harness without the parachute. If you ever have to use it you'll love and hate it. You'll hate it because it will crush your balls. You'll love because it can pull you out of the jungle when there isn't a suitable landing zone. You clip onto a rope and up, up, and away. The armory will issue you AK-47's and magazines. I suggest you all go the firing range and re-familiarize yourselves with them. You can keep your Browning Hi-Power pistols as they're manufactured by Belgium. I have map packets for each of you along with a suggested equipment list and a list of prohibitive items. Any questions?" No one in the team responded. "Good. Major, would you like to say a few words?"

"I understand this is your first SOG mission, right? As members of the Studies and Observation Group, this is what you've been training for. Understand this; you won't be on your own. We will devote every asset at our disposal to ensure your safe return. The terrain you will be operating in is the same terrain you're used to. The only difference is a line drawn on a map. It is essential that we obtain intelligence on the NVA capabilities in Cambodia. We desperately need actionable information on troop strength, supply routes, and supply depots. You will supply that information. You will be monitored twenty four hours per day. Help is only a radio call away. The best of luck to you."

"Thank you, Major," said Sergeant Brown. "If there are no other questions then go get your new equipment and familiarize yourselves with it. Sergeant Holt report to the TOC for the aerial overview at 1400 hours."

Major Jung walked over to Holt and extended his hand. They shook hands vigorously. "Good to see, Sergeant. I've kept an eye on you, Sergeant Soujac also. I heard you were wounded again?"

"Yeah, a bit of bad luck on a patrol. I'm really glad to have you aboard, sir. It'll be nice knowing you'll have our back."

"So all healed up and fit for duty?"

"Yes, Sir. Good to go."

"That's great. I'm going to see if I can hitch a ride on your aerial overview. Good to see you, Sergeant." With that comment, he returned to Sergeant's Brown and Banter.

As the squad went to the supply room, Sergeant Evans asked Holt how he knew the new commanding officer.

"He was my company commander back at the 25th. He needed time commanding a grunt unit to get a promotion. Guess everything worked out for him. He's a good guy. He looks out for his men. You'll like him."

At the supply room, they received their Belgium rucksacks and were issued reconditioned AK-47's. Holt chose an AK with a folding metal stock for himself. The rucks were stuffed with filled AK magazines.

"You'll want to go to fire off some rounds to get used to these. They're heavier and the rounds pack a little more punch. I have something else that might interest you," said Sergeant Simmons.

He went to a shelf and came back with some jungle boots. "These are French Legionnaire jungle boots. They're a little lighter than ours, and, in my opinion, dry out quicker. Try them on and walk around with them. We sprayed them with camo paint to tone down their tan color. If you don't like them, just bring them back. But I've used them and I like them."

"Did you run any patrols into Cambodia?" asked Holt.

"I did my time across the fence. It's not that different. Beaucoup gooks, that's all. Remember, you ain't there to fight. Just snooping and pooping. Rely on your Yards. They know what to do."

The men sat on benches and tried on the boots.

"I like these; they're lighter, more like sneakers," said Ryan.

"They're more like the NVA boots. Completely different lug pattern. It'll confuse the gooks," Simmons said. "Good luck to you boys. I'll see you before you leave."

The men returned to their barracks, they immediately disassembled the AK's, and gave them a thorough cleaning. They examined each magazine, removed the bullets, cleaned each one, and reloaded the magazines. Finally, they spray painted the surfaces with a mottled green camo pattern and wrapped the rifles with scraps of camouflage netting. From a distance they AK's looked like tree branches.

"Okay," said Holt. "Tomorrow we'll test fire the AK's. We'll run through about ten mags each. Then we'll come back clean everything again and assemble all our gear and be ready for inspection. For now, let's get some chow. I'll do the flyover with Rick. When I get back, me and Doc will go and alert the Bru. In the meantime, study the maps. I want everyone to know where we're going and where we are at all times. Sound good?"

At the mess hall they ate cheese burgers and French fries. In the back, Holt saw Major Jung huddled with the senior NCO's and several other junior officers from the air squadron.

"I never realized all the planning these patrols encompass. I guess they gotta get everyone on board; the over flight, the helicopters, and the artillery guys," said Holt.

"When there's a patrol out just about everyone is on twenty four hour alert. If we get into trouble they scramble everyone," said Mike.

"Has anyone of you guys been into Cambodia?"

"I did one patrol," said Mike. "Didn't find anything. Just walked around. At first, I was scared shitless, but you settle down. Like Sergeant Brown said: it's pretty much routine shit, just with more gooks around. We didn't go in with any Yards, just Americans. I kind of like having the Yards along."

"Bru," said Holt.

"What?"

"Call them Bru."

"Yeah, right, Bru."

Holt and Evans were at the TOC at 1400 hours and were met by Sergeant Brown and Major Jung. They all carried web gear and rifles. Sergeant Brown had a 35MM camera with a telephoto lens.

"Let's head over to the helipad. I have three potential sites in mind. Each landing zone has its advantages and disadvantages," said Sergeant Brown.

They all piled aboard a well-used UH-1 "Huey" unmarked helicopter. It's skin showed numerous riveted patches covering bullet holes. Holt and Evans sat on the left side and the Sergeant and the Major sat on the right side. The door gunner gave Holt a thumbs up. The Huey spooled up and left the runway. They traveled due west and within five miles, they crossed the Cambodian border. They turned north and about twenty minutes in, Brown pointed out the first proposed LZ. It was a sandy beach bordering a river. They were over the second site within ten minutes; it was a rectangular clearing bordered by elephant grass. The third and final site was a clear circle bordered by tall trees. At each site, Sergeant Brown leaned out of the helicopter and snapped about a dozen photos with the motorized camera. Holt passed his binoculars to Sergeant Evans.

They returned to base. The entire flight took a little over an hour.

At the TOC, Sergeant Brown gave the camera to Robbie to have the film developed.

"While we wait, I'll show you the LZ's on the map," said Sergeant Brown as he rolled out a large scale map on the table. Each proposed site was circled in red grease pencil.

"When are we taking off?" asked Holt.

"You'll take off before sunrise and arrive at the LZ at dawn. You'll have the sun at your backs."

"This is clearly the best landing zone," Holt said pointing at the sandy beach site. "However, the NVA usually try and camp at a place with access to fresh water. That could be a problem."

"Agreed," said Major Jung. "I don't like this circular site. It looks like it can only handle one ship at a time. It would work if you were only taking eight men: four Americans and four Montagnards."

"That's something to think about," Holt said, while studying the map. "The third site can handle two ships," Sergeant Brown said. "You

come in over the elephant grass and land nose to tail."

"One ship would offer advantages. A lot quicker in and out," mused Holt. "If we took four Americans, who would we leave back?"

"Mike would stay back," said Evans. "He's already been across the border; he won't mind. John Davis will be a problem. He's going to get all pissy, especially if his cousin is going."

"Look, let's take a break," Sergeant Brown said, "I got the pilots coming over. We'll find out how much they can carry getting in and out of the LZ's. Grab some coffee and we reconvene in twenty minutes. We should have the photos by then."

"If you guys are heading to the mess hall, bring back some donuts. Cookie usually has some in the afternoons."

As Holt and Evans walked to mess hall they both lit cigarettes.

"We could take the six of us and no Bru."

"Holt looked at Evans. "Really? You want to leave the Bru behind?"

"Not really."

"Neither do I. They're good. That fucker Phang is like a blood hound. He's better on point than I am. And I think I'm pretty good."

"Well, fuck it. Let's see what the pilots have to say about it."

They returned to the TOC with two large coffees and a box of donuts covered with crystal sugar, fresh out of the fryer .

Two pilots from the aviation detachment and Sergeant Banter had joined the group. They were hunched over the table studying the photographs with magnifying glasses. Holt set the box of donuts on the table. Everyone grabbed for a fresh, hot donut.

"We've kind of agreed on the rectangle landing zone for the reasons mentioned earlier. Which do you like?" asked Sergeant Brown.

"I'm fine with that," said Holt. "How many guys can you comfortably carry?"

"Depends," said one of the young pilots. "How much do you porker's weigh?"

"We're thinking ten guys. Six Americans and four Bru. Figure the Americans weigh one fifty a piece and seventy to eighty pounds of gear that would be about nine hundred pounds and five hundred pounds of gear, fourteen hundred in total and another seven hundred for the Bru. Say twenty two hundred in total," Holt said.

"We can do that. It will be snug but we carry more than that on resupply missions. We'll put the second bench in. Five on each bench."

When Holt and Evans got back to the barracks Holt knew something was wrong. The men were sitting apart and not talking.

"What's going on? Why aren't you getting your gear together?" asked Holt.

Sergeant Smith walked up to Holt with his eyes downcast. "I need to talk to you in private."

"Is it about the team?"

"Yeah, sort of."

"There's no 'sort of', does it concern the team or not?"

"Yeah, it does."

"Then spit it out. We have no secrets amongst the team."

"I ain't going on a cross border mission. I did one already and that's one too many."

Sergeant Evans started to say something but Holt put his hand on his arm and squeezed. "What do you mean you're not going? Viking got the mission and that means you're going."

"You'll go without me and that's that. These missions are illegal. Don't believe all the shit they're telling you; it's about all the support we have. We'll be on our own over there. And it's not only me, John feels the same way; he's not going either."

"Is that true, John? You not going either?"

John didn't answer. He just sat on his bunk and hung his head.

"Answer me, God dammit."

"No, I'd rather not go," said John, his voice just above a whisper.

Holt balled up his fists and could feel his face turning red. "I'm going outside with Sergeant Evans to have a cigarette. You got five minutes to think this over. Be very careful with what you decide."

Holt turned and steered Evans outside. He fished his cigarettes out of his pocket and offered one to Evans and lit both. He took two deep drags before talking.

"This is bullshit!"

"Why didn't you tell him he's was staying behind?"

"Because we don't get to pick and choose our missions. We have our orders. This is what we volunteered for. And now he doesn't want to do it? Fuck him."

"What are you going to do?"

"Send them both over to Banter, let him handle it. In any event, he's off the team. I can't trust him anymore."

"Banter will bust them down and kick them out. You know that, don't you?"

"What do you suggest?"

Evans finished his cigarette before speaking. "No, you're right. What if he wants to court martial them for disobeying orders?"

"I doubt it. This is an all volunteer unit. He'll ship them off to an airborne unit. Shit, they'll wish they would have stayed if they get sent to the 101st up in the highlands."

Holt finished his cigarette and field stripped it. "Do you agree with me?"

"Reluctantly, I agree. You got no other choice. The two of them are fucking assholes if they think this is going to turn out good for them."

"Do me a favor, run up to Banter and let him know what's happening. I don't want him to be blindsided."

"Sure, good luck."

Holt took a deep breath and composed himself before going back into the barracks.

Smith and Davis stood when he walked in.

"Leave all your shit here. Report to First Sergeant Banter. He'll decide what to do with you. In any event you're not coming back here. You're both off the team."

"That's bullshit! You can't do that! We were here long before you were," said Smith.

Holt took a step closer and said, "Get the fuck out of here. Now!"

They both walked away without saying a word.

Holt went to his locker to get his bottle of Jack Daniels and poured himself a double shot. He held up the bottle but both Ryan and Doc declined. He sat at the team table and lit a cigarette.

"What's going to happen to them?" asked Ryan.

"Don't know. If Banter's in a good mood they'll both get busted and sent off to a line grunt outfit. Probably one the airborne units up north."

Holt swirled his whiskey in the glass. "Did you guys know about this?"

Doc Blaze looked at Ryan before answering. "Not a word. This is the first we're hearing about this."

"John didn't say anything to me," Ryan said. "He was always a bit sketchy about this whole Special Forces thing. But I thought he was solid."

"I'm sorry you guys are going to get split up, but it was his decision," Holt said.

"I saw him talking to Sergeant Smith before, but I didn't think anything of it. If I had known, I would have talked him out of it," Ryan said.

"It's his decision to make, not yours."

"What will happen now?" asked Doc.

"As far as I know the patrol is still on. The four of us will go out with six Yards, Fuck, I mean Bru. The funny thing is, I was going to ask Smith if he would mind staying behind."

"You could have just said that?"

"He had to open his mouth first. This is the Army. Since when do we have a choice of what we do?"

Just then Sergeant Evans opened the door and the room was flooded with sunlight.

"What happened?" asked Ryan.

Evans paused to lit up a cigarette. "At first it was quiet, then all hell broke loose. Banter ripped those guys a new asshole. You were right Holt. He busted them down a rank and he's sending them to Nha Trang for reassignment. They're out of the Special Forces, both of them. He won't let them even come back for their personal stuff. Robbie's coming over to pack up their shit. He's really pissed."

"We still going out?" asked Holt.

Evans just shrugged. "He wants to see you in ten minutes. I guess you'll find out then."

Holt brushed his teeth to get the whiskey smell off his breath. He put on his beret and left the barracks.

As he walked towards the TOC, Holt dreaded the confrontation with First Sergeant Banter. Somehow he felt responsible for the betrayal of Smith and Davis. At the very least, he believed he would be classified as an ineffective leader.

As he went through the door, Robbie just pointed at Banter's office. Holt knocked on the doorframe before entering. He removed his beret and stood before Banter.

"Have a seat Sergeant. Tell me what the fuck happened?"

Holt told the story without emotion. He included every detail. "I'm sorry Top, I had no idea this was coming."

"They gave you no idea they were dissatisfied with the assignment prior to this?"

"None. I thought everything was fine. If I may ask where are they now?"

"At the airstrip, waiting for a flight to Nha Trang. When we're done here, Robbie will go back with you and he'll pack up their stuff."

"What will happen to them at Nha Trang?"

"They'll get reassigned to a line unit. Probably an airborne unit up north."

"I doubt Smith will enjoy being a Spec Four as a line dog."

"He brought it upon himself. I don't understand that Davis kid. He's only been with us a short while."

"If it's any consolation, Top, his cousin didn't see this coming either," Holt said quietly. "Is the patrol still on?"

"Yes, how do you want to play it?"

"I've already spoke with the team. We'll go with four Americans and six Bru if you agree."

"That will be fine. You seem to enjoy working with the Montagnards."

"I do. So far they are top shelf. We are learning a lot from them. Their jungle craft is superb. The point man, Phang, is the best I've ever seen. He can't read a compass or a map but point him in the right direction and he just takes off. Absolutely fearless. Claims he can smell the VC."

"VC?"

"I know there's no VC anymore but to them VC and NVA are all the same."

"Maybe we'll keep your team small for a while; just you four and your Yards. But don't go getting too attached to them. I don't need you going all Asiatic on me."

"I've been accused of that. I like it over here. I got nothing at home waiting for me. I plan on staying through my enlistment then we'll see what happens."

"I thought you were married and have a kid at home?"

"Marriage was annulled and the kid isn't mine. It's a long story. Buy me a couple of drinks at the NCO club and I'll tell you the whole story."

"I look forward to that."

"Thanks Top for your understanding. I thought I was getting my ass handed to me."

"I don't see any of this was your fault. Shit happens."

"Tomorrow, I'll go to the Montagnard compound with Doc Blaze and alert them. Then we'll head over the range and fire up the AK's, come back and pack up our gear. We'll be ready the day after tomorrow."

"Stop by the club tonight. I want to hear the rest of your story."

CHAPTER 13

Into The Dark Kingdom

Holt woke up with his head throbbing and his throat raw. He slipped into some flip flops, walked to the small refrigerator, and pulled out a beer. He cracked open the can, took a long pull, and lit a cigarette.

"Hair of the dog?" asked Evans.

"Feels like I fucking ate the dog," Holt moaned. "Fucking Banter can drink. I feel like shit. I must have smoked two packs of cigarettes last night."

"What did you two talk about?"

"Just swapped war stories and shit. He's not a bad guy. Do you know he did over eighteen cross border patrols? Most of them up north. Some of them in the A Shau Valley. Claims he even did a couple into North Vietnam.

"The A Shau Valley is the stuff nightmares are made of. I heard some of the old timers talk about it. Some patrols were inserted and never heard from again. Just vanished." Evans lit his own cigarette before continuing. "Glad we're down here and not up in that hell hole. I'll take jungle over mountains any day."

Evans studied Holt. "The beer helping any?"

"Yeah, it is. But I need some grease in my stomach. Some greasy eggs and bacon." Holt looked around. "Where is everybody?"

"Doc's over to the infirmary stocking up his kit for tomorrow and Ryan went to breakfast with some guys from the Echo team."

"How's he doing?"

"Ryan? Okay, I guess. He's really pissed at his cousin. Says he doesn't want to talk about it."

"That bullshit just came out of the blue yesterday. Caught me by surprise. Did they say anything to you?"

"I heard it when you did."

"Both of them made a big mistake. They're going to hate being regular grunts. Thirty days out at a time, eating nothing but C Rations. We're spoiled back here. Good chow, a bed to sleep in. Five day patrols and then five days off. They'll be begging to come back."

"That will never happen. They burned that bridge to the ground. Get dressed and let's get some chow."

Holt was wiping his toast in egg yolk when he saw Doc Blaze. "Doc, grab some coffee and come join us."

"Saw you at the club with Banter and some of the other top dogs," Doc said as he sat down. He leaned forward with a napkin. "Here, let me get some of that brown off your nose."

Holt pushed his hand away. "Banter wanted to buy me a drink for some reason. Didn't know it was going to turn into a late night bull session. Anyway, we need to go down and alert the Bru about tomorrow. Bring your kit and you can hand out lollipops and bandages. Win over their hearts and minds."

In a borrowed jeep, they rolled into the Bru compound. They walked over to Sangh's bunker. He was sitting outside drinking coffee and smoking a cigarette. He was wearing a Creedence Clearwater Revival concert t-shirt and a brightly colored loin cloth.

"Good morning Trung Si Holt."

"Good morning to you too." Holt watched as Doc set up his kit at a wooden table. He was soon surrounded by Bru children begging for candy and cigarettes.

"How come I never see any women here?"

"Women go inside when Americans come."

"Smart. Anyway, I wanted to tell you we're going out tomorrow. Five, maybe six days."

"Where?'

"Cambodia. Four Americans and six Bru. I need your best men. You and Phang, definitely, and four others. Tell them there is bonus money for Cambodia. No fighting. No kill VC, just go and look."

"Okay," was all he said.

"Another thing, we all carry AK's, no M16. Can your men fire the AK 47."

Sangh rolled his eyes. "See those boys with Bac Si. They all can shoot AK. Better than you, maybe."

"I'll come and pick you up at sunrise."

Sangh held out his wrist displaying a Seiko watch.

"At six AM," Holt said.

Sergeant Phang joined them. He wore a black t-shirt emblazoned with the SOG logo, a grinning skull with dripping blood from its teeth. He also wore a colored loin cloth. Holt offered him a cigarette while Sangh spoke to him. Phang smiled showing his stained teeth.

"Have you both been to Cambodia?"

"Many times. We go there to hunt."

"Hunt?"

Phang drew his finger across his throat. "Kill VC."

"Tell him no fighting, just looking. Make sure he understands that."

Sangh spoke and Phang's smile turned into a frown.

"Tell him he gets bonus pay."

Phang shrugged and walked away.

"Phang likes to kill VC. VC kill his family," Sangh said.

Holt nodded. "Do you have family here?"

"VC kill my wife and children in Hue while I was with Americans."

"I'm sorry to hear that. You're a long way from home."

"We all are. You too, long way from America." Sangh studied his face. "Or maybe you home now. You like Vietnam." It was a statement, not a question. "Maybe you stay and fight VC with Bru."

Holt stared into Sangh's eyes for a long moment. He saw nothing but sadness and anger. "Who knows. Tomorrow morning at six AM I'll come get you. Remember, we stay gone five or six days."

Holt walked over to Doc Blaze. "You about done here?"

"Sure, let me just pack up. These kids are really cute, aren't they?"

"Yeah, adorable," Holt said, remembering Sangh saying they all knew how to fire AK 47's.

"What's with Phang and Sangh? They're dressed up like Laurel Canyon hippies."

"Casual Friday."

"Friday? Is it Friday?"

"I have no idea what day it is. Let's go. We need to get to range to test fire our AK's."

After the range, the four men assembled in the barracks to pack up their gear. Holt studied the list of items supplied by Sergeant Banter. He always found it soothing to pack his ruck sack.

First came the AK 47 weighing eight pounds and twenty 30 round magazines at one and half pounds each. Then the McGuire Extraction Rig which replaced the normal web gear suspenders weighing about four pounds. The shiny steel D rings were spray painted flat black. Attached to the rig was a 9 mm Browning Hi-Power automatic and in a separate pouch the screw on silencer, weighing a total of three pounds. Taped to the left strap was a Marine K Bar knife weighing ten ounces.

Holt set the Belgian Paratrooper rucksack which weighed a little over four pounds on top of his footlocker. Each of the three outside pockets held a one quart canteen. A fourth canteen and canteen cup hung off the belt of the extraction rig. Secured to the bottom of the ruck was a ground cover and poncho liner with weighing three pounds. On tabs between the canteens two M18 smoke grenades were hung weighing nineteen ounces each. On each side of the rucksack was strapped a flexible two quart canteen. Each filled canteen weighed four pounds. The water weighed sixteen pounds.

Inside the ruck Holt packed his food. The men had cannibalized various C-Ration meals and packed a combination of conventional C Rations and LRRP meals. Holt also packed a one pound package of beef jerky. The combined weight of the food was approximately fifteen pounds. Holt and Evans carried a coiled twenty five foot length of thin nylon rope. On his belt, Holt had two standard ammunition pouches holding two M26 hand grenades with two more clipped to the outsides of each pouch. Weight of the grenades were eight pounds. An empty seven pocket ammunition bandolier held three golf ball sized Belgian V40 mini hand grenades in each pocket. Weight of the twenty one mini grenades was a little more than five pounds. In total, Holt and Evans were carrying over ninety pounds of gear.

Stuffed into their pockets and the rucksack were a compass, a code book, insect repellant, camo face paint, spare socks, water purification tablets, medical bandages, and a packet of morphine ampoules.

Holt and Evans studied their packs. Holt lit a cigarette.

Holt lifted his pack and groaned. "Too much," he said. "Shit can the ground cover and liner. We'll never use them. Leave four of the M26 hand grenades behind. That saves us about eight pounds."

"We forgot the Claymore's, they weigh three pounds apiece," Evans said.

"Ah fuck," moaned Holt. "You're right. You and me will carry a Claymore mine and each of the Bru will carry one. That's eight in total. That's more than enough."

"As it is, we're only carrying two gallons of water. I wish we could carry more."

"Two gallons won't last us five days. We'll need to find water when we're out there," Holt said. "Let's take a break and see how Ryan is doing." Ryan was fiddling with his radio. "I wish I had more time with this." Ryan was issued a brand new AN/PRC77 radio. It replaced the infamous PRC25, the Prick 25. The newer radio with battery weighed only twenty pounds, five pounds lighter than the Prick 25. It was all solid state electronics instead of vacuum tubes with an increased range of five miles with the three foot bush whip antenna. It also came with a ten foot long range antenna which was said to operate up to fourteen miles. The designation AN/PRC stood for Army Navy Portable Radio Communication.

"It's pretty much the same as the Prick but it's a helluva lot lighter. These Special Forces guys get all the new toys," Ryan said.

"You just heard me say dump the poncho. You don't need to carry grenades or a Claymore so your weight will be about the same."

"And this battery lasts a lot longer so I'll only need to carry one spare. They claim the handset is waterproof, but I'm still gonna wrap it in plastic to make sure."

"Good. The Bru can carry some spare batteries. Doc, how you doing?"

"I'm just about done. I went through my field kit. I got just about everything to handle any conceivable field trauma."

"Alright, let us sit for a minute and go over things. We all have our maps. We know where we're going. We have our individual emergency radios if we get separated—just don't get separated. We're there for reconnaissance only. We are to avoid combat at all costs."

"Just make sure the Bru know that," Evans said.

"I told both Sangh and Phang. I worry about Phang; he's a stone, cold killer. NVA killed his family. Sangh's too, up in Hue. Sangh seems okay, but Phang is another story. Sangh just gotta keep him on a tight leash." Holt paused to get a cigarette. "One thing we all understand; we all come back. We come back together or we don't come back. No one gets left behind."

They all nodded in agreement.

"Relax until chow. Write your letters home, take a nap, or whatever. After chow we'll check our gear once more, have a few beers and get to sleep early. We got a four AM wake up."

It was still early when Holt went to sit outside by himself. He wore a green t-shirt, cut off fatigue pants, and flip flops. He watched as the sun set over the mountains in Cambodia. He thought of the long letter he had written to Janet. It was a sappy letter. He inquired about the baby and her. He included some pictures taken before their last patrol. He looked fierce in his tiger stripe fatigues and camo face paint. He jokingly asked her for any hints in applying his makeup. He sent her another picture wearing his green beret and fatigues adorned with patches showing his recent accomplishments. He just about begged her to continue to write him. He didn't tell her that her letters were the only connection to a world he had given up and abandoned. He didn't mention he felt adrift in a world of violence and darkness. He lit another cigarette and closed his eyes.

He was startled when the screen door opened.

"Do you mind some company?" Sergeant Evans said holding out a ice cold can of Pabst beer.

"No Rick, not at all. Thanks," he said taking the beer.

They sat in silence for a moment.

"You nervous about tomorrow?" asked Evans.

"Not really. As Sangh says, one jungle same as another."

"It just got me spooked that Mike would give up everything rather than do the patrol. Davis, I can understand, he was just a kid. But I thought Mike was different."

"Who knows what they were thinking? We'll be okay. Just recon, remember."

"Do you ever think about getting killed over here?"

"Holt laughed. "Shit, I've been wounded six times. It's all I think about. Then I remember the gooks telling me I can't be killed."

"You believe that shit. Spirits and ancestor ghosts?"

"Why not? It works for them."

"I got just over a year left in the Army. Six months here and six months stateside. Maybe I'll extend and get an early out."

"You have plans stateside?"

"I have a girl that says she loves me—wait, here's a picture."

Holt took the photo and saw a beautiful girl with long brown hair parted in the middle. Next to her was Evans with equally long hair.

"She's a knockout; you, not so much. You two were hippies?" "Yeah, kind of. It's great in northern California. Really laid back. Lot of good music and great weed. It's peaceful, not like here." he took a deep breath and let it out slowly. "I figure I'll head back to school and finish up."

"I never saw you smoke weed?"

"I won't do it over here. Got to stay sharp. Focused."

"I really don't know how long we'll be here. They're starting to draw down the Special Forces. We might end up in Thailand." Holt drank some beer. "You know, I listened to the lifers talking the other night. They all know this war is lost. The South Vietnamese will never hold off the NVA. Once we leave, it's over. I feel bad about the Montagnards though. I mean, what's going to happen to them when we pull out? Sangh knows we'll leave some day. Says they'll go back to the mountains and just keep on fighting."

"I'm going to head on in and try to sleep. Maybe I'll ask Doc for a pill, something to help. I got the jitters."

"You want to stay back?"

"Me! No way. I'm no coward. I'll be fine once we're in the bush."

"That's how I feel. I like it out there."

"Fuck Holt, you're getting to be more gook than American. Watch yourself or you'll end up living with the Yards up in the mountains."

"I could think of worse things."

They got mortared that night sometime around two AM. The squad ran for the bunker in their underwear. They grabbed their rifles and a bandoleer of ammo. They sat in the damp, moldy bunker listening to the explosions. Dirt fell from the roof with each explosion. It was three AM before the all clear sounded.

"Fuck it. I ain't getting back to sleep. I think I'll get dressed and see if they got some coffee brewing at the TOC," Holt said.

Holt stripped off his t-shirt and underwear and slipped into his tiger stripes. He walked to the TOC and entered inside. He wasn't prepared for the activity he found.

"Sergeant Holt, I got your maps ready," said Sergeant Banter. "How you feeling?"

"Ready to go, Top."

"Good man. Mess hall will open up at four. Until then take a load off. You got everything memorized?"

Holt tapped his temple. "Got everything right here. Maps, codes, and call signs. Like I said, I'm rock steady."

"You just remember, no cowboy shit out there. Reconnaissance only. Make sure the Yards know it too."

At four AM Holt met the squad in the mess hall. They sat down to a large breakfast of fried eggs, sausage, bacon, and a small mountain of home fries. Holt was mopping his plate with toast when Banter walked over.

"When you guys finish up go get your maps and call signs. You can leave your dog tags, wallets, pictures, and rings. We'll put them in the safe."

As Banter walked away, Ryan said, "Shits getting serious know."

"You good?" Holt asked.

"I'm as cool as a mule."

"I'll assume that's a good thing. You got the Prick working?"

"My prick's working fine," he said, grabbing his crotch, "and the radio too."

At the TOC, Robbie met them with a battered three quarter ton truck and drove them to the Montagnard compound. Even though they were early,

Sangh had the men ready. Holt was surprised to see four of the Bru dressed in North Vietnamese uniforms. Sangh and a young boy no older than sixteen were dressed in tiger stripes.

"What's up with this?" Holt asked Sangh.

"Better we look like VC if we meet them. We surprise them. Maybe take prisoner and make big bonus. But then, maybe Phang kill and no bonus."

"You've done this before?"

"Many time. We go Cambodia, Laos maybe ten times or more."

Holt pulled out his cigarettes and offered one to Sangh.

"Those epaulettes he's wearing, is he supposed to be an officer?"

"Yes, he Captain, Dui uy. Phang speak perfect VC. Fool VC. Phang also speak French. This your first time in Cambodia?"

"Yes," Holt said.

Sangh said something to the Bru. Phang replied and they all laughed.

"Phang say you cherry boy."

"Cherry boy, that's good. That's funny."

"You relax. VC no can kill you," Sangh said indicating Holt's face. "Sangh take care of Americans. No one die."

"Remember we go and look only. No fighting."

"American say we go snoop and poop. No fight."

"Phang knows that? He's okay with that?"

Sangh nodded. "Sometime Phang get excited and no can stop him killing."

"Let's hope he doesn't get excited." Holt turned to Robbie. "Okay, Robbie, let's go."

Their first surprise came at the airstrip. Instead of the pilot they briefed with there was a Vietnamese Captain standing next to an aging Sikorsky H-34. The Sikorsky was a ungainly machine with a large bulbous top. The pilot and copilot sat high above the ground. Instead of a powerful turbine engine the Sikorsky was powered by a nine cylinder, radial, gasoline engine.

"What the fuck is this?" Holt asked.

"It's your ride, I guess," Robbie replied.

"No fucking way! This thing is ancient. Christ, look at it... it's all beat up. You see those riveted on patches? That's all from bullets. There must be dozens of them. Where did this thing even come from?"

"We've used them before. The Marines use them all the time."

"That's supposed to make me feel better? You ever been to a Marine base? It's like going back into the stone age. I was surprised I didn't see dinosaurs outside their perimeter. The Marines are still using WWII shit, for Christ's sake. And look at the pilot. Tell me he ain't more than seventeen."

"You never can tell the age of these gooks. He could be seventeen or he could be seventy."

"This is bullshit!" Holt said. Turning to Ryan he said, "Get me Top on the line. This fucking thing reeks of gasoline. I'm afraid it's going to blow up sitting right here. What's that green shit dripping from the bottom?"

Holt talked to Top expressing his concern. As he listened his face reddened. He sighed and handed the handset back.

"Top says Team Georgia called in a Prairie Fire and all air assets have been diverted to them. This is what we got. This is all that's left."

"We ain't getting any air support going in?" asked Evans.

"We are supposed to hook up with some Cobras when we near the LZ."

"Does this guy who's flying this piece of shit even know where the LZ is?"

"Ricky, you know as much as I do," Holt said.

The engine slowly came to life and they watched it belched out large clouds of black smoke. The blades began to turn faster and the ship began to rhythmically rock back and forth. It groaned and creaked ominously.

An American Lieutenant appeared from the other side of the helicopter and ordered them to get aboard.

"Who the hell is this guy?" Holt asked.

"Never saw him before," said Evans. "He is wearing a beret, though."

"Well, that makes all the difference."

As they began to walk to the ship, a jeep pulled up and a young Captain jumped out and waved his hands dramatically at the pilot. He made a slashing gesture across his throat and the pilot shut down the helicopter.

He walked up to Holt. "Who's in charge here?"

"I am, Sergeant Holt."

"Stand down until further notice. You might be needed elsewhere. Wait here."

Without any additional explanation he got back in his jeep and drove off.

Robbie who was parked with the truck walked over to Holt. "What's going on?"

"Do you know that guy? Where are all these officers coming from? He just told us to stand down," Holt said. "What are we supposed to do?"

"Stand down and wait, I guess."

"What a cluster fuck," Holt said. He shrugged off his rucksack and went to light a cigarette. Smelling the gasoline fumes he thought better of it and he walked with Robbie back to the truck.

"I'll tell you what... I'll go back and see what's up and then I'll come right back. You guys want anything while I'm back there?" Robbie asked.

"Some coffee, if they have it," said Holt.

CHAPTER 14

Hurry Up And Wait

Robbie returned about thirty minutes later and he jumped from the truck. "Give me a hand. I got a tarp, we can rig up some shade for you."

The men strung the canvas tarp from the side of the truck suspended on a couple of poles. Robbie dragged two large silver urns to the tail gate. "There's coffee and ice cold Kool aide. I got some cinnamon donuts in the cab."

He went to the cab and came back with a large, paper sack filled with donuts and a stack of Styrofoam cups.

"These are fresh out of the fryer." Robbie waved the Vietnamese pilots and crew over. Everyone crowded around the urns helping themselves to donuts and drinks. The Bru kept their distance from the Vietnamese air crew.

"Team Georgia went dark. There's no communication from them in the last hour. The officers are debating on sending you in on a Bright Light mission," Robbie said.

"'Bright Light', what's that?" Holt asked.

"A rescue mission."

"Then why don't they just say that."

"There's a code for everything. Anyway, everyone is debating what the fuck to do. Georgia was in heavy engagement when they declared the Prairie Fire. Then, nothing. Their over flight can't raise them and can't see anything on the ground. He does have their last known position marked," Robbie said in one breathless statement.

Holt got another cup of coffee and donut and sat against a tire in the shade of the tarp. Robbie sat next to him.

"Robbie, you did cross border missions, right? Has it always been like this?"

"I did three patrols into Cambodia. I got wounded on the third. They offered me a desk job and I snapped it up. I'm a short timer now and I can't wait to get home."

"It seems like every team we insert gets hit almost immediately and has to be pulled out."

"It has gotten worse. There's thousands of NVA in Cambodia and Laos. Landing zones are few and far between and they got trail watchers and scouts watching each one."

"Fuck," Holt said as he lit another cigarette. "I'm beginning to think Smith and Davis had the right idea in bailing out."

"Guys aren't extending their tours anymore. That why they started recruiting from the line companies, to fill out the ranks."

"Let me ask you, how many teams are we supposed to have?"

Robbie scratched his head. "Hmm, maybe twenty or more."

"And how many do we have?"

"I'm not really sure. Maybe, eleven or twelve. And those teams aren't full strength."

"Where are they? I've never seen that many guys in camp."

"They are assigned to different FOB's, Forward Operating Bases. At some point you'll get assigned to one too."

Holt noticed Phang staring at the Vietnamese with a look of obvious hatred.

"Sangh, please, go speak to Phang. We don't need any trouble here." He turned back to Robbie. "Where did those officers come from. I never saw them before."

"You won't see them around camp. They all hang out at the intelligence shack planning missions. They don't mingle with the enlisted men. Every once in a while they'll ask to go on a mission. They need time in the field in order to get their CIB. Can't be a Green Beret without a Combat Infantry Badge."

"Yeah, everyone wants a CIB, but no one wants to earn it." Holt took a long drag on his cigarette, "if they're gonna send us, in they better decide soon."

"Some of the officers think it's a waste sending in another team to rescue a team that's obviously dead."

"That's bull shit! If I was out there I'd like to think someone would come after me. If nothing else to bring my body back."

They sat in silence for a moment. "Robbie is that your first name or last name?"

"One name, just like Cher."

"Who?"

"Cher. You never heard of Sonny and Cher, the chick with the long black hair, 'You Got Me Babe'.

"Oh yeah. You don't wear any badges, what rank are you?"

"Sergeant, E5. I don't like wearing any identification." he looked around cautiously, "some of my trading activities are questionable. Don't need to advertise my name."

"If all the teams are named after states; how did we get the name Viking?"

"You know any states that begin with a V?"

"Vermont," Holt said.

"We don't use all the state names, some we skip."

"Why's that?"

"They only like state names with no more than three cymbals," said Ryan.

"'Cymbals'?" asked Holt.

"Yeah, cymbals like Alaska. A-las-ka, get it."

"You mean syllables," said Robbie.

"Ugh. Whatever."

"Where did you go to school?" Holt asked Ryan.

"Why?"

"No reason." Holt looked at Robbie and rolled his eyes.

At the TOC, Sergeant Banter stormed through the door and threw a file on his desk.

"What's up Top?" asked Sergeant Brown.

"Fucking officers are all up at G2 jerking each other off. They're trying to decide about sending in a rescue team to find Georgia." He stared hard at Sergeant Brown. "They're debating the merits of committing another team," he shouted at the room. "What fucking merits are there? We got a team in trouble; we got to help them." He searched his desk top for his cigarettes. "Fucking assholes."

"Sarge, I know you're upset but you got to keep your voice down."

"Yeah, I know better. Have we heard anything from them?"

"Not a peep. Maybe they went to ground and are waiting until it's safe to transmit. The Covey over flight says he hasn't heard a word."

"If Covey is overhead, they would break squelch to let him know they were still alive."

"Captured?"

"I doubt it. But, you know, maybe. Our guys know what the gooks do to them if they're captured."

Banter was chewing on his thumb and looking at the maps when Major Jung walked in followed by two Captains.

"Top, we have to decide if inserting another team is even feasible given the time of day," Major Jung said.

"We should have got them airborne as soon as Georgia called the Prairie Fire."

"Who would go in if we did authorize it?"

"Viking. They're sitting on the airstrip ready to go."

"Viking? Who's the team leader?"

"Sergeant Holt."

Major Jung sat in a chair and rubbed his hands across his face.

"I know Holt is your boy, but he's there and he's ready to go."

"I know Sergeant Holt and that has nothing to do with it, and I don't like you implying it does."

"I meant no offense, Major."

Major Jung took out some chewing gum. He extracted a stick and took his time unwrapping it. When he put it in his mouth, you could see his jaw muscles working.

"All right, send them in."

Sergeant Banter drove himself to the air strip. He skidded to a stop in a cloud of red dust.

"Get your maps out and gather round. You're going in to find Georgia. Hopefully they're holed up someplace." Banter spread his map on the hood of the jeep. "This was your LZ, forget that. You'll land about fifteen klick's north," he said pointing at the map. "Georgia's last known position was further north about eight klick's, right here. Circle it in red. You'll land and proceed eight klick's north and pick up their trail." He took a deep breath. "If they're dead, retrieve their bodies and bring them home. If not, like I said find their trail and try and contact them."

"Maybe their radio took a shit."

"They still have their emergency radios. No one's been able to raise them. We got rules in Cambodia. We're not supposed to go more than fourteen kilometers from the border. We can't use artillery or fixed wing aircraft, just helicopters. But I'm telling you right now, if you find them and need support, fuck the rules."

Holt finished folding his map. "Everything else remains the same: radio frequencies, call signs?"

"No change." Banter put his hand on Holt's shoulder and looked into his eyes. "Do this for me. Bring those boys home."

Holt and the team got into their gear and walked to the helicopter. A South Vietnamese Major was finishing up his briefing to the pilot regarding the change of plans. He walked away without acknowledging the Americans.

Holt walked over to the pilot. "We all good?"

The pilot smiled broadly. "Sure, we all good. How you say, same shit, different day."

"Is this piece of junk going to make it there?" Holt said.

"No worry GI. This is good ship," he said with his big, beaming smile.

The team settled in the interior. Holt clasped his hands and bowed his head, sucking on his lower lip.

"Are you praying?" Evans asked.

"I don't pray. God ain't helping us. It's all on us. I'm just trying and go over everything."

"Well, if you don't mind I'll say a little prayer."

"Can't hurt."

The helicopter started and began to rock back and forth. The noise was incredible. It slowly began to rise and move forward then it settled with a thud. The pilot shut the engine down.

The door gunner turned and said the ship was too heavy. The men all piled out and stared dumbly at the helicopter. They would have to wait for a second ship to become available.

Holt sat with his chin cradled in his hand.

Sergeant Banter walked over to Holt. "Don't get too comfortable, we got another ship on the way. Split up your team, five to a ship. You want to go over the maps again?"

"Top, relax. We got this. If they're out there, we'll find them."

"I almost got the mind to go with you."

Ryan turned and looked at Top with widen eyes.

"What? You don't think I can still hump the boonies with you pups?"

Ryan stammered an answer, "No Top, I wasn't thinking that."

"I could still walk you children into the ground and still have enough juice for a night at the EM club."

"No doubt. But I would feel better knowing you're back here looking out for us," Holt said.

Twenty minutes had passed when Banter announced their second ship was inbound. If possible, this second H-34 looked more beat up than the first. There were several bullet holes in the tail boom patched with just green hundred mile per hour tape.

Holt, Ryan, Phang, and two Bru loaded into the first helicopter. Evans, Doc Blaze, Sangh, and the remaining two Bru got on the second ship. This time the ship lifted smoothly. The pilot dipped the nose and went forward, he gained altitude, and turned west. The second ship followed. Holt sat in the open doorway with his feet resting on the steps. He looked out and marveled at the absolute beauty of the countryside below. It appeared as an unbroken carpet of lush green jungle. They flew at about three thousand feet and the air rushed over them cooling their bodies. After about forty minutes of flying, the door gunner tapped Holt on the head and pointed down. Holt saw a small field of elephant grass with thick jungle on its western side. The helicopter began to descend.

As the helicopter spiraled down to the open field, Holt looked for any sign of enemy activity. As the helicopter hovered two feet off the ground, Holt and the men jumped to the ground and ran towards the jungle. The second ship dropped the rest of team and they followed Holt into the jungle. When the ships left, the silence was overwhelming. Phang walked forward with two Bru to take point. Holt indicated they would wait ten minutes before proceeding.

Holt watched as Phang stared intently into the jungle. Phang placed his rifle on the ground and slipped out of his rucksack. He withdrew a machete, got up, and darted into the jungle. Holt turned to Sangh who indicated they were to stay put. After several minutes, which seemed like an eternity, they saw Phang emerge from the jungle carrying a severed head.

"Two VC watch trail. Both dead now," he said as he casually threw the head into the grass.

"Jesus Christ! What the fuck—"

Sangh leaned forward and whispered, "Trail watchers. Phang kill them."

"Why did he cut their heads off?"

"So they don't scream?" Sangh said, looking at Holt as if it was a stupid question.

"Yeah, okay, fine. Ryan, call in the all clear. Tell them we're proceeding eight klick's north. Tell them two enemy KIA."

Holt followed Phang and the three Bru all dressed in North Vietnamese uniforms. Behind him was Ryan and Sangh then came Evans, Doc, and the remaining Bru walking drag. They walked for fifteen or twenty more minutes then stopped to listen for ten minutes. They walked in single file with about ten feet between each man. After a while, the sounds of insects and birds returned which Holt took as a comforting sign.

Although shaded from the sun, the heat and humidity was still stifling. The air was thick and heavy with moisture. Sweat pooled under their arms and ran down their sides.

Holt wiped his face with his light cotton towel he kept wrapped around his neck, smearing his camouflage face paint. He took off his cut down bonnie hat and scratched at his short hair. Before starting again, Holt drank from his plastic canteen. The thin chain holding the cap to the canteen had been removed so it wouldn't make any noise.

Up ahead Phang signaled he was moving out. The jungle thinned out a bit and they were able to make good time. The moist ground muffled their footsteps and they proceeded silently. After a half hour, Phang raised his hand,

and they all stopped. Holt walked up to Phang. Phang pointed ahead and said, "trail." They moved forward cautiously and stood looking at a well worn trail about three feet wide. It ran west to east.

Holt took out his map and looked. There was no trail indicated. He wanted to mark it on his map. Phang leaned over him and took Holt's red grease pencil and drew a line. "Here on map."

Holt marveled at the Bru's ability to move through the jungle unaided by maps and compass. Phang leaned into Holt and whispered, "We go now. Two more hours and we find Georgia."

Holt peeled the cover back and looked at his watch, it was 1400 hours. They had made good time.

They crossed the trail and the last Bru in line swept away their boot prints with a leafy branch.

They walked another ninety minutes and stopped. Phang said, "I take two boys and find team. Then I come back for you. You wait here. Okay?" Holt looked at Sangh and they both nodded. They watched as the three Bru silently melted into the jungle; they seemed to dissolve into the leaves. The remaining seven men formed into a tight circle and waited. They sat in complete silence. To their right rear were some large rocks, and in front was long, wavy grass. The overhead branches put them in dappled sunlight. With their camouflage fatigues and face paint they felt their concealment was good.

The men took turns eating. Holt ate some beef jerky and drank from his canteen. He finished with a John Wayne bar, the hard, tropical, bar of chocolate which was impervious to heat. Holt watched as Sangh unwrapped a large green leaf containing a ball of seasoned rice and fish. Sangh ate the rice, chewing slowly and deliberately. He discarded the leaf.

Holt peeled back the cover from his watch, thirty minutes had passed. He crawled to the edge of their perimeter and unbuttoned his pants. As he kneeled urinating, he watched the jungle. Nothing stirred except the birds in the overhead branches. Mosquitoes fluttered about his face and settled on the small pool of urine. He scooped up a hand full of dirt and covered the urine. He had been told the North Vietnamese had special teams of men and dogs used exclusively to track the inserted teams. He rubbed some dirt above his knees where he had splashed himself. He settled back into his spot between Ryan and

Sangh. He sat with his rifle across his chest held by the sling. The buckles had been wrapped and taped with torn cloth to muffle sound.

The men waited. Forty minutes passed.

A small stone hit Holt in the chest and he looked to his right to see Phang silent as a wisp of smoke.

Phang walked over and got to his knees. He whispered in Sangh's ear. Sangh hung his head and grunted.

"Phang find the place where Georgia fight. Two Bru killed in fight. One Bru executed by VC; tied up and shot in head. No Americans. VC take them."

"Is he sure?"

"Yes."

"Shit," Holt said softly. "Did he find a trail?"

"Yes. Two boys stay with bodies. We go now?"

"Yes, we go." Holt turned to Ryan. "You heard?" Ryan nodded. "Okay, call it in. Tell them we will attempt to follow trail to see where the Americans have been taken and if they're still alive." He turned to Phang and told him to lead them to the bodies. He leaned against Sangh, "I'm sorry about your friends."

"We all die some day. It is the nature of life."

They walked quickly through the jungle, Phang assuring them there were no enemy soldiers in the vicinity. In thirty minutes, they reached the site of where Team Georgia fought and died. The wet leaves that overhung the pathetically small defensive position still held the smell of cordite and blood. The ground was littered with hundreds of expended shell casings. The surrounding trees were slashed and peppered with grenade fragments and bullet strikes..

Three dead Bru lay on the ground stripped naked. Blood pooled beneath their bodies.

Phang's men emerged from the trees and walked over to stand beside Phang.

Phang pointed to a clearly discernible trail. "VC take Americans and one Bru prisoner. We must go fast."

Phang went to the head of the column and started down the trail.

"Does Phang speak English or not?" Holt asked.

"Sangh shrugged. "Maybe. He's very strange. We should go now. He say hurry."

"Glad I'm in charge of this patrol or otherwise I'd think they were," Holt said to Ryan. "Follow Phang."

They followed Phang and his three men dressed like NVA soldiers down the trail. The trail narrowed and gave every impression of being an animal trail. Branches, leaves, and vines brushed against their shoulders and heads. They moved silently, their footsteps muffled in the soft, wet, forest debris. After a few minutes Phang stopped and held up a clenched fist. He lowered both arms. The patrol spread out in the shelter of the jungle.

Holt and Sangh walked forward to Phang. Phang whispered something and Sangh nodded agreement.

"What?" asked Holt.

"Phang said VC camp just ahead. Americans are there. He will take his men into camp and tell them he was sent to take prisoners north. We move forward and when time come shoot VC."

"How does he know where their camp is?"

"He know."

"Will they believe him?"

"Maybe. Maybe not. He speaks like VC. No matter. We kill all VC."

"Tell Phang we want a prisoner. An officer. Big, big bonus if he gets an officer."

"Sure. I tell him but if Phang get excited he can't control himself."

CHAPTER 15

Rescue And Reward

The men spread out on line and carefully moved forward. They stopped when they saw a clearing about ten feet in front of them roughly forty feet across. Around the perimeter were lean top's built of poles and ponchos. Twenty or so NVA soldiers rested in the clearing. The last lean to on the left was a cage made of bamboo. To the right was the Bru prisoner. He was tied between two trees his arms and legs extended outward in the shape of an X. His body was covered with knife cuts oozing blood down onto his legs. To the right of the Bru was a cooking fire attended by three soldiers with various blackened pots. They could smell the cooked rice, spices, and fish.

Holt watched as Phang spoke to his men. They all nodded. Then Phang squared his shoulders and boldly walked into the NVA Camp. One soldier went for his rifle and Phang barked some orders at him. The soldier hung his head and returned his rifle to the ground.

Phang walked into the center of the clearing and said something in a loud voice. A soldier got to his feet and came out of a lean to. As he walked towards Phang he finished buckling his belt. A polished leather holster hung from the belt emblazoned with a red enameled star.

"Uh oh," whispered Sangh. "He captain, Phang captain. No good."

Holt looked to his left and right. All the men lay concealed with their AK's pointed at the clearing.

Phang said something to the Captain in a stern voice. Then his demeanor changed, he smiled and took a step forward and extended his hand. The NVA captain looked over his shoulder at the bamboo cage. Several of the NVA now stood, looking at Phang, none had their rifles ready.

As the Captain looked back at Phang, Phang grabbed his hand and pulled him towards him. Phang viciously kneed him in the groin. The captain collapsed to his hands and knees. Phang clubbed him with the stock of his AK. Phang's three Bru fired into the NVA to their front. On cue, Holt and the remaining patrol fired at the NVA to the left and right. The noise was deafening. Tracers streaked through the enemy encampment. In a matter of seconds it was over. The NVA lay sprawled on the ground dead or dying. They never got off a single shot.

Holt walked with Sangh into the camp. Holt watched as the Bru casually walked amongst the NVA firing a single shot into the their heads.

Phang walked to the tied Bru. As he did, he said, "You want prisoner, you have prisoner." When he reached the man, he cut him down and cradled him in his arms.

"Evans, you, and Doc check on our guys then help Phang," Holt said. Sangh stood next to Holt and they both watched Phang. "That's Phang's friend. He was a good man," Sangh said. "A good fighter. He like a brother to Phang."

"We'll help him and get him back."

"Too late; too many cuts. No blood left."

Phang bent down close to his friend and whispered in his ear. He then covered the man's eyes and shot him in the head with his pistol.

The shot jolted everyone and they all turned to look at Phang. Phang gently laid his friend down and ripped a poncho from a lean to and covered him. He slowly walked back to Holt and Sangh.

As Phang approached the NVA Captain, he withdrew his knife. Holt stepped forward but was restrained by Sangh.

Phang showed the knife to the Captain, grabbed him by his left ear, and slowly sliced it off. He shoved the ear into the Captain's mouth and walked away. The Captain spit the ear out and howled in pain. He clamped his hand to the side of his head and continued moaning. Blood seeped through his fingers.

Evans and Doc Blaze had freed the American prisoners and helped them over to Holt. They were severely beaten; their faces were swollen and bloody.

"That's the motherfucker who beat us."

"What's your names?" Holt asked.

"Sergeants Jackson and Tollen."

Holt bent over and picked up the ear and handed it to Sergeant Jackson. "Here's a souvenir. Where are your boots?"

"They took them from us."

"Evans, look around, and see if you can find their boots. Doc, patch them up and get them ready to move. Ryan, let them know we got our guys and we're on the move to the PZ."

"Why not just land the chopper here?"

"Nah, we made a lot of noise. If there are any gooks around they'll be coming here."

Evans returned with two pair of boots. "Found them by the fire."

"All right, get your boots on and be ready to move out." Holt looked at his map and showed Ryan the pickup zone. "Right here, Ryan. We need two birds and cover fire."

Phang was at Sangh's side. Holt showed him the map. "Phang, take us home."

Phang pointed to the NVA captains pistol. "You sell pistol and give money to families of dead Bru."

Holt looked to Phang. "I will. But right now we need to go."

As if to emphasize the point a Bru ran from the forest. "Beau Coup VC come."

"You heard him, let's go."

As they left the camp they replenished their ammo from the dead NVA. Holt shoved several North Vietnamese stick grenades into his belt. The two wounded Americans picked up AK 47's.

They left on the same trail they came in. Phang set a brisk pace. The wounded Americans needed help walking.

After ten minutes of walking they could hear the NVA chasing them.

"Faster!" Holt shouted.

"Sarge, these guys are barely alive; they're all beat up," Ryan said.

"Alright, give me a minute to think." Holt was panting like a dog and knew the two American prisoners couldn't go any faster. "Here's what we'll do. Evans, you, Doc, Ryan, and Sangh go ahead with those two guys and the gook prisoner. When you get to where the fire fight was, where the Bru bodies are, go fast for another twenty minutes, due east. That's the PZ. I'll stay with

Phang and his men and hold off these bastards. Get on that fucking chopper and go."

"We ain't leaving without you," Evans said.

Holt shoved him hard in the chest. "You'll do exactly as you're fucking told. I'll be right behind you." Holt turned to Ryan. "We all can't get on one chopper anyway. Make sure they call in a second chopper. Tell them my men are dressed as North Vietnamese soldiers and not shoot them. Now go!"

"Sarge...."

"God damn it, go now. You're wasting time. Just make sure they know we're ten or fifteen minutes behind you and not to leave us behind. I'll contact them on the emergency radio. Now go!"

Holt watched them walk off down the trail. He turned to Phang. "Me, you and them. We stay behind and kill VC. We kill them all. Okay?"

"Okay, we kill VC." Phang spoke to his men and they began to lay out four Claymore mines in a staggered pattern along the trail. They placed the detonators in the mines and laid out the electrical cord as they ran further down the trail. They ran seventy five feet and stopped. Phang and two Bru went on the left side of trail and Holt and the fourth man stayed on the right side.

They heard the North Vietnamese soldiers before they saw them. When they did see them, they detonated the first two mines. Fifteen hundred steel ball bearings slashed through the NVA shredding the first six men into a bloody cloud. The enemy was stunned. As the smoke cleared, they regrouped and came forward, the next two mines were detonated killing another three men. Holt and Phang rose up as one and walked forward firing their AK's on full automatic. More soldiers fell dead.

They ran down the trail and reached the site of Team Georgia's battle. Again, they moved to either side of the trail and waited. This time the NVA were more cautious. They were moving slower down the trail. When they came into view Phang stood up and fired.

vPhang's bullets cut down the first five men. The remaining members of the team fired off to the sides of the trail where the NVA took cover.

Two of the Bru walked into the jungle shooting from the hip. Tracers were visible streaking through the trees. Leaves hung suspended in the air cut from branches by the bullets. For every tracer Holt saw, there were four other conventional bullets. He was amazed anyone could survive the Bru onslaught.

A lone NVA soldier, with bayonet extended, sprang from the trees and charged Phang from behind. Holt took aim and killed the man with several well placed shots. Phang whirled around, startled by the attack behind him.

When he saw the dead soldier he looked at Holt and smiled.

Holt accompanied by a Bru went into the jungle on the trails right side and began killing any NVA foolish enough to remain behind.

Holt was puzzled; the NVA attack seemed disorganized and half- hearted. It was so unlike his previous encounters with the enemy.

The NVA soldiers scattered in the jungle and their pursuit ended. Holt heard the first helicopter land and called to Phang to move out.

The Bru were searching the bodies and removing anything of value.

Holt hollered again. "God damn it, let's go. We need to move out now." He saw the Bru picking up some newer looking AK's. "Phang, now!" Holt shouted.

Once on the trail heading to the PZ, Holt got out his emergency radio. He changed the frequency on the URC-10 to match the air assets. "Eagle One, Eagle One, this is Viking One Zero. We are heading to the pickup zone, need you ASAP, how do you copy?"

"Viking One Zero this is Eagle One. We copy. Inbound now. Pop Smoke upon arrival."

"Eagle One, I have four indigenous personnel dressed as NVA. Don't shoot them. Please confirm."

"Roger that, Viking One Zero. Four indigs dressed as NVA. We copy."

Holt was surprised to hear an American voice on the transmission. He thought they would be picked up by the South Vietnamese Air force.

Holt stood off to the side and waved the Bru forward. As Phang passed Holt grabbed him on his shoulder. "Do not go into the clearing. I must go first. If they see you they will shoot you. Understand?"

Phang nodded and started down the trail. Holt grabbed his web gear. "Tell me you understand."

"Yes, I bic," he said using the Vietnamese word for understand. "You better understand," Holt muttered under his breath. Holt took one last look back and then followed the Bru. They ran for fifteen minutes before the clearing was visible. Holt doubled over with his hands on his knees. He was breathing hard through his mouth. Sweat poured off his face streaking his camo face paint. Bile rose in his throat and he spit on the ground. When he stood up straight, a wave of dizziness passed over him and he staggered. The Bru seemed unfazed by the run and looked at him quizzically.

Holt ignored their looks and walked to the clearings edge. He took out his radio. "Eagle One, we are at the clearing. Where are you? Over."

"We are above you? Viking. Pop smoke. Over."

Holt took a M-18 purple smoke grenade, pulled the pin and threw it into the clearing.

"Viking One Zero, I see Goofy Grape, over." Smoke grenades were used not only to mark a units location but gave the helicopter pilots wind direction and wind speed. Essential elements in making a safe landing.

"Eagle One, that's affirmative, come get us, over."

A Huey helicopter came from the west, behind them, and overflew the clearing. It made a lazy circle, turned back to the clearing, and began to descend. As it did an AK fire erupted from the wood line. Holt and Phang's group fired into the jungle. Eagle One pulled up and headed east. "Viking One Zero, Snakes in bound to suppress ground fire."

"Wait! Tell those fuckers we are shooting AK's too and not to shoot at us," Holt screamed into the radio.

"Viking One Zero, please use proper radio procedure. Snakes are aware of your location. They will make every effort not to shoot you. Over."

Two AH 1G Cobra helicopter gunships swooped down firing their mini guns into the tree line. The six, rotating, electric controlled barrels, firing at the rate of six thousand rounds per minute tore the trees to shreds. The air was filled with gun smoke and falling jungle debris. They made a second, slower pass, firing off a barrage of 2.75 inch, 70MM rockets. The garish, open sharks mouth, painted on the nose of the helicopter was clearly visible. Right on the Cobra's tail the Huey transport ship came in for a landing.

Holt and the Bru ran for the Huey. They hunched their shoulders and lowered their faces to avoid the swirling down draft of the helicopter blades. Holt stood to the side as the Bru loaded aboard then climbed into the cargo hold. As the helicopter began to rise it was peppered with enemy gun fire. Bullets slammed into the tail boom of the helicopter. The crew chief was firing his M60 machine and was thrown violently back against the helicopter bulk head as a bullet hit him square in the chest. He slowly sat up and ripped open his field jacket displaying a bullet caught by his ceramic body armor. He turned and looked at a bullet hole in the bulk head that had missed his head by inches. He smiled broadly and went back to firing his machine gun.

Holt sagged back against the vibrating wall of the helicopter and dug out his cigarettes. He lit one and passed the pack to the Bru. He gave the pilot a thumbs up, closed his eyes, and inhaled deeply. His hands were shaking violently. He gripped his hands together to conceal the tremors.

When they landed back at base camp the crew chief couldn't wait to show the pilots his damaged body amour. Holt took one of the older AK's from the Bru. He withdrew the magazine and cleared the weapon. He gave it to the crew chief.

"Hang this up in your club compliments of Team Viking." When the pilot came over Holt said, "I really want to thank you guys. You did a great job. Sorry about the radio shit. I was a little bit excited back there."

"No problem. Just be careful. You never know who's listening. Some desk jockey hears some shit and next thing you know you're on report."

They shook hands and Holt and his men walked over to Robbie and the waiting three quarter ton truck. As the Bru climbed into the truck, Holt asked Phang how many VC did he think they had killed.

"Forty four," Phang said without hesitation. "Twenty three at the camp and twenty on the trail."

Holt smiled at Phang who was once again speaking English. "Forty four it is. You did good Phang. You and your men are number one. Big bonus coming."

Phang leaned close to Holt. "You save Phang's life on the trail. You shoot VC. Phang will remember that. You number one too. Here, for your big man," he said, handing Holt a packet of documents and letters he took from the dead soldiers.

Holt thanked him and got in the truck next to Robbie. "What a shit show. It really sucked ass," he said as he lit a cigarette.

"Really? Wait till you see Top. He was fucking ecstatic. Not only did you rescue those two guys, but you got a NVA Captain as prisoner. He was so happy, I thought he was going to wet his pants. Those Cobra pilots reported thirty kills. Everybody is happy."

"I'm glad he's pleased. That's why we do this, to make Top happy."

"Hey fuck you. When Top's happy, we're all happy."

"Robbie, when you get the chance, go see the Bru. They stripped those gooks of anything of value."

"Beau Coup souvenirs. Shit, now I'm happy too."

They dropped the Bru at their compound and proceeded to the TOC. Holt walked in and dropped his rucksack and AK. He knocked on Tops door. The First Sergeant came from behind his desk and greeted Holt warmly, vigorously shaking his hand.

"You did a first rate job out there, Sergeant. Absolutely first rate. I couldn't be happier. Go grab some chow and a shower. You smell like ass. When you're done come back and give Robbie your after action report. Body count," he asked.

"By the numbers, forty four. That's an actual count by the Bru. They'll be looking for a big bonus."

"And they'll get it. The rescue of two POW's and an officer as prisoner; they'll get a huge bonus. I'll see to that."

"Don't forget the families of the four Bru that were killed."

"Already in the works."

Holt shook his head sadly. "Fucking gooks. They tortured one of them to death. Cut him to pieces. Just for fun. I'll never let them take me prisoner. Never!" Holt's eyes started to tear up.

Top put his arm around Holt. "You're back home now. Go get something to eat and we'll talk later. The Major will want to talk to you too."

"Maybe they'll have some bacon. I'd really love a big bacon sandwich right now."

"You head over to the mess hall. I'll call ahead. You'll get your bacon sandwich."

"With mayonnaise. A lot of mayonnaise?"

"With mayonnaise, son. With all the mayonnaise you want."

True to his word the First Sergeant had called ahead. Holt was greeted warmly at the mess hall.

A slim Vietnamese girl in a bright yellow sun dress brought over a carafe of coffee with cream and sugar.

"Food cooking. I hear you big hero. Get number one service," the girl said.

"What's your name?"

"My name is Lu," she said. "Too bad you smell bad. I take you to my place and love you long time, but you stink."

"Maybe next time?"

"Maybe next time you not be hero," she said slyly as she walked away.

Holt fixed a steaming mug of coffee and lit a cigarette. As he finished his cigarette, the mess Sergeant himself walked over with a sandwich stacked high with freshly cooked bacon and slathered with mayonnaise.

"For the next few days you and your team are golden. Enjoy it. It won't last long," he said. "You boys did really good out there. You earned everything you get."

"Thanks Sarge, I really appreciate it."

With his belly full Holt walked back to his barracks. He entered and threw his ruck on the floor and placed his AK on top of it. Evans, Ryan, and Doc jumped up form their bunks and hugged him, slapped him on the back and handed him an ice cold beer.

"Fucking asshole. Just had to stay behind and play the big hero," Evans said.

"Somebody had to make sure you guys got out."

"Tell us. What happened?"

"Later, at the club. I need to get a shower. Everyone keeps telling me I stink."

"That's grunt stink, my friend. They're just jealous."

"Grunt stink or not, I just want to get rid of it."

"How come you smell so bad? We weren't out that long," Evans asked.

"Fear sweat. It's different. It's thick and greasy," Holt said as he walked toward the showers.

CHAPTER 16

A Question Of Value

Holt came back from his shower and was toweling off. Evans sat by himself at the table. His radio, tuned to the Arms Forces Network played softly in the background. Jim Morrison was singing 'People Are Strange'.

"Sarge, you got a minute?" Evans asked.

Holt pulled on some cut off fatigues and a black t-shirt. He slipped his feet into his Ho Chi Minh sandals. "Sure. Where is everybody?"

"Doc's at medical replenishing his kit and Ryan went to get some radio batteries."

"And left you alone to talk to me."

"Yeah. That's about it."

Holt got a beer and sat down. "So, what's up?"

"What do you think about these missions we've been pulling?"

"In what way?"

"We were talking and it seems Mike and John made the right decision. These fucking missions are becoming more absurd as time goes on. I mean, ten of us on the ground up against hundreds of gooks. We've been lucky so far but our luck can't hold out forever. Every fucking time we end up running for our lives." He paused to light a cigarette. "You came from a line company; which is better?"

Holt leaned back in the lawn chair and rubbed his eyes with both hands. "There's pros and cons to both. We live better here. Chow is better. For the most part, no one fucks with us. In a line company you stay out for thirty days or more and all you eat are C-Rats. Basically, you're all alone with just your squad. You know how the jungle is. You can't see more than ten feet.

You know the other guys are there but for all intents and purposes it's just you and your squad. The whole purpose is to engage in combat. Find the enemy and kill them. We try and do the opposite. We try and avoid combat."

"Maybe that's how it used to be. Not anymore. Cambodia is crawling with hardcore NVA, thousands of them. You heard about Alabama? They inserted and a hour later they vanished like they never existed. All of them gone." Evans stared at Holt. "I don't like the cross border shit. What happens if we vanish? What do they tell our parents?"

"Killed in action or missing in action in South Vietnam. Body unrecoverable."

"Fucking 'Studies and Observation Group'. Sounds like we're librarians."

"When you signed up for SOG, you signed the same papers as I did. What we do is secret. Can't talk about it," Holt pulled an imaginary zipper across his lips. "Do you want out?"

"I don't know what I want. My girl writes me. Tells me she's having doubts about the war. Even the politicians are talking about ending the war; pulling us out. What I do know is I don't want to die in a war that everyone thinks is immoral. This is bullshit. You used to be able to wear your uniform with pride. Now they tell you to change into civilian clothes before you leave the airport."

"Americans don't have the stomach for a long protracted war. After Tet, everyone thinks we're losing." Holt stopped and lit another cigarette. "Does Doc and Ryan feel the same? Were you elected to speak on their behalf?"

"Sort of."

"We should have a few down days to figure things out. The four of us should talk."

Richard Evans wasn't the only person having doubts. First Sergeant Banter sat in his office staring at a map. He closed his eyes and massaged his temples. He was interrupted by a knock on his door. He looked up and saw Major Jung in his doorway. The Major's shoulders practically filled the opening.

"Top, you have a minute?"

"For you, always. What's up, Sir."

The Major saw the open bottle of Jack Daniels on the Sergeants desk.

"A little early isn't it? You're still on duty."

"I'm on call twenty four seven. It's never too early," he said pushing a clean glass across his desk and pouring a healthy, two finger shot into the glass.

"Maybe you could have a vodka and orange juice and at least disguise it," the Major said as he picked up his glass and swirled the contents.

"Do I look like a college girl on spring break?"

"No Top, you don't."

"What can I do for you?"

"I have some good news that might brighten your day."

"And I have nothing but bad news that will certainly darken yours."

The Major groaned. "You go first."

"We currently have eleven teams. We have eight, six man teams and four, four man teams and one team of just two men. That's team Georgia and we're losing them. Eight teams are assigned to three different forward operating bases and we have three teams here."

"Wait, why are losing Georgia?"

"They're being sent home. Apparently, if you were a POW you get sent home."

"But they were only held prisoner for a day."

"Doesn't matter. The regulations are clear."

"So, when they leave how many men do we have left?"

"Sixty four. We should have one hundred twenty. And to answer your nest question, there are no replacements in the pipeline."

The Major contemplated his drink.

Sergeant Banter continued. "I was thinking of reducing the six man teams to four man teams. That would give us two more teams."

"For a start, let's do that."

"That's easy. Consider it done. The problem is the orders we're getting from Saigon. Those desk jockeys are living in their own world. They're giving us assignments as if we're at full strength. I'd have to break the teams down even more to fulfill all their requests. We're short on medics and team leaders. Team leaders are supposed to be E-7's, Sergeant First Class. Only two teams are being led by E-7's. I have two team leaders who are E-5, Sergeants and the rest are led by E-6 Staff Sergeants. Half of them have less than three months time in grade."

"What about the recruitment program; the one Weaver and Holt came in on?"

"With all this talk of drawing down troop strength and turning the war over to the Viet's that program has dried up. Training in the states has been reduced to six months and even with that we can't count on replacements. And before you ask, I could cannibalize our rear echelon staff and not even make a dent in our requirements. And where would that leave us? We need staff back here to coordinate operations."

"I knew things were bad but—"

"Up north, things are even worse. I just heard, three teams just vanished. Two went into Laos and one into the A Shau Valley. All three, just fucking vanished without a word. Every team inserted into Laos gets shot up and comes out under a Prairie Fire extraction.

The Major grunted and took a sip of his drink.

"And here's the cherry on top of this shit cake. I just received orders. Saigon wants Team Viking re-inserted to assess the NVA presence where the prisoners were released."

"When?"

"Tomorrow."

"That's impossible. I have orders to conduct an awards ceremony for Viking and to hand out promotions. That was my good news."

"Fucking Army. The left hand doesn't know what the right hand is doing," Top spat out, as he drained his drink.

"Plus, they're supposed to get a three day in-country R&R for the capture of that NVA Captain."

"Shit! Robbie, stop playing that God damn rock roll music and get Sergeant Holt. Have him report here, pronto!" Top shouted.

"Sorry Top. They cancelled the hillbilly station. Not enough of you old-timer's around, I guess."

"Just turn off that fucking jungle music and get Holt."

"Yes Sir. I'll go get Holt right now."

Banter rubbed his forehead. "Do you see what I have to put up with, Major? Smart ass E-5's listening to boogie music all day long."

"I don't think it's called jungle music or boogie music, Top. Some of the men might take offence at that."

"But I shouldn't be offended when that little turd calls my music, hillbilly music. Hillbilly music my ass. It's America's music. It tells the story of Americans. Am I right, Sir?"

"I wouldn't know. I'm Korean."

"Korean, huh? I was in Korea too. Now that was a fucking war! We were sold out by that gutless puke Truman. He should have let MacArthur roll on into China and we wouldn't be in this mess. You mark my words, Major, the politicians will sell us out here just like they did in fucking Korea."

The Major watched Banter top off his glass and sighed. "I believe we're getting off topic, Sergeant."

"Right! We were talking about music. Do Koreans listen to music?"

The Major leaned his head back and closed his eyes.

"You okay, Sir?"

"I might be getting a headache."

"Here, let me freshen your drink. This will cure that headache."

Robbie found Holt and Evans in the barracks drinking beer and shots of Jack Daniels.

"Holt, Top is with the Major, they want to see you right away."

"You have to be kidding. I'm a little buzzed. Should I get dressed."

"You're fine. Get going," he said ,"ASAP."

"Robbie, wait a minute," Holt said as he got the Russian pistol from his locker. He handed it to Robbie. "How much can you get for this? And don't bullshit me."

Robbie turned the pistol over and examined the holster. "Wow! This looks brand new. If I was in Saigon, I could get a thousand dollars easy. Up here in this waste land, seven hundred fifty."

"I need six hundred dollars, the rest is yours. It's for the families of the Bru that got killed on team Georgia. Phang found this and I promised him I would sell it for him."

Robbie found a empty sand bag and put the pistol inside. "You'd better get going."

"Evans, I'll talk to Top about our conversation."

Holt entered Top's office and had to endure the critical inspection of the sergeant.

"Is the uniform of the day, Hobo chic? Sergeant Holt, have you been drinking?"

Holt saw the bottle and glasses on the desk but thought better of mentioning them.

"Yes Top, I have. And my intention was to continue drinking. I thought I was off duty."

"You're in the Army! You're never off duty. I'll tell you when you're off duty. Sit down. As long as you're drunk, you can have a drink with us."

Logically, that doesn't make any sense, Holt thought.

Top poured each a healthy shot. "There's good news and bad news. The Major has the good news and I have the bad news. Which do you want first?"

"Belay that, Top. I'll take care of the bad news. Don't worry about it," Jung said.

Holt looked from one to the other thoroughly confused.

"Roger that. Before we begin, I have a question. What happened to that gook Captains ear?"

"What ear?"

"The Captain; he's missing his ear."

"Must have lost it during the battle."

"He said one of the Yards cut it off."

"That's news to me."

"Who did it? That murderous little prick Phang did it. Didn't he?"

"I can't tell them apart. They are all just little brown people to me."

"Bullshit! I might believe that from someone else, but not you. You love those little people. You look out for them."

v"Is that Captain upset about his ear?"

"Of course he's upset! Someone cut it off!"

"I wish you could have seen what he did to the Bru prisoner. He's a fucking animal and lucky to be alive."

"Enough, we don't need to discuss his ear anymore," interjected the Major.

"If there's no bad news, you had mentioned something about good news, Major?"

"Tomorrow there will be an awards ceremony and promotions for Sergeant Evans, Specialist Blaze and Specialist Davis. You'll each be awarded the Bronze Star for Valor for your actions regarding the release of the two American prisoners. Sergeants Phang and Sangh will be awarded the Vietnamese Cross of Gallantry for their actions. The citation will read the event took place in South Vietnam. So Sergeant Holt, this will be your fifth Bronze Star?"

"Yes sir, I believe so."

"Very impressive for someone so young," Major Jung said.

"Sergeant Evans is being considered for his own team. Do you think he's ready?" asked Sergeant Banter.

"Ah, well, there is something to discuss," Holt said.

"What might that be?"

"Maybe I could get some coffee?"

"Robbie, bring in some coffee for Sergeant Holt. Is there anything else I can get you? Some donuts, perhaps?"

"You have donuts? Sure, I'll take some donuts."

When the coffee arrived, Holt thanked Robbie and pushed his cup towards Top. "Maybe you could Irish this up a bit?"

Sergeant Banter frowned but he poured a shot of Jack into Holt's cup.

"If there's nothing else, please continue."

"You mentioned donuts?"

"Forget the fucking donuts."

"Sure. Sorry. I just thought donuts were offered. Anyway, we were talking, the team and I, about... about the risk involved in our missions. The extreme risk of going into Cambodia for so little accomplishment."

v"Since when do staff sergeants question their orders?"

"Sergeant Banter, let's hear what Sergeant Holt has to say," Major Jung interrupted. "Sergeant, continue."

"I'm not questioning the orders; this was a discussion amongst the team. If you'd rather not hear about it then we'll just forget it."

Sergeant Banter leaned back in his chair and blew a perfect smoke ring towards the ceiling. "No, please, by all means, continue Sergeant."

Holt felt the tremors begin in his left hand and slid it flat against his leg. "Half the time we get shot out of the LZ and can't land, the other half we're compromised within twenty minutes and have to be extracted. We already know there are thousands of NVA across the border; why not just bomb the shit out of them and be done with it."

Holt looked at Banter and the Major and realized he should have kept his mouth shut. He gripped his leg tighter to quell his shaking hand.

"Anything else, Sergeant?"

"Utilize the border bases that we have. Run the patrols from there. Catch the gooks when they cross the border and bomb them or use our artillery. This way the men at least have the support they need." Holt ground out his cigarette and sagged backed into the chair. He realized any goodwill he had developed with the two men had probably vanished.

After an uncomfortable silence the major said, "What's wrong with your hand?"

"My hand?'

"Your hand, it's shaking."

"It's nothing. I'm nervous. Talking to officers makes me nervous."

"Sir! When you address an officer you say, 'Sir', Shit bag," Sergeant Banter growled.

"Sir, there's nothing wrong with my hand, Sir. And I'm no shit bag, Top, and you know that."

"I want you to go see the Doctor when you leave here. Not the medic but the Doctor. I'll call him and let him know you're on your way. You're dismissed Sergeant. We'll take what you said under advisement."

When they heard Holt leave the TOC the Major hollered to Robbie. "Call medical, tell them Sergeant Holt is on his way for a physical exam."

"Do you believe the balls on that pup. Telling us how to run the war," snapped Banter.

"What the fuck, Sergeant. You said the same thing to me, not ten minutes ago."

"I've earned my right to offer my opinion. It's my job to provide council. Squad leaders obey orders and keep their mouths shut. It's my own fault for coddling these mutts."

"These mutts, as you call them, risk their lives everyday obeying our orders. They should have the right to offer their opinions when it's their life on the line."

"Back in my day—"

The major cut him short. "Back in your day, I'm sure things were done differently. By the way, we have a new Captain coming tomorrow. He's supposed to head up operations but I have other plans for him. I want him to go to An Hoc and take charge of the camp. Maybe we'll send Holt and his team with him. Put his border patrol theory to the test."

"An Hoc, you mean the Dog Bone? That shit hole? It should have been closed long ago. It's virtually indefensible."

"That's the point. Saigon wants our recommendation whether to keep it open or not."

Holt walked into the medical bunker and reported to a bored looking medic. "Sergeant Holt, I'm supposed to see the Doc."

"What's the problem?"

"Nothing."

The medic began to say something but instead waved Holt to a chair. "Have a seat and the Captain will be with you shortly."

After ten minutes Holt was called to see the Doctor, a young Captain with curly blond hair and steel rimmed eye glasses. The Doctor stared at Holt's face for a minute, then down at his legs.

"Is this about your wounds?"

"No, Sir. I'm fine. My hand shakes from time to time. The Major was concerned."

"Your hand shakes?"

"My left hand. My forearm twitches and it travels down to my hand. Just sometimes, not always."

The Doctor examined Holt's arm. "I can't see any damage to your arm. Are you nervous?"

Holt shrugged.

"Are you scared? It would be natural to be scared over here."

v"Not really."

"Take off your shirt."

Holt took his tee shirt off and stood in front of the doctor.

"Jesus Christ, your left arm appears to be the only place you haven't been injured."

The Doctor listened to Holt's heart and breathing. "Your lungs are clear and your heart beat is regular. What am I supposed to do with you? How's your vision? Blurred at all?"

"No, sir. Everything's fine. It's just my hand. And as I said, it doesn't happen all the time. Doesn't happen on patrol, mostly back here at base camp. You know, dealing with Top and the officers."

"Understandable. I shake when I have to deal with Top too. He can be rather gruff." The Doctor tugged on his ear. "As far as I can tell you're fine. Without any further testing, I can see nothing wrong with you. Do you want additional testing?"

"No, Sir. Just relay your findings to Major Jung. That's all."

"Yes. I'll do that."

As Holt left the Captain's office, he called after him. "Sergeant, try and not get wounded anymore."

"Yes, sir, I'll try. Believe me, it's not intentional."

Robbie knocked softly on the Major's door. "Sir, the Doc just called and said Sergeant Holt is fine. Cleared for duty."

"That's it? Cleared for duty? Where is he? Get him on the phone for me."

"Doc said he was going to the officers club and if you needed any additional information he'd be happy to buy you a drink and discuss the matter further."

"Is today some holiday that I'm not aware of?"

"It's quiet, Sir. People take advantage of the down time."

The short walk to the club left a thin sheen of sweat on his body. In the dim interior of the club, the hot, humid air was stirred by two, slow moving overhead fans. A small group of junior lieutenants sat at the far end of the bar. They looked visibly uncomfortable with the Major's presence.

Major Jung saw the doctor sitting alone writing on a pad.

As the Major approached the captain slid the pad into his pocket. "A letter to my wife."

"Sorry to interrupt you. I wanted to talk about Sergeant Holt."

The captain cut him off. "He's fine. Good to go."

"About his hand?"

"Not a problem. He says you make him nervous, you and Sergeant Banter. Without further examination, I can't find anything wrong with him."

"What do you suggest?"

"Suggest? I suggest we send him home, him and everyone else in Vietnam."

"I'm being serious, Captain."

"So am I." The Captain signaled the barman for two more beers. "I'm not interested in your opinions about the war. I'm concerned about my sergeant."

"You ever see that boy's body?"

"No, why."

The Captain lit a cigarette and offered the pack to the Major, who declined. "You should. He looks like someone's failed science project. There's barely a inch of his body that hasn't been punctured by shrapnel, bullets, or knives. I'm surprised the only thing shaking is his hand. I'd be terrified of going out in the jungle again."

"He was drinking in the afternoon."

The Captain held up his bottle. "As we all are. I imagine he thought he was off duty. You sound like Claude Rains in Casablanca, 'I'm shocked. Shocked to learn that gambling is going on in here.' Everyone drinks."

"Your insolence is bordering on insubordination."

"Don't be so naive. Half your senior NCO staff are functioning alcoholics and the other half are just alcoholics."

Before the Major could comment, the Captain continued. "Don't take offense at this, but I really don't report to you. And I'm not concerned about my rank. I am a fully licensed medical Doctor. I have certificates and diplomas up the ass to prove it. As such, the lowest rank I can be is Captain. I'll doubt I'll get much higher. The Army paid for my medical school and I owe them four years. I'm only two and a half years in. Three more months over here and twelve months in the states and I'm out. I'm not about to make the military a career. If I wanted to, I could send your Sergeant home right now. I could easily justify it by his body alone. But I won't. I'll continue to do my part. I patch these boys up and return them to duty. And then I sit right here and wait for the same boys to come back. And again, I'll sew them up and send them back out. And why do I do it? Basically, I'm a fucking coward. I obey my orders without question and count the days until I go home." The Captain took a long pull on his beer. "I'd like to return to writing my wife. She's still under the misguided impression that I am an honorable man."

CHAPTER 17

Vung Tau

The next morning, after breakfast, the men stood around waiting for the awards ceremony to begin. They stood trying to find some shade. It was just after nine o'clock and it was already eighty six degrees. There was a problem causing a delay. A South Vietnamese Special Forces Major refused to participate upon learning he was to present his awards to Montagnards. He stormed off angrily back to his waiting helicopter leaving Major Jung standing by his jeep.

"Fucking little turd," Major Jung muttered. "Have the men assemble by the TOC and let's get on with this," he said to Robbie.

Holt, Evans, Davis, and Blaze were given their Bronze Stars as a group; the citation being read for all their awards. Major Jung paid special attention with the presentations to Sergeants Sangh and Phang, praising their bravery and their devotion to the Special Forces. He pinned their medals to their uniforms and posed for photographs with the two Bru warriors. He handed Sergeant Sangh a thick brown envelope.

"Your bonus payment for rescuing the two Americans. Please tell your men how grateful we all are." The two Bru beamed with pride.

Next came the promotion ceremony. Richard Evans was promoted to Staff Sergeant. The medic, Andy Blaze, was promoted to Specialist Sixth Class and Ryan Davis, Holt's RTO, was promoted to Sergeant.

After the promotions the men were dismissed. Holt was called over to Major Jung.

"Sergeant, for capturing a prisoner, you and your team are getting a three day in-country R & R in Vung Tau. Robbie will have your orders at the CP at

1330 hours. Your flight leaves at 1400. Standard jungle fatigues, fully patched, and berets are authorized. You can wear civilian clothes in Vung Tau if you have them. Major Jung extended his hand. "Congratulations. Have a good time. Relax and try to stay out of trouble."

"Thank you, Sir. I know the guys will really appreciate it. I do too. We need it."

Holt walked to the barracks and swung open the screen door. "Shit, shower, and shave boys. We're got three days in Vung Tau. We leave at 1400 hours. Shine your boots and get your berets out."

Ryan looked puzzled.

"1400 hours, it's two o'clock, asshole," Holt said.

"Yeah, I know that. You don't have to call me names. Anyway, I don't have to do any of that stuff. I showered and shaved this morning and I just came back from the crapper."

"Thank you for letting me know that. Now that you're a Sergeant you'll need to know the men serving under you are having regular bowel movements. As a matter of fact, I want you to keep a log of the teams bowel movements. Turn it in to Doc at the end of each week."

"Really?"

"Yeah, it'll help Doc track the well being of the team."

"You're kidding me right?"

"Doc, help me out here."

"He's right. It'll take that job away from me. He's not asking you to examine the shit, just note the time of everyone craps."

"With rank comes more responsibility," added Holt.

Holt sat down and removed his boots. He examined his feet then got out his K-Bar knife.

"What are you doing?" asked Doc.

"I need to trim my callous'."

"With a fucking combat knife? What are you stupid. You'll tear your feet up. I'll do it for you."

Doc got a scalpel from his kit and sat in front of Holt cradling his foot.

"Your feet are as scarred up as your face. What the fuck happened to you?"

"I know, Doc. It's tragic. When I came into the Army I had beautiful feet. They were as soft and smooth as a babies. Now look at them."

As Doc worked on Holt's feet Robbie came into the barracks with a small bundle of mail and distributed it to the men.

"Sarge, I sold that pistol already. Some goober officer on the flight line bought it."

"Thanks, Robbie. Hold on to the cash till I get back from Vung Tau."

Holt examined the letter he received. It was from Janet and smelled of perfume. He slit it open with his knife and quickly read it. The envelope contained a picture.

"Is that from your wife?" asked Doc.

"Former wife," Holt said handing the picture to Doc.

"God damn, she's beautiful. Is that your kid she's holding?"

"No. The kid ain't mine and neither is she."

"What the fuck are you doing over here when you got her at home?"

"That's just it. She's at home and I'm here. She says she's thinking of going to college. Her mother and grandmother will watch the kid. She'll soon be one of the college chicks protesting the war and sucking hippies dicks."

"You miss her?"

"I miss a lot of things."

Holt lit a cigarette and continued to stare at Janet's picture.

"She's part of a life that doesn't exist anymore."

"But you still write her?"

"She's proof that a normal life still exists even if I ain't part of it," Holt paused, "let me ask you a question. Now that you're an E-6, do you think they'll take you off the team? Maybe move you up to battalion?"

"Naw. Getting promoted was just a reward for getting them prisoners back. If I got moved off the team I'd lose the promotion and go back to E-5. You need a whole lot of specialized training to be a E-6 medic which I don't have."

"I know what you mean. If I ever return to the states I wouldn't be in Special Forces no more. Over here they let me play Green Beret because they need the bodies. As long as they need boots on the ground in Vietnam I'm good. As soon as they don't, I'll be shipped off, back to some grunt unit to serve out my time."

"They tell you that?"

"No, but I'm not stupid. I know what Top thinks of me and the other Vietnam recruits. We serve a purpose but we're not real Green Berets. Right now they're so understaffed they're happy to have me. But that won't last. When things return to normal, I'll be gone."

"Then why stay? Shit, I'm beginning to wonder what I'm doing here myself. These missions are becoming more insane by the day. I hear stuff from the other medics. Things like whole teams going missing. Just swallowed up by the jungle never to be heard from again. Hell, half the time we can't even land anymore. Fucking NVA is on the ground waiting for us. The whole idea of going cross border is bullshit."

Doc stopped scraping at Holt's feet and admired his work.

"All done. All the callous' are gone."

Holt studied his feet. "Good job Doc, thanks."

"Next time, just call me. I don't ever want to see you hacking at your feet with a filthy combat knife."

"I hear rumors too. I heard they're thinking of reducing the teams to two Americans and six Yards."

Doc turned his head away and blew a stream of smoke at the ceiling. "That's fucking nuts. Even the Yards won't go along with that."

"I know. Even Sangh expressed his feeling on the current situation. I wouldn't be surprised if one day they just pack up all their shit and move out. I know for a fact they got beau coup weapons and ammo stashed away. Half the shit we capture never gets turned in. They make a lot of money providing souvenirs for sale. And they get paid in Piaster's or greenbacks. Not the useless Military Payment Script. They're not stupid either. They've been fucked over by the French before us. They know they got to provide for themselves."

"Do you trust them?"

"I do. I wouldn't trust the South Vietnamese. Not one bit. Things get tough; they'll cut and run. If they won't defend their own country, how are we supposed to win this war?"

"There are some good units."

"Really? I haven't seen any. Their officers are incompetent. They get promoted based on who they know, not on ability. The government in Saigon doesn't have the support of the people. They're all Catholic in a Buddhist country. There are factions throughout this country that are hell bent on the over throw of the government. If the United States didn't support Saigon there would be more coup attempts. The government wouldn't survive without our support. As soon as we leave the North Vietnamese will roll right through this country. And believe me, we will leave. The protests at home are getting too big, especially after Tet. It's just a matter of time."

"And yet, you re-upped to stay here."

"It's like Top said, it's the only war we got. And it's the only thing I've been good at. What else am I going to do?"

"You could go home to your wife and kid."

Holt lit another cigarette before answering, "That's not going to happen. She's moving on to a normal life. She wants and deserves a life I can't provide."

"That's where you and me differ. When I'm done here, I'm done. I'll finish my time back in the states, I'll get out and go to school. I'll grow my hair long and protest the war. But right now, I think we should get ready for Vung Tau. We all could use three days off."

After lunch the team waited for their ride to Vung Tau. They wore clean fatigues adorned with all their patches and their berets. They each carried a small bag with an extra set of clothes and toiletries. Concealed under their shirts they had their Browning pistols and two extra mags of ammunition. The saw a helicopter land and taxi over to the refueling point. The crew chief got out and waved them over.

"You guys heading to Vung Tau?"

They all nodded.

"You're going to love it. Beautiful beaches, good restaurants, bars, and plenty of clean, available women. Just be careful with your money. It goes quick."

The pilot, a young warrant officer, asked for their orders. "Everything's in order. They're fueling the ship as we speak. Flight time is about an hour. Sit back and relax and we'll have you there in no time at all."

When they landed at Vung Tau they were greeted by a young Special Forces sergeant driving a plain three quarter ton truck.

"Hop in the back. We got a place set up for you. It's a small villa that we maintain for guys in town. Right now it's empty. You'll have it all to yourself."

Holt sat in the back with the team. Their drive drove quickly through the outskirts of town and soon they were in Vung Tau proper. Swerving through the choked streets, they barely avoided pedestrians and the small motorbikes that seemed everywhere. A haze of exhaust fumes hung over the streets. Obeying horns, traffic lights, and Vietnamese officers directing traffic appeared to be optional.

The streets were lined with small shops open to the sidewalks selling cheap souvenirs, clothing, assorted black market cigarettes, beer, and soda. Food carts and stalls competed for space each topped by large, brightly colored umbrellas. The war seemed far away.

Americans crowded the sidewalks dressed in fatigues, summer khaki uniforms or cheap, Post Exchange civilian clothes.

Bar girls dressed in miniskirts or shorts posed in the doorways of the bars. They made lewd gestures to attract the soldiers who crowded together for security.

Finally, they arrived at a walled compound and drove through two large rusting metal gates manned by two fierce looking Nung guards and stopped in the cobblestone parking area.

"This is it boys," their driver said. He waved his arms to encompass a two story, stone house with two massive columns framing the doorway. The courtyard was shaded by large palms and crowded with exotic plants in large, painted clay urns. Two more Nung security guards sat on the porch cradling M-16's.

Inside, the lobby was set up like a small hotel. The check in desk was off to the right and manned by a young Spec 4. He held out his hand and said, "I need your orders." He opened a large ledger and wrote down their information. When done, he handed their orders back to them. "Keep your orders on you at all times. The MP's sometimes like to harass the combat troops on leave. If you do get into any trouble, and please don't, give them this card. It instructs them to call us instead of locking you up."

They each examined the card before slipping them into their pockets.

"You need to leave any weapons here." Before they could object, he said, "No exceptions. No weapons allowed downtown. Hand them over and we'll secure them."

They removed their pistol belts and handed the clerk the Browning pistols. Holt watched as they were secured in a locker behind the desk. Each was tagged with a number and the clerk handed them a numbered plastic disc. "You'll get them back when you leave."

He pointed through an open doorway. "Back there is the bar and restaurant. The food is great and is available all day long. The drinks are strong and the beer is cold. The girls working the bar are not bar girls so behave yourselves. You can flirt with them but that's about it. Any questions just ask. We want you to be safe and enjoy yourselves."

"What if we wanted to stay in one of the hotels downtown?"

"That's up to you, but I don't see why you would. It's safe here. You got to pay for your food and drinks but over wise it's free. Which one of you is Sergeant Holt?"

Holt stepped forward and was handed a sealed, thick, brown envelope. "That's from a Sergeant Banter." The clerk gave them each a key. "We're empty right now so you'll each have your own room. You'll have to share the two bathrooms. Any questions? If not go clean up. Your first drinks are on us. Enjoy yourselves."

"So, what's in the bag goose?" said Evans.

"Goose?" said Holt, looking at him oddly.

"Yeah, Goose, Granny Goose. Granny Goose potato chips. They're a big seller on the west coast. Everyone knows Granny Goose."

"Never heard of them."

"That's bullshit. You never saw the Granny Goose commercial?"

"I just said I didn't."

"See, there's this cowboy riding down a trail and he's stopped by two Mexican banditos. They got the bullets draped across their chests and the big floppy hats. They stop this guy and says, "You may not believe this but I'm Granny Goose." And the Mexicans say, "What's in the bag goose?" He then tells them about Granny Goose potato chips and how good they are.

"Sounds kind of racist. Like all Mexicans are bandits."

"They're fucking good potato chips, is all I'm saying."

"Fucking good potato chips. Is that how you'll talk when you get home?"

"My old man works on the docks. You think I haven't heard that word every day since I was born."

Holt sighed. "I'm sure your father has a very colorful vocabulary."

Evans pointed at the envelope. "So, I say again, what's in the bag goose?"

"I don't even know how this all got started. It's an envelope, not a bag." Holt opened the envelope. He held up a stack of cash and a note. "It says have a good R & R and stay out of trouble."

Holt counted the cash. "It's four hundred dollars. Now why would Top give me four hundred dollars?"

"You mean to say, why would Top give each of us one hundred dollars?" Evans said.

"Yeah, maybe," Holt said as he handed each of them a stack of bills. "I'm going up to my room, unpack, take a shower and then head to the bar."

They all agreed on that plan.

Entering the bar and the first person they saw was the bouncer. He was an enormous black man standing tall at six foot six inches, weighing at least two hundred and seventy five pounds. His shaved head glistened under the lights. He wore a cloth eye patch over his left eye. A bright red scar ran down his forehead beneath the eye patch and continued down his cheek.

"Will you look at that! I've never seen a bear dressed in clothes working at a bar," Ryan said.

"Lower your voice," Holt said. "I don't want any trouble from that guy."

"I'm just saying. That fucking guy is enormous."

A waitress came to their table. She was a slender, Vietnamese girl wearing a yellow sundress. Her long, black hair was pulled back and flared onto her shoulders.

She came over to Holt and leaned in against him. Holt put his arm around her waist. He felt the warmth of her body against his.

"Baby San, you are so beautiful, I could just pour sugar all over you and eat you up."

She leaned over and whispered in Holt's ear. "I sweet enough, no need sugar."

Her warm, moist breath in Holt's ear sent shivers down his body.

She took their drink orders and walked away. Holt watched the sway of her hips as she left.

"Boys, I'm in love."

"Uh oh, the bear is coming over," Evans said.

He stood at their table and all four had to look up to see his face.

"I heard we had some new arrivals." He saw their SOG patch beneath their left pocket. "Yep, you all the wild boys from that rough country along the border. You enjoy yourselves in Vung Tau but while you in this establishment you need to behave. These girls here are good girls, not bar girls. They'll flirt with you but at closing time they all go home. We understand each other?"

"Sure thing Master Sergeant, we'll behave," Holt said, speaking for the group.

"Hey Sarge, can I get a picture with you? You're the biggest guy I've ever seen," Ryan said.

"You sure can, little fella."

Ryan handed Evans his Kodak Instamatic camera and stood next to the Master Sergeant. The Sergeant draped his hand around Ryan's shoulder. Ryan's head barely came up to the Sergeants chest.

"If you don't mind me asking, how did you lose your eye?" Holt asked.

"Didn't lose it. A B-40 rocket took it." the Sergeant looked at Holt's face. "Seems like you've seen some shit yourself?"

"You should see the other guy. You're still here, huh?"

"Normal Army, I would have been discharged. But they kept me on. I got eight months until full retirement. We look after our own." He winked at them with his good eye and turned away. "You wild children have fun."

The waitress returned with their drinks. When she leaned over Holt could see the top of her white, lacy bra.

"What's your name?"

"Cara, it mean precious jewel."

"Well, Cara, that you are. You take good care of us and we'll tip you beau coup. Okay?"

"Your name?"

173

"Holt."

"Okay Holt, I treat you number one."

When she left Holt said, "I'm am so fucking horny right now. I need to get laid or get drunk."

"Drunk tonight, get laid tomorrow," said Doc Blaze.

"Sounds like a sound plan."

CHAPTER 18

A Chance Encounter

The next morning they met for breakfast in the bar. Unfortunately, Cara was not there. They ordered a meal of eggs, bacon, and fried potatoes with coffee.

"I'm going to meet up with you guys later. I got a friend over at the 36th Evac hospital that I want to see," said Doc Blaze.

"I guess we'll hit the souvenir shops in the morning and the bars in the afternoon," Holt said.

Ryan looked at Holt's clothes. He was wearing a pair of faded khaki shorts, a dark green tee shirt and his Ho Chi Minh sandals.

"I don't want to look like a GI. I need to get some clothes," Ryan said.

"Ryan, that's one of the dumbest things you ever said. You're a twenty year old male in Vung Tau. Do you honestly think anyone will think you're not a soldier?"

"I could be a tourist."

"What kind of fucking nut job, tourist would come to Vietnam?"

"Maybe I'm a journalist."

"What? Your high school paper sent you to Vietnam to do a story on the war?"

"It could happen."

"C'mon, we'll use Top's money and buy you some clothes. Maybe some black pajamas and a conical straw hat so people will think you're a local."

"More likely, a deserter," Evans added.

After a morning of rummaging through the souvenir shops, clothing stores, and black market stalls, Evans and Riley decided to head to the bars.

Holt said he wanted to see the beach and made plans to join them later. On Front Beach Holt sat at an open air bar and ordered a steaming bowl of Pho, a traditional noodle soup containing broth, rice noodles, herbs, spices, and slivers of chicken. He also got an ice cold bottle of beer 33.

As he finished his soup he looked at the tables scattered across the patio. There, under one of the brightly colored umbrellas, he saw someone he recognized. He paid his bill, took his beer, and walked to the table.

"Uh, excuse me, Lieutenant Green is that you?"

The attractive, dark haired women looked at him with a frown on her face. "Oh," was all she said. She turned to her friend, another women with pale blond hair. "Kathy, this is Sergeant Holt, he was a patient of mine back at Cu Chi."

"I didn't know if you would remember me."

"Kind of hard to forget you. I see your scars have faded a bit. What are you doing here?"

"Three day R & R."

"What did you do to get an R & R at Vung Tau?"

"Freed some American POW's and captured an NVA Captain."

"You're still in combat? I thought you were getting out of the Army?"

"I re-enlisted and joined the Special Forces."

"Seems about right."

"Do you mind if I join you for a minute. Can I buy you ladies a drink?"

"Suit yourself," Lieutenant Green said, turning her face away.

Holt signaled the waitress for another round of drinks and sat down across from Lieutenant Green.

"I wanted to thank you for taking care of me."

"I was just doing my job. If it wasn't for your face, I wouldn't even remember you. You'd just be another body on a bed."

"That seems a little…"

"What? Harsh? Is that the word you're looking for?"

"Yeah. I guess."

"When I was first over her, I thought it would be nice to meet someone I cared for. See them back home and see what they made of their life. Instead, I run into you… someone who'll never go home. You'll stay here until you're killed. All I did with you was repair a piece of equipment and return it to the field. You're just that. A military issued part that I serviced and repaired."

"This isn't going the way I expected when I saw you."

"What did you think would happen? A tearful reunion? We'd hug each other and maybe you'd get a piece of round eyed pussy? You look shocked. Isn't that what you grunts call us? Round eyed pussy."

"Maybe I should go. I didn't mean to upset you."

"You're not upsetting me. I've come to terms with what I do. I can't tell you how many times I've sat up at night with some teenage boy crying and terrified of returning to the field. And then there are guys like you; so damaged and warped that you've come to enjoy this shit, the violence and the death."

Her friend put her hand on her arm. "Alright Andi, that's enough. We should go."

"You're right. We should go." She was a little unsteady as she got to her feet. As she gathered her things she turned and looked at Holt. "Enjoy your war, Sergeant."

Her friend looked at Holt and said, "I apologize. She's had too much to drink. She's not usually like this. Good luck, Sergeant."

Holt nodded and watched them walk away.

The waitress returned to clear the table. She watched the nurse's leave. "American girls are stuck up. No like GI's. Go find a Vietnamese girl. You look like big hero. Kill many VC. Vietnamese girls love American heroes. You go and have good time. Enjoy Vung Tau."

"Good advice. That's what I'll do," Holt said. He lit a cigarette and looked at the ocean. He turned his face to the sun and closed his eyes.

The three days passed quickly and before they knew it, they were on a helicopter on their way back to Katum. They were driven straight to the command bunker.

"Hope you boys enjoyed yourselves because you're going out tomorrow," Top said.

"Where are we going?" asked Holt.

"Back to that area where you picked up those two assholes that got captured. We're landing you twelve klick's east of the border. This way you can walk in undetected." Top gathered up some papers on his desk and handed them to Holt. "Here's your maps, call signs, and codes. We already briefed your Montagnard buddies. They'll be ready at 0600. Go get your shit together and get a good night's sleep."

"Not much of a welcome back."

"You've goofed off for three days, now it's time to go back to work. I hope this isn't an inconvenience for you, Sergeant."

"No, I think it fits into our schedule."

"Now, get the fuck out of here. Be back after chow for your final briefing.'

As Holt gathered up his things he said, "Thanks for that envelope, Top. It was much appreciated."

"I don't know what the fuck you're talking about."

"The envelope with the—"

"Hey, shit for brains, I said, I don't know what you're talking about."

As Holt walked out he said, "Well, thanks anyway."

"You're welcome," Top mumbled softly.

"I heard that," Holt said.

"Asshole!"

"I heard that too."

After chow the men returned to the TOC for their final briefing. The helicopter pilots were there along with representatives from the artillery battery.

Major Jung pointed to a large scale map of Cambodia. "Remember this, you are not to go more than fourteen klick's into Cambodia. Anything past that and we won't be able to provide air or artillery support."

"Do the gooks know that?" asked Sergeant Evans.

"I'm sure they do. That's why we don't expect you to find any large units within the fourteen klick sector. What we do want is for you to scout out any likely avenues of approach a large unit would take to cross the border. Unknown trails, water sources, things like that. In this way we can move resources on our side of the border to intercept those crossings. Sergeant Holt, any comments?"

Holt blushed at being singled out for comment.

"Sergeant?"

"I agree, it sounds like a good plan."

"I thought you would be happy."

"I am."

"Good. If you're happy, then we're all happy. Go get some sleep. You'll be woke at 0430, breakfast at 0500. You'll gather you're Montagnards at 0600 and lift off at 0700."

As the room cleared Holt approached Major Jung. "Why the change in tactics?"

"It's what you suggested. We tried to accommodate your concerns."

"Really?"

"No. The change was in the works prior to your comments."

"Then why didn't you just tell me instead of letting me make an ass of myself."

"Because it was amusing to watch. And also, like Top would say, we're not in the habit of adjusting tactics to meet sergeants requests."

Robbie woke them at 0430 and they dressed quickly. At the mess hall they loaded their gear into a waiting three quarter ton truck and went inside to eat.

At the air strip, they applied their camouflage makeup and watched the air crews go through their pre flight check.

Holt watched and smiled as the Bru applied the camo face paint to each other making war like designs similar to American Indians. Top arrived in a jeep and went to speak with the pilots, he then came over to the squad.

"You guys all set? You have everything, maps, code books, and all your gear."

"Yes Top, we double checked everything this morning," Holt said, amused at the concern shown by the First Sergeant.

"Davis, you got your call signs and radio frequencies all memorized?"

"What? Oh yeah, I got everything right up here," Ryan said tapping his forehead.

"Make sure it stays there." Top shifted on his feet unsure what to say next. "Be careful out there. No fucking heroics. Just scope out the area and get you asses back here in one piece."

"Sure thing Top. Don't worry about us, we know what we're doing. Just snooping and pooping."

"I ain't worried about you assholes. It's just, one of you gets hurt, it's a shit load of paper work for me."

"Agreed, whatever we can do to make your life easier," Holt said.

"You're taking two ships. Five to a ship. When you hit the ground, un-ass those choppers and make yourself scarce."

Holt saw one of the pilots twirl his arm above his head.

"Okay boys, time to go. Ryan, you me, Phang and two of the Bru in the first ship. Evans, you Doc and Sangh and the other two in the second ship," Holt said. "See you on the ground. We all come home together."

"No one left behind," Evans added.

Holt sat on the floor behind the pilot on the right side leaning up against the door frame. Ryan sat across from him on the left side. Phang and the two young Bru sat on the canvas seat, Phang stared impassively out the door. He seemed lost in deep thought. They flew north for a bit and then turned west. Holt closed his eyes and let the vibration of the big turbine pass through his body. A feeling of dread washed over him and he shivered convulsively. Phang looked at him oddly and nodded as if they shared a secret. Holt smiled back.

They flew at three thousand feet. The air was cool and crisp. The jungle passed beneath them like a like a featureless green ocean , unbroken except for slashes of streams that twinkled blue in the sunlight.

Holt looked to the west and saw dark swirling clouds over the mountains in Cambodia and worried about rain. Air extraction in the rain would be difficult if not impossible.

A change in altitude signaled their decent. They were passing over a sea of elephant grass that stretched for miles. Somewhere in that mess was their landing zone. The choppers made a quick decent and touched down, flattening the grass in two large circles. Holt and the men jumped out and ran about twenty feet away and threw themselves to the ground. The helicopters seemed to defy gravity and sprang straight up and made a sharp turn to the east. The whole departure took just seconds. The pilots would make two or three false insertions away from the team in an attempt to conceal the real LZ.

In the silence after the choppers left, Holt was once again consumed by an ominous feeling of dread and despair. He heard Ryan on the radio saying one word, "Touchdown."

They stayed on the ground, motionless for several minutes before rising. Holt retrieved his compass and map. He noted the black dot that indicated their LZ and wrote the time of the insertion. He rose on his tip toes and strained to see the wood line three kilometers to the west. The wood line ran south to north. He signaled Phang to come close.

He pointed at the map to show where they were. "Go one kilometer west, then turn south and go six kilometers south."

Phang nodded and got his two Bru and started off. Before he left he put his hand on Holt's shoulder and whispered, "It will be alright. We can't change what is already written."

Holt said to Sangh who stood by his side. "I guess today he understands and speaks English. Do you know what he meant?"

Sangh shrugged. "Maybe."

"Who are the two kids with him?"

"Little Phang's. One and two," Sangh said.

"They seem very young."

"They good boys. Good trackers and good fighters. They hate VC."

They proceeded in single file, Holt behind the third Bru followed by Sangh, then Evans and Doc Blaze and the remaining Bru. Holt marveled at Phang's ability to traverse the wild, unknown area. He seldom used a compass or map. Holt assumed he navigated by the position of the sun.

They moved silently and slowly, stopping often to listen. The sounds of the cicadas and other insects was comforting. Here in the dry grass and open sunlight the mosquitoes were not a problem... the heat was. They all sweated profusely.

They stopped after an hour to take a break. Holt wiped his face with his green towel and took a swig of warm water. With all the technology available, Holt wondered why they couldn't invent a canteen that would keep water cold. Holt looked at his watch, it was 1030 hours. They had turned south and would walk for another hour or so before turning west into the jungle. Once in the jungle, they would stop for lunch. Holt heard Ryan calling in a sit rep. He looked up at Holt and smiled. He would call in the situation reports at predetermined times. While they were out, the command center would be manned twenty four hours a day for instantaneous communication. At some point in their patrol they would have to relay messages through the Air Force forward air controller, called Cubby. The new PRC 77 radio, all though much improved over the PRC 25, was still limited in range.

Up ahead he saw Phang get to his feet and start off. Holt thought, as he always did, who actually was in charge of the patrol.

Walking through the elephant grass was more like swimming. The grass was five to six feet tall. If your sleeves weren't rolled down the grass would leave thin cuts, just like paper cuts, along any exposed flesh. Their arms were covered by the spidery, white scars of these cuts. The cuts, painful as they were, were not the main problem These open cuts could easily become infected leading to debilitating open sores.

You moved through the grass by extending a gloved hand, parting the leaves and sort of sliding along. Any trail they left would soon be covered as the grass resumed its normal position. Holt kept about a fifteen foot interval between himself and Phang's group. Ryan was directly five foot behind Holt, and the remainder of the team was spread out behind them. During the walk, Ryan kept the radio's antenna bent over his shoulder for concealment.

Ryan whispered to Holt, "I'm sweating like a pig. How's my makeup? I feel I must have wiped it all away."

"Always worrying about your makeup. You look fine. You might need a touch up when we stop for lunch."

They walked in silence for another two hours before making a right turn and heading west towards the jungle. Holt desperately wanted a cigarette. On these patrols, besides making enemy contact, he dreaded his nicotine addiction. He dug into his side pocket a got out a hard candy. He removed the cellophane and placed the candy in his mouth. He handed one to Ryan. He placed the wrapper into his pocket.

Another half hour brought them to the edge of the jungle. He heard Ryan call in. "Going Tarzan," was all he said.

Holt looked at him. "Tarzan?"

"Yeah, Tarzan. Going into the jungle."

They soon found a concealed place to stop. They formed a tight perimeter and settled down to eat. Coming from the grass field into the jungle was like entering a dark room. The heat and the moisture was oppressive.

Sound was deadened by the wet foliage and the air itself seemed to have weight.

Holt got a foil package of beef jerky from his trouser pocket and a plastic bag of crackers. He watched as Ryan opened a can of chicken and noodles with his P38 can opener. Although they carried the dehydrated LURP rations, they seldom ate them during the day. They required too much preparation. The biggest detriment was they required a lot of water to prepare. They tried to save the LURP's for when they had a certain source of water.

Holt tore a piece of the thick jerky and began to chew. As he did, he studied his map. He took out his pen and marked the spot where they entered the jungle. He entered the current time. They would walk west for half a klick, then turn south again, and then go another three klick's. At that point, they should cross the trail that led to the POW camp.

Holt looked at Sangh who sat next to Ryan. Sangh was eating a meatball-sized chunk of rice and vegetables. He saw Holt watching him and extended his hand offering Holt some rice. Holt declined and returned to staring into the jungle. Above him, in the tree tops the birds chirped and the leaves rustled with other tree bound animals. He wondered if there were monkey's overhead. He remembered back in the Wolfhounds, he told one of his squad that the NVA trained the monkeys to attack them. He smiled at the memory. He missed his old squad and hoped they were all doing well. There wasn't much need for silence in the jungle when you traveled with a full company of men. You could smoke and talk, cook your food and make coffee. Here, on patrol, in Cambodia, the silence they had to maintain was oppressive. He let out a long breath. He caught Phang's attention and tapped his watch. Phang started off without question. The team followed in their single file formation. In three hours they should be at the trail.

At 1600 hours Phang stopped the column and walked back to Holt. They had arrived at the trail that would take them to the POW camp. Holt marked the location on his map and made additional notes in the small spiral bound notebook he carried. Holt told Phang they would rest here for half an hour then proceed west to see what lay beyond the camp. He heard Ryan radio in that they had reached 'The Great Escape' and would head towards California. Holt smiled at the reference to the 1963 World War Two movie. If the NVA were listening in they wouldn't be able to decipher this coded language. He barely understood it.

"Did you go over all this crap with someone before we left?" Holt whispered in Ryan's ear.

"We decided we would use states to indicate direction and movies for locations."

"How did you come up with the movie titles?"

"We knew where we were going, so we picked out a bunch to use." "Don't you think you should have told us about the code words?" "It's all written down in my code book," he said tapping his breast pocket.

Holt took out another hard candy and sucked on it, longing for a cigarette.

Holt showed Ryan the map. "We're five kilometers in from the border. We'll go another eight until we bump up against the limit."

"I thought the limit was fourteen kilometers?"

"Fuck, we're just guessing how far we've gone. I'd rather be short of the limit, than over it. Believe me, no one is going to volunteer to come help us. We don't need to give them a reason by stepping over some arbitrary line on a map."

"That makes sense. Did you know that in the early days, Bull Simons redrew the map extending the border of South Vietnam further west so that the Special Forces could legally operate in Laos?"

"Yeah, those were the good old days. But to get to our problem, once we get there, do we go south or north? They left it up to our discretion."

"North would be closer to base camp," Riley said as he picked his nose.

"Please don't pick your nose while you're talking to me. It's disgusting."

"Another three or four days out here and we'll all be disgusting. I can smell you from here and we've only been out half a day."

"You're right. Just turn your head away."

"Fine, if it bothers you so much. So which way south or north?"

"I'll let Phang decide."

"Should I tell the other guys?"

"Do that. Tell them ten more minutes before we head out again."

As they walked deeper into Cambodia the jungle became more dense. Barely any sunlight found its way through the tree tops. They were left in perpetual gloom. Moss, mold, and decay covered everything. Vines of every diameter snaked their way up trees and across the branches. The poked out of the ground like the decaying fingers of buried corpses. The only good thing was that the ground was so soggy they were able to move silently. The damp earth silenced their footsteps. One of the trailing Montagnards did his best to erase any indication of their passage.

At 1600 hours Phang emerged from the shadows and told Holt he had found a place to stop for the night. Holt took it, not as a question or suggestion, but as a statement of fact. Phang took Holt to a small grassy knoll, flat on top and surrounded by small stunted bushes.

"This is good. Good work, Trung Si. We'll stop here." Phang walked away without saying a word.

They settled into a small perimeter on the top of the knoll. Eight men manned the outer ring with Holt and Ryan in the center. They would be on fifty percent alert and slept in two hour shifts. Holt and Ryan would take the same two hour shift manning the radio. Holt knew he could trust the men to stay awake on guard. If one of the Montagnards fell asleep they would be punished severely by Phang or Sangh. Phang would probably kill the man for the offense.

The men set about placing their Claymore mines in a defensive ring around the perimeter, then settled in to eat their evening meal.

Holt had a can of pork slices and ate each of the four slices on a saltine cracker. He ate slowly and chewed each bite thoroughly. He drank a half of canteen of water to wash the meal down. He wiped his mouth on his sleeve.

Ryan volunteered to take the first radio watch. Holt leaned back against his rucksack and closed his eyes. He was totally physically and mentally exhausted from the days march maintaining a constant state of alertness and complete silence. They had crossed many trails during the day. Most were old and un-used but several indicated fresh travel. Holt tried as best he could to indicate the trails on his map but knew their location was only approximate. Finally, he pulled his boonie hat over his eyes and went to sleep.

When Ryan woke Holt, it felt as if he had just closed his eyes. Ryan leaned close and whispered in Holt's ear. "I just made the Sit Rep. remember, break squelch twice, they'll respond the same way."

Holt nodded and lifted his watch which was looped through the button hole of the flap covering his left breast pocket. He peeled back the fabric covering the luminous dial and saw it three minutes past ten, 2203 hours. The darkness was complete. He could barely see the men spaced around him. They appeared as black lumps against the dark shadow of the trees. The birds had quieted, replaced by the fluttering of bats in the upper branches. Holt took pleasure in the noises of the insects and tree frogs. If they quieted, it meant that men were about.

Holt started to reach for a cigarette but stopped and smiled. Instead, he reached for a hard candy. During his guard shifts, Holt would compose long letters to Janet and have imaginary conversations with her in which he played both parts. In these conversations his life was good. They were together. A wave of sadness washed over Holt and he wished he was home.

CHAPTER 19

The Second Day

They woke the next morning at 0600.

Ryan busied himself changing radio batteries. He leaned close to Holt. "I gotta tell you Sarge, being out here in Cambodia, miles from nowhere, miles from help, scares the shit out me. When I was a kid our parents used to tell us kids stories about clowns living in the woods outside of town and about how they would kidnap kids and torture them. We all knew it was just bullshit to keep us kids from going into the woods at night, but it still scared me. And now, being out here with just the ten of us, I'm scared all over again."

"Clowns in the woods are scary. I hate clowns. They should put a bounty on their heads and hunt them for sport. At least out here you got a gun."

"Yeah, but here the clowns got guns too."

"I know what you mean. I sometimes think this whole SOG stuff makes no sense. We lose a lot of guys and gain what. We already know the jungle over here is filled with NVA. Just bomb the shit out of the Ho Chi Minh trail and get it over with."

Holt finished the water in his canteen and switched them around so he had a full canteen on his belt. "I'd kill for some hot coffee and a cigarette about now. Let's eat something; I want to be on our way by seven."

"Which way?"

"West."

"I'll call it in."

Holt listened to Ryan on the radio.

"Heading to California until we hit the coast. Will advise."

Holt watched the other team members eat breakfast. He held up seven fingers and they all acknowledged.

At 0900 Holt could see the jungle thinning up ahead. He saw a large patch of open sky. The air cooled and there was a slight breeze. They came to the edge of the jungle and saw a large flat stream in front of them. The stream was shallow but at least thirty meters wide.

Holt walked forward with Ryan, Evans and Sangh.

"What do we do?" asked Evans.

Holt studied his map. "Here's the stream on the map, but there's no indication of how wide it is. I certainly wasn't expecting this. We ain't crossing this. It would take one guy two or three minutes to make it across. You'd be out in the open and exposed the whole way across." Holt looked at Phang. "Which way?"

"No good here. Too muddy, leave too many tracks, we go back to solid ground and turn north."

Holt rubbed his lips They were dry and cracked. "Agreed. Take a ten minute break and we'll head out."

After walking for twenty minutes, Phang came running back.

"VC come."

"How many?" Holt said.

"Three, maybe four."

"Are they following us?" Phang shrugged.

Holt made a quick decision. "We turn here, go north."

After ten minutes of walking at a quick pace Holt heard a muffled cry of "Shit."

He looked back and saw Evans holding his hand to his face, blood seeping through his fingers. A large, thorny vine had ripped across his face leaving a deep cut across his cheek.

Holt walked back. "How bad?" he asked Doc Blaze.

"Missed his eye, but cut his cheek pretty bad. Just let me throw a bandage on it and he'll be good to go."

"Hurry, Doc. We gotta keep moving." Holt turned to Phang. "Phang, take the little Phang's and walk drag. I'll walk point. Make sure we're not being followed."

"If VC go to river they'll see our tracks."

"Can't worry about that now. We have to get out of here and put some distance between them and us."

"I kill VC?" Phang asked.

"Can you do it quietly?"

Phang tapped the sound suppressor on the end of CAR 15 and smiled.

They walked ten minutes, stopped and waited. They heard nothing.

Phang appeared out of the trees. He looked at Holt and drew his finger across his throat. He walked past Holt with the two Montagnard boys and resumed his position at point. Holt noticed one boy examining a severed ear.

Holt heard Riley on the radio. "We met four unexpected guests. They had to be evicted." Riley turned to Holt. "They want to know if we're compromised."

Holt thought for a moment. His first thought was to say yes and arrange to be extracted. But he told Riley, "Tell them we'll Charlie Mike," using the military phrase for 'continue the mission.'

"Are you sure, Sarge?"

"Yeah," he said reluctantly, "for now."

Holt's stomach was in knots. He was sure Phang had concealed the bodies but wondered when the soldiers would be missed. If they were a point element for a larger force they would be missed quickly and they would be searched for. The team's tracks by the stream were clearly visible and could be followed easily. They could have gooks on their heels right now. Holt chewed at his finger and desperately tried to think clearly. Holt had already expressed his doubts about the cross border missions and his call for an early extraction would be questioned. But if they were being followed, was he just setting them up for a disastrous enemy encounter? He didn't know what to do. For now, he decided, they'd just Charlie Mike and drive on.

At noon, they stopped to eat. Phang took the two boys and scouted the rear. The jungle thinned and they were now able to see through the trees. The trees still blocked the sun but on the ground the vegetation became sparse. Small, coarse bushes and clumps of plants and grass replaced the thick, choking jungle. If they could see through the jungle so could the enemy. They sat in a shallow depression and waited for Phang to return.

Holt's fatigues were soaked with sweat and the sour smell of urine and ammonia hung over him like a cloud. Holt looked back where Phang had gone.

Sangh, sensing his concern and whispered, "Phang be okay. VC no catch."

Holt smiled weakly and drank from his canteen. He offered it to Sangh who declined.

For some reason, a wave of nausea passed through Holt and he shivered uncontrollably.

Sangh gripped his shoulder and squeezed. "It okay, if VC come we kill them. If more VC come, they die too."

Holt looked into Sangh's eyes and was calmed.

"Why does Phang cut the ears off the dead?"

"Phang say, if body not whole, then no go to heaven."

"Do you believe that?"

"I believe many things. Catholic things. Buddha things. Nature things. We all part of one world. If Phang believes that, what does it matter. Phang is a strange man consumed by rage. I don't think Phang is a happy man."

"You've said that before." Holt remembered his conversation with Nurse Green. "Do you think I'm a happy man?"

"No. You a man without a home. Cannot be happy until you find where you belong. Buddha say, 'A man who has nothing, has nothing to lose.' Maybe that why you so brave."

"You think I'm brave? You're wrong. I'm scared all the time. I'm scared right now. You Sangh, are a brave man."

"Like you, I have nothing to lose. I have no family and I have no home. When it really counted, I couldn't save my family. I don't fear death, I welcome it. Maybe when I die I get reborn and be a better man."

"Rebirth? That's Buddhist. Are you a Buddhist, Sangh?"

"Maybe sometimes, maybe not."

Phang returned and reported there were more VC in the area but they were not searching for them. "Maybe they cross river and go to base camp."

"How many did you see?"

"Many."

Holt asked Sangh, "How many is 'many'?"

He flashed his extended fingers on both hands three times. "We should go."

They continued north. They spread out their intervals to twenty feet. They separated into two columns. They moved silently through the shadows. The terrain became more forest than jungle.

Holt was asked once, "what's the difference between forest and jungle." His reply was, "it's obvious to anyone that's been in both and if you have to ask you've probably been in neither."

They moved quickly over a forest floor covered with a matted coating of wet, rotting leaves and moss that concealed their footprints.

At 1530 they stopped again for a break. Holt wondered what purpose they were serving. They were moving away from any NVA concentration. Should they not stop and try to find their base camp? He knew Ryan had called in the position of the NVA reported by Phang, but what use was that information to the higher ups that was worth the risk of their lives. There was no artillery barrage or air strikes called in on the position. Was the information just noted on a map somewhere, soon to be forgotten? If all the enemy sightings gathered by other patrols were posted on maps maybe that gave some indication of enemy movement and future plans. Holt had to believe that what they doing made a difference, even if it was a small difference.

Holt looked at his map and his notes during the break. Further to the north the map indicated nothing but jungle. To the west there were mountains but ahead, lay only an expanse of unbroken, green forest.

Evans crab walked over to Holt and crowded in next to him. He looked down at Holt's map.

"What's ahead?"

"According to this, more trees."

"Where do you think they get the maps from?"

"Most of these are left over from the French. I guess, in the past no one really cared what was out here. From the air what can you see? Just a bunch of jungle. Maybe that's why we're here, map making."

Evans winced and touched his cheek.

"You okay?"

"Hurts like hell. Doc says I need some stitches. He's worried about infection."

Holt signaled the Doc to come closer.

"Doc, do what you need to do with Evans. Stitch him up."

"You sure? It will take about twenty minutes."

"Time is the one thing we have. We got nowhere to be and plenty of time to get there."

Doc peeled the bandage from Evans face and wiped the wound with Betadine solution. He then gave him an injection in his cheek.

"That should numb the area in a minute or two." He prepared his needle and thread. "I'll be careful with the stitches so you don't look like Holt."

"The medic that treated me stapled my face together," Holt said.

"Quit your bitching, he did a good job."

As Doc worked on Evans Phang came over to watch. After a moment he said, "I go look ahead."

"Phang relax and rest. You must be tired," Holt said.

Phang said something to the young Montagnards and they all laughed.

Phang scurried off with one of the boys.

Holt asked Sangh why they laughed.

"Phang said they will scout ahead while Grandfather rest. Boys thought that funny."

"Grandfather? I'm twenty three. How old are the boys?"

Sangh rolled his eyes. "Fifteen, maybe sixteen. Parents dead. No one knows."

Holt shook his head sadly. "They should be in school, not fighting a war."

"War is what they know."

Holt turned his attention back to Evans. He watched as Doc put in six, small stitches. When he was done, Doc Blaze sat back and admired his work.

"Really nice, Doc. I mean, really good work."

"In training, after class, some of us practiced stitches on fruit. I remember stitching up bananas and oranges. Got really good at it."

Doc replaced Evan's bandage after smearing the wound with antiseptic.

"That will do it."

"We'll head out as soon as Phang returns," Holt said.

Phang returned excited.

"Come now. You look. We found something."

They walked a few minutes and saw a break in the forest.

Phang signaled a halt and waved Holt forward.

Holt walked forward and stood on the edge of a large gorge about one hundred meters wide and seventy five meters deep. At the bottom of the gorge was a dry river bed. He leaned over the edge and saw the almost vertical walls of the gorge. He pulled out his map.

"Shit! This fucking thing ain't on the map," he said to Phang. He signaled the team forward.

Holt got on the radio and called it in.

"What have you found exactly?" was the response.

"I told you, it's some sort of gorge."

"Be more precise. Is it a gorge, a ravine, or a canyon?"

"What? I don't know. What's the difference?"

"Wait one."

Holt turned to Ryan. "Who the fuck is this moron?"

"Some Lieutenant I think."

"Fucking guy is an asshole."

After a short wait the Lieutenant came back on the radio.

"I doubt it's a canyon. What you're describing is too small. It's probably a gorge or a ravine. Is there water on the bottom?"

"No. I said it once was a river but it's dry now."

"So maybe at one time it was a gorge."

"Does it make a fucking difference?"

"Watch your language. Maintain proper radio procedure. And yes, it makes a difference. I just looked it up. There's a difference between these geographical things. What am I supposed to tell Six? I have to be precise. Can you get to the bottom?"

"No. I told you the walls are vertical. We don't have ropes or climbing gear."

"Can you use vines?"

"To climb down? No, we can't use vines."

"There should be vines that you could use."

"We have to move. I'll call back in ten minutes," Holt said ending the call.

"What a fucking idiot! Ryan call back and get your buddy on the phone. Tell him to get Top. I ain't talking to that asshole anymore."

After several minutes Ryan handed Holt the handset. "I got Top on the line."

"Who was that moron?"

"Watch your mouth, this is an open line," Top cautioned.

"Sorry." Holt repeated what they found. "The ravine runs true, west to east. We'll find a place to set up and observe for a day or two. Then we'll follow it and see where it goes."

"What's at the bottom?"

"If I had to guess, I'd say it's compacted gravel. Looks like it could support heavy traffic."

"Are you sure of your position?"

"Sure, plus or minus."

"I'll have Cubby fly over and mark your position. I want sit reps every hour on the hour."

"If it runs true east, we'll follow it until we cross the border and arrange for extraction."

"Roger that, out."

Sangh stood next to Holt. Holt pointed east. "Tell Phang to find us a place where we can observe this thing."

Sangh went to speak to Phang.

"I hope you're not in trouble with that Lieutenant," Ryan said to Holt.

"Fuck him in the mouth and feed him fish," Holt said.

"What?"

"It's a saying, a Greek saying, or so I'm told."

"It makes no sense but I like it."

After letting Phang get a few minutes ahead, the team followed. They walked in the tree line skirting the ravine. After a few hundred meters they saw Phang.

"Phang say we stay here. I stay with you. Phang and the boys will set up listening posts over there," Sangh said indicating to the forest behind them.

Holt examined the terrain. It would be tight but with some digging they could create a shallow depression hiding them within some bushes and grass.

"Okay. Tell Phang okay. Hey, let me ask. Sometimes Phang speaks English, sometimes he don't. He does speak English, right?"

"Yes, sometimes."

The team set about preparing their position. While the team dug, Ryan was on the phone with their over flight.

"You're about a mile out. Come south west," Ryan instructed. Ryan strained his body to see Cubby. "Mark! You are right over us. Can you see the ravine?"

"Not really. There are trees everywhere."

"Tell him we're in a forest. There should be lots of trees," Holt said.

Ryan shushed him with a wave of his arm.

"Okay. It's down here. From what we can see it runs a true west, east line. Mark it and give us the coordinates."

The pilot responded with coordinates and Ryan wrote them in his note book. He repeated the coordinates and Holt marked them on his map. "We were only about a kilometer off; not too bad. At least, we now know where we are."

"A kilometer is pretty far off."

"Give or take," Holt said as he drew a line on his map. He saw Evans leaning through the bushes and taking pictures of the ravine with a Minolta 35mm camera.

"Where did you get the camera?" Holt asked.

"Top gave it to me. I've been taking pictures all along. I've already taken a full roll of pictures. Didn't you notice?"

"No, I didn't. Why are you taking pictures?"

"Top asked me to document the patrol. Maybe he wants pictures of the unit in action. If you didn't notice then I got some good candid shots."

"If anything happens, make sure you destroy that film."

"What's going to happen?"

"Gooks might happen, that's what."

By 1800 hours they had finished their position and began preparing their evening meal. Holt dug a foot deep hole and placed his stove at the bottom. He lit a chunk of C4 explosive and boiled a pint of water. It wasn't dark yet and the hole would conceal any flame. He poured the boiling water into the foil packet of LURP rations. He stirred the water into his chicken and rice and let it sit. The other men prepared their own meal using the concealed flame.

Sangh took out a large ball of rice, vegetables, and fish wrapped in a large leaf and began eating. Holt offered Sangh some of his food. Sangh took the spoon and tasted it. Holt offered more and Sangh made a face and shook his head.

The men sat silently and finished their meal. It was still light enough that Holt risked boiling some more water for coffee. He added the foil packets of coffee, cream and sugar and stirred the mixture. He poured some into the cup that Ryan extended and leaned back against their foxhole.

"It's good to have a hot meal," Holt whispered to Ryan. "What did you have?"

"Chile."

"Don't be farting all night and giving away our position. Phang says the gooks can smell us just as we are; don't go adding to the smell."

They set the guard roster at two hours apiece. They would start guard at 1800 and end at 0600 hours. Holt drew fourth shift. So, he settled back to sleep.

CHAPTER 20

The Natives Are Restless

The night was uneventful. The woke at 0600 and prepared breakfast.

Holt ate some beef jerky, crackers, and cheese. He made some more coffee and longed for a cigarette.

The rest of team stretched, scratched, and yawned in the early light of dawn. Ryan moved a few feet away, unbuttoned his trousers, and urinated into the bushes. He returned to the hole, wiping his hands on his pants.

"Looks cloudy today. We got some dark clouds north of us rolling down south. We might get rained on today."

Holt wiped some leaves from his damp fatigues. He finished his coffee and got up to stretch.

"This wasn't a bad spot but I don't want to stay here again. We'll move east and set up again. We'll spend the night and the day and after that we should be close to, or over the border. We'll find a clearing and get out of Dodge. They can do what they want to this place. Bomb the shit out of it as long as we're long gone."

"What if they want us to stay and observe? They might want us to do a bomb damage assessment report."

"They can send in another team now that they know where this is. We don't have enough food or water for an extended stay. And I doubt we're going to find water up here."

They saw Phang and the boys approach their position. Evans got his camera out.

"Don't take pictures of the Bru unless you ask them. They might think you're trying to steal their soul or some other bullshit," Holt cautioned.

Phang came over and squatted next to Sangh and spoke to him.

"Phang said, no VC here. He wants to know if we're staying here." Holt shook his head. Obviously Phang wasn't speaking English today.

"Tell him we're moving east and we'll find another place tonight."

Holt turned to his team. "Let's fill in this hole and get ready to move. Ryan get on the horn and let them know what we're doing."

They moved off with Sangh in the lead followed by the Americans. They walked to the edge of the ravine. Phang and his boys were about twenty yards ahead and off to the right providing flank security.

They walked for about three hours and took a break. They resumed the march until noon. They hadn't seen any trails or any indication of enemy activity. It's as if they were the first humans to have travelled this forest.

The day was hot and humid and they were all soaked with sweat. When they stopped, Holt wiped the sweat from face and reapplied his camo face paint. His shoulders ached from the heavy rucksack straps.

A jolt of fear went through Holt as the sounds of the birds and insects stopped. Ahead of them they could see two figures approaching them. To the right Holt saw Phang.

Holt heard two muffled snaps and the two men crumpled to the ground. The Bru went to the fallen men and leaned over them. They cut the ears off the men. The boys then took the AK's and ammunition and slung them over their backs. They stripped the bodies of food and canteens. They cut off the patches on the uniforms and handed the patches and some documents to Phang.

"Shit, what the fuck?" Holt whispered.

They waited until Phang came to them. He handed Holt the patches and a bundle of paper.

"Just two. No more VC. The boys hide bodies. We keep going."

"Are you sure?" Holt asked.

"Sure. Just two."

"Ryan, call it in and let's keep moving."

Evans came up and walked by Holt's side. "This is fucked," he said. "Those two guys weren't just out here themselves. They were either coming from some place or going somewhere. They had to be part of a larger group."

"Agreed. My guess is they were going somewhere. Whoever they were going to join is behind us. That's what I think."

"Why do you think that?"

"It's better than thinking that we could be walking straight into a larger group. Maybe they were watching a clearing ahead and it was change of shift."

"The NVA works in shifts?"

"I don't know. Just saying." Holt yawned. "I'm fucking exhausted. The heat and humidity are kicking my ass today."

"Maybe the Bru boys were right. Does Grandfather need a nap?"

"Fuck you."

They walked for another hour until Phang signaled them to a halt. Phang came up to Holt and Sangh. "Big trail, maybe thirty meters south. Beau Coup boot and sandal prints."

"How many men?" Holt asked.

"Beau Coup, maybe fifty."

"How old?"

"Fresh. Maybe three, four hours old."

"Are you saying they have been walking along side of us for three or four hours?"

Phang shrugged.

Holt wiped his over his eyes. "Show us," he said.

The men turned south and walked through the forest until Phang stopped them.

"Ahead," he said pointing.

"You guys wait here. Phang, take me to the trail."

When the trail became visible, Holt told Phang to wait and stepped out onto the trail. Holt looked back towards the west and turned to look to the east. The trail was clearly visible and extended as far as Holt could see. He knelt down and placed his hand against the ground. It was still damp. The prints had to be fresh or they would have dried and hardened in the heat.

Phang and Holt rejoined the team. They gathered around Holt. The Bru boys provided security.

"Let's take a break and try and figure this out." Holt drew a line on the ground. "Those prints are fresh. I don't know how many, but there's a lot of them. They appear to be heading east like we are. Maybe they know we're here and are trying to set up an ambush in front of us. Maybe not. Six or seven klick's and we should reach the border. Hopefully the forest breaks out into the grassland like when we came in and we can get the fuck out of here. If it doesn't, then we got some more humping to do. There is no fucking clearing indicated on the map. That don't mean anything, because that grassland we landed in wasn't on the map. I say we head south and get around those gooks who are ahead of us. We find an open space and call for extraction."

"Top wants us to observe that ravine for a few days. You going to tell him we want out?" Evans said.

"That's exactly what I'm going to say. They know where the fucking ravine is now. What good will it do to observe it if it puts us in serious danger? And now, as a bonus, we got this trail to report."

"We got food, water, and ammo enough for two or three days. He's not going to like us for pulling out early," Ryan added.

"That's true. He's going to be pissed. Any suggestions?" Holt asked.

The men were silent.

"Sangh, what do you think?"

"You in charge, you decide. We do as you say."

"Phang?"

Phang stared back impassively.

"Christ, I wish we knew what was ahead of us."

Sangh spoke to Phang. "Take one boy and look ahead. Maybe three hours. Maybe find a clearing. Send boy back and he bring us to you."

"Phang, I can't ask you to do that. It's way too dangerous."

"You not ask me, I," he paused, searching for the word, "I volunteer."

Holt looked at his watch. "It's 1530 now, you'd never make it back before dark."

"I send boy back when sun up."

"Here, take this," Holt said handing Phang his emergency survival radio. "It's only good for short distances. Use it when you are coming back so we don't shoot you. Turn it on here and press this button to talk. Show Little Phang how to use it."

"I use before, no problem."

"Your English is good today."

"Your English, not so good. Learn to speak Bru," Phang said as he and Little Phang disappeared into the trees.

Holt looked at Sangh who smiled.

Holt addressed the team. "We need a place to stay the night, it can't be far or Phang won't find us."

"Go where you want, Phang find you," said Sangh.

"There's a small depression back about fifty feet. If we dig it out it will be big enough for all of us."

It took about an hour to enlarge the hole to three feet deep with dirt piled up on all sides.

"You think the hole is big enough?" Doc asked.

"That's what your mom asked me when I was home on leave," Holt replied. "I told her it would be fine."

"Christ, what are you? A thirteen-year-old boy? You gonna start telling fart jokes next?"

"Just trying to lighten the mood," Holt said.

Holt spoke to Top. "We found a well used trail," he read off the coordinates, "we're setting up here tonight to watch it."

"Why aren't you at the ravine?" Top questioned.

"We were observed. We had to move. According to Phang, there are Beau Coup VC in the area and they are aware of our presence."

"Are you requesting extraction?"

"There is no clearing for a chopper. We'll move tomorrow and will advise then."

"I ain't happy about this. Sit Reps, every hour," Top growled.

Holt ended the call and took out his map.

"Gather round," he said spreading the map on the ground. "We got four points where we're certain of our location. First was our LZ when we landed, second was when we left the elephant grass and entered the jungle. Third was the old POW camp. And fourth was our position at the ravine when Cubby overflew us. They're all marked on the maps, make sure you got the same coordinates." Holt pointed at his map, "I figure we're somewhere around here right now give or take."

"Give or take what?" Evans asked.

"A few hundred feet. We can't be off by much." Holt took out a hard candy and popped it into his mouth. He offered the bag around. Sangh and the Bru boys greedily took two each. He continued, "We can't go north, we're blocked by the ravine. We can't go east, the gooks are up ahead of us. West will only bring us deeper into Cambodia. That leaves south. We'll head back to the POW camp and find our original pickup zone and get the hell out of here. Comments?"

Evans stroked his chin as he studied the map. "We cut our mission short and Top will be pissed. The Major too."

"Top is already pissed. Look, it's my call and I'll take the heat when we get back, but I want to make sure we're all in agreement. So if you got any suggestions, let's hear them now."

"Sangh?"

"It's good."

"Ryan?"

"I'm with you Sarge. I want out of this shit hole."

"Doc?"

"The sooner the better." "Evans?"

Evans hesitated and looked down.

"Evans, speak up. I know exactly what's bothering you. You just got another stripe and you're due for your own team. You don't want to piss Top off." Holt met his eyes and held his stare. "Okay, so let's say this is your team, it's all up to you. What are we doing?

"We head back in," he said softly.

"What? Say it like you got some fucking hair on your balls."

"We head back."

"And when Top holds your feet to the fire?"

"I'll tell him, I agreed, we all agreed, it was the only course of action."

"Does anyone remember Top's last words to us, 'No fucking heroics.

Get your ass back safely.' That's what he said. Okay, so now he's got a big hard on because we found a ravine with a hard surface road at the bottom and a new trail. Great! We did our job. We got them marked on the map; bomb this place and be done with it. You know that asshole Lieutenant wanted us to swing down to the bottom of the ravine on vines. That's the type of shit we're dealing with here." Holt paused and took a drink from his canteen. "Look around you, this place hasn't been touched. Everywhere else we've been there are bomb craters everywhere, shattered trees, and scorched earth. But not here. The gooks know the same thing; that's why they are here. This is a virgin forest. I ain't ending up as one of those teams who goes missing. Just fucking vanishes like they never existed. We did our jobs and now we need to find a way out."

Holt looked at each man in turn. "Alright, let's settle in and wait for Phang. We got a long night ahead of us. At dusk we'll put out our Claymore's, fifty percent alert."

The men moved about their position and got comfortable.

"This hole is tight, but it should work for tonight," said Doc.

"Your Mom said that too."

This time, Doc laughed.

At 0445 the emergency radio by Holt's ear crackled to life.

"It's me, Phang. I come in, don't shoot. Say okay."

"Phang we hear you, come on in," Holt said.

"It's pitch black out. How the hell did he find us. I swear that guy must be part bloodhound."

"I had an old hound dog that could—"

Holt cut him off. "Not now Ryan."

As Phang and Little Phang collapsed in the hole, Holt was stunned to see Phang was soaked in sweat and breathing hard. Phang never appeared affected by the weather or exertion.

"Phang sit down, you okay. You want some water?" Holt asked.

"I okay. We must go. VC come. Many VC come. Maybe fifty or more."

"Breath Phang, take a breath. How much time do we have before VC get here?"

"Maybe forty or fifty minutes. Phang set booby traps then run here."

Holt got his red-lens flashlight out and shown it on his map. "The POW camp, can you get us there?" Phang nodded.

"We go to the VC camp and then go to the LZ. Remember the first landing zone where we kill beau coup VC."

"Yes." Without consulting a compass, Phang held out his arm and pointed south. "Camp this way. We walk fast, maybe one full day. But we go this way." He turned his body forty five degrees and pointed. "Go right to landing place, maybe fourteen hours. We no stop. We go now."

Holt thought, *shit, he's right. Why go to the camp? Just go straight to the landing zone.*

"Alright, everybody, ruck up. Ryan, tell them we're being chased by gooks and we're running. Tell them where we're going. They have the coordinates already. Phang are you okay? Do you need to rest?"

Phang looked at Holt strangely. "No, Phang okay."

They retrieved their Claymore mines and were gone from the hole in three minutes with Phang leading the way.

"I'm glad to be out of that hole, it smells like piss and sweat," Doc Blaze said.

"Jesus, Doc, now you're just setting me up," Holt said.

It began to rain.

CHAPTER 21

Run Through The Jungle

They headed off at a slow jog, close to each other, almost touching. Phang led, his arms hanging straight down, holding his Car 15 by the carrying handle.

The sound of the rain on the leaves removed the necessity of noise discipline. It was as if they were running inside a snare drum.

Holt could barely see Phang. He was just a jumble of blurred shadows. Holt settled into a steady pace, lulled into an almost meditative trance by the pounding of his feet. He ran without thought propelled by fear. He breathed hard through his nose matching his breaths to his pace.

They all ran from the danger behind them. The sound of Phang's booby trapped Claymore mines barely registered. It was just another jungle sound but it did confirm they were being followed.

After an hour Ryan shouted, "God dammit, Sarge! We need a break."

"Phang, stop," Holt said to the shadow in front of him.

Phang stopped and looked at Holt blankly. "VC behind us, they no stop."

"Phang we have to rest, ten minutes," Holt wheezed the words through gasping breathes. Drool and spittle hung from his mouth.

Ryan moved forward until his shoulders touched Holt. "I got to catch my breath and call in a sit rep. There's no way we can run like this all day."

"Fucking Phang, he's like a machine. That fucker has been awake for twenty four hours and he's not even breathing hard," Holt said doubled over, his hands on his knees retching up yellow bile.

"This is worse than Ranger training," said Doc. "They made us do twelve miles in full packs. We had to complete it in four hours."

"In Advanced Infantry Training we had to do twenty five miles, but they gave us seven hours to do it," Holt said. "That's the pace we need to maintain. If we do, we can be there tonight."

"Sarge, we gotta think this through. Say we get there tonight, they ain't going to pick us up. We'll have to spend the night in the open," Ryan said, his breathing returning to normal. "We need to time our arrival at the PZ. Getting there at night ain't gonna do us any good."

"You're right. Let me talk to Sangh and Phang."

Holt explained the situation. Sangh spoke to Phang in Bru or Vietnamese or whatever language they spoke amongst themselves. To Holt, it all sounded like ducks fucking.

The conversation grew animated and finally Sangh said to Holt, "Phang say we go to the pickup place now. That if we stop and VC find us we'll never get away. He say go to pickup, dig in, and wait till morning. If we fight, then helicopters can help us. Out here we'll be on our own."

Sangh's plan sounded better. They would be at a known location. Holt was torn between the two plans. Both had risk.

"Alright Sangh, I agree with Phang. I don't want to be caught out in the woods miles from the PZ. We keep moving until we get to the PZ. We should have air support there and artillery if we need it. But he has to set a pace we all can maintain. We ain't Bru, we can't run like you guys. We have to stop and rest from time to time."

Holt saw Phang handing out small green leafy packets to the Bru. They put the leafs into their mouths.

"What are they chewing?" Holt asked Sangh.

Sangh took a little packet out his pocket and handed it to Holt. Holt handed it back.

"Betel Nut," Sangh said. "It give you energy. You try?"

"I know what Betel Nut is."

"You chew and spit. Try?" Sangh said, extending his hand.

"No thanks, but I do have an idea."

Holt called Doc to his side.

"The Bru are chewing Betel Nut. No wonder they can run all day. They're all jacked up on that shit. Don't you carry amphetamines?"

"Yeah. Why?"

"Well, wouldn't that help us?"

"I don't like giving that shit out. It can be addictive. It's only for emergencies."

"You don't think this is a fucking emergency?"

Doc dropped his pack and withdrew a small tin of pills. He showed it to Holt.

Holt had stories about the drug use of the Special Forces and sure enough Doc had a variety of pills. It was rumored that some Green Berets took steroids to bulk up. But Holt had not seen any indication of steroid use. He himself had gained about fifteen pounds, but that was from the good mess hall food. Even with the weight gain he still only weighed a hundred and forty pounds. Most of the other men back in camp were about the same. Hardly the massive, muscled, monsters depicted in Sergeant Rock comic books.

Doc held out his hand. "It's twenty milligrams of dextroamphetamine. It says right here 'to be used for forty-eight hours of enhanced combat readiness.'"

"Fuck, Doc, what are you waiting for? If this ain't an emergency, what is?"

"Alright, one pill each."

He handed out one pill each to the Americans. "It should start working in a few minutes."

Holt saw Sangh watching him.

"It's our version of Betel Nut." He turned to Phang. "Okay, let's go."

Doc got into his ruck sack and said to Holt, "What a fucking war. We got the Bru jacked on Betel Nut and we're all wired on speed. This sucks."

"We're just a bunch of junkie monkeys running through the jungle," Holt said.

They took off at a fast walking pace. Within minutes Holt felt a jolt of energy course through his body. His fatigue diminished, his confidence returned. He knew it all came from the drug but didn't care. He now knew they had a plan.

Above them, the sky lightened considerably. What they could see through the trees was dark gray. Dawn was breaking.

They walked for two hours before taking a break. Holt was tired, they all were. But he wasn't exhausted.

Holt took a deep pull from his canteen and noticed it was almost empty. He couldn't remember if this was his third or fourth canteen. They would need to find water. Strapped to his ruck sack were two, two quart, collapsible canteens. If he, and the men, carefully rationed their water they might get by until the morning.

Holt checked his compass and saw they were on a south west heading. At some point, they would leave the forest and enter the thicker jungle growth. Their progress would slow but so would the NVA.

They resumed their quick pace. The blackness of the night subsided replaced by shades of gray. Soon the sun would be fully up and with it the debilitating heat.

Two more hours and it was twelve noon, 1200 hours. They would stop for a ten minute break to eat something. They formed a tight perimeter around a small stand of trees. Each of the men ate their food in silence, too tired to talk.

Holt leaned in close to Doc. "Even with the speed, I'm beat to shit. Any chance of another pill?"

"I won't even consider it until this evening and don't ask again until then."

Holt was breathing hard through his mouth. He concentrated on breathing through his nose and slowing his breaths. He pulled some jerky from his pocket.

"Eat something else besides that shit. It's full of salt and will only make you thirstier. Here take this," Doc said, handing Holt a can of chicken and noodles.

"I can't take your food, Doc. I got plenty."

"Just take it. Jesus, what a whiny little prick you can be sometimes," Doc hissed.

Holt opened the can and took his spoon from his shirt pocket. He licked the spoon clean and scooped out a large spoonful.

As he chewed he turned to Doc. "Do you think we're doing the right thing, heading in early?"

"Damn straight I do. What the fuck more could they want? We found two large, all weather trails and plotted them on the map. And now we're being chased by gooks. What the fuck are we supposed to do?"

"I got a feeling Evans doesn't agree."

"He just made rank and he's looking for his own team. He's afraid of fucking up."

"If he gets his own team he'd better learn to think for himself."

"He's afraid of Top and what he thinks."

"You know, something just came to me that we didn't consider. The NVA have radios; what if they called ahead and arranged a blocking force?"

"If there are gooks ahead of us Phang will spot them and we'll just go around them."

"We're giving Phang a lot of credit. We're putting him in charge of our lives."

"I trust Phang. He's a tiger. Out here, he's the predator, not the prey." "I hope you're right," Holt said while chewing on a cracker. "I figure, we'll go another two hours and take a break. Maybe send Phang and Little Phang out ahead of us and scout around. I'll walk point."

"No you won't. You get one of the Yards to walk point. That's their job."

Holt looked to his side and flicked a leaf with his finger. "Leaf leeches. God, they're disgusting."

"They're just trying to stay alive in the jungle like the rest of us. They usually live on worms and small bugs. They suck them dry. We must seem like a bonanza for them."

"They make my skin crawl. They're revolting."

"Just part of nature, bitch. Don't get your panties in a wad," Doc said.

"Don't wear panties just like you. I wonder why they don't issue us jock straps. You know, to hold the boys up close."

"Same reason we don't wear underwear; the elastic would rub you raw," Doc said. "We're out here in some God forsaken, prehistoric forest being chased by murderous gooks and you're thinking about underwear?"

"I knew a guy named Parker. He was terrified of getting wounded. Wore a flak jacket and a steel cup. Got shot through the neck and bled out."

"Talking to you is like having lunch with the grim reaper."

"Maybe we should wear those little G-strings like the bar girls wear. They look comfortable."

"You want something pulled up between your ass cheeks, be my guest. I'm fine with going commando."

Holt looked at his watch. "Time to move out."

"Thank God. You know what your problem is? You need to get laid. That's your problem." "You may be right."

"You take my advice, I'm a doctor. Or at least out here I am. Give me a minute and let me check Evans bandage."

"Is he getting a Purple Heart for that?"

"I'm putting him in for one. Whether he gets it or not is not up to me. Any objection?"

"I'm with you. If we bleed out here we get a heart."

Ryan was close behind Holt on this leg of the march.

"On your sit reps, do they say anything?" asked Holt.

"No, they just mark it down. Why do you ask?"

"I was just wondering. Aren't they concerned about us? I thought the TOC was on full alert when a team was out?"

"Right about now Top is cracking the seal on a new bottle," Ryan said.

Holt looked at Ryan. "I know you're just kidding. Top wouldn't drink when a team is in the field. The Major would have a fit if he caught him."

"He'd have to catch him first." Ryan looked around. "Jesus, this is boring. I swear we passed that tree before. We're moving like a herd of stampeding turtles."

"I keep forgetting you're a country boy. We are moving along at a good clip. That's the speed talking."

"Maybe. I do feel better though. You know when I get home, I'm going to beat the shit out of my recruiter. He made this all sound like it would be one big adventure. Like going camping with your friends." He slapped at a mosquito. "This is some kind of scary shit."

"That it is. When's the next sit rep? Ask them to drop off some cold sodas."

"Shit, I would kill for an ice cold Dr. Pepper."

They walked in silence for a while. "Next time we take a break they want Cubby to do an over flight to mark our position."

"Is he up there all the time?" "Supposed to be."

Holt saw Phang raise a clenched fist and drop to the ground.

The column of men got down and faced outwards. In the silence of the forest Holt could hear his heartbeat in his ears. His drug dilated eyes stared out into the gloom.

Phang crawled forward with the little Phang's and disappeared into the shadows. Minutes passed like hours. The sweat rolled down Holt's face. He dare not move to wipe it. Inches from face he saw a leaf leech raise its body sensing for the warmth of Holt's body. It twisted and turned and dropped to the ground. It was impossible to see it on the forest floor.

Phang and the two boys reappeared walking upright. He held up two fingers and drew his hand across his throat. Holt shuddered.

Holt rose from the ground and walked to Phang. Phang leaned in close. "Two VC, I kill."

"Were they looking for us?"

"Maybe, not sure. We turn, go west now. One hour and turn again."

Doc stood behind Ryan. "See, I told you. Phang is the ultimate predator. He smells the NVA before we could even see them."

They followed Phang forward until he signaled another stop.

Holt and Ryan were besides the bodies of the NVA that Phang had killed. Holt looked down at the bodies. One lay on a rock with his head leaning back. His throat had been cut to the point that his head was almost severed. The second boy lay on his stomach and appeared unharmed.

"Jesus, look at them, they're just boys. They're no older than the Bru boys," Holt whispered to Ryan. "They're no different than the Bru or, for that matter, the South Vietnamese."

"The Bru are darker skinned and their noses are a little flatter," Ryan said, missing Holt's point.

"Two kids walk down a trail and meet. They immediately fall into a murderous rage and try to kill each other because they're wearing different uniforms. This is fucking nuts. It's crazy. The north hates the south and they both hate the Montagnards because they live in the mountains. They kill each other because of politics or skin color. And we're stuck in the middle of this shit. We don't belong here, yet, here we are."

"Sarge, are you okay?"

"I'm fine, Ryan. I'm just tired."

"Phang's moving out again. We should go."

They followed Phang as he led them west. After a hour they turned south again.

Holt questioned his purpose. Phang led the patrol. All he did was read the map and work the radio, but Ryan did ninety percent of radio work. This patrol would get along fine without him.

They stopped at a stream. It was ten foot wide and about three foot deep. It ran cool and clean over a gravel bed.

Phang tasted the water. "It's good," he said.

One by one the men stopped and filled their canteens and crossed the stream. The Americans added their iodine based Globaline tablets to their water. The tablets dissolved in less than a minute but left the water with a distinct taste of iodine.

They continued south. The forest turned to jungle. The undergrowth was thicker and tangled vines and clumps of bamboo slowed their progress. The humidity increased and sweat covered their bodies. Flies and mosquitoes buzzed around their faces.

Ryan slapped a mosquito on his face, the sound loud and sharp as a gunshot.

Holt turned and looked at him.

"Sorry," Ryan said.

"Don't worry about it. The gooks know where we are. We just gotta keep ahead of them."

Holt couldn't tell if it was still raining. What little portion of sky he could see through the jungle canopy was gray. Water dripped continuously from the trees. The ground was covered by matted leaves and twigs. Vines were everywhere. Some vines were thin as a pencil, others, as thick as your wrist. They snaked up the tree trunks and curled around the bushes and across the ground ensnaring your feet. They didn't walk; they plodded through this mess, one foot after another in a mind-numbing repetitive march to nowhere.

Up ahead, Phang stopped and signaled to get down. When he turned back to look at them, his face was filled with sadness.

The air was split by a massive explosion. Phang and the Bru boys were vaporized in a cloud of blood, flesh, and bone.

Immediately following the explosion, the air was filled with thousands of pieces of shrapnel sending leaves, twigs, and bark raining down upon them. Then the jungle erupted in automatic weapons fire.

Holt was thrown backward. He stumbled to his feet shouting, "Get up! Get up! Attack them! Attack! Attack!"

Holt ran forward firing his Car 15 on full automatic. As he emptied one magazine, he ejected it and slapped in a fresh one in one fluid motion. He ran forward firing left and right breaking right through the ambush. He was followed by Sangh and the two remaining Bru. They smashed through the NVA positions and sent the enemy scurrying off into the jungle.

Evans, Doc, and Ryan got to their feet and staggered forward.

"What the fuck is wrong with you guys? I know they taught you in Ranger school to attack an ambush. If we allowed ourselves to get pinned down we would have been done," shouted Holt, his ears still ringing from the explosion.

"Jesus, Sarge," Ryan stammered.

"Never mind." Holt turned. "Sangh, check the bodies. Be quick. We have to get out of here. They'll be more coming."

Sangh pointed to a long piece of twisted wire and followed it.

As Holt stepped forward he saw the remains of the Bru boys. All that left was a smear of blood and tattered cloth pinned to the trees and bushes. He looked around for their weapons but could find nothing. Three men gone, turned into a pool of blood and a mash of flesh and bone. There wasn't anything to retrieve, nothing to bring home.

Sangh found the mine. It looked like the base of a fifty gallon barrel packed with explosive and nails.

"It must have been command detonated. Phang must have saw it but it was too late. That explains the look he gave us. He knew he was done." Holt examined the crater left by the mine. "From the size of the explosion and the damage it did I'd guess it was packed with more than twenty pounds of explosive and whatever shit they threw in for shrapnel," Holt said.

Holt pulled out his compass and shot a quick azimuth. "Sangh, we need to go south west. We need to get of here quick before they regroup and come after us. Ryan call this in and be quick about it. We need to Di Di. I'll take point."

They started to jog through the tangled jungle. There was no time to mourn the loss of Phang and the boys. They were gone and nothing would bring them back. They were still alive and had to move on.

After an hour they had to stop. All were exhausted, panting, and gasping for air. Evans was doubled over on his hands and knees retching. Over Doc's objection, the Americans took another amphetamine capsule. The Bru stuffed their mouths with Betel Nut. Holt swallowed half a canteen in two or three long gulps. He wiped his face with his towel. His camo face was long gone, smeared across his face in streaks of green and brown.

"Did you get a hold of Cubby?" Holt asked Ryan.

"Couldn't raise him," Ryan said, his eyes bulging from fear and the speed.

"Shit! Try them again next break," Holt said, chewing on his thumb nail. Holt jabbed a finger at Ryan. "Let them know we're running and will need extraction."

"I did, Sarge."

"Just make sure they don't forget."

CHAPTER 22

A Long Scary Night

Holt dug through his pants pocket and pulled out a John Wayne chocolate bar. He unwrapped it and bit off half. He chewed the hard, crumbly chocolate into a pulpy mass and swallowed it. He took a final drink from his canteen.

"We go now Trung Si. VC come," Sangh said.

"Yes, we go," Holt replied. "Alright, everyone on your feet. We got two, three hours tops to the trail and the PZ."

"Sarge, I'm beat. Can't we rest more," Ryan whined.

Doc Blaze was standing adjusting his pack.

"Holt's right. We need to move out."

Holt looked at Evans who was sitting back on his legs wiping his mouth.

"Evans, let's go."

Evans started to say something and Holt was upon him in two steps. He roughly grabbed his combat harness and pulled him to his feet. He was filled with an irrational rage.

"Not a fucking word. We're moving out now. You don't want to come, then sit your ass back down and wait for the gooks to come. The rest of us are going."

Holt reached into a pouch on the back of his belt and got the sling for his rifle. He attached it to the front triangle sight and the rear butt stock. He slung it over his shoulder. As he started walking, he got his Browning pistol and screwed on the silencer. He moved off down the game trail at a fast walking pace.

Sangh and the Bru boys were behind him, followed by Ryan, Doc, and Evans. They kept this fast pace for an hour before stopping for a ten minute break.

"Ryan, anything?"

"Yeah, I got Cubby," he said holding out the handset for Holt.

"Cubby, do you know where we're going?" Holt said foregoing proper radio procedure.

"Yeah, I know."

"We'll be there in about two hours. It's 1400 now. Can you arrange for an extraction?"

"There is a storm moving in from the east over the mountains. You'll have maybe a hour of daylight left. At dusk, with a storm, you might have to overnight in place."

"Unacceptable. We need to get out."

"I'll do my best."

"Wait one. Is there anything closer?"

"Not that I can see. Nothing that will take two ships. Stay on course and Charlie Mike."

"We don't need two ships. We've had three KIA. We can get on a single ship. We'll dump our gear if we have to."

"Stay on course. Out."

"Motherfuckers! I swear, I'm going to shove this pistol up Top's ass if we get back."

"You mean, when we get back, right, Sarge?" "Yes Ryan, That's what I meant."

Sangh saw the look of concern on Holt's face and stood by his side. "Sangh, we might have to spend the night out here. If so we'll have to dig in and Alamo up."

"Alamo?"

"Sorry, the Alamo, it's a place in America."

"I know Alamo, it's in your Texas."

Holt smiled at him. "That's right, Texas."

"I want to see Texas someday."

"I hope you get there. Let's move out."

The trail they were following became more pronounced. Holt debated whether to stay on the trail or move off into the jungle. They were taught never to walk a trail but for the speed offered it was too good to pass up. Up ahead he saw three shadows moving through a gap in the trees. He signaled the men off the trail. He put his fingers to his eyes, pointed forward, and held up three fingers. Sangh started to rise but Holt placed a hand on his shoulder.

He crouched in the bushes and waited.

As the men got closer, Holt rose and walked towards them. The men were so startled they just stopped. He shot the first man three times in his chest and pushed him aside. He pushed the silencer under the chin of the second man and fired. The third man turned and ran. Holt shot him three times in the back and he stumbled and fell to the ground groaning and writhing in pain.

Holt signaled the team to rise and move out. As he walked by the third NVA, he shot him in the head. The silencer barely made a sound.

"Phang is in him," Sangh whispered to the boys. "Phang is with us. We will be alright."

They walked steadily for a half hour when the trail suddenly veered off at a ninety degree angle towards the southeast.

Holt got his map and Ryan and Sangh came to look over his shoulder. Holt orientated the map correctly and pointed.

"Look, we're here." He drew a line with his finger. "The trail is heading right towards the POW camp. If we go straight ahead, due south, we'll hit the trail that took us from our landing zone to the POW camp. That LZ is now our PZ."

He waited until they both agreed. "That means if we continue south west, on a diagonal, like we're doing, we'll get to the PZ quicker. It can't be far now, maybe an hour, a little bit more."

Ryan looked to where Holt indicated. "Shit, Sarge look at the jungle. It looks all most impassable."

"It's just jungle, I've been in way worst," he lied. "Don't forget, we're the baddest motherfuckers in this jungle. We're Green, fucking, Berets. This is our home. We live here."

"The NVA also live here," Ryan said.

"Fuck them. The NVA are all from city's or farms. They had to adapt to the jungle just like us. Joseph Conrad wrote in The Heart of Darkness, that the jungle was no place for white men." He looked at Sangh and said, "No offense."

Sangh shrugged. "None taken."

"That's bullshit. We own this jungle. Now if we were up against the Viet Cong, I might be worried. They grew up in the jungle. But these dickheads from the north are no better than us. We're bigger, stronger, and have better equipment. Tell the guys to take ten and then we'll move off."

"Okay, Sarge. I feel better now. I'm wired tight as a string. You're right, fuck these gooks." Ryan looked at Sangh, "Sorry, I didn't mean..."

Sangh just held up his hand.

Holt watched Ryan walk back to the team.

"Pretty good speech," he said to Sangh.

"Did you believe it?"

"Not a word. Right about now, I'm scared shitless. I'm exhausted, hungry, and have only the faintest clue as to where we are."

"No, you good. We go this way, as you said, and we get helicopter home."

"What if we can't get out tonight?"

"Then we fight. Can you get help?"

"Maybe we could get Puff or some artillery. I'm not sure."

"You eat something. You need strength."

"You're a good friend, Sangh." "You and me, brothers."

Holt dropped his ruck and got out a tin of crackers and a packet of jerky. He replaced his empty canteen with a fresh one. As he ate, he checked the map again. He looked at the jungle ahead of them.

Everything in the jungle was designed to hurt or kill you. There were spiders whose bite could swell your arm to twice its size and close up your throat in minutes. There were snakes whose venom could kill you in two steps. Thorns tore at your flesh and vines tripped and tangled you. The smell was overpowering. It smelled like rotting vegetation and death.

Every surface was covered in mold spores and moss. The air was thick with humidity and made breathing difficult. And the heat was like walking in an oven. In the brightest sun it was still dark and dank. He would never master the jungle but he could survive here.

After ten minutes they started off again. Holt walked point. Holt thought of Phang. If Phang could fuck up and walk into an ambush, what hope of survival did he have? He wasn't as good as Phang; no one was. At best, he could only see ten feet in front. There could be a company of gooks dug in and waiting.

Holt began to doubt his plan. It was obvious they were running to a pick up point. They were heading to the most obvious choice. The NVA wasn't stupid; you had to respect them. They camped in this area and knew all the clearings where a helicopter could land. Was this expected and were they making a huge mistake? Holt shrugged off his paranoia. This was the plan and for the time being they were committed to it.

He knew the amphetamines were fucking with head. But he knew he couldn't maintain this pace without them.

Ahead, lay every conceivable plant imaginable. It was a world of green. You couldn't force your way through the jungle. You swam through it. He pictured the old Tarzan movies with white men slashing through the jungle with machetes. It was ridiculous. The effort of using a machete would exhaust you in minutes. You had to adapt.

Holt walked with his arm extended parting the vines and branches and moving silently between them. He kept his Browning pistol pointed in the direction of travel. He would occasionally check his compass heading. There were no visible landmarks to aid navigation. He felt enveloped in the jungle growth and had to fight down the fear of claustrophobia. The leaves closed in and brushed his face as the thorny vines clawed at his shirt and trousers. He breathed deep and plodded on.

He counted his steps and let the careful placement of his feet calm him. He looked at his watch; it was 1530. He called everyone to a halt. High above him in the jungle canopy, the rain started.

Sangh pushed past Ryan and stood by Holt's side.

Holt was staring at his compass.

"Are we lost, Sangh?"

"No, we good. Soon."

"How soon?"

"One hour, less maybe."

Holt looked up. "It's raining. If it's dark and raining, no helicopters."

Holt turned to Ryan. "Cubby?"

"Refueling. He'll be back on station in twenty."

"Did he confirm our position?"

"Give or take."

"Give or take what?"

"A few hundred feet. It's the best he could do."

"Have we heard from Top?"

"Cubby is relaying our messages. He said they know we're looking to get out."

Holt holstered his pistol and smeared his face with insect repellent. He offered the small bottle to Sangh.

"Bugs don't bother Bru like you. You smell different."

"Do we smell better or worse than Bru?"

"Different."

"You could make a career in diplomacy when all this is done. We'll move out in five minutes."

"I take point; you rest."

"No. We can't afford to lose you. I'm expendable, you're not. Let's hope it's no more than an hour."

They marched on. The rain continued. In a triple canopy jungle, like this Cambodian wilderness, the trees grew in staggered heights. The first layer, called the scrub layer, consisted of shrubby plants, bushes, and tree saplings. Next was the understory where small trees grew up to twenty feet. Finally, there was the upper canopy where the trees were over a hundred feet high. It was the overgrowing branches of the upper canopy that filtered the sun and rain. The rain didn't so much as fall as seeped through the branches and leaves. Hours after a storm water would continue to fall from the trees.

It was here they plodded on through tangled vines and thorny bushes, their footsteps softened by a spongy layer a decaying leaves and moss.

Thirty minutes passed and Cubby was back on station.

"Viking Six, this is over flight. I got your position pegged. You are approximately thirty minutes out. Over."

"Over flight. What about extraction?" Holt responded.

"Negative. A team, twenty miles north, has declared a Prairie Fire and all air assets are diverted to their location. I should be able to arrange artillery support and I'll try to scare up Puff if you need it. How are you fixed?"

"We've got plenty of supplies, but we're running on empty."

"Understand. Snuggle in and I'll watch out for you. Keep the faith. Over flight, out."

Holt gathered the team around him. "We got about thirty minutes to go. We'll be spending the night. Another team nearby called a Prairie Fire, so that's that."

"So they got everyone's attention and we're hung out to dry," Evans said.

"We'll be fine. We get there and dig in. Look on the bright side, we got beau coup ammo and grenades. We got food and water and we should have artillery support. Over flight is also trying to get Puff on station."

"This cross border shit sucks. This mission has been fucked from the beginning," Evans said.

"When you get your own team, you can tell that to Top. Until then, please keep all your negative shit to yourself. No one needs to hear it. We dig in and wait for dawn. Got it?"

"Yeah, I got it," Evans said with a petulant whine to his voice.

Holt, followed by Ryan, walked to the head of the column.

"What's up with Evans? Why is he acting like a pissy, little cunt all of a sudden?"

"He's just stressed out. We all are," Ryan said.

"Team leaders don't get stressed out. And if they do they don't show it to the team. Let's get moving and get the fuck out of here."

Before moving Sangh set out two grenade traps across their trail.

Forty five minutes later, Holt saw a break in the upper canopy. They moved forward and found the trail. Twenty meters due east was their clearing. They walked down the trail and stopped at the clearings edge. It was as they remembered it, a circular break in the jungle about a quarter mile wide.

"We'll dig in here, a trench across the trail with our backs to the clearing. Sangh, you and the boys start the trench and we'll drag some logs over."

They dropped their packs and set about preparing their position. They found a fresh fallen tree and dragged it in front of their hole. The branches were still pliable and the leaves were moist and green.

They placed six trip flares forty to fifty feet from their position and to their sides. Four Claymore mines were placed twenty feet out, two covering the trail and two off to the sides. They stacked the remaining mines in front of the log as a last ditch measure.

They continued to dig. The ground was soft and digging was easy; they kept expanding the hole until it was ten feet long, four foot wide and three feet deep. They were able to kneel in the hole, lean against the edge and place their rifles on the log.

"This is good earth," Ryan said scooping up a handful of dirt. "Look at it; it's rich, dark, and damp. It's almost like compost. You could grow anything in it."

"Look around you. We're in the middle of a jungle. Everything does grow here. Every conceivable plant in the world is growing here," Holt said.

"You know what I mean. You could clear a patch of ground and grow vegetables and raise stock. This could be a beautiful country if it wasn't for the war."

"That's all the farmers want to do. Tend to the earth and live in peace. Unfortunately, politicians have other plans."

Holt climbed from the hole and walked in front of it. He walked back twenty feet. He couldn't see the team. Their position looked like another patch of vegetation.

He dropped back into the hole. "It's perfect, you can't see a thing."

Holt sat back in the hole and looked over at Sangh. Sangh sat with his hands pressed flat together and his fingers against his forehead. He saw Holt looking at him.

"I pray for Phang. I pray he finds the peace he never had in life."

"Phang was a warrior."

"Phang had a hard life. He told me he killed his first man when he was twelve."

"How did that happen?"

"After the big war over Americans leave Japan men in charge until the French came back. One day a Japan man come to Phang's village. He was drunk and tried to rape Phang's sister. She only ten years old. Phang kill him. Ten Japan men come to village to punish Bru. Bru kill all men and cut heads off. Bru go to where Japan men live and throw heads over wall. Japan men never come back to village. Frenchmen return and force Bru to work at rubber tree place. Bru kill French and go to mountains to live. Find good place to live. Secret place that no one can find. VC kill many French and Frenchman leave. Americans come back to fight VC. Special men, like you, come to Bru and ask for help fighting VC. Phang help Americans since then. He once say, killing only thing he good at."

"Not a good way to grow up," Holt said.

"Maybe now Phang at peace."

"I hope so. Phang was a good man, a good warrior, and a good friend."

He rummaged through his pack and took out a can of C-Rations. "We should eat and try and rest. We got a long night ahead of us. When Cubby comes back I'll signal him with a flashlight and see if he can spot us. Maybe he can lay in some artillery."

Holt opened his can. It was beans and little hot dogs, commonly referred to as "beans and baby dicks."

Sangh had dug a one square foot indentation in the foxhole wall.

"We cook our food there," he said. "No fire visible."

Holt took out his C-Ration stove, a short can with holes punched in the sides. He broke off a piece of C-4 plastic explosive and rolled into a golf ball sized ball. He placed it in the stove and lit it. It hissed into a blue white flame. He placed his can of food on top of the stove. After just a minute the meal was bubbling. He removed the can and stirred the contents. The others had prepared similar cutout's and were cooking their food.

Holt leaned back against the foxhole and scrunched up his knees. He ate his meal with a can of saltine crackers. He felt the moist earth against his back.

"I'm making some coffee, do you want some?" Ryan asked.

"That would be great," Holt said. He remembered his friend Mercado and the delicious coffee he would make. "Spanish coffee," he called it. A delicious mixture of coffee, vanilla, and cinnamon. It was a night time ritual he shared with Holt. Mercado would be home by now. Holt hoped he got his Bodega in Spanish Harlem and was doing what he loved. He could picture it as Nick would describe it: old men sitting at tables in the sun playing dominos, inside, the restaurant smelling of steam and spices. On the patio, there would be tables with colorful umbrellas and a guitar player playing soft Spanish ballads. Couples would sit drinking ice cold beer and eating fried plantains. Holt missed Nicky and his old squad. He promised himself he would write him when they got back. As much as he missed him, he was glad he wasn't here. Nick did his part and deserved the life he dreamed of.

Cubby returned and interrupted Holt's thoughts.

Holt looked into the darkening sky and saw Cubby to the north.

"Cubby, this is Viking six, can you see my light?" Holt blinked his flashlight.

"Got you spotted Viking Six. I can see you clearly. Do you want to spot and adjust some artillery fire?"

"Affirmative."

"Shot out."

The team heard the shell as it passed overhead. Holt could barely see the explosive flash about four hundred meters out and two hundred meters to the south.

"Tell them to drop one hundred and two hundred to the right."

Holt could clearly see the explosion three hundred meters to their front.

"Mark that target Alpha. I'll make all adjustments from Alpha if needed. And make sure they fuse for ground explosion. Don't need any tree bursts."

"Roger that. Stay safe. I'll be on station for the next four hours looking out for you."

"Cubby, how's the Prairie Fire? Is it out yet?"

"No, those boys are in deep shit. Three kilos and four whisky's. Still burning strong. The natives are angry and out for blood."

"Roger that, Viking out," Holt said. He gave the handset back to Ryan. "Did you hear that? Evans is right about these patrols, they're fucked."

As the night came upon them, the forest came alive with the sounds of insects, frogs, and lizards. Above, in the branches of the canopy, monkeys and birds settled in for the night. Bats fluttered through the sky hunting.

Off in the distance, north of them, they heard a small muffled explosion.

"Grenade trap," Sangh whispered. They all sat and waited.

"VC find second trap."

"I guess they did," Holt said. His heart was pounding and he wiped his sweaty, shaking hands on his pants leg.

"I'd hoped we outran them and they gave up."

"VC Come tonight," Sangh said emphatically.

It started to rain again, a soft persistent rain.

CHAPTER 23

Lights And Whistles

At 0100 Holt finished his guard shift and tried to sleep. The hole wasn't big enough to stretch out so the men sat with knees bunched up leaning against the mud side.

Holt was comforted by the grunting of the bull frogs. Then, there was nothing. Dead silence. Holt came fully awake in an instant.

Sangh leaned into Holt until their shoulders touched and pointed.

"See, out there, lights."

"I see them. What's going on?"

"VC come."

Holt stared out into the jungle and watched the small pinpricks of light.

"Flashlights?" he asked Sangh.

"I think yes. VC try to get ready to come at us." "But they have to realize we can see the lights." "Maybe they try and scare us."

"It's working. Ryan, get me Cubby." Ryan handed Holt the radio handset.

"Cubby, this is Viking. Can you see the lights out in front of us?" "Yeah. I was just going to call you. What's going on?"

"Who the fuck knows. I've never seen anything like this." "You want me to light them up?"

"Do it."

A minute passed and Cubby came back on. "Shot out. Group of six."

After several seconds the team heard the shells scream overhead. The jungle lit up in six furious explosions.

"Splash down," Holt said. "Adjust, drop twenty, and fire for effect."

The fire base fired three groupings of six shells each. The jungle exploded with the concentrated volley of eighteen shells. Shrapnel, traveling at supersonic speed, lay waste to a hundred yards of jungle, toppling trees and spreading a storm of fallen leaves and branches. Thick, pungent clouds of cordite smoke spread through the trees and watered their eyes.

"Cubby, good job."

"At your service. Gotta go and refuel. Cubby 2 will be on station, call sign, Nightrider."

"Cool name. Don't you have a call sign?"

"Wolfman, but Cubby will do."

"Wolfman it is. Thanks and hurry back."

"Nightrider will take good care of you. I'll be back for extraction at dawn. Wolfman out."

At 0230 the lights were replaced by whistles.

"I can't stand the whistles. They scare the shit out of me. I'd rather have the lights."

The team, on full alert stared into the darkness. The sound of the rain hid any sound. A trip flare to their left snapped and burned in a brilliant white light. Shadows moved through the trees.

"Hold your fire, let them get closer," Holt said.

Ryan shoved the handset at Holt. "It's Nightrider."

"Nightrider, Viking Six, Target Alpha, drop seventy five, fire left and right."

Seconds passed. "Shot out. Duck down and cover your ears."

Holt counted off the seconds. Seven seconds and a line of twelve explosions ripped across their front. In total, it took twenty eight seconds. Shrapnel sizzled overhead.

"Two guns firing, six each," Holt said.

"Are you sure?" asked Ryan.

"Not really; I'm just guessing."

"Viking Six, Nightrider. Gun crew warns they are getting close. Can't guarantee accuracy in this rain."

"Understood. That trip flare you saw was only fifty feet out. I'm hoping that was just a probe. I'm guessing at the distance of main force."

"Are you declaring a Prairie Fire?"

Holt looked at Ryan then at Sangh.

"Not yet. Big guns seem to be holding them."

Holt leaned forward in the hole. "Doc, Evans, how you doing?"

"I got movement off to the side. Could be my imagination or my ears ringing. Can't be sure," Evans said.

"Stay alert."

"Four hours till dawn," Doc said. "This really sucks ass. I am so over this bullshit"

"Could be worse. We got plenty of ammo, water and food. And we got this beautiful hole to hide in," Holt countered.

"How many do you think there are?" asked Ryan.

"Sangh, how many?" said Holt.

"Two hundred," Sangh said without pause.

"Jesus Christ! We're outnumbered ten to one," Ryan said. In the dark they both looked at Ryan.

"What kind of fucking hillbilly school did you go to? Did they teach math there?" Holt said.

"Ryan, it's closer to thirty to one," Said Doc. "That's even worse!"

"Considerably worse. Ryan why don't you call that in and let Nightrider know. Tell him to pass it on to Top. Let that grizzled, old fuck know what we're up against," Holt said.

Even in the dark, Holt could see Doc roll his eyes.

"Nightrider says he going to see if he can get Puff out here."

"Movement," hissed Evans.

"Where?"

"To my front, about twenty yards."

"Evans get your M-79 and put a few rounds out there," Holt said. "Everyone, pass down your M-79 rounds to Evans."

Evans fumbled with his pack and got the grenade launcher strapped to the side. His hands were shaking.

He loaded and fired off a round and immediately fired a second.

The small explosions illuminated a small group of men scurrying back into the safety of the jungle.

"How the fuck did they get so close without us hearing them?" Evans said.

"They gotta be sending out small groups to probe us. Evans, you watch your side. Sangh, tell the boys to watch their side, and the rest of us will watch the front," Holt ordered. "Ryan, let Nightrider know we're being probed on all sides and they're danger close."

"If they weren't sure where we were, they are now," Doc whispered to the group.

Holt looked at his watch. "0315. We just got to hold out until dawn and pray it stops raining." Holt took a gulp of water and his hands trembled holding the canteen. "Three more fucking hours," he said to himself.

Holt arranged the Claymore detonators on the small shelf they had dug into their hole. He also placed his hand on the six hand grenades he had lined up.

"Ryan, get Nightrider up."

Holt was breathing hard as he spoke to the over flight.

"We need another bunch of shells to our front, like before, but drop another seventy five."

"Viking 6, that's really close, are you sure?"

"I assume you guys want to come in and pick up survivors and not bodies. Just do it. I take full responsibility."

"Shot out."

The team crouched lower in their hole and waited. A line of explosions ripped the jungle in front of their position. But this time it was different. In the midst of the explosions, men charged forward firing as they ran.

Green tracers flew over their heads and others impacted the log barrier. The team fired back on full automatic into the line of men. The NVA fell but kept on coming. The noise was overpowering. They couldn't hear themselves scream.

The gun flashes illuminated the foxhole in a bizarre, strobe like effect. Time passed in jerky images.

Holt fired off two Claymore's and fifteen hundred steel ball bearings tore through the advancing men. The charge faltered and broke. The NVA stumbled back into the jungle.

"Fuck you and your fucking whistles," Holt shouted. "Fucking bunch of pussies!"

Nightrider was shouting on the radio. "What's your status?"

"Nightrider, calm yourself, we're okay."

"Shit! It looked like you were going to be overrun. All I could see were tracers and explosions. They looked close."

"They were but we're good for now."

"I'm calling in Puff. I ain't taking any chances. I've never lost a team and I ain't starting now."

"We'll do our best not to spoil your perfect record."

"I meant—"

"Not to worry. Puff would be good." Holt handed the handset back to Ryan. "Fucking Cubby pilots are all crazy."

"Puff on station in fifteen mikes. Stay cool until then."

"Lay out your ammo and grenades. We still got three hours to go." Holt noticed Doc fiddling with Ryan's shoulder. "What's up, Doc?"

"That's one I never heard before. Something nicked Ryan's shoulder. Could be a piece of shrapnel or a bullet. Whatever it was, it's good for a heart."

"That's good. We're too close now. I made a mistake putting those two remaining Claymore's out on an angle. Seems they like coming at us straight on. How's everybody fixed for ammo?"

They counted their ammo and reported in.

"Good. They only used about fifty men. They won't make that mistake again. If they come at us again, they'll throw everyone at us."

"Maybe they'll wait until dawn and try to bag a helicopter," Evans said.

"Sarge, there's someone out front," Ryan said.

They all turned to see two men crawling up to a wounded soldier and starting to drag him back. Evans started to raise his grenade launcher.

"Evans, stop. Don't be a dickhead. Let them get their wounded," Holt said.

"Are you nuts? You think they would let us do that?"

"I have no idea what they would do. What I do know is that we ain't them. We don't shoot wounded."

"You shot that guy back on the trail."

"He was too far gone. He was missing part of his head. I did him a favor."

In twenty minutes they heard the drone of Puff approaching. Puff, the Magic Dragon, sometimes called Spooky, was a converted Douglas AC-47 cargo plane. It's side bristled with three General Electric, six barreled mini guns, firing through the side windows and the cargo door. It carried massive amounts of ammunition and it was said to be able to fire a bullet every square inch of a football field at the rate of six thousand rounds per minute. The pilot would dip his left wing and fly and elliptical circle over the target firing a stream of bullets that a appeared to be a solid, red streak of flame. No target supported by Puff had ever been overrun.

"Viking 6, this is Nightrider. I'm turning you over to Puff, call sign Razorback. I'll circle above."

"Razorback, this is Viking 6. Any chance you're from Arkansas?"

"I am, why do you ask?"

"Woo, Pig, Sooie."

The pilot laughed. "Are you a fellow Hog?"

"No. Just happen to know some folks who are. Glad you're here."

"Our pleasure. Can you mark your position?"

"We have survival strobe lights. I'll mark the front and sides of our hole. Let me know if you can see them."

"Sangh, you got your strobe light? Good. Put it out on the side. Evans mark your side and we'll mark the front."

Five strobe lights blinked upwards.

"Got you sighted, bright and clear. Would you like us to introduce ourselves to your neighbors?"

"Have at it Razorback. Put the fear of God into those mothers."

In one of the most foolish and unbelievable incidents of this encounter a large caliber enemy machine opened up on Puff from across the open field.

"Hold on Viking. Let me just take care of this."

Puff altered his turn and flew over the machine gun emplacement and hosed it down with several hundred 7.62 mini gun bullets. Several small secondary explosions obliterated the machine gun crew.

"Sorry for that interruption, Viking. Let's get back to work."

Puff made a lazy turn north, flew over the teams hole, and dipped it's left wing. A solid stream of tracers hit the ground surrounding Viking's position two hundred yards out. The pilot, who controlled the guns, alternated the mini guns, literally shredding the jungle like a wood chipper. The sound could best be described as tearing apart a long section of Velcro. The display was amazing considering that four regular bullets were interspersed each phosphorus tipped tracer round.

The team watched in awe as a shower of leaves, twigs, and branches fell to the ground. Several small trees toppled over.

"Alright, Viking. Your friends have been warned. We'll stay with you till dawn and watch over your extraction."

"Thanks, Razorback. Nice to have you around."

Holt let out a sigh of relief. "That should hold them until dawn."

"No," Sangh said. "VC come one more time. They know that with dragon overhead, they must get in close. They fire from front to get us down and come from the sides. They know we just few men and once in close they can kill us. Move Claymore's to sides. Me and boys will take this side. Trung si Evans and Doctor take other side. You and boy take front."

"Did he just call me a 'boy'?" asked Ryan.

"Quiet! Are you sure Sangh?"

"It's what I would do."

"The airplane and the cannons had to hurt them. Maybe they just left."

"They want to kill you and stop teams coming to Cambodia. They willing to risk men to do it."

"They had better be quick about it. It's maybe two hours to dawn."

"They move close now. Come in one hour."

Holt sagged back against the hole.

"If Sangh's right, we're still in deep shit," he whispered to Ryan.

"Why would he call me a boy?"

"What is wrong with you? We got more important things to worry about."

"But—"

"He called you a boy because you look like you're twelve years old. You don't even shave yet."

"Yes I do."

"What, once a week? You've been trying to grow a mustache since I met you. God damn it, I don't want to talk about this now. Get me Razorback."

Ryan worked the radio while mumbling under his breath. "Here," he said, in a petulant manner.

Holt took the handset. "Fucking moron," he mumbled.

"Razorback, how close can you get to us?"

"Why? What's going on?"

"Our Bru guide says the NVA are working in close to avoid your fire."

"How close do you want?"

"One hundred feet on all sides."

"That's danger close. It takes a real pro to get that close. A little bit of wind up here and my aim could be off."

"I trust you."

There was silence for a minute.

"Viking 6, I need you to say it loud and clear what you're requesting." Holt repeated his request.

"Viking, I'll start one hundred yards out and work my way in as close as I can. Put your lights on and get down. First sign of the NVA and we'll drop flares. Keep an open line and holler if I get too close."

In the cabin of the gunship the pilot scrubbed his hands across his face. "That fucking guy is nuts. Mike, you heard him?" he said to the co-pilot.

"I did, loud and clear."

"Dave?"

"Heard him," said the navigator.

"Alright, here we go."

The pilot dropped his wing and began circling the teams foxhole. As he fired, thousands of bullets spewed from the guns in a solid red, luminous, stream of fire. He slowed to a hundred and seventy-five miles per hour and descended to two thousand feet. He dipped the wing even lower. He fired a short burst and seeing it was accurate, fired an extended burst. He guessed he was seventy five yards from the foxhole.

On the ground, the NVA had been patiently and silently working their way through the jungle towards the teams position. Sensing that they had been detected, they began their attack early. They started with a barrage of Rocket Propelled Grenades. The RPG screeched through the air trailing spray of sparks and passed overhead, exploding behind them. In seconds, the gunners were reduced to bloody pulp as the mini guns of Puff tore their bodies apart.

True to his word, the pilot ordered the disbursement of flares. Three large MK-24 canister flares were pushed from the ship igniting in a brilliant burst of two million candle power. On the ground, night became day.

In the brilliant, white light of the flares Holt saw groups of men advancing on either side. He gave the order to fire.

On the left, Sangh and the two Bru boys calmly fired controlled three round burst into the advancing soldiers. Evans and Doc Blaze fired into the men on the right.

The same jungle which made travel so difficult for the team now entangled the feet of the advancing NVA soldiers. The stumbled and tripped over vines and branches tore at their faces. Unable to properly aim their weapons they fired wildly.

Six soldiers left the jungle and ran down the trail leading to the foxhole. One soldier knelt and carefully aimed his RPG. He was able to fire before Holt shot him. The rocket hit the log directly in front of Holt.

Holt was thrown violently against the back wall of the hole. He felt a searing pain in his left shoulder and chest. It felt as if someone pushed a red hot poker through his flesh.

Ryan was thrown back with Holt. His hands grasped his throat with both hands and slumped over.

Sangh, seeing what happened, turned and killed the NVA running towards Holt.

Holt struggled into a sitting position. His ears were ringing and his head reeling. He couldn't see straight. The pain in his shoulder was overwhelming. He doubled over and vomited. He rose and sat back on his legs. Vomit drooled from his mouth onto his chin and shirt. He wiped his mouth and as he did he saw Ryan. He grabbed him by his web gear and pulled him to a sitting position.

"Doc, Ryan's been hit bad."

Doc pried Ryan's fingers away from his throat and great gouts of blood spurted forward. The blood pulsed two or three more times, then stopped.

"He got hit in carotid artery. He's gone." He let Ryan slump back and resumed firing.

Holt dumbly searched for the radio. His body felt lopsided and uncoordinated. He found the handset and screamed, "Prairie Fire! Prairie Fire!"

He slumped forward and pushed himself up again. Six soldiers ran towards their hole. Holt couldn't find his rifle so he pulled his Browning pistol out and fired. On his left, Sangh fired controlled bursts and brought down four men. Holt shot the remaining two with his pistol. One fell against the log and struggled to rise. Holt shot him in the head, spraying bits of blood, bone, and brain matter over Sangh and himself.

The Bru boys fired their Claymore and brought down six men. Evans fired his Claymore and shredded three more.

All this time Puff had been circling their position firing their mini guns and dropping flares. The air reeked of cordite, blood and feces from the shredded bodies.

The firing tapered off and then stopped. Holt sagged back and passed out.

Holt woke to Doc ripping his shirt open. "What happened to you? Why didn't you say anything?"

"I'm alright, work on Ryan."

"I told you before, he's dead."

"No. He'll be fine. He's just sleeping. He's tired."

Doc pulled the radio from Ryan's body. "Evans, get on the horn and call in a medi-vacs. Holt's wounded."

"Cubby, we need a medi-vacs and immediate extraction."

"I heard your call for Prairie Fire and called it in. Help is on the way. Where is Viking six?"

"He's Whiskey India and we have another Kilo India." "Okay, what is enemy status?"

"For the moment, all quiet. Puff put a hurt on them."

"A Mike Force is inbound and Medi-vacs behind them."

Helicopters started landing one after another disgorging the Mike Force, which was a quick reaction team of forty indigenous personal and four to six Special Forces personal.

They quickly spread out forming a perimeter around the team and advancing into the surrounding jungle.

Cobra attack helicopters prowled the edges of the clearing searching for any enemy foolish enough to fire on them.

A tall, lanky American walked over to Holt and knelt by his side.

Holt looked up and smiled. "Joe, Joe Jenkins, how you doing pal?"

"From the looks of things, better than you."

"I'm okay. Do you have a smoke on you? My cigarettes are all bloody."

"I do," he said fishing out a pack of Kool's from his shirt pocket. He knelt over Holt and lit it.

Holt inhaled deeply. "You brothers and your menthol cigarettes. What's up with that?"

"You don't want it?"

"No, no, I'm just saying. So what do they have you doing?"

"I'm on the Mike Force. It's a lot better than running SOG patrols. You should try and get on it."

"Top's probably going to have me burning shit after this."

"Why's that?"

"He's pissed we cut the patrol short. We found a couple of new trails and ran into some gooks. They chased us all the way here and finally caught up with us."

Jenkins surveyed the dozens of dead NVA surrounding their foxhole. "Fuck him. It's easy for him to criticize, sitting back at a desk. We'll spend the afternoon counting gooks and searching their bodies. We'll let him know what happened out here."

Doc Blaze came over and knelt beside Holt.

"You in pain? Need some morphine?"

"No, I'm fine. Could use another smoke though. How's Ryan? Haven't heard a peep out of him."

Doc looked into Holt's eyes. "I told you, he's dead," he said quietly. "Yeah, dead. I remember now."

Doc looked up. "Your ride is here. I'll go get a stretcher. You'll be on your way to Cu Chi in no time."

Holt was carried to the waiting helicopter and slid inside. He saw them place Ryan's body next to him. He was wrapped in a poncho. One of Ryan's arms had come loose and lay on the floor. Holt reached over and held Ryan's hand for the whole ride back.

CHAPTER 24

Hoc Minh

Holt's arrival at the 12th Evacuation Hospital at Cu Chi was uneventful. He was rushed into surgery and his wounds were attended to with professional skill. In two weeks, he was healing nicely. Being mobile, he was encouraged to walk the hospital grounds, which he did on a regular basis. He asked about Lieutenant Green and was told she had been transferred to Cam Ranh Bay.

On his fourth day in the hospital, a colonel he didn't know came by to give him a Purple Heart medal. He started to get up but was told by a lieutenant to lay back down, that it would make for a better picture. In barely five minutes the ceremony was complete, and the colonel and his entourage left the ward.

He became a voracious reader and waited for the Red Cross Donut Dolly each day. Her arrival was proceeded by the sound of the squeaky wheels of her book cart. She was a cute, Irish girl with dark hair and piercing blue eyes.

He flirted with her every day, all to no avail. She did save the new arrival of books for him; he was reading a book a day.

He read everything. Kurt Vonnegut became a favorite author, along with Richard Brautigan and Dalton Trumbo. He read westerns by Louie L'Amour and Elmore Leonard and books on Buddhism, and all the classic Hemingway novels.

At 10 AM every morning he had physical therapy to strengthen his shoulder and chest muscles. After therapy, he would return to the ward, strip off his hospital pajamas, and sit outside in a pair of shorts and slippers and read. His skin darkened to a deep, rich walnut color.

Unexpectedly, Sangh came to visit him and they talked for two hours. Up to that point, Sangh was his only visitor.

In the afternoon, he would give himself a sponge bath and sit and write long letters to Janet.

He was content and in no hurry to return to his team.

After fifteen days Major Jung came to visit. He brought some magazines and a carton of Marlboro cigarettes. He found Holt sitting outside.

"I was here for a meeting and thought I'd stop by," he said.

"I appreciate it, Major. I was beginning to think you guys had forgotten about me."

"We're going through some changes back at base camp. I thought you might be interested. The cross border patrols are being put on hiatus for a while."

"Really?"

"Yes, really. Seems a cross border patrol into Laos captured a prisoner. Turns out he was Chinese. You can't imagine the diplomatic shit storm that erupted. We all know the North Vietnamese have Russian and Chinese advisers. Hell, there are even rumors of East Germans and Cubans up there. But they all swore they don't operate south of the DMZ. But we're not supposed to be in Laos and that's the problem. This guy is telling anyone who will listen that he was captured in Laos. We deny it of course, but—"

"So what happens now?"

"We behave ourselves for a month or two."

Holt lit a cigarette. "We've all heard the stories of the White Cong, left over French officers leading the VC in the South. And of course, there's the Black Cong, American deserters working for the Cong."

"I heard those stories too. But they're just rumors, this is fact."

"Where does that leave us?"

"By us, I guess you mean Team Viking? Viking is being disbanded. Evans is being assigned to an A Team in the Central Highlands and Doc Blaze is moving up to Battalion. Once you return to duty you'll be put on an A Team yourself."

"Am I being demoted?"

"Not at all. It's a lateral move. The A Teams are our primary business in the south. I'm just trying to find a good team for you. One other thing, during the debriefing, Evans really stood up for you. Told Top in no uncertain terms he stands behind all your decisions. He said without your leadership the entire team would have been lost. He told Top it wasn't his call to second guess a team leader in the field. By the way, Top got promoted to Sergeant Major. He's going up to Nha Trang to work at the Recondo school."

Holt nodded his head.

"One other thing. Two nights ago Sergeant Sangh left. He took about forty Bru fighters and twenty civilians with him. I heard he came to visit you? Do you know anything about his departure?"

"He may have mentioned something about taking some leave time."

"And it didn't occur to you to inform us?"

"Was he under some legal obligation to stay?"

"That's not the point."

"He told me a story. During the Khe Sanh siege there was a group of Special Forces and about three hundred Bru and a hundred South Vietnamese Rangers holding an outpost at Khe Sanh village which sat on Route 9, about three miles west of the combat base. They were attacked by the NVA 66th regiment. After several days of heavy bombardment and ground attacks, they were in imminent danger of being overrun. The Marines at the combat refused to come to their aid. They were on their own. So they broke out and fought their way to the Marines. When they reached the base, the Marines refused to let the Bru enter. The Special Forces and the South Vietnamese were allowed entry but the Bru were not. The Marines said they were afraid there were VC within their group. They were left outside the base with no defense's and most were killed by the NVA artillery. Men, women, and children. He said this wasn't the first time they were abandoned by the Americans. Now that Nixon is president and has begun the withdrawal of American troops, he fears it will happen again. The Americans will pull out and leave the Montagnards defenseless."

Holt paused to light a cigarette. "He said they have been persecuted by the North and South alike. Both the Japanese and the French have hunted them. They only allies they have ever known are the Green Berets and now we are planning to leave. He told me about a place deep in the mountains of Laos where they will go. He made it sound almost mythical, like Shangri- la. There the Bru will be safe. That's what he told me."

The Major stared at Holt intently. "Why did he tell you all this?" "He trusts me," he stated flatly. "I've known for months they have been stock piling weapons and ammunition. I didn't think it was any of my business. I'm new here, I thought it was business as usual. They've made and sold souvenirs for years. With that money they have prepared for their departure."

"Where did they get the weapons?"

"From dead North Vietnamese. They pick up the debris of war and kept it."

"All that should have been turned over to us." Holt shrugged.

"Did he leave any way to contact them?" the Major asked.

"Now that's the strange part. He was very mysterious. He said that if I ever wanted to join them, I would be able too."

"What do you think he meant by that?"

"Don't know. I never gave him any impression I did. He thinks I'm a man without a home, out of step with my own country. He said I would never be considered a real Green Beret, that I would always be considered an 'outsider.' And when I return to the states I would be let go. I agree. Top once referred to us recruits as 'shake and bake' berets. I know that at home I have no future with the Special Forces. I'm only useful here as another warm body. I've known that all along. It's been made clear to me by some of the old timers."

"You're probably right about that. That could change with the proper recommendations. And, I tend to agree with Sangh's assessment of you. I doubt if you'll be happy at home. Not after your experiences over here."

"You may be right."

"I don't understand any of this. You've only been here nine months. We have Special Forces that have been dealing with the Montagnards for years. Why come to you?"

"What makes you think I'm the only one they've confided in? There are a lot of guys over here that think the Bru have gotten a raw deal. Maybe more than you think."

"I want you to get in touch with him."

"And how would you suggest I do that? And if I could, what would I say to them? Is he wrong? Do we have any plans to help them when we pull out? Are we going to take them home with us?"

The Major lit his own cigarette, took one puff and threw it to the ground. He ground it out with his boot. Holt reached down and put the butt in the coffee can he used as an ashtray.

"If this rebellion spreads we're in deep shit. All our camps are manned by the Montagnards," the Major said.

"'Rebellion'? I would hardly call this a rebellion. It's a little late in the game to be thinking about this. This had to cross your mind. I know you trust and admire the Montagnards. Aren't you concerned about what's going to happen to them?"

"Why now? What prompted this?"

"Phang's death really tore up Sangh. Maybe that was the flash point for him."

"This conversation isn't over. The doctors said you'd be released in two weeks. Get back to base camp and I'll have your next assignment ready for you."

When the Major left, the Red Cross girl poked her head through the door.

"Danni," Holt exclaimed, visibly brightening. "I was hoping you'd come by today."

"I have some new books for you."

"So, you were thinking of me. I knew you liked me."

"I like your interest in books. I don't know you well enough to like or dislike you."

"You have to get to know me better. I'm really a very nice guy."

"Your conversation with the Major seemed very intense."

"Oh him. He's an asshole, a well-meaning asshole but an asshole none the less. Being an officer and being an asshole are synonymous."

"I have the equivalent rank of a second lieutenant. Does that make me an asshole?"

"I don't know you well enough to make that determination," Holt said using her own words against her. "That's why we should get better acquainted. Have dinner with me."

"I don't date enlisted men."

"It wouldn't be a date; it would just be dinner."

"It's out of the question."

Holt's eyes turned down and his face pouted.

"It's my face, the scars, isn't it?"

"Oh for God's sake, that's pathetic. How many times have you used that line? Has it ever worked?"

"It hasn't yet. It's a work in progress and needs to be refined. In a couple of weeks I'll be returning to my unit; can I write to you?"

"I thought you were married?" "Divorced."

"You're awfully young to be divorced."

"You see how interesting I am. I'm like an onion consisting of many layers."

"Well, I won't be peeling off any layers in the near future. I'll see you tomorrow Sergeant Holt. You should stay out of the sun. You're getting dark enough to be a native."

As she walked through the door she stopped and looked back over her shoulder.

"Do you have a first name, Sergeant?"

"Yes, maim, I do. It's Donald."

"That's a nice name, you should use it more often."

"It's a good name for a duck."

Two weeks later, Holt was released from the hospital. On his last day, Danni gave Holt a present. It was a new copy of Farley Mowat's book, 'Never Cry Wolf.' Inside there was an inscription wishing him well and a slip of paper with her military APO address.

He boarded a helicopter to Camp Katum and arrived at 1400 hours. He walked to the command post and asked the clerk where Major Jung was. He was told that the Major was unavailable and he should report to the first sergeant.

"Hey, where is Robbie, the clerk that was here before?" asked Holt.

"Don't know any Robbie. The First Sergeant's office is back there."

Holt knocked on the door frame and entered the office. He placed his orders on the desk.

"Sergeant Holt, reporting for duty."

"Stand at ease, Sergeant."

Top read his orders. "Holt! What kind of fucking name is Holt?"

"No idea, Top. It's American, I guess."

"It don't sound American."

Holt stared at Top's name tag stitched onto his shirt above his right pocket. It was about thirty letters long and seemed to contain every letter in the alphabet.

"Do you find me particularly attractive, Sergeant?"

Holt was startled. "What?"

"I said 'do you think I am attractive?'"

"I really don't have an opinion. You're okay, I guess."

"Then why the fuck are you staring at me, Sergeant?"

"Oh, I was trying to read your name."

"My name to you is Top. Quit fucking eyeballing me."

The First Sergeant paged through Holt's file.

"This is your third year over here. What is fucking wrong with you? Why aren't you back home fucking college girls." Holt looked perplexed.

"Don't bother to answer that. I'm really not interested. The Major will be back at 1600 . Report back to him. You can leave your gear out front."

Holt thought about going down to Mama San's bar in the village, but realized he didn't have enough time. Instead, he went to the NCO club and had two large ice teas and a cheese burger.

At 1600 hours he stood before Major Jung.

"You met with our new First Sergeant? First impressions?"

"Well, he didn't threaten to rip off my head and piss down my neck. That was promising."

The Major chuckled. "He's old school, you gotta love him."

"He's delightful. Intense, yet warm and caring. We should treasure him."

The Major shuffled through some papers on his desk and handed Holt his orders.

"You're being assigned to team 107, call sign Boston. They are up at a place called Hoc Minh, two kilometers east of the Cambodian border. You head one squad and your friend Joe Jenkins will head the other. The squad leader positions are usually E-7's, but we are short on them right now. The team is led by Master Sergeant Cox who is about to retire. The team and the camp is under the command of your old platoon leader, Lieutenant Mason, newly appointed to Captain. He joined us about two months ago. This will be his first command with us. I hope you help him out in any way possible."

"Sounds good, Sir."

"The team leads a Mike Force of forty to sixty Montagnards so you'll be right at home. Your squad is a mix of experienced men and new guys. Your gear is packed and waiting for you at the supply room. Your flight leaves at 0900 so you can get it in the morning. You can meet up with Captain Mason at the officers club at 1800 hours. You'll be allowed in to meet with him. Any questions?"

"No sir. Nothing right now."

"I have one. Where are all your medals and citations? They weren't in your locker."

"I send all that stuff home to my ex. She said she'll hold on to them for me."

"Very well. You are dismissed Sergeant. Good luck at Hoc Minh."

"I do have one more question, Major. What happened to Robbie?"

"He was getting short so I transferred him down to MACV, it's the Military Assistance Command Vietnam, in Saigon. It gives him a chance to sell all his stuff before he goes home."

"Yes sir. I know what MACV is. Thank you."

Holt arrived at the club and was stopped at the door by a large, black Sergeant. He was allowed to enter when he explained he was meeting someone and was expected.

The officers club were much nicer than the enlisted mans club or the NCO club. The table and chairs matched, the bar was a real bar not one constructed out of wood planks and crates, and the best thing of all, it was air conditioned. The waitresses were young and dressed in western clothes.

He saw Captain Mason sitting at a table by himself. He walked over and greeted the Captain warmly.

"Congratulations on your promotion, Captain. It's well deserved. I have to ask though, how did you end up here?"

"Same as you I suppose. Major Jung recruited me."

"Have you met our First Sergeant?"

Mason laughed. "Yes, I had the pleasure. He said I was a young and wet behind the ears pup who had better listen to and take the advice of my NCO's if I wanted to stay alive. I assured him I would."

"Major Jung says he's old school. I guess that explains a lot. I'm glad we'll be working together again."

"Yeah, Hoc Minh. I haven't heard too much about it except that it's a real shithole. Can't argue; it's my first real independent command. What have you heard?"

"It sits across a major NVA infiltration route. Gets shelled nightly. Has a bit of a morale problem. The men there feel like they have been abandoned."

"There's supposed to be a warrant officer and a master sergeant to help run the A Team. I doubt I'll get involved much with you guys. There is also a artillery lieutenant who doubles as the executive officer to help with camp operations. I guess I'll play it by ear and see what happens."

A waitress came by and took their drink order. She was slim and very attractive. Her long, black hair was pulled back in a loose pony tail. She wore a western style sundress with yellow and pink flowers on it. The top two buttons were undone exposing a hint of cleavage. Holt breathed in deeply.

As she left Holt said, "My God, she smells great."

"I would imagine she reports back everything she hears to the NVA."

"I'm well aware of that. It's an unfortunate fact of life over here. These poor people are caught between two opposing factions. They do what they got to do to survive. So let me ask you, are you making the Army a career?"

The Captain snorted. "No, definitely not. I got eighteen months left. This assignment will look good on my resume. Plus, I think I'll look good in a beret. How about you?"

"I haven't thought that far ahead. I got about twenty-two months left. Plenty of time to make that decision."

Their drinks arrived. When the waitress left they resumed their conversation.

"How's your wife?" the Captain asked.

"Ex wife. She's okay. She writes me and I write her, that's about it. If I remember, you're married, right?"

"Yes I am. When I told her on leave that I was coming back as a Green Beret she wasn't too thrilled. I explained it was safer than being in a line company. I won't be going out with you guys. I stay in the rear with the gear."

"That's something, knowing you're there looking out for us."

They ordered another round of drinks and some cheeseburgers.

"Did you hear about that chink they caught up north?" Holt said.

The Captain looked around before replying. "The big brass are terrified that China will enter the war like they did in Korea. They got three hundred thousand men on their border with North Vietnam."

"The North Vietnamese hate the Chinese as much as they hate us. They got bad history with China. They'll take all they can get from China but they don't want China directly involved in the war. They'll just end up fighting them when we're gone."

The conversation turned to Delta Company. The Captain filled him in on all the men they knew. They both teared up when discussing Sergeant Camp.

After several more drinks, Holt said he had to go.

"I have to find a place to sleep tonight and get my gear squared away. I'll see you in the morning at chow. It's great to see you again. I really mean that."

"Get a good night's sleep, Sergeant."

CHAPTER 25

The Dog Bone

Holt met Captain Mason in the mess hall at 0730 hours. They sat together drinking coffee.

"Major Jung says my first assignment is to give him a no bullshit assessment as to whether the camp should remain open," Mason said. "It's ironic that the first decision I have to make about my first command is whether to end my command."

"Maybe he's just playing with your head. I guarantee that he's already made his decision about whether to keep the camp open or not. Maybe he wants to see what you come up with on your own."

"The higher you get in rank, the more bullshit you have to deal with. Nothing is straight forward. Everyone is playing games. You're always being assessed to gauge your potential for advancement, especially, if you're an officer."

"I don't have that worry. I have at least three years before my next promotion. And in three years, who knows where we'll be. Nixon says he's going to end the war. His political career depends on doing it."

Mason looked at his watch. "It's about time we head over to the airfield. You have all your stuff?"

"I'm like a fucking turtle; everything I own is on my back. I got all my combat gear in my pack and all my clothing in my duffel bag. I'm all set."

Outside the mess hall, a young specialist waited for them in a jeep. Holt noticed the drivers fatigues were pressed.

"The new First Sergeant wants everyone to wear pressed fatigues in base camp," the driver said to the unasked question.

"You're new here yourself?" said Holt.

"Just graduated Special Forces training at Fort Bragg. I've only been here a few days."

"How old are you?"

"Nineteen. When I got here, Top made me the Major's driver."

Holt leaned forward and said to the Captain, "According to Top, that makes him more of a Green Beret than you or me."

"Hey, what's that supposed to mean?" the driver asked.

"Nobody was talking to you. Mind your own fucking business," Holt growled.

The driver put the jeep in gear and jolted forward sending Holt back against the seat.

"Stop the fucking jeep," Holt said. He got out and replaced the driver and drove off leaving the driver running after them.

"Fucking little weasel, pencil dick. Can you imagine this bullshit, pressed fatigues."

The Captain laughed. "This should be an interesting assignment. I forgot how much fun you could be."

At the air strip they pulled up next to a waiting helicopter.

"This our ride?" asked Holt to a soldier lounging in the doorway.

"If you're going to Hoc Minh, it is."

Holt threw his rucksack and duffel bag into the cargo hold which was stacked high with cartons of C-rations and crates of ammunition. He took the Captain's gear and did the same.

"We're running late. The co-pilot got the shits and we're waiting for his replacement," the door gunner said. "Shouldn't be too long. Help yourself to some cold drinks."

Holt fished a can of ice tea out of a cooler and watched indifferently as the driver staggered up to them.

"Why did you have to do that?" the driver said as he gasped for air. "I'm all sweaty now and will have to change my fatigues."

"I did that to teach you to show the proper respect. Do I look like some fucking REMF that you can mess with?"

"I didn't mean anything—"

Holt cut him off. "Get out of here. Next time you'll know better."

The door gunner laughed and lit up a cigarette. "So, what did you guys do to get assigned to the Bone?"

"The Bone?" Holt asked.

"Yeah, everyone calls Hoc Minh the 'Dog Bone.'"

"Why?"

"You'll see once we get there. So, are you being punished?"

"Not that I'm aware of."

"If the asshole of the world had its own asshole, that would be Hoc Minh."

"I don't understand," the Captain said, "it holds the high ground, doesn't it."

"It's on a hill, a big hill. It's about three hundred fifty feet high. Unfortunately, it's surrounded by bigger hills and all those hills are held by the NVA. That's why it gets shelled, mortared, and rocketed every day and night. We fly up there every other day and every time we land we catch shit. Usually, it's mortars and small arms fire. Just look at this ship as an example; it's been hit over eighty times by bullets and shrapnel."

Holt and the Captain saw the numerous patches of hundred MPH tape and riveted aluminum panels covering the body.

"This old girl is going to be taken out of service soon. She needs a complete overhaul. The tail boom is ready to fall off," he said as he patted the side affectionately.

"The co-pilots door is all shot to shit," Mason noted.

"Yeah, his side amour saved him that day. Back here I got a half inch steel plate welded to the floor. Gotta protect the family jewels," the gunner said, grabbing his crotch. "Oh goody, here comes the officers, fashionably late as always."

The pilot and co-pilot stepped out of the jeep, two young warrant officers in their early twenties. Each had long drooping mustaches and hair way beyond regulation length.

Holt nudged the Captain and pointed out the large Grateful Dead, 'Steal Your Face' decal. on the back of the pilot's helmet.

"Okay, gentlemen, lets load up and get flying," the pilot said.

"Where do we sit?" asked Mason.

"We're carrying a full load today. You'll have squeeze in on the left side. One of you will have to sit on the floor and the other gets the bench. I'll land going uphill and you'll jump out," the pilot said.

"Jump out?" asked Mason.

"Bobby, explain to these guys the landing procedure while we do the pre-flight check. Where's Carl?" the pilot said referring to the crew chief.

"Taking a dump. Here he comes now."

Holt and Mason squeezed in next to the C-rations.

The door gunner walked up to them. "We'll land on a slope of land. It's like a finger that runs from the base camp down to the valley floor. We can't actually set down because of the slope. You'll have to jump out. When you hit the ground run straight ahead and get your asses in the ditch. They'll be somebody there to guide you to the camp and help with your gear. We then fly over the camp and push all this shit out. You got five seconds to un-ass the ship. If we spend more than a minute over the camp that's a lot. You got all that?"

"This should be interesting," Holt said.

"I can't believe no one told you about the Bone. It's a mini Khe Sanh. You guys are under siege up there. You sure you didn't piss anybody off to get this assignment?"

Holt just smiled and lit a cigarette. As he settled in, he noticed where the floor had been hammered down over several bullets holes.

The door gunner got into his body armor over his Nomex, fire retardant flight suit, and climbed into his compartment.

The pilot started the helicopter and it rocked back and forth as the blades gained momentum. The door gunner leaned out of his compartment and looked backwards as the helicopter backed out of its parking space. The pilot drifted sideways over the runway and turned the ship into the wind. Being heavily loaded as they were, the pilot dropped the nose and proceeded down the runway gaining speed. He then gently lifted the helicopter, gained altitude, and turned west.

Holt looked at the door gunner who was moving his head to the sounds of the AFVN, the Armed Forces Vietnam radio station which played the top forty. With his helmet on and the tinted visor down, he looked like a giant insect.

Captain Mason nudged Holt's foot and pointed ahead.

Holt turned and saw the co-pilots helmet. It had a large sticker on the back that said, 'Stop Screaming, I'm Scared Too.'

They flew at three thousand feet. Holt marveled at the lush, green jungle beneath them. Occasionally, they passed over villages surrounded by the square geometric patterns of rice paddies. It looked like nothing had changed in hundreds of years.

After about twenty minutes the gunner shouted into Captain Mason's ear.

"The pilot is going to circle the base a couple of times so you get the lay of the land."

The base was on top of a hill that looked like an enormous, upended pound cake plopped dead center in a valley. Larger hills surrounded the camp, some as close as a half mile. A large stream ran down the valley floor from Cambodia into Vietnam. To the south side of the stream was wide dirt road. The valley floor was pockmarked by over lapping bomb craters.

From this view it was obvious why it was called the Dog Bone. The base was a large rectangle sitting east to west. At each corner of the rectangle were circular concrete bunkers.

The hills south of the camp twinkled with bright lights followed by the lazy arc of green tracer rounds searching out the helicopter.

"Your welcoming committee," the gunner shouted as he fired his M-60 machine gun at the flashes of light.

The pilot turned the helicopter back towards the base, lining up on the grassy finger of land that lead up to the camp. As he neared the ground and slowed, the door gunner shouted, "Get out, get out! Jump now!"

Holt grabbed his duffel bag and jumped from the helicopter followed by the Captain. He hit the ground and rolled. He got to his feet and was momentarily disorientated. He saw the ditch and ran for it. Machine gun bullets snapped over his head. Several mortar rounds exploded showering them with dirt.

They huddled in the ditch until greeted by a young specialist.

"Welcome to the end of the world. Follow me," he said, leading them up the trench. He made no offer to help with their bags.

Holt could see the helicopter hovering over the camp with boxes and crates being kicked from the doors. In less than a minute it was gone.

Mercifully, the machine gun fire and mortars ended.

They made their way down the trench and a barb wire barricade was pushed aside. As they entered the compound, they were confronted by a flurry of activity. Men swarmed the helicopter drop zone bringing the C-rations into a supply hut and others loaded crates of ammunition into the armory. A clerk came out of the TOC, grabbed the red mail bag, and scurried back inside. As he entered two men emerged. One was tall and gaunt and the other, by contrast was, was beefy and short. They walked up to Mason and Holt. The heavy set man wore fatigue pants and a dark green t-shirt, He was constantly was looking around, his eyes darting back and forth, and sweating profusely. The painfully thin man wore shorts and a dark brown t-shirt, stained with sweat.

The thin man extended his hand. "Hi, I'm First Lieutenant Thomas Greer. I'm head of the artillery detachment and I guess, also, your executive officer. You can call me Spider, everyone does."

Mason thought the nickname was appropriate given his appearance and was surprised to hear the name came from a famous basketball player.

"Do you play basketball?" Mason asked.

"No, I never have. I did a little research. Couldn't find any basketball player named Spider. Maybe they call me spider because I'm slender."

Slender would be an exaggeration; he was a skeleton covered with skin.

"And you?" Mason asked the other man.

"I'm Master Sergeant James Cox. But you don't need to know my name. I got six days left in this shithole and I'm gone. And I don't plan on being above ground for any of those six days."

Someone dropped a carton and startled the sergeant. "In fact, I've been out in the open for too long. The Lieutenant here can show you around." He went back inside the TOC.

"What's his story?"

"Like he said, he only has six days left here. He's really jumpy."

"Isn't he supposed to be in charge of the A Team?"

"Is he? I didn't know that. We only got the A Team about a week ago. I thought your man was in charge."

"This is Staff Sergeant Holt," Mason said. It was the first time Holt was acknowledged. "I guess maybe he is in charge."

Holt nodded in greeting to the Lieutenant.

"What does the Master Sergeant do then?"

"Uh, that's a good question. He handles communication and logistics I guess. Look, maybe we should go inside and continue this conversation. The gooks might mortar us again."

"Does that happen often?"

"All the time. No set schedule. Day and night. The mortars and the rockets we can handle, but they have big guns set up across the border. That's the real worry. Come on inside and I'll show you your quarters."

Mason turned to Holt. "Sergeant you'd better come along, you can meet the team later."

The Lieutenant led the way. They passed through a two inch steel reinforced door that opened effortlessly and silently. Inside Mason was pleasantly surprised. The TOC was clean, neat, and orderly. Light bulbs hung from the ceiling enclosed in wire cages.

"Most of the buildings were part of an old French fort. The TOC here is built with four foot reinforced concrete walls and ceilings. Most everything else is the same way. That's your desk straight in front. Mine is to your left. Your quarters are over there, through that door in the corner"

He opened the door into a spacious room. To the right was a bed with a real mattress hung with mosquito netting. Opposite it was a desk fashioned out of a sheet of plywood. Against the wall were two lockers with shelving between them and a foot locker. The Captain placed his bags on the bed and they returned to the TOC.

"Did you notice? You have your own radio and a mini fridge?" "Yes, very nice. What's this over here?" the Captain said pointing to a thin cabinet laying across two saw horses.

The Lieutenant produced a key and opened the cabinet. The cabinet was about four feet long by three feet wide. It was bordered with three inch walls and covered by a hinged top. The inside was painted white and a large scale rendering of the entire camp was drawn with meticulous detail. There were numerous red switches placed throughout the board.

"This is the command detonation board. This is a detailed drawing of the camp. Those switches control charges placed strategically at various places. In

255

case the gooks break through you can flip a switch and blow shit up. Here you can see the four circular bunkers at each corner. The bunkers have C-4 charges placed in each of them. Inside the circle is a switch. You flip the switch and the bunker will be destroyed. The other switches are for the various structures in the camp. This is top secret. No one outside the TOC knows the camp is wired to self destruct. You and I have the only keys to the cabinet."

"Jesus, what if you bump a switch by mistake?"

"The board isn't armed yet. To arm the board you have to flip this master switch under this protective red cover. Once the board is armed, you'll see all the lights. Each light is a charge."

The Lieutenant handed Mason a key on a chain.

"Wear this around your neck twenty four seven. Never take it off. I guess it's alright your Sergeant knows about this, but he can't tell anyone."

"I'm standing right here. You can speak to me," said Holt.

"No offense intended."

"None taken."

"Sergeant Holt, are you one of those new recruited Green Berets?" asked Master Sergeant Cox.

"Yes, I am."

"The Special Forces are going to hell I tell you. I joined up during World War Two. Now that was a war. Served in Korea too. Fought the chinks. Now here in Vietnam. Don't know what to call this shit. How many languages do you speak?"

"English, that's about it."

"I speak fluent German and passable Russian."

"That must be very useful over here," Holt said indifferently.

"Young fucking pups, think they know it all," Cox said walking back to his desk.

"What was that about?" asked Mason.

"Ignore him. Like I said, he's jumpy. If we could get back to the board. The south and west walls are manned by our Montagnard contingent, about two hundred men. The north and east walls are under the command of two companies of South Vietnamese Rangers. Both groups have American advisor's attached to them. We hardly ever see those guys. They live with their troops. This bunker here, the one with the chain link fence around it, has some Air Force guys in it. Again, we never see those guys. I assume they monitor enemy radio traffic. Their bunker isn't wired for destruction. If we get over run they're on their own. Any questions, so far?"

"How about re-supply?"

"Oddly enough we're not lacking in anything. We have tons of ammo and food. The only thing we're always short of is water. We're on strict water rationing here. We have rain barrels set up all over the place. I haven't had a decent shower in over thirty days. I take a whore's bath every night, you know, wash my pits and crotch and that's it. When it rains, you'll see the guys come out of their holes and scrub down. I don't enforce shaving or haircuts. I don't care what you wear as long as you do your job. I hope you won't be introducing any changes in that regard."

"Like I said, it's all going to hell and back. In my day we shaved everyday using ice water."

They all turned to look at the Master Sergeant.

"It looks like he hasn't shaved in two weeks," commented Mason.

"He does keep his hair close cropped though," the Lieutenant said.

"I can hear you. I keep my hair short so I don't get lice. One guy gets them, we all do."

"Is lice a problem?" Mason said to Greer.

"No. Not that I know of."

"What are the problems here?"

"Boredom. There is nothing to do. Most men are here on a thirty day rotational basis but I swear they have forgotten about us. Some guys have been here over ninety days. We did have the beginnings of a drug problem but we squashed that quick. Drugs will not be tolerated in any form. Any new guy coming in, his bags are searched. All personal packages received are subject to search."

"Is that legal?"

"Who cares? They can file a complaint with the Inspector General when they leave here. We don't have a race problem. Blacks and whites get along fine. The South Vietnamese are another story. They hate the Montagnards and the Yards hate them. Two weeks ago the Viet's shot a Montagnard that wandered into their area. In reprisal, the yards showered them with grenades killing four. Since then, the South Vietnamese refuse to leave the camp. Any patrolling is done by the Montagnards and they have to be bullied into going out. But now that your A Team is here maybe things will change."

"If no one will leave the camp, what purpose do we serve here?"

"To stop infiltration from Cambodia. Occasionally, we get calls to fire artillery support. But there are bigger bases that can handle that. Just by being here we have stopped all traffic on the road down there. So I guess we have stopped supplies coming across the border, at least in this area."

"I've been told that this camp is indefensible."

"Oh, we can defend ourselves. We have plenty of fire power, but if the gooks really wanted this camp they could take it. The only thing stopping them is our artillery and the air power we have available. We're not situated in the best of places. We have larger hills all around us and the NVA hold most of them. The hills get shelled and bombed on a regular basis but the gooks are dug in so well it really doesn't affect them. They've been working on their defenses since World War II. It would take a massive ground assault to drive them out. A real Iwo Jima type of assault and the brass in Saigon aren't going to risk massive casualties at this stage of the war. At least, not here."

"Do you want to give me a tour of the outside now?"

"Let's take a break. In honor of your arrival we got a barbeque for lunch, just cheeseburgers and stuff like that. Usually, we exist on C-rations so this is special. The men are really looking forward to it."

"Alright, we'll continue after lunch."

CHAPTER 26

Bombs And Boredom

As Holt walked to the team barracks he was amazed to see the evidence of the enemy bombardment of the camp. Every concrete structure showed the effects of shrapnel and bullet strikes.

One building had the corner blown out. Large chunks of concrete lay like tumbled blocks on the ground. Twisted rods of rusting rebar re- enforcement jutted from the sides. The ground was uneven with craters hastily filled in with gravel and dirt. Sandbags were slashed by shrapnel spilling dirt onto the ground. One smaller bunker was completely destroyed, its roof caved in and the steel door hanging off its hinges, scorched by fire. As he neared the teams living quarters he was apprehensive of the minimal protection it had. There were four rows of sand bags stacked about four foot high running around the perimeter. The roof was nothing more than thin sheets of corrugated, galvanized, rusted steel plating. As he opened the door, the hinges squealed in protest. Inside it was dark and smelled of mildew, sweat, and cigarette smoke. The room was filled with men dressed in shorts or Army issued green skivvies and little else.

His friend, Staff Sergeant, Joe Jenkins hollered a greeting.

"Don, how are you? Welcome to the bone."

He rushed forward and extended his hand.

"Jesus, this place is a fucking dump. What did you do to get sent here?"

"Who knows. C'mon, let's get you settled in. Your bunk is back here," Jenkins said, grabbing Holt's duffle from him. "My squad is on the left and yours is on the right."

As they passed the men, Holt nodded in greeting. The men appeared indifferent to Holt's arrival.

"We're right through here," Jenkins said indicating a doorway which led into another room. "I'm over here and I got you set up on the right. Bunk, mattress, two wall lockers and a foot locker. I also scrounged up a helmet and flak jacket for you. I figured you wouldn't have any yourself."

"Helmets and flak jackets, what the fuck?"

"Believe me you'll wear them when you're walking outside. You never know when the gooks are going to shell us."

"That happens a lot?"

"Every fucking day. Sometimes, like today, a half dozen shells, other days two or three hundred shells."

"You're shitting me?"

"Last week, just after we got here, we were shelled for three hours. I thought I'd go insane. Scared the fucking crap out me. The gook have howitzers across the border. Big motherfuckers. Russian made, 152 MM, ML-20's. They got a range of over seventeen kilometers. They sit just past the fourteen kilometer boundary and fire away at us. They got forward observers and radios up in the hills. They got us zeroed in by now. We can't fire back since they're beyond the fourteen klick's self imposed limit."

"Shit. So what do you do?"

"We sit in the bunker and pray. By the way, our bunker is right through the back door. If the shelling starts, run quick or you'll get trampled by the stampede. Everybody comes right through here. We keep working on the bunker adding more sand bag layers and wooden flooring but it's still a hell hole. Stinks like rat turds and piss."

"How are the guys?"

"I was able to pick my own team and I picked out yours too. They're a good bunch. Most of them are Fort Bragg trained. You might catch an attitude about that shit at first. But I did my best and told them all about you. They got a few patrols under their belts but I would say limited combat experience."

"I guess I should meet the men."

"Go ahead, I'll start unpacking your bag if that's okay?"

"That's fine Joe. Appreciate it," Holt said as he started for the barracks proper. He stopped and turned back. "Hey what's the story with that Master Sergeant Cox?"

"Who the fuck knows. Met him once when we first got here. He stays in the TOC. Tells everybody he's too short and isn't taking any more chances. We're on our own here."

As Holt entered the barracks he saw that there were eight bunks on each side, only ten were occupied. There were two large picnic tables and benches in the center of the room. Bare light bulbs were strung from the center rafter. A mismatched variety of lamps and fans were around each bunk. Homemade shelves housed radios, paperback books and magazines. He did notice one luxury, a large electric refrigerator sat in the back next to a door. Inside, it was stocked with soda and beer.

"You guys want to gather around and I'll introduce myself," Holt said, sitting at one of the tables. "My name is Staff Sergeant Holt. Like Sergeant Jenkins, I'm an in country recruit into the Special Forces. If that's a problem with any of you, please feel free to shove that straight up your ass. This is my third year in Vietnam. Just by looking at me you can tell I've been in the shit. To me, you're all are FNG's until you prove different. You can think of me as an FNG if you want. I have to prove myself to you just as well. I'm not interested in your names or life stories now, that will come in time. What I do need to know is who is my RTO?"

A young, blond kid raised his hand. "I am Sarge, Specialist Donnelly, Jack Donnelly."

"Alright Jack nice to meet you. We'll be working close together. One thing I want to emphasize, our primary job is to survive this place. I don't want to hear any bullshit about love for God and our country; no flag-waving crap. To the higher ups we're just expendable pieces they move around a big board. I consider you my brother and I'll do my best to get you home in one piece. Your life comes first and the mission second. There is no fucking mission at this stage of the war that's worth dying for. Any questions? None? Okay, good. I'll leave you guys alone and you can discuss what an asshole I am. That's okay, I expect that.

Hopefully, your opinion will change. One other thing, is that soda and beer for everyone?"

"It's for the barracks, Sarge," Jack said. "We all chip in. Help yourself."

Holt got out his wallet and peeled off a ten dollar MPC note and put it on the table. "Here's my contribution."

As Holt walked back to his room, he stopped and got two cans of RC cola.

He tossed one can to Jenkins and asked, "The bottles of Jack?" "In your foot locker."

Jenkins got two canteen cups and handed one to Holt. Holt poured a healthy shot into each and added some cola.

"So, did you hear? What did you think?"

"You did good. You addressed all the issues. You were firm but—"he paused and wiggled his hand— "but not too firm. They're good guys. They all are. We'll get along fine."

"It's the same speech I give all the new guys, almost word for word."

"They'll warm up to you. It won't be a problem."

"The Captain said something about a barbeque? I guess in the mess tent where ever that is."

"They cook sometimes. We mostly eat C-rats. No one gathers together. Creates too big of a target. I'll send two guys over to grab the burgers and whatever else they got. We'll eat here."

"Sounds good. After chow, maybe you can give me the nickel tour so I can get the lay of the land."

"Absolutely."

"I have to tell you, Joe. I'm glad you're here. It's nice to have a friend."

"Who said anything about being your friend? Why do you keep saying that?"

They sat around the picnic table eating cheeseburgers and drinking pop. The men were subdued around the two senior Sergeants. They mainly chatted amongst themselves.

Jenkins spoke up and recounted the story of Holt's last mission. Of how they were surrounded and hopelessly outnumbered and how Jenkins arrived in the nick of time to save Holt's life.

As the story progressed, Holt looked away and rolled his eyes.

"That story is a perfect example of what I was saying earlier," Holt said. "According to Top, we should have evaded the gooks and stayed out. I think that old fuck has forgotten what it's like to be running for your life. It was my decision to make and I took the heat for it. That's probably why I ended up here."

A few of the men nodded solemnly.

"You've seen a lot of action Sarge?" asked a kid who introduced himself as Phillip Humphrey. Humphrey had a lilting Jamaican accent, caramel colored skin, soft curly hair and the brightest green eyes Holt had ever seen.

"The biggest was at the old French Fort when I was with the Wolfhounds. That's where I got this," Holt said pointing to his face.

"Holy shit, that was you? We all read about that back at Bragg in the Stars and Stripes," said Humphrey, who Holt found out was the teams medic. "The article said eighteen guys held out for a week and ended up killing over three hundred NVA soldiers."

"There might be some exaggeration there. We did have artillery and air support," Holt said.

"That's some crazy Alamo shit," said a young E-5 sergeant named Eugene 'Gino' Butler, another member of Holt's team. "Didn't they give you the Congressional Medal of Honor?"

"No, not hardly," Holt laughed. "Over a open channel, I disobeyed a direct order. Everybody heard it. Fucking Major wanted me Court Martialed."

"What was the order?" asked Charley Pratt, a rifleman on Holt's team. "The fucking, scumbag Major wanted us to leave the wounded behind and make a run for it. To a man, all eighteen of us said no. When I told him, he went ballistic."

"What a prick," said Paul Woods, the fifth and final member of Holt's reduced A Team.

"Yeah, he was a grade A moron. In the end, he was relieved of his command."

Holt pushed himself away from the table. "Joe's going to give me a tour of this toilet. We'll talk later. Ready Joe?"

"Yeah, grab your flak jacket."

They left the teams talking amongst themselves.

Holt grabbed his web gear, flak jacket, and CAR 15 carbine. He placed a worn and battered helmet on his head and met Jenkins at the front door.

"Jesus, Joe, this jacket smells like BO. You couldn't find a clean one?" "It's the best I could find. You'll smell like the rest of us. The tour starts right here. See these plastic barrels at each corner, fifty gallons each. They're built three feet off the ground and the roof gutters run right into them. The water tastes rusty from the roof panels. We mainly use this for washing and shaving. We plan to enclose them in sand bags. Back there is Spider's pride and joy. Our latrine. Notice, you don't smell any shit burning? Spider had the engineers dig a twenty foot deep trench. He built the latrine around the trench. It's an eight hole masterpiece. Once a week we throw some lime in it. No smell and no shit burning. It's his own design of a septic system. The ARVN's and the Yards got their own latrines. This one is just for the Americans. There are piss tubes all over the camp. You saw the TOC. On either side is the supply bunker and the medical bunker.

Next to the medical bunker is the kitchen. It's not often anyone cooks for us. Like I said, we mainly eat C's and LURP rations."

"How big is the camp?" Holt asked.

"It's about fifteen hundred feet long and four hundred feet wide. Running down the middle are the four gun pits for the howitzers. We got two 105's and two 155MM howitzers. On either end are two more pits for our big mortars, two 81MM's. The artillery guys got their own bunkers dug in around the guns."

Joe pointed to the camps corner. "At each corner is a circular concrete bunker. They give the camp its nickname. Those fuckers take a beating. The ARVN's man two and the Yards man two."

"Who built this place?"

"The French back in the fifties. They did a decent job; the concrete on the bunkers is three to four feet thick. They just picked a lousy place. The hills overlook us. Those hills to the south and the west are infested with NVA. The north and east sides aren't as bad. Did Spider tell you the South Vietnamese Rangers won't leave the camp?"

"He mentioned that. Said that the Montagnards and them got into it a while back."

"That was some wild west cowboy shit. The Yards run some patrols, but only at night. They claim the NVA are digging trenches up to the camp. We tried running some patrols in the daylight but as soon as we stepped outside the wire we got mortared. Now, we just sit on our asses."

"Why would anyone want this shithole?" Holt said.

"It overlooks that road in the valley. At night, sometimes, you can hear the trucks coming in from Cambodia. We fire up flares and the artillery guys shoot at them but when we do the gooks in the hills pound us. They want us to stay in our holes like good little rats."

"What's that?" Holt said indicating a large bunker surrounded by chain link fence.

"Let's walk a bit. Don't stand in one spot for any length of time. They got snipers out there. They're not too good but you never know."

"That's gotta be more than nine hundred yards. They would have to be excellent shots."

They started walking towards the fenced in bunker.

"This is the spook shack. See all the antennas on top. Supposed to be run by the Air Force but you never see the guys. When you do, they're all wearing civilian clothes or fatigues with no patches. They have their own supply choppers and their own generator. Speaking of generators, I have to show you Spiders other accomplishment."

They walked to the back of the TOC where a large squat bunker sat.

"We got two industrial diesel engines that run the generator. They alternate running twenty four hours a day. They're encased in four feet of reinforced concrete. On top of that there are four stacks of sand bags. They fly in diesel fuel one a week."

Holt looked around. "You know, this isn't that bad of a place. If the gooks ever wanted to take it, it would cost them."

"Spider is a weird fuck but he really does his job. We got more ammo than we could ever use. We have C-Rations stockpiled. The only thing we don't have is water. They can't bring in enough. Even with all the rain barrels, we're always running short."

"Too bad we can't pump it up from the stream below."

"I'm sure Spider has thought of that."

Off to the left, in the hills, several sparks of light caught their attention.

"Oh shit! Incoming!" shouted Jenkins.

They started to run back to their barracks when the first shells hit. The explosions were deafening and the concussive wave knocked them to the ground. They were covered in a cloud of dirt. The shells came in groups of three. The next three blasts landed in front of the artillery pits.

"It's not their artillery. It's their mortars. They got a shit load of Chinese 82 mm's. Over here, there's a trench," Joe shouted.

They got up and ran to a trench leading from one of the gun pits. They threw themselves into the trench and lay flat on the bottom.

Outside, there were three more blasts that shook the earth. The ground heaved beneath them. Their bodies rose from the ground and were thrown back down. They could hear the sizzle of shrapnel slicing through the air. Another volley was fired and they were thrown against the sides of the trench. Suddenly, there was four deafening booms as the base's howitzers answered the mortars. The vibrations of the big guns rippled through the ground and shook dirt from the trench's sides on them.

After what seemed like hours but was only minutes, the shelling stopped. The camp guns continued to fire.

When the howitzers stopped they both stood and peeked over the lip of the trench. Rolling clouds of dust and gunpowder covered the camp. It was later reported that over thirty shells hit the camp with minimal damage. "That's a lesson learned," said Jenkins, "never walk outside without knowing where the closest bunker is. Sorry, that was my fault. I should know better."

"No harm done," Holt replied.

Like a gopher city coming awake, men poked their helmeted heads up from trenches and out of bunkers. The stench of cordite assaulted their senses.

Holt opened his mouth and worked his jaw. "My ears are still ringing."

"Welcome to the Dog Bone. It's a shit hole, but it's our shit hole. We call it home," Jenkins said.

When they entered the barracks they saw Doc Humphrey examining Charlie Pratt.

"What's going on?" Holt asked.

"Charlie got thrown to the ground by one of the explosions. I'm just checking him out."

As Holt went to sit down he stumbled a bit.

"When I'm done with him, I'll check you." "I'm fine, Doc."

"Alright Charlie, you're okay. Sarge, sit down and let me take a look at you."

"I said I'm okay. No need."

"Let's get one thing straight right now. When it comes to things medical, I'm in charge, not you. Is that clear?"

"Sure. Didn't mean to step on your toes. Check away."

"The concussive force of an explosion can kill you just as good as shrapnel. Total body disruption is the most severe and potentially fatal injury. Burst ear drums, ruptured blood vessels in the eyes, lungs and stomach problems can occur hours after exposure to the shock waves of a blast." Doc held a thin flashlight up to Holt's eyes as he talked. "Half the guys I saw back at Bragg had some degree of hearing loss, tinnitus, or vertigo. If you're close to a blast, your brain can crushed up against your skull. Your internal organs can be slammed around inside your body. There are stories of guys being killed by the blast wave and not a scratch on them. When they open them up to do an autopsy their insides look like jelly."

Doc poked and prodded for a few minutes and declared Holt fine.

"I want you to take it easy for the next day. Try and get some rest. Lay down and rest your eyes." He turned to Jenkins. "What the fuck were you doing, wandering around with no idea of where a bunker was?"

"I was just showing Holt the camp."

"Next time, start your tour by showing him where the bunkers are located. You guys got lucky this time." As Doc packed up his kit, he continued. "Walking around like some FNG's." He shook his finger at Jenkins. "You know better than that, Joe."

"In all fairness to Joe, he did admit he fucked up." "You both could have been killed."

"That's right," said Holt, "you almost got me killed. We're even now for you supposedly saving my life."

"Why the fuck am I getting yelled at?"

CHAPTER 27

The Nick Name

Over the next three days they were mortared unmercifully. The attack on the third day lasted over three hours. More than four hundred 82MM mortar shells hit the camp with deadly accuracy.

The camps howitzers and 81MM mortars were ineffective in stopping the barrage.

The western mortar pit was hit destroying the mortar and killing one American and wounding two others.

The artillerymen performed valiantly, manning their guns throughout the bombardment, exposing themselves to the deadly shrapnel in defense of the camp. Spider, to his credit, never abandoned his men. He stayed in the gun pits directing the return fire. He looked absurd. His scrawny body clad in green shorts and blue beach flip flops wearing his outsized flak jacket and a helmet that appeared too large for his head.

Fixed wing aircraft were called and bombed the surrounding hills with anti-personnel bombs and napalm. It had little effect in suppressing the enemy fire.

Holt and his team sat huddled in the bunker behind their barracks. Jenkins and his team were on a work detail and didn't make it back to the bunker.

"Shit, I hope those guys found cover," Holt said.

"I saw them run for the TOC; I think they made it," said Doc Humphrey, his face showing his concern.

"Are you sure Humpty? You saw them, right?"

"I saw them running but shit man, I was running too."

A nearby blast threw the men against the bunker walls. Sand and dirt fell from the ceiling choking them.

Holt sat doubled over, his head on his knees hugging his CAR 15. He raised up and lit a cigarette with shaking hands.

"How do the gooks take it when we bomb them. This shit is driving me crazy," he said.

"Imagine if the gooks had planes and napalm. This fucking war would be over. We'd pack up and go home," said Jack Donnelly protectively cradling his radio.

"Any news, Jack?" asked Holt.

"Here, listen for yourself. Everyone's screaming on the net all at once. Can't make any sense out of it. Radio discipline is all shot to shit."

"What time is it?" Eugene Butler shouted.

"1430," Doc responded.

"What time is that? Speak fucking normal."

"Two thirty, asshole. You're in the Army. Quit thinking like a civilian."

"Fuck you, Doc," was his curt reply.

"We've been down here for ninety minutes. How the fuck much ammunition do those fuckers have," Jack shouted over the sound of the continuing explosions.

"I tell you, since Tet these bastards seem to have more ammo than we do," Holt said.

"Why are they bothering with this shit hole. Aren't there better places to attack?" moaned Paulie. "I can't stand this shit. Even the fucking rats have left the bunker."

A nearby blast sent the concussive wave spilling through the front of the bunker knocking them all backwards. One wall bowed in menacingly.

"Hand me a jug of water," Holt said.

There were five one gallon plastic jugs of water stacked on top of two cases of C-Rations in the back of the bunker.

Holt drank deeply from the jug and poured some water on his towel and scrubbed his face. He passed the jug around. Holt opened his mouth and worked his jaw around. His ears were ringing and his eyes hurt. He lit his sixth cigarette.

Doc fished out a Newport and passed the pack to Charley.

"I don't smoke," Charley said as he got out a cigarette and lit it.

"You just said you didn't smoke."

"What are you? My fucking mother? Smoking can't be any worse that sitting here breathing in sand and concrete dust."

Holt rubbed his hand through his hair releasing a small cloud of dust. "Can we get our hair cut here?" he asked.

"I got some clippers in my locker. You want me to run in and get them?" Gino said.

"Could you Eugene?"

"Jesus, Sarge, I was just kidding. And call me Gino; everyone else does."

"About the clippers, Gino?"

"No, I got clippers. I was kidding about getting them."

Several more blasts rattled the bunker.

"You know, I don't like my name Charlie. I want to be called something different. Charlie sounds too goofy."

"Why don't we just call you by your last name, Pratt. That's short and sweet?" Holt said.

"Pratt will do for now. But I really want to put some thought into this."

"Well lets all discuss this; it's as good as time as any," Holt said.

"Where are you from?"

"Florida."

"That's no good. Too many syllables. Doesn't roll off the tongue. What city in Florida?" "Tallahassee."

"That's even worse. Does anyone have any suggestions?"

"Now Spider has a cool name. How about something in the insect world. How about Beetle?" Gino said.

"Naw, he's a comic book soldier. I need something like Spider though," Pratt said.

"I got nothing," Doc said.

Just then another mortar round hit close by slashing the bunkers sand bags and sending clouds of sand falling from the ceiling. The men moaned.

Donnelly held up the radio handset. "Someone's calling for a medic."

Doc Humphrey started to rise and Holt told him to sit his ass down.

"You ain't going out there and run around looking for somebody. You'll end up getting your own ass blown away," Holt said.

"This sucks major ass," Doc said. He looked at his watch. "It's been over two hours and they ain't letting up."

"Does your name have to be a insect?" Paulie asked.

"What? Oh, are we back on that. No, it doesn't have to be insect related. Hey, how about Spike?"

Gino looked him over from top to bottom. "Nothing about you says Spike. Keep going."

The shelling picked up intensity. The explosions were almost continuous, one on top of the other

"You know what this reminds me of, back home in Pennsylvania," said Paulie.

"You get shelled much back home?" asked Pratt.

"Let me finish, asshole. In Pennsylvania, in Altoona. We got coal mines. Every once in a while there's an accident in the mines and these guys gotta get dug out. Just like us sitting in this bunker."

"Oh sure, it's just the same. The only difference is we're in Vietnam getting shelled by the NVA, not buried alive in a coal mine. Other than that it's exactly the same. What a fucking doofus!"

"Who you calling a doofus, asshole. I'd rather be a doofus from Pennsylvania than some sort of redneck, cracker from Florida."

"I ain't no cracker. I live in the capital city, shit for brains."

"That girlfriend you get letters from, is she your cousin? You fucking your cousin, Cracker?"

"Why you motherfucker… I'll rip you apart," Pratt said throwing himself upon Paulie.

The two tumbled to floor rolling about each other. Suddenly, Paulie yelped in pain and shoved Pratt off him.

"This wild, redneck, motherfucker bit my ear off," screamed Paulie. The team pulled the men apart.

"Knock it off!" shouted Holt.

Doc examined Paulie's ear. "Your ear is fine; he just bit it. You're bleeding a little. Don't be such a baby."

"Jesus Christ, you're letting this shit get to you. Calm the fuck down," Holt said.

Holt leaned back and lit his twelfth cigarette.

"Both you assholes were trained at Fort Bragg, right?"

"Yeah, that's right. What of it?" Pratt said defiantly.

"Didn't they teach you hand to hand combat. Big tough Green Berets, rolling around on the floor like two high school assholes on the playground. One of you should be dead right now. Fight like that out in the jungle and a gook will rip you a new asshole with his bayonet."

Both men stared at the floor petulantly.

"He started it," whined Paulie.

Pratt leaned in close to Paulie till their noses almost touched and snapped his teeth.

"You see that; he's crazy. He's like a wild animal." Paulie said pushing Pratt away who continued to snap his teeth.

"God damn it, that's enough," Holt said. That's it, I got your nicknames, the two of you. Pratt you are now Gator and Paulie, you are Tuna from Altoona."

"Sarge," Paulie began to protest.

"Quiet!" Holt shouted. "It's done. Gator and Tuna, everyone agree?"

"Who the fuck cares as long as this shit is done," Doc said.

"Does everyone agree," Holt asked again.

The squad all agreed. "Tuna and Gator," they said in unison.

"I kind of like mine," said Gator. "It ties into Florida."

"Hope your cousin likes it. She'll be whispering it in your ear while you're fucking her," said Tuna.

Gator started to rise.

"Sit back down," Holt said. "This is over between you two. You assholes are friends; act like it. Besides, cousin fucking happens in Alabama, not Florida. Hey wait, do you hear that? The shelling stopped."

They sat motionless for a few minutes until the all clear sounded and they stumbled from the bunker. They emerged into the sunlight looking like clay people. They were all covered in a fine, powdery gray cement dust.

As they stood upright, the first time in over three hours, they blinked their eyes myopically in the blinding sun. They stared in wonder at the devastated camp. The back of their barracks was blown apart.

The ground showed the numerous craters of the mortar explosions. Shrapnel littered the ground like shards of broken glass.

The TOC had been hit several times and large chunks of concrete were blown away exposing the rusting re-bar. The heavy steel door was pockmarked with dozens of shrapnel hits and scorched black by flame.

The largest devastation was reserved for the Spook Shack. The NVA spotters in the hills did an excellent job directing and adjusting the mortars. More than forty strikes hit the compound. The chain link fence lay in ruins. The upright galvanized poles were twisted and bent. The fencing was reduced to useless coiled bundles. The bunker was devoid of its antennas which were ripped from the wired supports. The roof was literally split open with one wall tilting precariously. The steel door lay on the ground torn from its hinges.

Eight men in plain fatigues and a German Sheppard emerged from the bunker carrying large olive drab containers. They waved everyone away and walked about twenty yards from the building. Several small muffled explosions came from inside and thick black smoke poured from the door and the shattered roof. Two flat black helicopters appeared and landed in the compound sending swirling clouds of dust into the air. The men and the dog hurried aboard and were gone.

"They didn't waste any time in getting out of here. The lucky bastards," said Holt.

"They got helicopters in here even before the dust off ships were called," said Donnelly. "Who the fuck were those guys?"

"Spooks! They carried what they could and blew up the rest," Holt said, shielding his eyes from the swirling dust clouds. "Come on, let's see if we can find Jenkins and his guys."

They started for the TOC and were happy to see Jenkins emerge through the door.

"Joe, are you alright?" hollered Holt.

Joe walked over and Holt wrapped him in a tight bear hug.

"Jesus, brother, I was worried about you."

"That was some scary shit. We were caught out in the open and ran for the TOC. Two of my guys caught shrapnel in the legs. Medi-vacs dust off choppers are in bound. Those fucking Spooks left in a hurry. Couldn't even be bothered to give our boys a lift to the hospital."

As they talked an artillery guy passed them carrying their wounded friend. Four others carried their dead friend wrapped in a poncho to the helipad.

Doc started after them. "I'm going to see if I can help."

As they watched Doc hurry after the wounded they saw Master Sergeant Cox leave the TOC carrying a duffel bag. His arm was wrapped in a loose bandage.

"That crazy old fuck! I think he cut himself with a piece of shrapnel. Told the Captain he was gone. Said he was too short for this shit," said Jenkins.

"Gotta be honest with you; I don't blame him. You want to head over to our barracks and see if it's still there? I think our room took a couple of hits. The ass end, our end, is all blown to shit," Holt said.

"Might as well. Shit, this place is a wreck," Jenkins said, looking at the smoldering ruins of the camp.

The damage to their barracks was confined to the Sergeant's room. The back wall was gone and the roof was peeled back. The lockers were turned onto their sides and the wooden footlockers were split open. Holt searched through his footlocker and was happy to see his two bottles of Jack Daniels were unharmed.

Holt hollered from the back. "You guys want to give us a hand. This place is beyond repair. We're going to move in with you hobo's in the low rent district."

Everyone pitched in and in just a few minutes Holt and Joe were settled into the two unoccupied front bunks.

Holt looked through the front door and saw the artillery men return from the airstrip.

"I'll be right back," he said. He walked out front and extended his hand to a young, blond Sergeant. "Sorry to hear about your buddy."

"Yeah, that was Jimmy. He was a good guy. At least it was quick. Got hit with a big piece of shrapnel in the head. Split his skull open. Doubt if he felt a thing. He was dead before he hit the ground," the Sergeant said, shaking his head sadly.

"We heard you guys firing all the time we were getting shelled. You got some giant, fucking balls."

"Just doing our jobs. Shit, man, you should have seen Spider. That crazy fuck was humping shells to the guns wearing beach flip flops. This fucking place sucks."

"What unit are you from?"

"Not supposed to say. Everything about this hell hole is top secret. Fuck it. Don't mean a thing."

"I know what you mean brother. If you need anything, let me know."

"I need a ticket out of this motherfucker, that's what I need."

"You and me both. I just wanted to let you know you are appreciated."

CHAPTER 28

It Couldn't Get Any Worse

It had rained overnight and turned the compound into a slurry of muddy cement dust and jagged pieces of metal.

After breakfast the men went about cleaning up and making what repairs they could.

Jenkins and Holt went outside and walked to the Spook Shack. They stepped over the rubble and poked their heads inside. They saw two banks of radios that had been destroyed with small C-4 charges and thermite grenades. The overhead fluorescent lights dangled from the ceiling. Shattered glass lay everywhere. Filing cabinets were emptied and left with their drawers open. Against the back wall were two bunk beds with torn and shredded mattresses.

"Man, I thought these guys lived better than us, but they actually had it worse," said Jenkins.

"There were eight guys in here. I guess they took turns sleeping," Holt said.

"That is foul. Imagine sleeping in a bunk that some dirty, sweaty guy just got out of."

Against one wall was a small refrigerator that someone placed a thermite grenade on top of it. It melted through the top and through the inside shelves.

"Let's get out of here. There's nothing of value left," Holt said.

As they walked back to the barracks they passed the artillery crew trying to replace ripped sandbags.

"Morning, gents. Hard at work I see," Holt said.

The blond Sergeant Holt had met stood up and wiped his face with a towel.

"Trying to salvage what we can. We lost a mortar yesterday. The same shell that killed Jimmy destroyed one of the 81's. Bent the tube all to shit. Nothing worth saving."

"Hang in there. It has to get better," Holt said with genuine sympathy.

As they neared the barracks, Gator poked his head out. "Captain wants to see you two. Pronto!"

"We're on our way. Gator, do me a favor, get some cold drinks and bring them out for the arty guys."

Gator made a sour face.

"Gator, please don't be a prick, just do as I ask."

As they walked to the TOC Jenkins said, "This can't be good."

"Don't be such a pessimist. Maybe it's good news."

Inside, the TOC had an air of urgency about it. All the radios were manned with men coordinating, artillery, air support, and resupply. Captain Mason and Spider had their backs to them studying the large scale wall map.

"You wanted to see us, Cap?" Holt said.

Mason turned. "Yeah. Go grab some coffee, it's fresh and someone made some donuts. They're not bad."

When they were settled in, Mason sat behind his desk. "We got a lot to go over. First, I got word on your two men. They're gonna be alright but they won't be coming back out anytime soon. We're not getting any replacements so I'm going to combine the two teams. Sergeant Holt will be team leader and Jenkins you'll be assistant. Any problems?"

"I'm good," said Jenkins.

"Me too," added Holt.

"The Colonel wants us to take a combat patrol into the hills, find and eliminate those spotters."

"That's easier said than done. Who knows where they are?" Holt got up and went to the map. "First we have to get out of the camp without being spotted."

"You'll go at night," said Mason.

"We have to cross no-man's land and get into the jungle. Maybe somewhere around here," Holt said pointing to the map. "Then we have to climb up and work our way west and hope we get lucky. The spotters have to have protection and will be dug in. They've been up in these hills since the French so you know they have underground bunkers and tunnels everywhere. They have to have at least a platoon guarding them. They have to be somewhere along this line here," Holt said tracing his finger along the hills. "They could be anywhere within two or three miles. Did the Colonel offer any suggestions on how we find them?"

"He just wants it done. I explained the difficulty in doing so but he wasn't interested in excuses, just results."

"That's the kind of concrete information that instills confidence. What size patrol?"

"I'm thinking maybe six Americans and thirty or forty Montagnards. Who'll lead the patrol?"

Without hesitation Holt pointed at Jenkins. "Joe will take it."

Jenkins looked at Holt with bug eyes.

"I'm just fucking with you. I'll take it."

"That's settled. When we're done here we'll go down to the American advisor's and fill them in. Let them know these are orders from the Colonel."

"I'm sure they'll be thrilled to cooperate," Holt said with little enthusiasm.

"Next up. I've been asked to put together a plan to evacuate the camp if it becomes necessary. That would only happen if the camp was in imminent danger of being overrun. We'd have to walk out. We'd never get enough helicopters in here to get everyone out. There's a small ARVN base twelve kilometers to the north east—"

Holt stopped him. "No way. I don't trust those fuckers. And you know they won't take in the Montagnards. They hate them."

"I'm aware of that," the Captain said. He showed no annoyance about Holt interrupting him. He got up and joined Holt at the map.

"There's an Australian FSB about twenty klick's due south. Right on the border like us. It's called Fire Support Base Adeline. They even have a mechanized unit with them. If we have to leave we'll split up. Our gooks will go to the ARVN base and we'll go to the Australian base. When we get close, maybe they can send out their tracks to support us."

"That sounds better," Holt said. "They have good beer too. Those big pint cans of Fosters."

"Ah, great. Then that will be the deciding factor."

"Are you being sarcastic?"

"How'd you guess?"

"It's just that in making a decision of this magnitude you have to consider everything. That's all I'm saying," Holt said softly.

"If it comes to it, Sergeant Holt, you'll take five of your guys and lead the artillery guys. I'll take the other four and lead the Command Post men. Keep in mind, these guys aren't infantry; they'll be scared and won't know what to do. You'll have to babysit them and keep them under control. We'll split the Montagnards. Let half of them walk point and the other half cover our rear."

"What do you think the chances are of us bugging out?

"If we get shelled again, like yesterday, almost certain."

"Those spotters are great. Did you see the Spook Shack? They hit it so many times it split in half," Holt paused and lit a cigarette. "Those guys didn't waste any time getting out of here. They had a dog with them. A big German Sheppard. Do they know something we don't? Speaking of getting out, what happened to Master Sergeant Cox?"

"Packed up and hauled ass on the medi-vacs chopper. Said he had a shrapnel wound. I'd miss him if I had any idea of what he did. Fucking guy was so jumpy he made Don Knott's look calm."

Spider joined them standing behind the Captain. "What's this about a dog?"

"The Spooks had a dog," Holt said.

"A dog?" Spider looked puzzled. "Was the dog a spy too?"

"The dog? Yeah, sure," Holt said.

"That's cool. A dog trained in espionage. Must be a smart dog."

"Spider, forget about the dog. Holt, go brief your men and I'll meet you in front of your barracks in twenty minutes. We'll head over to the Montagnards."

"Hey Captain, throw on some tiger stripes and wear your beret. Let these guys know we're one of them."

As they left, Spider was telling the radio operators about the spy dog.

As they walked towards the Montagnards the Captain said, "I may have the shortest command in the history of the Army. I sometimes wonder if Major Jung was setting me up by sending me here."

"I doubt if he was fucking you. But I'm sure he wasn't telling you everything. He's a Major and you're a Captain. Shit rolls downhill. I'm sure the Colonel fucks him, who in turn gets fucked by the General. Don't take offense, but I try and not wonder why officers do the things they do. It's the fucking Army."

"Do you think I fuck with you?"

"Sure you do. This patrol, I know it's the Colonel's idea. You pass the orders to me knowing full well it's a waste of time. A dangerous waste of time that might get somebody killed. But you do it. I mean we ain't going to get anywhere close to those spotters. It's like hunting for the proverbial needle, only the haystack will be guarded by dozens of NVA. it's a shit assignment. You know it and I know it but the colonel wants it done. So that's that."

They entered the Montagnard area and climbed down into the wide trench studded with sandbagged bunkers.

"Where's your Dai uy?" Mason asked.

A Montagnard pointed down the trench line. They all stared at Holt.

They continued walking past the indigenous troops. Some were on guard and others squatted around cooking fires. They all turned and stared as they walked past.

"Why are they all staring at us?"

"It's you Captain," Holt said, "you're a very handsome man. The Montagnards are very impressed with physical beauty."

"I'm sure that's it. There he is, up there past the next bunker." They walked up to the captain in charge of the CIDG.

The Civilian Irregular Defense Group was a program started and implemented by the Special Forces. Basically indigenous civilians were recruited and trained and formed into militias to protect their villages. They were used throughout Vietnam as paid mercenaries.

The CIDG Captain was a tall, extremely sunburned man with close cropped brown hair that was bleached by the sun. His face was the color of worn leather and had the same texture. His name was Shawn Peters.

As Mason explained the mission the Captain frowned.

Captain Peters shook his head. "I don't see that happening. Going into those hills is a one way ticket. There are hundreds of NVA up there all dug in.

You'd need a battalion of men to be successful and even then the casualties would be high. I can't see wasting my guys on some wild goose chase. You'll never find those spotters and if you do find and kill them they'll just be replaced."

"Those are my orders, Captain," Mason said.

"I'm not under your command. I take orders from MACV," Peters said.

"That's where my orders come from too. Can we step into your bunker and discuss this privately?"

They left Holt outside. He leaned against the bunker and fired up a cigarette. He looked to his left and saw a group of Montagnards staring at him. He looked at them and smiled and touched his hand to his boonie hat in salute. They looked away. They talked among themselves and soon turned back to Holt.

A Montagnard sergeant walked towards Holt. He extended his hand and smiled. "You are Sergeant Sangh's demon friend?"

Holt looked surprised. "How do you know Sergeant Sangh?"

"He is, how do you say? My cousin. Yes, he my cousin."

"I like to think of Sergeant Sangh as a friend but I'm not a demon."

"No, no, he say you good demon and VC no can kill you. He say you good man and friend to the Bru and can be trusted."

"Look at me. Do I look like I can't be killed?"

"I see many VC try and kill you but here you are, still living," the sergeant said pinching Holt's arm for emphasis.

Holt pulled his arm back. "Do you know where Sangh is?"

"He go home," the Sergeant said pointing north.

"Where?"

"In the mountains. He find new home for Bru people. He said you are destined to help."

"You, my friend are crazy. I am a Sergeant and I'm not destined to do anything but stay alive and go home."

"He say you are home and will help Bru."

"Sangh chewed too much Betel Nut. He made a mistake. I'm not a good demon or a bad demon. I'm just a man."

The small Sergeant just shrugged and smiled.

"Seriously, go tell your friends that Sangh made a mistake. Hey wait, can you find Sangh?"

"You want to find Sangh? I may can help. But he in secret place. It take many days to find."

"For now, just tell everyone what I said."

Holt watched him walk away and lit another cigarette.

"What were you and my Sergeant talking about?" Captain Peters asked.

Holt was startled. "I didn't see you come back. Your Sergeant is fucking nuts. He thinks I'm some sort of demon."

"The Bru are very superstitious people. Maybe to them you look like a demon."

"I would appreciate it if you would convince them otherwise."

Captain Mason joined them. "For the time being our patrol is on hold. MACV is clarifying our orders. Captain Peters is correct. Apparently the Colonel doesn't have control of the CIDG. We'll wait and see what happens."

Captain Mason shook hands with Captain Peters. "Shawn, it was very nice meeting you."

A young Sergeant stuck his head out of the bunker. "Captain Mason, I have an urgent call for you."

Captain Peters remained outside with Holt.

"Don't let the Yards spook you. I've had to learn to work around their superstitions. In a lot of ways they are still very primitive."

"We all got our superstitions. I don't know a grunt alive who doesn't carry a talisman of some kind."

Peters reached into his fatigue shirt and produced a gold locket. "Picture of my wife and kid."

Holt looked at the photo. "Beautiful woman. The baby kind of looks like Winston Churchill."

"Fuck you Sergeant. All babies look like Churchill."

Holt took a silver dollar from his shirt pocket. "My girl gave this to me when I first came over here. Hasn't stopped me from getting wounded but I'm still above ground."

From inside the bunker they heard Mason explode in rage. "God dam it! Fuck! You gotta be kidding me! When? Those cowardly motherfuckers, I'll be right back."

Mason stormed from the bunker. "Those fucking South Vietnamese Rangers are taking off."

"What?" asked Holt.

"Those fuckers are leaving right now. I have to get back and stop them. Holt stay here. Captain Peters said he'll show you around." Mason took off, running back to the TOC.

Peters took out his cigarettes and offered one to Holt. He lit both with a silver zippo lighter.

"If those assholes got a mind to leave, your Captain won't be able to stop them. This is not good. I'll have to split my force. Half my men will take over the north wall. Mason will have to babysit them. They need an American officer to work the radios." Peters looked around and sighed. "This fucking dump ain't worth saving. If the gooks want it so bad, let them have it."

"Aren't we stopping traffic on the road?"

"We're just a fucking minor inconvenience for them. We haven't stopped anything. Fuck it, it don't mean a damn thing. C'mon, I'll show you around. We'll let the rest of the Yards see the demon."

When Holt returned to the TOC, Mason was still fuming.

"Those fuckers were gone by the time I got back. They must have been planning this for days. I already spoke with Shawn. He's sending half his men to the north and east walls. I'm going to have to go and stay with them. I told the Colonel and at first he thought I was lying to him, to what purpose I don't know. He said he'll court martial the American advisers."

"They left with the gooks?"

"They left and never said a word to anybody. Motherfuckers deserve to be court martialed!"

"Wow! I never heard you curse before."

"Not going to be the last fucking time. Of that I'm certain."

Behind them one of the RTO's was waving the radio handset. "It's a Major Jung and he doesn't sound very happy."

"Stick around for a minute, this should be good."

While Mason was on the horn Spider came into the TOC, sensing the mood he did a quick about face and left.

"What the fuck was he wearing?" asked Holt.

"A Hawaiian shirt. He got a whole bunch of them when he was on R & R."

Holt laughed. "This place is nuts," he said under his breath.

He watched Mason. It was apparently a one way conversation. Mason leaned his head away from the handset and grimaced. He looked over to Holt and smiled weakly. When he was done he walked back to Holt.

"The advisor's are trying to cover their ass. They said they told me the camp was indefensible and said we should abandon the camp immediately. The lying cocksuckers. I've never even spoken to them. The first day I arrived I asked to meet them and they declined."

"Was the Major pissed?"

"He wasn't happy."

"Look on the bright side, you made a new friend today. Shawn and Charles sitting in a tree—"

Mason cut him off. "Charles?"

"That's your first name isn't it?"

"I prefer Mason just like you prefer Holt. Am I correct Donald?"

"Point taken. If I may continue, Shawn and Charles sitting in a tree—"
"Sergeant, please go fuck yourself."

"Solid advice, Sir. The patrol is cancelled, I assume."

"You assume correct. I'll be over with the Montagnards if you need me."

"If you want I'll hang with the Yards."

"If I'm needed here I'll call you. For now they need an officer to get them squared away not a demon Sergeant."

"Oh, you heard about that?"

"Surprisingly, I heard it from the Major and not you."

"Not worth mentioning. Those little fuckers are insane. You should get along good with them."

"Dismissed Donald."

Holt saw Spider in one of the gun pits and walked over to him.

"I love your shirt Spider." It was the most garish shirt Holt had ever seen. It was all swirling, bright colors with bare breasted hula girls, palm trees, and splashing dolphins.

Spider pulled it away from his chest. "Yeah, I love it too. Got it in Honolulu on R & R. My wife thinks it a little too X-rated what with all the bare titties."

"You're married?" Holt said incredulously.

"Yeah, I'm married. Why do you say it like that?"

"I just thought you were married to the Army."

"Fuck no. I'm just here for the GI bill. Gonna finish up college when I get home. I'm a double digit midget. Seventy nine days and a wake up." When Holt walked in the barracks he asked Tuna, "Did you know Spider is married?"

"Fuck yeah. Did he show you a picture of his wife? She's a world class, number one, piece of ass. Got tits out to here," he said lewdly holding his hands out from his chest. "She's absolutely gorgeous. A fucking centerfold babe for sure."

"I'd crawl over a mile of broken glass just to smell her farts," Gino said.

"That's disgusting," said Holt.

"What? The fart part?"

"No, not at all, the broken glass part."

"So, what's this about the gooks leaving?" asked Doc.

"Their fucking in the wind. Gone baby, gone. The Yards are taking their place. It's all for the good. You can't trust Marvin the ARVN."

"This is bullshit. Why are we even here then? They won't even fight for their own country," Donnelly said.

"Jack, that's a good question, unfortunately it's above our pay grade."

"Fuck those cowardly cocksuckers."

"That's right, fuck them in the mouth and feed them fish," Holt said.

"What the fuck does that mean?"

"Still trying to figure that out. One of the guys in my old squad used to say it all the time. Said it's an old Greek expression."

"Greeks! Those butt hole fuckers?"

"He claimed that wasn't true. Although we said we believed him, no one wanted to take a shower with him."

CHAPTER 29

But It Did Get Worse

Somewhere around 1600 hours it started to rain. Inside their barracks, the team realized the damage was more extensive than they previously thought.

There were numerous shrapnel holes in the roof. Water seeped in and collected on the floor. The screens were torn. The only dry spots were at the front of the barracks. The men moved their bunks and lockers closer to the door.

Holt stood at the door and watched the artillery men who seemed unconcerned about the rain. He had considered inviting them to use the barracks when it rained but then realized they were better off staying where they were.

They had rigged up ponchos extending from their bunkers and sat in lawn chairs smoking and drinking coffee. When building their bunkers they had placed thick plastic sheet between each layer of sandbags. Their bunkers were effectively water proof.

Donnelly came up to Holt and said, "Captain wants you up at the TOC."

Holt followed him back inside and got his carbine and web gear.

At the TOC, Captain Mason greeted him warmly which put Holt on alert.

"Just made fresh coffee and we found some real cream that Sergeant Cox had squirreled away. The donuts are a little crusty but still good," the Captain said.

"Donuts and coffee? Should I just bend over now or drink my coffee first?"

"Don't be so dramatic; it's nothing bad. Shawn just called…"

"Shawn, your new buddy?"

"Yes, that Shawn. With his Montagnards spread thin he asked if your team could man the corner gun pits."

"Sure. No problem. They're probably drier than our barracks. The barracks are leaking like a sieve."

"Bring all your gear with you. We still might have to bug out at a moment's notice. If the gooks are planning anything this rain provides the perfect opportunity."

"I guess air support is out of the question?"

"We might be able to get a Spooky up but no helicopters will be flying except medi-vacs. Who knows what the fixed wing guys will do?"

"There are ten of us. Three guys in each bunker. I'll leave Doc with Shawn. He should be safe there. The Yards can man the fourth bunker."

"That's a good idea. I'll stay in the fourth bunker with the Montagnards. I wrote down the call sign for each bunker and all the radio frequencies. Each bunker has its own radio. If we do have to leave either take the radios with you or destroy them. Don't forget to destroy the fifty cal."

"Uh, duh. This ain't my first rodeo, cowboy," Holt said.

"Just saying, alright?"

"I'll stop by the arty guys and make sure they know what to do. Where's Spider?"

"I sent him over to the Montagnards while I'm here at the TOC."

"They will love his shirt."

"I made him change into fatigues and put on some boots. You all set then? Keep in constant contact and good luck."

"You too, Charles."

Holt stopped at the artillery pits. "You know, I never asked your name. I'm Holt."

The blond Sergeant extended his hand. "My name is Winston but everyone calls me Winnie."

"Alright Winnie, here's the deal…"

Holt went on to explain the situation in detail, focusing on the bug out plans.

"Pack up all your personal shit. Keep your web gear and M16's handy. Make sure you have at least three meals and four canteens. Pack all the ammo and grenades you can carry. If we have to boogie, I'll come back and get you. I'll get you out of here. Just follow my orders and do what I say. Any questions?"

"Appreciate it."

"Can you destroy these guns if need be?"

"We got thermite grenades and C-4. We can fuck them up good."

"Good. Monitor your radio. If, for any reason I can't get back to you, hook up with the Captain and Spider. They'll get you home."

"Understood," Winnie said. He was all business. "God help us all," he said solemnly.

In the barracks Holt divided the team.

"I'll take Donnelly and Gino with me. I'll take the south west bunker. Tuna, you, Gator, and one of Jenkins guys take the south east bunker. Joe, you take the bunker on the north wall. Take all your shit. Carry as much food, water, ammo, and grenades as you can. We might not be coming back here. Just plan as if we're not."

"What about all the ammo we're leaving behind?" Jenkins asked.

"If we bug out, they'll blow the crap out of this place. The jet jockey's will use it as target practice. They won't leave anything standing."

"You think it will come to that?" asked Gator.

"I hope not but... Listen, if the order comes, we meet back here. If we get separated, find the Captain. We'll be okay. We got like two hundred Montagnards with us. Those boys can fight. Any gooks wanna fuck with us they'll regret it. We'll tear those fuckers up. It should take us two days to get to the Aussie Fire Support Base Adeline, but it could be longer."

They climbed down into the Montagnard trench system loaded down with all their gear.

"Tuna, you guys are down there," Holt said pointing to his left. "Do a commo check with the Captain as soon as you get set up. We're at the other end of the trench."

In the middle of the trench they met Captain Peters. "Captain, this is Doc Humphrey, everyone calls him Humpty. I'll leave him with you. Please take good care of him—"

Doc interrupted. "Just call me Doc. No one but Holt calls me Humpty."

They shook hands. "Good to have you aboard, Doc. Our medic is set up in the next bunker. Go make yourself at home." He turned to Holt. "Thanks for filling in." He shook his head slowly, "What a fucking mess this is. Did your Captain talk to the Aussie's?"

"As far as I know."

"No problem with my boys?"

"The Yards? No, they got no problem with the Montagnards," Holt said.

"Fucking South Vietnamese, racist motherfuckers." "Did you know Sergeant Sangh?"

"Your old Sergeant? Heard of him, never met him. He was part of the CIDG before he hooked up the SOG program. He's well respected among the Bru."

"Not like him to just take off like he did."

"The Montagnards know they ain't welcome by the Vietnamese. Now, with us withdrawing troops they got to look out for themselves."

"Your men are still loyal though?"

"To us? For the time being. They're not going to leave if that's what you're worried about. They hate the North Vietnamese as much as they hate the South."

"If they were to establish a homeland, where would it be?" Holt asked. "Shit, it would have to be way up north in central Laos. Away from the Ho Chi Minh trail. I can't see any other place."

"Yeah, I think you're right, " Holt said. "I guess I better go and get settled in."

As they walked down the trench line they passed groups of Montagnards who all stared intently at Holt.

"These guys give me the creeps," Gino said. "Why are they staring at you?"

"Long story."

The small Sergeant that Holt had spoke to earlier stopped Holt.

"You guys go on ahead, I'll be right along," Holt said.

"I have gift for you," the Sergeant said. He held out a small leather bag hung on a rawhide string.

"What is it?"

"It's for good luck. It will keep you safe."

Holt took off his hat and bowed his head allowing the Sergeant to place the amulet around his neck.

"Thank you."

"Thank Sangh, it gift from him."

"Thank Sergeant Sangh when you see him."

"You thank him yourself someday," the Sergeant said as he turned and walked away.

"This is a weird fucking place," Holt said to himself as he walked to the bunker.

When he reached the bunker he stopped and examined the outside. The exterior concrete was pockmarked with dozens of bullet and shrapnel strikes. Holt stepped up on a sandbag and looked at the top. There were several deep gouges from mortar hits but the bunker was still sound. He knocked on the steel door.

"Lucy, I'm home," he said. He went inside. The air was damp and cool. The bunker had an inside diameter of about ten feet. In the back were two worn cots. In the center of the bunker was a 50 caliber, M2 machine gun. There were dozens of boxes of 50 caliber ammunition stacked around the gun. Across from the door was a small table and stool. There was a PRC 25 radio sitting on top of the table with three fresh batteries. Under one of the cots were three cases of unopened C-rations and a five gallon water jug.

"Not bad," Holt said, looking around. "Did you check in yet?" Holt asked Donnelly.

"Yeah, we're four by four."

Gino was at the 50 cal. "You gonna check the head space and timing on the gun, Sarge?" he asked.

"I have no idea how to do that." Gino gave Donnelly a look.

"Don't give me any of your Fort Bragg bullshit. If you know how to do it, just go ahead and do it," Holt said.

Gino walked in front of the gun and unscrewed the barrel. He screwed it back in until he heard a series of clicks. He backed off two clicks. "Righty tighty, lefty loosey," he said as he worked. He opened up the receiver cover and pulled the charging handle back a bit. "Gotta make sure the firing pin ain't exposed." He held up a thin machined rectangle. "This is the Headspace Go, No Go, gauge." With the charging handle pulled back he inserted the gauge. "No Go," he said. He backed off the barrel one click and inserted the other side of the gauge. "Go." he said. "Now I'll check the timing."

Holt, bored with procedure, turned away, and lit a cigarette.

"All done," Gino said proudly. "Next time you can give it a try, Sarge."

"I wasn't paying attention. It's your job for the foreseeable future. You're the fifty gunner from now on. Good work."

"Cool."

"Yeah. Cool," Holt said as he moved to the gun port. "It's still raining."

"You don't need a weatherman to know which way the wind blows," Gino quoted.

"Gino, you surprise me. You like Dylan?"

"Why are you surprised?"

"I just thought you were a country boy. I figured you for a Merle Haggard or Willie Nelson fan."

"I'm from Columbus; it's a big city."

"How did you end up here?"

"The draft was taking everybody. No jobs in Columbus if you were classified 1A. I figured I'd enlist before the draft got me. I didn't plan on the infantry. I must have scored high on one of the aptitude tests. I got talked into airborne and I did well at that. I was approached about Special Forces and figured why not? All the way Green Beret and all that rah, rah shit and here I am."

"You got a girl back home?"

"Had a girl. She started college and got caught up in the anti-war movement and suddenly I was an oppressor of the masses. I figure she's a hippie girl now sucking Jodie's dick. How about you, Sarge? You got somebody waiting for you?"

"Believe it or not I was married. She had a baby. Didn't work out."

"You have a kid?"

"She has a baby. It's not mine. It's a long, boring story. Short version is guy meets girl. Girl gets pregnant. Guy marries girl and girl's parents get marriage annulled."

"Sounds like a complicated story, if you ask me."

"It is. Parents thought I was good enough to give her my name but not good enough to stay married to. Her father actually had the balls to tell me the best thing that could happen is that I get killed over here and she would become a war widow. Fuck him! I ain't dying in this place. I got somewhere around three months left until my leave. Maybe I'll go home, maybe I won't."

"But I thought you get letters from her?"

"We still write each other but she has her own life now." Holt changed the subject. "So are you staying in the Army?"

"Don't know yet. Maybe."

Holt peered out the gun port, "Going to be dark in awhile. If we want to cook our food we should do it before it gets dark."

Holt lit another cigarette. "You know it's funny; we make all these important life altering decisions in such a haphazard way."

"I was just thinking about that. The only reason I'm in Special Forces and here is because it was easy. Basically, someone else decided for me. Fucking Army takes advantage of the kids. They find out what you think you want and offer it to you." Gino looked around the bunker, "This is the first time I'm away from home. The only time I ever left Ohio. I miss my family."

"That's okay. You should miss your family."

"It's not that. It's like when you go away to sleepover camp. You're stuck there and can't leave. I feel like a baby telling you I'm homesick."

"This is just like camp. You're with a bunch of guys you don't know, sleeping out, cooking over an open fire and hiking all day. It is camp; if everything at the camp was trying to kill you, including the councilors, and your only goal was to survive and go home."

"Man, I made a mistake."

"Join the Army and see the world they said…" Holt said lighting another cigarette.

"Yeah see the world. Now I'm stuck in some fucking bunker that smells like cat piss surrounded by thousands of gooks that want to kill me." "You know Sarge, I haven't really seen any combat before this. I've never really saw a NVA soldier up close," Donnelly said. "What if I panic? I mean, shit, I'm fucking scared all the time."

Holt continued to stare out across no man's land. "It's normal to be scared. We're all scared. You'll do fine. You're well trained. Just do as I do. If I fight, then you fight. If I run, you better damn well run faster than me."

Holt held up his hand for silence. "Did you hear that?" "What?" asked Donnelly, a tremor in his voice.

"I don't know. It sounded like scraping. Like someone is digging out there."

Holt looked onto the barren ground. He turned and un-strapped the M79 grenade launcher from his rucksack. He took two high explosive rounds and stepped outside the bunker. Once outside he thought he saw a puff of dirt about two hundred feet out. He aimed the M79 and fired a round and reloaded.

The grenade exploded and a man sprung from the earth. He fired again, and then two men rose and started running towards the trees. Gino fired a long burst from the fifty cal machine gun. The sound was deafening. Dirt kicked up around the fleeing soldiers and one fell. The Montagnards joined in the firing and hundreds of rounds were fired at the NVA soldiers. Both fell to the ground and did not move.

Holt ran into the bunker and grabbed the radio handset from Donnelly. "Red 6, Red 6, this is Viking 6." Captain Mason answered immediately.

"Red 6 when was the last time anyone was out in no man's land? I think the gooks are digging trenches out there. We just killed two a few hundred feet out."

"Viking 6, you say two hundred feet? We'll fire some mortar rounds, observe and adjust."

Behind them they could hear their mortars fire. After a moment Holt saw the explosions.

"Red 6, drop ten and fire for effect."

A dozen more 81MM mortar bombs exploded where the soldiers had emerged from the ground.

From the hills, the NVA answered with their mortars.

Six explosions fell short of the trench line. The enemy adjusted and fired again. A dozen rounds fell around the bunker and the trench to their left. They choked as clouds of dirt swirled into the bunker. They could hear shrapnel pinging off the bunker's sides. Dust and sand fell from the roof.

The camp's howitzers returned fire. Holt watched and saw explosions in the hills.

"Right twenty five," Holt hollered into the handset.

"We have it."

To the left of the enemy mortar position, about two hundred yards, Holt saw six enormous flashes.

"Shit, rockets, get down now!" Holt screamed.

The big 122MM Chinese rockets trailed a thick plume of smoke and impacted around the TOC. The ground shook with the impact.

"What the fuck was that!?" Donnelly screamed.

"Big, fucking, Chinese rockets. They have about fifteen pounds of explosive. That's why they're so loud. Stay down," Holt said.

Holt peeked through the bunker firing port and saw dozens of flashes in the hills. He turned to get his helmet and remembered he left it and his flak jacket in the barracks. He looked at Gino who had his ears covered and was working his jaw back and forth.

Gino yelled at Holt. "My ears keep popping."

"That's the blast wave. Keep your mouth open."

Holt searched the floor and picked up his cigarette butts. He pinched off the filters and handed two to Gino. "Stuff these in your ears. They should help. Give two to Donnelly."

Donnelly winced when handed the filters. "Oh man, you had these in your mouth."

"They weren't in my mouth you moron. Oh, fuck it, then don't use them. Use your own!" Holt yelled above the explosions.

"I don't smoke, I told you that," Donnelly whined.

"I've seen you smoke."

"Not all the time. Smoking's no good for you."

Both Holt and Gino looked at Donnelly and began laughing.

"Why are you laughing? Oh, I get it," Donnelly said and laughed.

They were all laughing when three more mortars rocked the bunker and threw them to the floor.

They stood on shaky legs and Holt looked out the bunker and saw a half dozen more rockets launched. He followed the smoke trail as it neared the camp.

"Rockets!" he shouted just before they hit.

They hit behind them and instantly a rolling cloud out dust and dirt engulfed the bunker.

"Get the captain on the horn," Holt said.

"I think they're targeting the TOC with those rockets. We've taken a bunch of direct hits," Mason said. "There's a big crack in the corner. I can see light through it. I called for air support but the fixed wing guys aren't flying. We might get some Cobras."

The barrage continued for more than an hour then suddenly shifted. Instead of targeting the camp, the NVA were now firing into no man's land.

Donnelly handed Holt the radio. "It's the Captain."

"What's going on? What are they shooting at?"

"Red 6, they are blowing up the wire out front. They're hitting our mines and flares. The barbed wire is being torn to shit. It looks like the fourth of July out front. They have to be preparing for a ground attack."

"Agreed. Hold tight. I'm going to request air support again. Maybe I can get Spooky up."

Holt relayed the message.

"Spooky?" asked Gino.

"Yeah, Spooky. You know? The gunship."

"You mean Puff?"

"Puff, Spooky, they're all the same. People call them different names. I like Spooky myself."

The NVA continued their bombardment of no man's land. Mines exploded and trip flares burst into light. The barb wire coils would get hit, spring closed and fly into the air and then fall to ground in a hopeless tangle.

"Do you really think they'll attack us?" Donnelly asked.

"Unfortunately, Jack, I do."

"When?"

"Anytime after dark. This shit was just to soften us up. The next bombardment will be followed by a ground attack from the woods. If they're going to do it, they'll do it while it's still raining. They know we won't get air support in the rain."

"What if the Montagnards leave like the ARVN?" Gino said.

"They won't leave. They ain't stupid. They know they got no place to go without us."

Holt dug into his cargo pocket and pulled out a package of beef jerky. "Gino, do me a favor and go into my ruck and see if you can find some crackers," Holt said.

"How can you eat now? I feel like I'm gonna shit my pants. I'm fucking scared."

"I'm scared too but I'm also hungry. I can't control being scared but I can do something about being hungry."

Holt opened the tin of crackers and laid them on some sand bags. He opened a packet of Kool Aide and poured some into his canteen and shook it. He passed the remaining Kool Aide to Gino.

"Go ahead and mix some up; we got plenty of water."

He tore off a large chunk of jerky and bit into a cracker. He held up the beef jerky again. "You sure you don't want any? It's just like having a Philly Cheese Steak back home minus the steak, hoagie roll, onions, peppers, and cheese."

"The cheese in a Philly is made from melted Cheese Wiz," Gino said.

"Fuck, maybe in Ohio. The real ones use Provolone cheese. That's a real Philly," Holt said.

Gino pulled out a small transistor radio and held it up. "You mind, Sarge?"

"Go ahead. I think the gooksters know where we are."

They sat in silence and listened to Peter, Paul, and Mary sing 'Leaving on a Jet Plane'.

When it was over Holt said, "That's a sad song."

They were all quiet.

"I hate this fucking place," Donnelly said.

CHAPTER 30

One If By Land

The rain continued as the sky darkened. Holt toyed with amulet bag around his neck.

"What's that thing?" Gino asked.

"It's a good luck amulet bag. A Katha. One of the Montagnards gave it to me."

"Why?"

"Who knows? You'd have to ask them. They're a very strange and superstitious people."

"Kind of backward if you ask me."

"What are you wearing around your neck?"

Gino fished the chain from under his shirt. "It's a medallion of Saint Michael, the Arch Angel. He's the patron saint of the military. I got it from my father before I left home. He said he wore it in World War Two."

"I rest my case," Holt said indifferently.

"What do you mean? You don't believe in God, the saints, and the Bible?"

"I believe in God and I guess the saints are part of the package. The Bible I can take or leave."

"How can you say that? The Bible is the word of God."

"No one knows who wrote the Bible or when it was written. Go to the library and look it up. Some say Moses wrote the first half 1500 BC and other parts were written three to five hundred years after Christ died. Who knows? Did you ever read the Bible? It has some bat shit crazy stuff in it. I used to have long conversations with our Chaplin. I used to ask him about some of the

299

insane stuff and loved to see him squirm as he tried to explain it. To me, the Bible is a novel, take it or leave it."

"Wow! I can't believe—"

"Incoming," shouted Holt.

They heard the thunk as the mortars were fired, followed by the whoosh of the rockets. it seemed the mortars were landing in no man's land while the rockets targeted the camps interior. Dozens of explosions rocked and heaved the earth. Shrapnel sizzled through the air at supersonic speed. Almost immediately the camp's artillery fired back.

"Those arty guys are nuts. They're standing out in their pits firing back. Christ, they have balls," Holt said.

The 122MM rockets were joined by the big Chinese supplied howitzers. The big 152MM, ML-20's fired from deep inside Cambodia were systematically ripping the camp apart.

One of the huge rounds exploded behind Holt's bunker. The men were tossed around like pinball's by the concussion. The bunker filled with the chocking smoke of cordite and dirt.

Holt got off the floor coughing violently. "Are you guys alright?"

"I hit my head against the concrete. I swear, I'm seeing double," Donnelly said.

Gino rose and fell against the sandbags supporting the fifty caliber machine gun. He wiped his hand against his forehead. "Shit, I'm bleeding!" he cried out.

Holt grabbed Gino's head and held it still.

"You got a bad cut over your eye. You might need some stitches but you'll be okay. Let me wrap it."

Holt went to rinse Gino's head with water.

"Stop! That's your canteen filled with Kool Aide. Don't use that," Gino said.

"Yeah, yeah, I'm sorry. Hold still."

Holt smeared the wound with some anti bacterial ointment and wrapped a field dressing around Gino's head. Blood seeped through the bandage. "Head wounds bleed a lot but it ain't bad." He slapped him on his back. "Good as new," he said.

"Gino," Donnelly called. As Gino turned Donnelly snapped his photo. "You should have left some blood on your face. It would have made a better picture."

"When did you get a camera?" Holt asked.

"Always had it. I've been taken pictures for days. I don't like all those posed tough guy photos. The candid ones are much better. I can't wait to get them developed. I'll make copies for everyone."

Outside the shelling continued. The artillery from Cambodia was dismantling the camp piece by piece. Enormous chunks of concrete were thrown through the air. A shell landed behind the Montagnard trench's and showered the bunker with shrapnel. They could hear screams for medics.

Between the explosions they could hear whistles from the woods.

"What the fuck is that?" Gino hollered to make himself heard.

"The gooks are getting into position. They use whistles to coordinate their movements. The fucking whistles always scare the shit out of me," Holt said. "Gino get behind your gun. Jack, check in with the CP. Tell them what we got."

Holt busied himself opening the cans of ammunition for the fifty cal and laying the belts across the sandbags.

"Remember Gino, short bursts. Don't fuck up the barrel."

"Don't worry. I know what I'm doing."

"Stuff the cigarette filters in your ears; it's going to get loud."

From the wood line a single green star cluster shot up and exploded showering the sky in green light.

"Get ready, here they come," Holt screamed.

The tree line came alive with running, shouting, screaming men. The enemy mortar barrage, like a wave, moved forward forcing the Montagnards from the trenches back into their bunkers.

The camps mortar crews poured fire down upon the running soldiers. The NVA ran forward heedless of their own safety. Trumpets blared from the forest urging the men forward. Explosions fell among them shredding their bodies, but still they came.

Gino fired a short burst and adjusted his elevation. He fired another short burst. Satisfied, he fired in earnest. The large caliber bullets tore the advancing men to shreds.

As the men neared the camps shattered defenses, they were ensnared in the ruins of the barbed wire and tangle foot wire. The tangle foot was a grid of barbed wire laid about a foot off the ground. Although ripped apart by the enemy mortars, it still tore at the men's ankles and legs. The attack slowed. The NVA had to stop their mortar barrage in fear of hitting their own men. Once stopped, the Montagnards poured from their bunkers into the trenches and poured fire upon the soldiers. Dozens fell.

Gino fired the fifty cal with deadly accuracy. The muzzle blast was like lightening inside the bunker. Brilliant, explosive light momentarily blinded Holt, Gino, and Donnelly. The noise was deafening.

"Feed me!" screamed Gino over the noise. "Feed me!"

Gino threw open the receiver cover and Holt laid in another hundred round belt of ammo. Gino slammed the cover shut and pulled back the charging handle twice and continued firing. Men fell in the open field.

Like a welcome avenging, angel Spooky appeared overhead, the drone of its engines barely heard above the battles noise. Captain Mason directed Spooky to take out the hidden mortar positions first. The crew of Spooky dumped large canister flares turning the night into day. They fired their mini guns at the enemy mortar flashes delivering a deadly torrent of fire at the enemy positions. The bullets poured from the mini guns in a solid stream of death. The mortars fell silent. They circled back to address the attacking men.

They flew in a slow arc over no man's land sweeping the ground with bullets spaced every square inch. No one survived. When they were done the ground was littered with over one hundred fifty bodies. The air reeked of cordite and blood.

"Jesus fucking Christ, that was fucking awesome. We tore those gooks apart," Gino shouted to be heard by their deafened ears.

"Gino, you are the angel of death," Holt shouted jubilantly, slapping Gino on the back. "You did great."

"Did you see me? I keep screaming 'feed me, feed me' and you did. God damn it Holt, you and me, we tore those fuckers a new asshole."

"We sure did," Holt said sagging back against the sandbags. He fumbled for a cigarette and lit it with shaking hands. "Jack, call in a sit rep, see what's going on."

Donnelly remained quiet. Holt looked and saw Donnelly slumped over against the wall. He was clutching his shoulder.

"What happened?" he sobbed. "I think I've been hit."

Holt crawled to him and pulled his hand away from his shoulder. Blood covered his shirt.

"You took a bullet to the shoulder. It's not too bad, you'll live."

Holt set about cleaning the wound and applying a field dressing. "How's the pain? Do you want some morphine?"

"No, not now, maybe later. I don't even remember getting hit. I just remember sitting here. Is it over?"

"It's over for now. They'll think twice before coming back. Let me call Doc."

Holt spoke into the radio and laid the handset on the ground. "Doc's working on some of the Yards. I told him I got the bleeding stopped. He'll be here as soon as possible. He said to give you a morphine shot; he doesn't want you going into shock."

Holt jammed the syrette into Donnelly's thigh and squeezed. Donnelly settled back and smiled.

"That's good! Whoa man, I'm okay now. Don't worry about me, Sarge."

"Gino, keep an eye on him. Let me get on the horn with Mason and see what's happening."

"Spooky is going to remain overhead as long as he can. He'll have a replacement here before he leaves. We'll have cover for the rest of the night," Captain Mason said. "We have fourteen wounded, ten Montagnards and three of the artillery guys and your guy. Two Yards were killed. The north wall didn't have any activity, it was all on your side. We got lucky. The gook artillery did a number on us. There's not much left standing. One of our howitzers was destroyed and another damaged. The TOC is a shambles. Saigon is debating what to do."

"Debating what?" asked Holt.

"I would assume whether we stay or not. Who knows what the fuck they're doing? Medi-vacs will be in at first light if not sooner; have your guys ready to go."

"Roger that, six. Glad to hear you're alright."

"Why do I hear shooting still coming from your side?"

"It's the Montagnards. I think they're shooting at the NVA wounded tangled in the wire."

"Get them to stop that."

"Fuck it, let them have their fun. They ain't gonna listen to me." "This country, this war, it's all fucking insane. Shit, who cares what they do. I'll let you know when the choppers are inbound. Six out."

Holt secured the radio and turned to Gino and Donnelly. "Medi-vacs will be here soon. I'm going to make some coffee, you guys want some?"

"Woo, I am flying right now. Don't feel a thing. I'm out of here, bitches. I'm gone and I ain't coming back. Say your goodbyes now because I'm gone."

"That's right, pal. You did good. But for now do you want coffee?"

"Shit yeah, I want coffee and some donuts too. Hot fresh donuts, please. Sprinkled with sugar. Don't forget the sugar."

"I'll see if I can scrounge you up a pound cake. Gino, call Doc and ask him if it's okay for Jack to eat?"

Holt set about making coffee. He got out the sugar and creamer packets and started the water to boil. He stirred in the coffee packets, added the sugar, creamer and some cinnamon. He opened the tin of pound cake with his P38. He divided the mixture evenly into three canteen cups.

"Doc said liquids only, nothing solid."

Holt handed the cups out and settled back to light a cigarette. "Where's my fucking donut?" Donnelly wailed. "I'm wounded and I want a donut."

"Doc says you have to wait until you get to the hospital and the nurses will give you all the donuts you want. They'll even feed you."

"I want nude nurses. I want naked nurses to feed me their tits. I want to suck on their titties."

"You make sure you remember that. Ask them politely and I'm sure they will do it for you," Holt said while twirling his index finger against his temple. "This boy is flying high."

"Man, I'd get wounded too if I could suck on nurses titties," Gino said.

"Wouldn't we all. I've been wounded a bunch of times and never once did I see a bare breast," Holt said. "But truth be told, I never asked. Maybe Donnelly will have better luck."

Holt settled back and drank his coffee and smoked.

Gun shots and laughter came from the Montagnard trenches.

"Sounds like the Yards are having fun," Gino said.

Daylight broke and Spooky went off station. They were happy boys having been credited with over a hundred enemy killed.

As dawn broke the medi-vacs ships arrived accompanied by six Cobra attack helicopters and two small Loaches'. The little observation helicopters flew at tree top level daring the enemy to fire at them. The Cobras prowled over head.

Holt walked with Donnelly up to the landing zone which was crowded with wounded and the dead concealed by clouds of billowing yellow smoke. It was all so surreal, like a psychedelic movie.

Donnelly was shaking his head to the beat of an unheard song. "Holt, I want more morphine. I want morphine and titties," he said.

"You have plenty of morphine. Don't forget to ask the nurses to show you their boobs."

"I won't. I'll get pictures and send them to you. Hey, I forgot my camera. You find it and keep it safe. Okay?"

"Don't worry about anything. I'll get all your personal gear. I promise."

Holt walked him to the helicopter and helped him in. Donnelly kept repeating, naked nurses titties over and over and bobbing his head to unheard music.

The helicopter crewman looked at Holt and asked, "What the hell is he saying?"

Holt shrugged and said morphine by way of explanation. The crewman smiled and gave him a thumbs up.

With the wounded and dead loaded, the ships rose in a cloud of swirling dust and the remnants of yellow smoke.

Holt saw Captain Mason at the edge of the LZ and walked with him back to the TOC. The TOC lay in ruins. Someone had already spread a large green tarp over the shattered roof. They stood out front and looked around.

"Not much left," Mason sighed.

Holt looked at the gun pits and saw one of the 155MM howitzers completely destroyed and the second one with its breach damaged. All that remained were the two smaller 105 howitzers and a single 81MM mortar.

"Gun guys took a beating," Holt said.

"Yeah, they did but they never left their post," Mason said. "Hey, I just remembered, didn't both your guys get wounded?"

"Gino, what's his full name? Eugene Butler I think. He got a cut over his eye. Said he didn't want to leave. Doc stitched him up and wrote him up for a heart. Doc said he was okay to stay if that's what he wanted."

"Fucking foolish guy. He should have gone in. This ain't going to get any better."

"What's next? Think we'll bug out?"

"Look around, what's left to defend? I'll hear from the brass later today. If we go, it will be tonight so get your guys ready. Twenty kicks to the Australians. It will take us at least a day and a half."

"If we really pushed, we might be able to do it in a single day." "That would mean we'd have to walk all night and I don't want to do that. We'll do five or six hours tonight and the rest tomorrow. Make sure your men are rested and fully re-supplied. Standby, as soon as I hear anything you'll know."

Inside, the TOC was a flurry of activity.

"Spider, what's going on?" Mason asked.

"I got the burn barrel going, all non-essential papers are already burning. If we get the order to bug out the maps and that box are the last to go. I'll keep the fire burning. I made a fresh urn of coffee and found four thermos'. We'll have some hot coffee to take with us."

"The firing board?"

"I checked all the circuits. Everything seems in order. Just give the word and I'll blow the bunkers and everything inside them."

"You'll be the last one out, you and Holt's team. Make sure you wear your boots. Everyone all packed?"

"They are and bitching like crazy. They wonder why we can't fly out?"

"How many do we have?"

Spider rolled his eyes for a moment. "Non infantry counting the artillery guys eighteen."

"That's three choppers. Let me see what I can do."

"They're really not road worthy, Cap. They'll be dragging ass the whole way."

"Make sure your boots fit. Road worthy or not, you'll be walking out with the rest of us."

"The Captain says you're a foolish young man. You should have got on the medi-vacs," Holt said to Gino.

"What's that expression of yours, 'Fuck him in the mouth and feed him fish."

"He's just concerned."

"I'm fine. My face is a little swollen and the stitches hurt a bit. Other than that, I'm good to go."

"Your funeral. Let's go through Donnelly's pack and get his personal stuff. That fucking moron wanted his camera to take pictures of the nurses boobs."

"You don't think he'll ask them, do you?"

"Oh, I'm sure he will. He was flying high and that's all he had on his mind."

"Hopefully they'll knock him out before he gets to open his mouth." Gino laid out Donnelly's equipment. "Not much here. He has some letters and a few photos, his camera and little gook radio. Here's a couple of rolls of exposed film and two rolls of new film. He got a deck of cards with fuck pictures on the back. What should I do with them?"

"They're all yours. I'll take his camera and film and you take his letters and photos. Throw the rest of his ammo and grenades into his ruck and I'll take it down to the yards and see if they want it."

"What about his spare fatigues? He got some clean socks, two pair, and his beret."

"If the fatigues fit you, keep them. I'll take a pair of those socks. Hold onto his beret, he'll want that back."

Holt sat drinking coffee with Captain Peters.

"How did your boys do last night?" Holt asked.

"Kicked ass and took names. They are some ferocious little fighters. I feel bad about the two dead. A couple of the big shells landed really close. That's how I got the wounded and the two killed. These fuckers never bitch. They just keep on keeping on."

"You wonder what will happen to them when we pull out?"

"I try not to think about it. It's fucking inevitable. We ain't staying forever. We've trained a shit load of them. The last I heard over forty thousand. I doubt the South Viet's will want to take them on. Maybe they'll just leave them alone."

"What makes you think the South Vietnamese will be in charge when we leave?"

"For a little while at least. They might make out better under the north. Hopefully, they'll just fade away into the mountains and everyone will just forget they're there."

"It's going to be a free for all when we leave," Holt said lighting a cigarette.

"It'll be a shit show that's for sure. The CIA has a whole bunch of militia trained and supplied down south in the delta. Buddhists opposed to the Catholics in Saigon. They use Cambodia for a sanctuary just like the NVA. They won't be quiet."

"What about us? Do you think we'll hang around?"

"By us do you mean the Special Forces?"

"Yeah,"

"We'll move to Thailand. I'm sure we'll keep our hand in somewhere."

"Are you already to bug out?"

"Soon as we get the word. You and your guys are coming with us?"

"Yeah, I got nine guys left."

The Captain nodded at Holt's throat. " I see they gave you a Katha?"

"Said it was from Sangh."

Peters held out his wrist. "When they give you a bracelet, you know you've been accepted."

Holt showed his wrist. "Sangh gave me one before he left."

CHAPTER 31

The Bug Out

Holt and Jenkins walked to the TOC together. They passed the smoldering ruins that once was their barracks.

"So much for home sweet home," Holt said.

"The place was a pig sty to begin with," Jenkins said.

"Agreed but it was our sty. I wonder what the Captain wants?"

Jenkins turned his head from the barracks. "About the bug out, I would imagine. Who's that guy walking towards us?'

"That's Captain Shawn Peters, the advisor to the Montagnards." Holt waved to Shawn. "Did you get any sleep last night?"

"Not really maybe an hour, not more than that."

Shawn joined them. "You boys took a beating up here, " he said by way of greeting.

Holt sighed. "Not much left. Look over there; they cracked open the TOC like a walnut. That was three or four feet of concrete plus sandbags on top."

"Keep in mind, that was French concrete poured by slave labor over thirty years ago. Water probably seeped in and weakened it. It was ready to come down by itself. It just looked good," Shawn said.

"Like a lot of French stuff; it looks better than it is."

They entered the TOC and were greeted by Captain Mason. "Gentlemen, we are leaving today. Give me a minute and I'll brief you. Help yourself to coffee and donuts. What isn't finished will be thrown out."

They busied themselves fixing coffee. The donuts were stale but still edible.

Shawn looked wistfully at the bank of radio equipment.

"It's such a shame to blow this stuff up," he said.

"Not worth much. We have no antennas. They went during the shelling," Mason said. "Do you need radios?"

"Always. We are always short of everything. Our supplies come through the South Vietnamese. They steal half of everything we order and sell it on the black market and then it ends up in the hands of the VC or NVA. They're profiting off this war while we do the fighting for them."

"We have four Prick 25's, one in each of the corner bunkers. You're welcome to them."

"Off the books?"

"Combat loss. The spoils of war," Mason said grinning.

"Better yet."

"Alright, let's get started. If you will gather round the map. We are going to start the withdrawal at 1200 hours. Three Huey's are coming in to take out the non-infantry support people. Spider convinced me they have no on the ground combat experience. They won't be able to keep up with us and will just hold us back. Along with the Huey's we'll have six Cobra attack helicopters and three Light Observation copters. They will cover the Huey's and when they are gone they will cover our withdrawal. We have about one mile of open ground until we get into the forest. They will stay overhead until then. The Australian's have told me that the entire walk to their camp is through forest and not jungle. They said it's like walking through a park. So hopefully we should be able to make good time. Any questions so far? None? Okay, good."

"Have your men pack up everything they can carry and destroy what's left. Holt, you and your team will stay behind with Spider. Once we're clear of the camp, Spider will blow the bunkers and you'll meet up with us. Holt put thermite grenades on all the fifties and Spider, spike the two remaining guns. Fixed wing aircraft will fly over and bomb whatever is left. Finally, when we get closer to the Aussies they'll send out a patrol to guide us in.

I doubt we'll make it to the Aussies in one day. We'll probably spend a night in the field. Shawn if you have no objection half your Montagnards will lead and half will bring up the rear. We'll stay in the center. Hopefully everything will go smooth."

Walking back to the bunkers Holt addressed Captain Peters. "I'll have two of my guys bring the radios over to you along with all the spares batteries we can scourge up. What are you going to use them for?"

"Internal communication and coordination. It should be a big help." "One other thing, some of my guys have expressed interest in working with the CIDG program. Is there any strings you can pull?"

"When we get to the Aussies give me their names. I'll see what I can do. How about you?"

"Joe and I have been talking about it. I'll let you know. Thanks Shawn, I'll see you later."

As Peters walked away Jenkins said, "When did we talk about CIDG?" "We will. We have to get out of this SOG bullshit. CIDG sounds good." "Alright but just don't make any commitment on my behalf. I have to think about it."

"Your choice all the way. When the Huey's come in I'll meet you at the TOC. Make sure your guys are fully loaded, ammo, water and food. See ya pal."

In the bunker Gino was finishing packing his ruck.

"I got a sack of stale donuts; lets brew up some coffee and relax. It's 1015 now, choppers are coming in at 1200. We'll move out at 1230. We have a nice walk ahead of us. Gino, are you up to carrying Donnelly's radio or do you want me to carry it?"

"I'll take it. I'm fine." "How's the head?"

"Stitches hurt a bit, that's about it. Doc said it will leave a scar. He said the girls go wild over a guy with a combat scar."

"That's what I keep telling myself."

Holt made coffee and they sat and ate donuts. Holt turned on Donnelly's transistor radio. The AFVN disc jockey was playing Sly and the Family Stone, 'Everyday people'.

"Let's sit outside and get some sun before it starts raining again," Holt said.

Holt lit a cigarette and looked out across the wasteland.

"Jesus, just look at all those dead fucking gooks. Good thing we're getting out of here. By this afternoon they'll start stinking to high heaven."

"Think their pals will come down and get them?" Gino asked.

"If they do they better wait until dark. The jet jockeys are gonna blow this place up." Holt took a deep drag on his cigarette and drank some coffee. "Coffee and cigarettes, what could be better?"

"Pussy," said Gino emphatically.

Holt laughed. "Alright, I'll give you that one. Pussy! Then coffee and cigarettes."

"You miss your wife?"

"Ex wife," Holt corrected him. "Sometimes. I got a long letter I wrote her that I have to mail. It's a fucked up situation."

"Maybe you'll get back together."

"Who knows? Sometimes she expresses interest in that and other times she tells me how excited she is starting college and her new life. She doesn't exactly say her 'exciting new life' includes me."

They sat in silence for a moment.

"How about you? What are your plans?" Holt said.

"Like I said, my girl is off at college fucking Jody so—"

"Jody! He's every guy back home fucking our women. I wonder how they got that name. Jody? Not a common name."

"Good as any I guess.. Supposedly, Jody started in World War Two and is the name for any guy back home that steals your girl while you're away," Gino said. He was quiet for a minute. "I got two hundred and thirty days left over here then I got another year to do back in the states. I ain't staying in. I was thinking about extending over here and going for an early out. Then I think, why am I in such a hurry to go home? I have no education to speak of so I'll just end up in some dead end factory job like my father. So, why not just stay in the Army? And that gets me depressed."

"You got plenty of time to decide. Not to change the subject but did you hear from Tuna and Gator?"

"Yeah, while you was gone. They're okay. Just some minor scrapes and cuts from shrapnel. Doc got them all patched up."

"Assholes. They should have gone back in with the wounded and you should have too."

"Water under the bridge, Sarge. Too late now."

"Let's hope you don't regret it. It should be okay. This should be an easy march to the Australian camp. The Montagnards are walking point and we'll be in the middle snug as bugs."

At 1212 the Huey's circled the camp accompanied by the Cobras and LOACH helicopters. The Huey's landed in the midst of a cloud of green smoke while the Cobras prowled over the hills. The spare radios were given to the Montagnards and Gino set two M14 TH3 thermite grenades atop the receiver section of the machine gun. The thermite grenades produced a blazing heat sufficient to burn through an engine block. They made quick work of melting right through the fifty caliber guns.

The TOC support staff along with the artillery guys ran to the waiting helicopters and boarded. The helicopters rose in a billowing clouds of smoke and swirling dirt.

The nine remaining men of the A Team met in front of the TOC. Spider came out of the TOC dressed in new fatigues and boonie hat. He shrugged on his ruck sack and hefted his M-16. Inside thermite grenades flashed and burned through the radios.

"Looking good, Spider," Holt said.

"I feel like a real soldier now," he laughed. "I set the timers for fifteen minutes; we'd better boogie."

Captain Mason and his RTO led the way out of the camp. They proceeded down the grassy knoll and turned south into a meadow of grass and trees. From the south and north walls the Montagnards surrounded them in a diamond formation. In the meadow they turned an watched as four, massive, ear shattering, explosions destroyed the bunkers. Without a word they resumed their march south.

The sun beat down on them without mercy. Soon they were all drenched in sweat.

Holt wiped his face with his filthy green towel. The towel stunk of sweat. In front of him he watched as Spider reached for his canteen.

"Spider, how many canteens did you bring?"

"Four, counting this one. Why?"

"Just go easy. You have to make that water last until we reach the Australians."

"I feel like I'm sweating out a quart of water every ten minutes." Holt handed him a salt tablet.

"Take this with another sip of water. Spider are you wearing underwear?"

"Of course I am. Why would you ask that?"

"When we stop for a break I'm going to cut them off you. No one wears underwear out here. They're probably soaked now. They'll chafe your skin raw. You'll end up with a painful rash around your waist, upper thighs and balls."

"You're kidding me, right?"

"No Spider, I'm not. Trust me. I know what I'm doing."

"Captain?"

Mason looked back at Holt. "I don't think it's appropriate for an enlisted man to be commenting on an officers balls. But to answer your question Spider, yes, take your underwear off."

They walked for over an hour and left the meadow area without incident. They took a short break as they entered the forest at 1430.

Holt walked up to Spider holding out his combat knife.

"Drop those pants and I'll cut off your drawers."

"Captain?"

"Let him do it, Spider."

Spider unbuckled his fatigue pants and slowly lowered them. Holt knelt down and grabbed the waist band and slowly sliced down through the left leg. "Damn it Spider, hold still or this will turn into a neutering." Holt cut through the other leg and pulled the underwear off through his legs. "There you go, all done and hardly any blood. I have to say, Spider you have the whitest ass in all Vietnam. If you look up the definition of alabaster there would be a picture of Spider's ass."

"If I wrote home about this no one would believe me," Spider said.

"Routine tailoring, jungle style. Happens all the time," Holt said handing Spider his underwear. "What do I want these for?"

"Hold on to them until we stop and you can bury them. We don't leave anything for the gooks to use."

"As if they would want my sweaty drawers."

"Save them and use them as toilet paper."

"I don't plan on shitting in the forest."

Captain Mason turned to Spider. "So, how does it feel?"

Spider put his arms out to his side and rotated his hips. "It feels good, actually. But what happens if you take a leak?"

"Just give little Spider a few extra shakes and you'll be fine. No one worries about pee spots in the jungle," Holt said.

Even though the forest was shaded the heat didn't relent; if anything the humidity was even higher. The trees soared overhead to majestic heights, their branches interwoven blocking out direct sunlight. The ground was dappled with shafts of sunlight's like golden spears. The forest floor was a mixture of fallen leaves and small broken twigs. The bases of the large trees were covered in moss and mold giving everything a green tint. Among the lager trees were smaller trees and bushes competing for sunlight. Vines of every description snakes up the trees. Some were covered with large thorns almost three inches in length. Smaller vines lay on the ground ready to snag and trip the unwary.

The forest was alive with insects. Beetles as large as a man's fist lumbered through the grass like small, armored vehicles. Snakes hunted roaches that could jump and fly six feet or more. And of course there were mosquitoes. They flew in clouds fluttering up against faces, ears, and eyes.

Holt wiped the sweat from his face. He noticed Spider slapping at his skin.

"Spider take this and lather up," Holt said, handing him a bottle of oily insect repellant. "Don't get any in your eyes."

Spider squirted a liberal amount in his hands and rubbed his face.

"Don't forget your neck and hands," Holt said as he lit up a cigarette.

"Can we smoke out here?" Spider whispered.

"Normally we don't but we're walking with two hundred guys so I guess it's okay. Kind of hard to miss us."

"It's amazing how quiet everyone is. I thought it would be a lot noisier."

"We're are all professionals. We know what we're doing."

Indeed, the Montagnards moved like silent, green wraiths. Their tiger stripe fatigues blended perfectly with the forest making them almost invisible. The forest floor, covered in a thick matting of decaying debris silenced their footsteps.

"We're making good time," Spider said.

"We are but we won't get to the Australian base by nightfall. Couple of more hours and the Yards will start looking for a NDP."

"What's that?"

"NDP? It means night defense perimeter. They'll find some place they like and we'll settle in. Hopefully it will be before dark so we can cook our dinner. I hate eating cold C's."

Holt got out some beef jerky and handed Spider a thick piece. "Chew it slow. The salt will help replenish what you're sweating out."

Spider bit off a piece and chewed it thoroughly. "This is good. It's soft and moist."

"Some of the shit you get is dried out and crumbly. This stuff is made by the Classic Jerky Company. They've been around forever. The Post exchange carries it. I always stock up when I get the chance. Coffee too. You can never have enough coffee. Tonight, when we stop, I'll make you coffee that you'll love. Got the recipe from a friend, Nick the Spic. A Puerto Rican guy who loved his coffee."

"He didn't mind you calling him a spic?"

"Do you mind being called Spider? It's a term of endearment just like your name. We're all brothers out here."

"Even me?"

"Even you, Spider. You got more balls than most guys I know. You and your gun boys standing out in those pits trading shells with the gooks took plenty of guts. You're no REMF Spider; you're hard core."

Spider turned his head away and blushed.

The silence was broken by two explosions and AK automatic weapons fire. The men threw themselves to the ground. Within an instant return fire from M-16's filled the air and overpowered the AK fire.

Holt lay pressed to the ground as green tracers whizzed over them barely inches above their bodies. A single RPG whooshed over them and exploded in the woods.

Spider started to raise up and Holt pushed his face into the moist earth. "God damn it Spider stay down."

The Montagnards rose up and charged the ambush. The two sides of the diamond formation came on line and began to fold themselves around the NVA enveloping them. They enemy was literally cut to pieces by the murderous fire of the Montagnards. The Yards swarmed over the NVA bunkers and into their trenches killing anything that moved. Grenade explosions rocked the air.

Another flurry of green tracers flew over them. Spider cried out and rolled onto his side his hands pressed against his eyes.

Holt covered Spider with his body and pried Spider's hands from his eyes. He saw the largest fire ant he had ever seen on Spider's right eye, it's mandibles deeply imbedded in his eyelid. Holt held Spiders head still and pinched the ant between his thumb and forefinger and pried it off. Immediately the eyelid began to swell.

"Spider, you're okay." Holt looked around and saw Doc. "Doc, when you get a chance come over here."

Doc low crawled on his belly to Holt. "What's up?"

"It's Spider's eye. I don't know what happened. He might have taken some shrapnel from that RPG."

Doc held Spider's eye apart. "Doesn't look like shrapnel, looks like something may have bit him or he got poked."

"Yeah, whatever. Is he gonna be okay?"

"His fucking eye is going to swell shut but he should be okay. Spider hold still," Doc said as he smeared the eye with a tube of bacitracin. "I'll have to cover your eye. It's almost swollen shut as it is."

As Doc set about wrapping Spiders eye, Holt, surreptitiously, took some pictures. Doc wrote the time and date of the incident in his notebook. "You'll be good as new in a few hours." He gave Spider two Benadryl tablets. "Take these, it will help with the swelling."

"Will he get a heart?" Holt asked.

"A Purple Heart? Sure he will. Whatever it was it happened in combat under fire."

The firing had stopped. There was now only an occasional single shot and grenade explosions as the enemy bunkers were blown.

As Doc crawled away Spider asked Holt, "I'm getting a Purple Heart? It felt like I got bit by something."

"Spider, do I look like a doctor? If Doc says it was shrapnel then it was."

"Really?"

"Like Doc said, it's combat related. Congratulations Spider. You got a good clean wound. Your wife will be proud of you."

"Oh I can't tell her. She must never know. Not until I get home and maybe not even then. I don't want her to worry so I told her I'm the executive office and all I do is paperwork back at base camp."

"Well, we better do our best to keep you alive." Holt sat back and lit two cigarettes and passed on to Spider. "Can I ask you a personal question?" "I know what you're going to ask. How did a guy like me get a girl like her? I saw a picture of your wife. I could ask you the same thing?" "Touché."

"No I didn't mean—"

"I didn't always look like this. Oh Spider," Holt said wistfully, "when I came over here I was beautiful, perfectly smooth skin. I never even had acne when I was a kid. And now look at me; I'm a fucking monster. I haven't been home since this happened. She knows about it and keeps asking for a picture without camo face paint but I'm afraid if I send her one, I won't hear from her again."

"But you're still married?"

"No, the marriage was annulled. But enough about me."

"I met Evelyn, that's her name, at a college party. She said as soon as she saw me she had to meet me. And after talking with me for ten minutes, she knew we would be married and spend the rest of our lives together. She still tells me that." Spider looked around before continuing, "She's the first girl I ever... you know. And she'll be the only girl I'll ever be with."

"Jesus Spider! Your life is like a fairy tale. If this was a movie people in the audience would be saying right now, 'okay, that guy is doomed.' When we get back to base camp you keep your ass in base camp. You need to stay out of harm's way."

"I told her about the nick name you guys gave me and she loves it. In her letters she calls me Spider."

In the background the shots and explosions stopped.

"What were those Montagnards doing?"

"My guess would be shooting the gooks, making sure they were all dead." Holt said. "Sit tight. I need to check on my guys. How's your eye feeling?"

"It hurts like a son of a bitch. It feels hot and It's throbbing like hell." Holt walked to his team. "How you guys doing?"

"Captain said the Yards walked up onto a bunker complex and surprised a bunch of gooks. Did you see those fuckers? They are fucking fearless. They just rolled over those NVA boys. Killed everyone of them and chopped them up," Gator said.

"I'm sure glad they're on our side," added Tuna.

Gino held up a finger and they stopped talking.

"Twenty Yards are scouting in front of us looking for a place to stop. We're going to stop while it's still light out," Gino said relaying the Captains message. "How far do you think we've come?"

"About eight or nine klick's. If we leave early tomorrow we should hook up with the Australians by noon," Holt said.

"Why do you think the gooks let us leave the camp without mortaring us?" asked Tuna.

"With the Cobra's overhead why risk a fight. They got what they wanted. The camp is theirs. As far as I'm concerned, they're welcome to it," Holt said.

CHAPTER 32

Thunder And Foster's

The Montagnards found a NDP location about one quarter mile south. The men passed through the ambush site that was littered with dead enemy soldiers. The bodies lay in a tangled mess outside their destroyed bunkers. All had been shot multiple times and some had been mutilated. The Montagnards striped the bodies of anything of value, boots, sandals, weapons, backpacks, and ammunition.

Captain Peters handed Captain Mason a packet of documents and letters taken from the slain soldiers. He reported that eleven NVA had been killed and his indigenous troops had suffered four wounded. The wounded were designated minor and did not require immediate medical extraction.

"The NDP is just ahead," Captain Peters said.

"Jesus, your boys did a number on these guys," Mason said.

"When they get their blood up, it's kind of hard to control them."

"Why do they cut the bodies up?" Spider asked. He had not been able to take his eyes off the bodies. He stared at them with grim fascination.

"Something to do with the body has to be whole to enter the afterlife. Who knows? In so many ways they are one step up from primitive savages. I don't question their loyalty but I do question their methods. I'm due for reassignment soon and I'm looking forward to it. I'm tired of living with them. I want to be around Americans again."

"Suggestions about the NDP setup?" asked Mason.

"My guys will provide the outer perimeter. I'll put out four LP's after dark. The listening posts will be at the compass points. We'll set out Claymore's and trip flares. You can get a good night's sleep. I'll set up with you guys in the center if that's okay."

"That's fine, Shawn. I figure we have about ten kilometers before we hook up with the Australians. If we get an early start we should meet them around noon. I would suggest as we get close to them my guys take point. Don't want any misidentification."

"Agreed. Sounds like a plan. How about we start off at 0700?"

"Sounds good. How are your wounded guys? Do you need my medic?"

"Couldn't hurt if he takes a look at them, thanks."

"Doc, go with Captain Peters and look at his wounded?"

"Tuna go with Doc," Holt added.

They reached the NDP location and watched as the Montagnards set up a tight circular perimeter. The Yards were not enthusiastic about digging. They scraped out some shallow fighting positions and then set about preparing their food.

"Do you want to dig in Captain?" Holt asked.

"I don't think that will be necessary. In forest this thick we don't have to worry about mortars. If we get hit it will be from line of sight weapons, RPG's and small arms fire. Maybe drag some of those logs over to provide some ground cover."

Doc and Tuna returned and took their place in the CP.

"Some shrapnel wounds and one guy was grazed by a bullet," Doc reported. "Tough little bastards, they're good to go."

"Even with the Montagnards providing security I think we should stand shifts," Mason said. "Two guys, two hours?"

Everyone agreed.

Holt opened his rucksack and got out a C-Ration meal, Beans and Baby Dicks, his favorite.

"Spider, what are you eating?"

Spider held the can up and examined it. "Ham and Lima Beans."

"They call them 'Ham and Motherfuckers'. It's garbage. Even the gooks won't eat that shit. I brought extra, let me see what I got." Holt sorted through some cans. "How about Meatballs and Beans or Beefsteak, Potatoes and Gravy."

"Meatballs and Beans sounds good."

"Sit back and relax, I'll do the cooking."

While the food was being prepared, Gino was fiddling with Donnelly's transistor radio. He finally got AFVN to come in clearly.

"Oh my God, that's The Dead," Spider exclaimed.

"What dead?" Gino said.

"The Grateful Dead. I got to see them when I was in San Francisco."

"You're a Dead Head?" Holt asked.

Spider held his arms out straight and started swaying to the music.

"Spider are you okay? What are you doing?"

"The Dead dance; you just let the music get hold of you and let it take you away. I saw them when they put on a free concert in the park. I had dropped acid and thought I was in heaven."

"You took acid?"

"Just a little bit. The first time I heard Jerry, I thought I was hearing the voice of God. He's incredible!"

"Captain, do you believe this guy? Spider, you are like an onion. The more layers we peel back the more we learn about you."

Holt went back to preparing their meal. He dug a shallow hole and placed his stove inside. He cut off a chunk of C-4 explosive and rolled it into a ball and put it inside the stove. The stove was nothing more than an empty can with holes cut along the sides to provide air. He opened the cans with his P-38 and bent the lid back for a handle. He lit the C-4 and it flared up beneath the can of food. He stirred the contents and within a minute the contents were boiling. He passed the can to Spider along with a tin of crackers. He then prepared his own meal.

Spider took a tentative bite of the food. "Not bad, not bad at all."

"Hot sauce?" Holt asked offering a bottle of Louisiana hot sauce.

"Thank you."

"What do you have Captain?"

"Chicken and Noodles with hot sauce."

"You two served together in the infantry?" Spider asked.

"Yes we did. The Captain was just a young pup, a butter bar when we met. I took him under my wing and taught him everything he knows. I probably saved his life," Holt said.

"And Sergeant Holt was a constant pain in my ass," countered Mason.

"More like a hemorrhoid. An annoyance that you learn to live with," Holt said smiling.

"A very large, annoying hemorrhoid."

"Did you guys see a lot of action?"

"Our fair share and then some," Mason said.

"I'm told experienced combat veterans form a strong bond."

"You should know Spider; you're part of the brotherhood now," Holt said.

"I appreciate that."

Holt finished his meal and dug out his battered tin coffee pot. "Coffee, anyone?"

"We're in for a treat Spider. I've been told Holt's coffee is legendary."

Holt set about making the coffee. He boiled the water and added three packets of coffee, six packets of sugar, and three packets of creamer. He let it boil for a minute and added some cinnamon and nutmeg. He poured a generous cup for Mason, Spider, and himself. He then sat back and lit a cigarette. "I've said it before and I'll say it again, coffee and cigarettes can't be beat."

"I've told you before, pussy is better," said Gino.

"And I agree Gino. But considering there is no pussy available I'll stick with cigarettes."

Spider laughed. "I know I'm going to sound stupid but I'm really enjoying this. It's just so fucking exciting."

"Do it every day and the excitement wears off leaving a dull throbbing pain," Holt said.

"But you keep coming back," Spider said.

"I got nowhere else to go." Holt turned away. "I got a pound cake and a nutmeg roll to have with coffee. Anyone?"

Mason caught Spider's eye and shook his head. Spider's face colored and he nodded.

They shared the desserts in silence.

That night the listening posts to the south and the east reported movement. They withdrew back into the perimeter. The NVA probed the southern perimeter. There was sporadic gunfire throughout the night but no large scale event. Two Claymore's were fired at some shadowy figures. In the morning the Montagnards found two blood trails leading south.

The men woke at 0530 and prepared a quick breakfast meal.

As Holt sat smoking Spider quietly said to him, "I need to use... the bathroom. Number two."

Holt called out, "Gator, do me a favor. Go with Spider and watch him take a shit."

"What?" Spider shouted. "Why would he do that?"

"Wrong choice of words. He ain't going to watch you, he's going to watch over you while you're indisposed. Go over there behind those bushes. Here, you'll need this," Holt said handing Spider an entrenching tool. "Dig a hole and bury it."

At 0650 Captain Peters informed Mason his men were ready to go. He had already sent out an advance patrol of twenty men to scout the area to the south along their line of march.

Captain Mason gave the word to saddle up and they moved out.

At this time of the morning it was still relatively cool. The temperature was in the low seventies. Above the trees storm clouds were gathering, rolling in from the mountains in Cambodia. They walked silently through the darkening forest.

Up ahead the twenty man patrol ran into a squad of NVA setting up an ambush. A quick and vicious fire fight broke out and the column halted. To the east a large group of men could be seen running in the forest.

The Montagnards immediately took off after them. Holt and his team took up positions in the broken Montagnard lines. Once again green tracers filled the air. Bullets impacted the trees showering them with bits of bark and falling leaves. Grenade explosions could be heard in the distance.

An enemy squad of sapper's had slipped past the Montagnards and closed in on the Americans. They each carried seven pound bags of explosive with a protruding fuse.

Three men broke from the group and ran towards Holt's team firing their AK's from the hip. One stopped pulled the fuse on his satchel charge and started to throw it towards the crouching team. He was cut down by a hail of bullets and the charge fell at his feet. It exploded blasting the man into small pieces. He disappeared in a red cloud of blood.

Holt and his men moved forward firing their CAR-15's. Two more enemy fell dead.

Holt kneeled next to a tree changing magazines. Two bullets hit the tree inches from his head. When he looked up he saw an enemy soldier taking aim at him. Before he could fire Gator shot him three times. Bullets passed through the man's jaw ripping off the lower part of his head. He dropped to his knees and Gator shot him a fourth time in the chest. Three other men broke cover and tried to flee. Nine CAR-15's firing on full automatic tore them to pieces. Holt, Gino, and Gator advanced towards the bodies while the remaining team members provided cover. Holt looked down at the bodies. They were so distorted by bullet impacts they looked like bloody sacks of meat.

Ten Montagnards emerged from the trees chattering excitably; they stopped when they saw Holt. They looked at the NVA and gave Holt broad toothy smiles. They quickly searched the remains and carried away any weapons and equipment they could retrieve.

Holt and the team walked back to Captain Mason and his command group. Jenkins handed Holt a lit cigarette.

"Why the fuck don't they leave us alone? We're leaving their area. Why don't they just let us go?" Jenkins said.

"They must really hate us to want to kill us so bad."

When they saw Captain Mason Holt held up his hand with his fingers splayed wide. "Five enemy KIA, we're fine."

It took twenty minutes for all the Montagnards to return. They were all very excited and it took an effort of their NCO's to get them under control.

"We need to take a break," Shawn said. "My boys are all jacked up. It's going to take a while to calm them down."

Mason looked at his watch and frowned. "It's almost 1100. We're behind schedule. I guess thirty minutes more won't matter."

Holt looked at the Montagnards. "Who are your NCO's?"

Shawn looked at a group of about twenty and shrugged. "Who the fuck knows? We pick the ones who speak the best English as NCO's and officers. In reality they function more as interpreters. The Yards pick their own leaders and that can change from day to day. We give orders to the officers and they pass them on. Then the orders are discussed; it's all done by consensus. If they all agree the orders are obeyed, if not, they change the orders. They kind of function independently, like they did today. Our orders are more like suggestions."

"They wouldn't bail on you like the ARVN's did?"

"They might. But they would tell us first and the reason why. They wouldn't just leave us on our own. I don't blame them. They've been fucked over so much they have to look out for themselves."

"What happens to all the weapons and gear they collect? Do you turn it in?"

"Naw, they keep it. For what purpose I don't ask. Why do you ask?"

"Sergeant Sangh told me they are stockpiling weapons and ammo for the day when we leave. He knows the ARVN will try and disarm them and they want to be ready. He said they want to establish an independent province under their control."

Captain Peters looked at Holt. He lit a cigarette and passed the pack to Holt. "He told you that? It doesn't surprise me. They tried once before. In September of 1964 they had plans to seize Ban Me Thuot in Darlac Province. In the spring and summer of 1964 the government in Saigon was changing hands daily. There was massive political unrest and attempted military coups. There were demonstrations by Catholics, Buddhists, students, and labor organizations. At the end of the summer, General Nguyen Khanh seized power by a military coup in Saigon. That's when the rebellion happened. There was heavy fighting between the Yards and the South Vietnamese. The Special Forces had the trust of the Montagnards and were able to broker peace but there has been tensions ever since."

"Why Ban Me Thuot?"

"The yards always considered it the capital of their nation. What's interesting is that the Montagnards were aligned with the VC in the forties and fifties. They helped fight the Japanese and then the French. Then Ho Chi Minh came along as the nationalist leader in the north. He wants a unified Vietnam. He doesn't want to share power with the VC. That's why the VC did the heavy lifting during Tet. They were decimated during Tet and for all intents and purposes are no longer a threat to Ho. Now, all we see and fight are NVA in the south. The Yards could switch allegiance if Ho offered them a better deal. It's a fucked up situation and our government doesn't seem to know what they're doing. The CIA isn't thrilled with Saigon and has ties with all the dissident movements and supplies them with arms and other assistance. They're spread throughout Cambodia and Laos and maintain their own private armies. This place is a nightmare of intrigue and conspiracy."

Holt just nodded.

"I'm surprised Sangh would mention any of this to you," Shawn said.

"Don't forget, he sees me as some sort of avenging demon. Maybe he thinks I'm here to avenge the Yards."

"Interesting," Shawn said. "Well, I better get my guys under control so we can move out again. Nice talking to you, Sergeant."

Captain Mason stopped Shawn. "The Australians say they have been waiting for us, and right now, their ass is hanging in the breeze. They want to know, and I quote, 'What the fuck is the holdup?' What should I tell them?"

"God damn Aussie's. Tell them the truth. Tell them we're fighting our way to them and if they're too scared to wait to go back to their camp and we'll find our own way."

Behind them they heard massive explosions.

"That's the Air force bombing our camp," Mason said. Lighting a cigarette he calmed himself before continuing. "I'll tell them to do what they think is best. Cocksuckers, we didn't ask for their help; they offered it."

Shawn waited and heard Mason repeat his message in more diplomatic terms.

"Well?"

"The bulk of their men are going to return to camp. They'll leave behind a six man SAS patrol to guide us." The SAS, Special Air Service, is the equivalent to the American's Green Berets.

"How far are they?"

"They said they heard the gunfire clearly so they can't be far. Maybe two klick's ahead. I'm going to send Holt's team ahead to make contact. If they see your Montagnards they might shoot at them."

"Agreed," Shawn said lighting his own cigarette.

Mason signaled Holt forward. "Take your team and make contact with the Australians. They should be about two klick's ahead on a heading of a hundred and eighty-six degrees. We'll give you a fifteen minute head start and then follow. I want frequent radio updates."

"Roger that."

"Be careful, everyone is on edge and we still have gooks crawling around. Your password is Tiger and they'll answer, Thunder."

Holt signaled his team and relayed the instructions. Within minutes they took off and disappeared into the trees.

They did the first kilometer quickly. They then slowed their pace and moved more cautiously for the remaining klick.

Ahead of them they heard gunfire. They could see green tracers through the trees. The AK fire was answered by the Australian L1A1 SLR. They moved forward silently until they could see the battle in front of them. Six Australians to Holt's right were pinned down behind a fallen log. One man appeared to be wounded and was being attended to by a medic. The four others were firing at the advancing NVA to Holt's left. No more than a hundred feet separated the two groups.

"Gino, call it in. We'll get on line and move forward. We're on their flank and they don't know we're here. We'll get as close as we can. Wait until I fire then open up."

Holt's team got on line and moved forward. The Australians were putting out a heavy volume of fire and the NVA advance faltered. Holt saw one soldier load up an RPG and start to take aim. Holt fired a short burst and hit the man in the chest. He fell backward and the rocket propelled grenade whooshed up and exploded in the overhead branches.

The entire team moved rapidly catching the enemy by surprise. They fired controlled bursts and watched the soldiers fall. Several tried to turn and run and were cut down where they stood. In less than a minute it was all over. Holt's ears were ringing. The forest was clouded by smoke and falling leaves. The smell of cordite and blood was overpowering. Holt's team walked through the bodies firing single shots into their heads.

As they neared the Australians Holt called out Tiger! Someone answered, "We see you."

"Tiger!" Holt said again.

"Fucking Thunder, mate. I said we see you."

As Holt neared the huddled group he said, "You must be the Aussie's sent out to save us."

A tall blond man wearing a sand colored beret stood and extended his hand, "That would be us. Consider yourselves saved."

Holt stood a full head shorter than the Australian. "You're a big one, aren't you?"

"Normal size I would imagine. Appears you may have shrunk a bit in all this rain.

"I'm Staff Sergeant Holt."

Holt's hand was engulfed in the Aussie's paw.

"And I would be Staff Sergeant Oliver Wilson. In Australia it's common for us to have a first name and a surname."

"Just Holt."

"Well, just Holt, where is the rest of your group?"

"They'll be with us shortly. We have over a hundred Montagnards with us. Will that be a problem?"

"Not for us."

"How's your man? Was he hurt badly?"

"That's Timmy, a new boy just out of the pouch. He needed to be blooded," Oliver said, looking over his shoulder at the prone man.

"So what happened here?"

"Those lads came out of nowhere. True, we may have been a bit lax in our security but we had it all under control. We would have finished them in short order."

"That's the way it looked to me, "Holt said.

"Truth be told, it was a fucking dog's breakfast, we're lucky you came along. It won't be reported that way but thanks all the same."

"A dogs breakfast?"

"A fuck up."

The Montagnards appeared silently and set upon the bodies.

"We should be taking in those weapons," Oliver observed as he looked sideways at the scavenging soldiers.

"Just let them have them. Oh, here comes Captains Mason and Peters."

Introductions were and Captain Mason asked, "What happened here?"

"It was a dogs breakfast, sir," Holt said quickly.

Mason looked at Holt and started to say something but stopped. "We'd like to be on our way Sergeant Wilson. Is you man okay to walk?"

Sergeant Wilson turned to his squad. "Doc?"

"Timmy's being a bit of a whinger but he'll walk." Mason looked puzzled.

"They speak weird English but you'll get the hang of it."

The walk to Camp Adeline took about thirty minutes and was without incident.

"The place used to be a former rubber plantation. The rubber trees begin on the other side of the camp. That big colonial house over there is where the command post is along with the officer's billet."

Sergeant Wilson addressed Captain Peters. "I'm sorry but we don't have room for your boys within the camp proper. But there are some prepared bunkers on the outer ring. Will that be sufficient?"

"That will be fine. We do need some resupply."

"My understanding is that your fellas will be bringing in resupply tomorrow. If you need anything until then just let me know. I will be your liaison while you are our guests. Sergeant Holt, if you will follow Sergeant Logan over there he'll direct you to a tent we have set up for you. If you don't have any plans we'd like you to be our guests for dinner at our compound."

"Shrimp on the barbie?"

"Steaks on the barbie and Fosters beer. I assume you boys are old enough to drink?"

CHAPTER 33

Meet Mr. Black

The first thing that struck Holt was that Camp Adeline was immaculate. It was as if someone had set a military installation in the middle of an urban park. On the way to their tent they passed under soaring majestic trees which shaded the installation in dappled sunlight. The walkways were laid out with military precision and appeared to be recently swept.

"This is the most beautiful Army base I have ever seen," Holt said to Sergeant Logan.

"We have the Colonel to thank for that, Colonel Smith," Logan replied. "He spends most of his time on camp improvements. He's not the most aggressive commander we've ever had. We seldom do any extended patrols and we don't mount any large scale operations. He lives in fear of a major enemy offensive against the camp. When we went to meet you we rode out in four APC's, armored personnel carriers. As soon as he heard the firing he recalled the carriers and left us to meet you. I guess he thought the firing was a prelude to an attack on the camp."

"Things are quiet here?"

"For the most part. We get mortared occasionally, nothing serious. My feeling is, as long as we leave them alone, the gooks leave us alone."

"How many men are stationed here?" Holt asked.

"A mixed battalion. We have about seven hundred and fifty guys. Infantry, artillery, armor and aviation. And of course two teams of SAS headed by a captain and a lieutenant. We're the colonel's red headed stepchild. He barely tolerates us since we don't report directly to him. We run patrols around the camp. But everything has to be approved by him so that we have artillery and aviation support. He keeps us on a tight leash. Now you lads, I understand, roam far and wide."

"That's our job. Too far and wide for my taste. We establish camps along the Cambodian and Laotian borders and man them with a variety of indigenous and South Vietnamese troops. We try and interdict the flow of men and material into South Vietnam."

"Have you done any cross border patrols?" asked Logan.

Holt ran his fingers across his lips. "Can't say one way or the other."

"Understood." They came up to a standard issue Army tent surrounded by chest high sand bags. "This will your digs while you're here. There's a pretty stout bunker out the side door if you need it." Logan pointed, "That will be the showers over there. I'll send someone by to escort you to the mess tent. We're having a barbie tonight in your honor."

"Look forward to it. What's your first name, Sergeant?"

"Liam."

"Thank you Liam. We'll see you later."

The men showered and sat outside to air dry. Holt was wearing shorts and his Ho Chi Minh sandals. Jenkins sat next to him wearing green GI underwear and shower flip flops.

"What do you think of our hosts?" Holt asked.

"What do you mean?"

"You didn't notice anything strange about them?"

"No, I didn't," Joe said warily.

"Nothing out of the ordinary. You didn't see that they're all clones of one another. They're perfect. They look like a Special Forces recruiters wet dream. All of them were six foot tall with a swimmers build, broad shoulders and chest. Short cropped sandy hair and blue eyes. They look like the result of some sort of Aryan genetic experiment."

"Maybe that's what Australians look like. Don't be a dick."

"You look at them and then you look at our crew. We look like cast offs from a ASPCA yard sale. Mutts!"

"Mutts or not, we saved their asses today. Maybe they could use a few more mutts."

"One thing we have in common, they have asshole officers. Liam was..."

"Liam?"

"Yes, Liam. Jesus, Joe I'm friendlier than you. I ask people what their first names are. I'm a people person."

"That's a new one. So tell me, what did Liam say?"

"He said the Colonel that runs this place is a real wanker."

"Wanker?"

"Yeah, like a dickhead. I'm trying to learn Australian slang. Get with it Joe."

"You have to admit, this place is gorgeous."

"They don't do much patrolling. Did you see those hills to the west that overlook the camp? I would bet they are infested with gooks. All dug in nice and cozy."

"Not our problem. We'll only be here a few days." Joe looked at his watch, "We should be getting dressed."

At 1730 another SAS clone came and escorted them to dinner. Holt and his team were dressed in relatively clean, standard issue, jungle fatigues complete with Green Berets.

As they walked their guide pointed out the essential features.

"Piss tubes everywhere, the shitter is over there. To the east and the west we have artillery pits and the helipad is on the northern side of the camp. We have twelve APC's and they are placed on the perimeter of the camp. Our mess tent is right down this road. Breakfast is served starting at 0700."

As they entered the mess tent all conversation stopped, then the Australians broke into thunderous applause.

At the front of the room Sergeant Wilson stood. "Boys, these are the American lads that pulled our bacon from the fire."

The applause died down and Wilson gestured them forward. They sat at a place of honor in the front.

"This is our whole contingent, twenty four SAS and an equal number of support troops," Oliver said. "I know you Americans have servants waiting on your every need but we don't stand on formalities here. Beer is on ice in the esky, help yourself."

Holt looked to where Oliver pointed and saw several large, olive drab, insulated coolers overflowing with American beer and large pint cans of Fosters beer.

They drank beer, smoked and talked about the day's events. At 1800 they were called forward to the serving line and were greeted by mounds of grilled steaks, potatoes wrapped in foil, baked beans, and other vegetables. A stereo system blared AFVN over loudspeakers.

After eating Holt intermingled with the SAS. At some point he walked outside to get some fresh air and quiet. Sergeant Oliver followed. The sat on a bench to the side of the door.

"All kidding aside, I want to thank you for what you did today." Holt lit a cigarette and said, "You would have done the same for us." "Can I ask, what happened at your camp?"

"The NVA wanted the camp and they took it. I was only there about a week. The camp was getting shelled on a daily basis. Accurate, devastating fire from the surrounding hills. They had a bunch of large guns across the border and those guns tore the camp to pieces. It made resupply and evacuation of the wounded almost impossible. The final straw came when the South Vietnamese pulled out without so much as a explanation. With them gone we were spread too thin to adequately maintain the perimeter. The NVA started a series of ground attacks. Resupply became impossible. We were short of everything, food, water, and ammo. Finally we had no choice but to abandon the camp. Either that or we would be overrun and everyone would die."

Oliver sat back and exhaled loudly. "Do you think it could happen here?"

"Your guess is as good as mine. I would say you need to get up in those hills and see what's going on."

"That's not going to happen. Our government won't stand for heavy casualties. Our involvement in Vietnam is becoming unpopular at home. Protests are mounting just like in the states. And now, your president is pulling out American troops. Talk is we'll be pulled out sooner than later." "The days of these isolated border camps are numbered," Holt said. "The helicopter units are complaining how costly it is to maintain them. They are losing too many ships and aircrew. To make matters worse the Special Forces camps are under the jurisdiction of the South Vietnamese government. They won't lift a finger in support. They despise the Montagnards and could care less what happens to them. When supplies are ordered about half shows up. The other half is pocketed by the generals in Saigon and sold on the black market. Our own supplies end up with the NVA."

"But surely your military would come to your aid?"

"You would think so. The 1st Division and the 25th Division were the closest units to us. The 1st is being pulled out and the 25th is spread too thin. They weren't about to mount a major offensive to rescue an isolated camp. We were pretty much on our own. The only ones we could rely on were our own Special Forces and the CIDG. But we couldn't wait for them. We were lucky we had you guys."

"This is not what I signed up for. We spend most of our time filling sandbags," Liam said.

Holt stood up. "Maybe it's time we rejoined the party. Hey, can I ask a favor? Is there any way I could get a set of your camo fatigues? They're pretty cool looking."

"Hmm," Oliver said scratching his chin. "That could be a problem.

Let me see if we have any in children's sizes." "How do you say 'fuck you' in Australian?"

Inside, Captains Mason and Peters along with Spider had joined the men. Spider was laughing and appeared to have already consumed an abundance of alcohol.

Captain Mason waved Holt over to him.

"Your team seems to be having a good time. It's good to see them laughing again," Said Mason.

"They needed this. What's up, Captain?"

"Don't get too drunk tonight. You have to report to the command post tomorrow at 10 AM sharp."

"What's this all about? Who's asking for me?"

Mason looked at Captain Peters and shrugged. "Just be there. Okay?"

"Sure. 10 AM. You can't tell me anything else?"

"I don't know anything else. Do me a favor, keep your wits about you and don't commit to anything without speaking to me first. Okay?"

"Yeah, sure, I guess."

At 10 AM, Holt walked up the flagstone path to the old French villa. He entered through the doors and looked around. He saw a clerk sitting in an alcove.

"I'm Sergeant Holt. I was told to report here at 10 AM."

"You can have a seat over there. I'll let them know you're here."

"Who are you going to let know?"

"Whoever answers the phone." After a minute he picks up the phone and says to Holt, "Down the hall on the right, room twelve."

Holt walked down the hall; the floor was some sort of polished stone. He was self conscious of his boots which were scuffed and faded to a light tan color. He sniffed at his armpit; his fatigues smelled damp and musty. At room twelve, he knocked and opened the door.

Inside he saw Captain Shawn Peters and another man dressed in civilian clothes. Shawn nodded to him and the other man extended his hand and said, "Sergeant Holt, great to finally meet you."

Holt shook his hands and said, "And you are?"

"Mr. Black."

Holt looked at him oddly.

"Joe Black. But please call me Joe." "And you are from…?"

"I work for the United States Agency for International Development, the USAID."

"Uh huh," said Holt. "What can I do for you, Mr. Black?"

"Please, call me Joe. May I offer you some coffee?" he said, pouring Holt a cup without waiting for a response. "Cream and sugar?"

"Please."

As Black prepared the coffee, he said, "Feel free to smoke if you want."

Captain Peters walked toward the door. "I'll leave you two to get acquainted. Nice seeing you again Sergeant."

Holt watched him leave without saying anything. He somehow felt betrayed.

Holt settled into a chair and lit a cigarette.

Mr. Black sat across from Holt and opened up a folder. "I have a copy of your 201 folder. I must say it's very impressive."

They sat in silence for a few minutes while Joe thumbed through Holt's personal folder.

"I have a proposal I'd like to make. I have an assignment that you would be well suited for, your team as well."

"Shouldn't they be here too?"

"I trust you will relay the information to them accurately. How would you like to come work with me for about thirty days."

"The USAID?"

"What? Oh, yes. The USAID, of course."

"No thank you. I appreciate the offer but I'm happy where I am."

"But you haven't even heard the offer yet."

"I'm trying to get into the CIDG program."

"I can arrange that, in fact I can guarantee that. That or any other assignment of your choosing. For your team too."

"Providing I first do this thirty day thing for you?"

"That goes without saying."

"What exactly would I have to do?"

"You know a Montagnard Sergeant named Sangh? I'd like you to make contact with him."

"I have no idea where he is. I wouldn't know how to get in contact with him," Holt said.

"I have a general idea where he might be. I just need you to find him and make introductions."

"I heard he was up north in central Laos." "That's where I believe he is."

"It's illegal to go into Laos."

"Tomato, tomahto. We have several small facilities in Laos."

"The USAID?"

"Yes. How long would it take you to walk one hundred miles give or take through the triple canopy jungle?"

"Anywhere from ten to fifteen days depending on the terrain."

"Oh, the terrain is quite rugged."

"I'm not really interested."

"I wish you would reconsider. You see, you've already been assigned to me on thirty days TDY."

"TDY?"

"Temporary Duty assignment."

"So if this has all been settled why even ask me?"

"I would much prefer that you sort of volunteer."

"Hmm," Holt said and lit another cigarette.

"There's more to my offer. First we would go to Thailand. If you want, I have arranged for you all to jump with the Thai Special Forces and earn your Thai parachute wings. That's just a little bonus. Second, you will all receive a seven day, all expenses paid, R & R in Bangkok. After the R & R, you and I will travel to northern Thailand where I will explain more about this assignment. While we're gone your men are free to enjoy the beaches of Thailand. So, what do you say?"

"Let me talk to my team and I'll get back to you."

"You have to be quick about it; we leave this afternoon," Joe said.

"You don't sound convinced. How do I convince you?"

"It's me you want, why do you have to involve my team in all this?"

"It will be quite an arduous journey. Working with men you already know would have its advantages."

"Put yourself in my position. A strange guy with an obviously phony name comes along with an absurd story and I'm just supposed to believe him and then convince my men to accept all this crap based on what?"

"Shawn knows me."

"My trust in Shawn has diminished greatly."

"How about Master Sergeant Carl Soujac? Do you trust him?" I'll have Carl meet us in Thailand and he can vouch for me. Is that good enough?"

"You know Slow Jack?"

"I do. We've worked together many times."

"Alright. You let me speak to Soujac alone without your interference and we'll see."

"Done. Just impress upon your men that all of this is highly classified and not to be discussed with anyone else. Be ready to leave at 1300."

Back at the tent he found Captain Mason sitting with his men.

Mason and Holt walked outside and sat on some lawn chairs under a huge banyan tree. Holt told Mason all that had transpired.

"So do you think this guy is from the CIA?" Mason asked.

"Duh? What gave it away?"

"The Special Forces works closely with the CIA. The whole SOG program is run in conjunction with them. So in effect you've already worked with them." Mason got a cigarette and offered the pack to Holt. "How do you feel about all this?"

"I feel there's a lot he hasn't told me. I mean, traipsing through the mountains of northern Laos with someone I don't know. How would you feel?"

"I feel somehow responsible for getting you involved in this. Shawn was asking a lot of questions about you. I should have known better." Mason scuffed his boot in the dirt. "Would you feel any better if I was involved in this."

"Yeah, I'd feel a lot better. I trust you."

"Well get your team together and I'll go speak to this Mr. Black. If he has you on TDY you don't have much of a choice."

"He didn't show me any orders. Who knows what he has?"

"I'll confirm his orders. As your commanding officer I have a right to see the orders."

Holt and the team stood outside their tent at 1300. The men were excited. They all had questions that Holt couldn't answer. Gino did confirm the working relationship the Special Forces had with the CIA. He explained it was told to them at Fort Bragg.

A jeep pulled up to their tent driven by an Australian PFC. Joe sat in the front and Captain Mason sat in the back with all his gear.

Mr. Black was all smiles. "Gentlemen, it's a sincere pleasure to meet you all." He addressed Holt privately. He indicated to Captain Mason. "I hope you see that I will do whatever is necessary to gain your trust. You wanted Captain Mason to come along, so you got him."

They walked through the gates of the camp to a waiting Chinook helicopter. They flew for forty five minutes and landed at a remote section of the Ben Hoa airbase where they immediately boarded an AC-47, Air America cargo plane.

Within minutes they were airborne.

CHAPTER 34

Shambala

They flew south west to avoid Cambodian airspace. Once in the Gulf of Thailand, they turned north west and flew direct to Bangkok. At a cruising speed of one hundred and sixty miles per hour the flight took about four hours.

On the plane Holt wrote a long letter to Janet. The men were cautioned not to seal their envelopes as all letters would be opened and censured before mailing. They could say they were on a temporary assignment in Thailand but nothing more.

The other men aboard the flight wrote letters, slept or read books or magazines.

They landed a little after 1800 hours and were whisked by truck to a house on the outskirts of Bangkok.

"Down the hall and to your left is where you can stow your gear and weapons," Joe said. "We have provided a change of civilian clothes for you. You can buy additional clothing at the shop at the hotel and charge it to your rooms. Please, don't go overboard. We do have a budget for this mission."

"We'll spend whatever we want," Holt said bluntly. "Fuck your budget."

Black sighed in resignation. "Sergeant, you'll join your men later. I have arranged for you to meet Sergeant Soujac this evening for dinner."

"How did you know our clothing sizes?" Holt asked.

"Sergeant, don't insult me. I know everything I need to know about you and your men. I've done my homework. Meet with Soujac and do yours. I'll expect your decision when you return from dinner."

"You'll get my decision when I'm ready to make it."

343

"Sergeant, you seem to believe you have more leverage than, in reality, you do. Make no mistake about this; if I want you on this mission, you'll be on this mission regardless of your feelings. As to your men, I can put together my own team in twenty four hours. The inclusion of your men on this assignment is merely a gesture I make on your behalf. Are we clear?"

Holt stared at Mr. Black.

"Are we clear?"

"Crystal," Holt said.

"Good. Please, pick out some clothing. You can take a quick shower and change in your room. Second floor, room 201. A car will take you to your dinner with Sergeant Soujac in forty five minutes."

Holt sorted through the clothing. A mixture of light-colored slacks and pastel colored golf shirts. They were each issued low top, Army oxford shoes.

"Everything okay, Sarge," Gator asked.

"Just peachy," Holt said, smiling weakly. He hoped his forced smile hid the feeling of desperation and helplessness he felt. "I'll see you guys later. Probably tomorrow morning. I have to meet someone tonight. Behave yourselves and stay out of trouble."

Captain Mason walked over to Holt. "I'm being put up in a hotel. I guess we'll talk later."

"I feel like Alice and I just fell down the fucking rabbit hole." Holt looked around cautiously, "Does anyone know where we are?"

"Saigon, MACV, must be aware of our temporary assignment. They would have to approve the orders."

"Promise me whatever happens you'll take care of the guys. It's me they want, not them."

"Are you having second thoughts about all this?"

"Are you kidding me? I've had nothing but second thoughts from the minute I met that jackass. Mr. Black! He didn't even have the decency to come up with a believable fake name. All this fucking bullshit is worse than the fucking Army."

"I promise, I'll look out for the men and you as best I can. You are still under my command."

"The shortest command in history."

Mason smiled. "Be that as it may, I'm still your commanding officer." Holt sat in the back of a black, Peugeot sedan and was driven to an older section of Bangkok. There were no brightly lit neon bars staffed with bar girls and strippers to be seen. They stopped in front of building with no name. The driver wordlessly pointed at a door.

Holt walked to the door manned by a large black man. "Good evening," he said. Holt detected a slight southern accent.

Inside the Maitre' D greeted Holt by name and walked him to a booth in the rear. They passed an enormous polished teak bar backed by lit shelves stocked with every conceivable liquor imaginable. The bar had few customers but most of the tables were full.

Sergeant Soujac sat in a corner booth and rose as Holt approached. He held out his hand. "Sergeant Holt, I knew our paths would cross at some point. How are you?"

"That remains to be seen."

"I was genuinely sorry to hear about the death of Sergeant Camp. Wendell was a good friend. He was given a posthumous promotion to Sergeant First class to increase his death benefits but unfortunately we could find no living relatives to distribute it to. His wife, such as she was, couldn't be found anywhere."

"He told me before he died, the Army was his family."

Soujac signaled the waiter with a wave of his hand. "I'll have another and my friend will have a Jack Daniels Woodford Reserve with Coke."

"With Coke?" the waiter asked.

"You should really try it on the rocks. It's a special blend," Soujac said to Holt.

"Sure, why not."

"You're not surprised I know what you drink?"

"Nothing surprises me anymore."

The waiter brought their drinks and Holt sipped his.

"It is good, very smooth, like cream."

"I thought you would like it. So, what can I do for you?"

Holt told his of his approach by Joe and the nature of the assignment.

"And you want to know if he can be trusted?" Soujac said as he reached for a cigarette. The waiter approached with a light but was waved away. "I've worked with him on a number of occasions. He is a man of his word. I trust him." "I don't understand what this is all about. Why me? What's all this crap about Sergeant Sangh and how am I involved."

"I understand you were a trusted friend of Sergeant Sangh. He was a prominent figure in the Montagnard rebellion in the mid sixties. You've heard of that?"

"I have."

"Apparently, Mr. Black feels you both can be of value to him. I'm sure he'll explain more when you accept this assignment."

"According to him the decision has already been made."

"MACV wouldn't have approved this assignment if they didn't believe in it."

"He said he can get my men their choice of assignment when all this is done. Can he?"

"That I can assure you. He has a lot of pull over here." Soujac caught the waiters eye. "Let's discuss this more over dinner."

"I'll have another drink," Holt told the waiter. "Make it a double. I plan on getting shitfaced tonight. One thing I want to ask you; is he really with the USAID?"

"That or one of the other alphabet agencies over here." Holt raised his glass and drained it.

The sedan was waiting to take Holt back to the house.

In the morning he woke with a throbbing head. He showered and dressed in fresh clothes. Downstairs he asked where he could get breakfast and was directed to a small cafe next door that catered to Americans. He ordered eggs over easy, ham, and fried potatoes. He also ordered a large glass of orange juice and coffee. When the juice arrived he drank some and then added a small bottle of airline vodka that he found in his room. He sat back, lit a cigarette, and drank some coffee. As he waited for his food he saw Mr. Black enter the café.

Black sat down and with no preamble asked how Holt's dinner went.

"It was fine. Sergeant Soujac gave you a glowing review."

"So you're in?"

"I love that you make it seem like I have a choice. Yes, I'm in. But I want to discuss my men first."

"What about them?"

"If any of the guys don't want to come along on this mission there will be no repercussions."

"Not from me. That I can promise."

"Next, I don't need an R & R. I want to get started right away. Today. You said we have to go to northern Thailand; then let's do it, today."

"Are you sure?"

"I don't need any bar girls; I'm married."

"I thought you were divorced?"

"Are you arc a fucking marriage counselor now? I'll take an R & R when I get back."

"You know, I have the simulated rank of major. I would appreciate the level of respect that rank accords."

"Good. You're a simulated Major. I'll give you simulated respect."

Black laughed. "This should be an interesting trip. How about jumping with the Thai Special Forces?"

"Afterwards. Let's get down to business. Today."

"Fine. Do you have fatigues with no patches?"

"Tiger stripes."

"That will do. We'll be gone for two or three days. Draw your weapons from the armory and meet me out front at 1100 hours. I'll let your boys know you won't be joining them."

At precisely 1100 Holt stepped outside the house into the sheltered courtyard. Black was waiting in an unmarked jeep driven by a young man wearing a gaily colored Hawaiian shirt and shorts. They drove in silence to a small airport where they bordered a de Havilland DHC- 4A, small STOL airplane. The STOL planes were built for Short Take Off and Landings. Their journey would take them to extreme north eastern corner of Thailand bordered by Laos to the east and Burma to the north, some nine hundred miles away. The flight time was a little over four hours. There were four other passengers on board who Joe said were Australian construction workers on contract with the USAID.

The interior of the plane was crowded with various crates and boxes of supplies.

Holt lay across the web seating and covered his face with his boonie hat and went to sleep.

Black woke Holt. "Fifteen minutes until landing. We has a strong tail wind the whole way so we made great time. You know, I'm always amazed at how you grunts can sleep, anywhere. anytime."

Holt turned and looked out a window to the mountainous terrain below. In the distance a small village blossomed like a weed in a city sidewalk.

Holt ignored his comment. "Does this place have a name?"

"Lamphang, although that may change in the future."

They landed on a small compacted dirt runway and taxied to a long cinder block building that functioned as the airport terminal. They boarded another unmarked jump and left the Australians to off load the plane. They rode about a half a mile into the town proper, if it could be called that. They stopped by a large, two story, stuccoed building painted a light tan color, fronted by a large covered teak porch.

"This is the hotel, restaurant, bar. We'll be staying here," Black said.

Holt got out of the jeep and stretched his legs. Holt looked down the main road, wide, rutted, and compacted, barely half a mile long.

"That large steel building is the supply depot," Black said, pointing to a building two hundred feet away. "Next to it is a compound for the construction workers. They have their own cooking facilities and bar. We discourage their use of the hotel. The hotel is for the use of the aid workers and other visiting dignitaries. Across the street is a row of shops. You can buy just about anything you may need. They have tailors, barbers, and clothing shops. They cater to the natives in the surrounding villages. In back of them is a similar row of shops."

Holt turned and noticed a young women coming down the steps of the hotel. She was of slender build with deeply tanned skin. She was wearing green shorts and a pale yellow t-shirt. Her light, blond hair was capped by a sweat stained tan baseball cap. She threw her arms around Joe.

"Joseph, so nice to see you again."

"Karen, let me introduce you to Donald Holt. He is a consultant on this project. Don, this Karen Mellings. She is the head of the USAID up here."

Karen looked Holt over from top to bottom. "You're a consultant Mr. Holt?"

"Please, just call me Holt. And yes, I guess I am. Pleasure to meet you," he said, shaking her hand.

"Karen, we're going to settle into the hotel. It's been a long and uncomfortable trip. I brought some things you asked for," he said, handing her a large package wrapped in brown paper.

"What did you bring?"

"T-shirts, shorts, and some toiletries. And some underwear. I had my secretary pick out the clothing and underwear. I thought she would get more practical items than I might have selected."

"Thank you," she said. She frowned seeing Holt get his carbine and web gear from the jeep. "I don't care for guns up here Mr. Holt."

"Neither do I."

"Do most consultants in your line of work find guns necessary?" Holt smiled weakly.

As they walked to the veranda they stopped.

"That's new," said Black indicating a brightly colored sign hanging from the rafters.

"It is new. They let me name the hotel."

"Shambhala?"

"It's the name of the legendary Tibetan paradise in the 1933 novel, 'Lost Horizon' by James Hilton."

"Hopefully, when we're done here it will be appropriate," said Joe. "Karen give us about thirty minutes and meet us on the veranda for drinks." It was more a statement than request.

"Are you her boss too?"

Black smiled. "I'm everyone's boss."

Holt was given a room on the first floor away from the other guests. He washed his face and hands and changed into some shorts and light colored buttoned shirt. He slipped into his Ho Chi Minh sandals. He locked his CAR-15 rifle and web gear in a cabinet and went downstairs.

Karen was sitting at a small, round, teak table with a tall glass in front of her. She took in Holt's heavily scarred legs and face. "Consulting appears to be a dangerous occupation."

"Most things in Asia are dangerous."

They were joined by Mr. Black. "Holt, you changed clothing. Good, you look much less threatening this way."

"If you say so, Joseph," said Karen.

A waiter came to take their drink orders. He saw Holt and grimaced. He leaned into Karen and whispered in her ear. She placed a hand on his arm and said something in Thai to him. He left looking back at Holt.

Holt raised his eyebrows.

"He said you look like a Buddhist demon."

"I get that a lot," Holt said.

"Are you a demon, Mr. Holt?

"Just a consultant—"

Black interrupted. "Karen, I want to brief Holt on the situation here. Holt, what you're about to hear is strictly confidential and highly classified. Do you understand?"

Holt nodded.

"Good."

Their drinks arrived. Holt looked dubiously at the ice.

"The ice is made from boiled water and all our food is brought in from American sources. We are quite civilized here," Karen said.

"If I may continue," Black said. "The Americans, under President Nixon, are withdrawing their forces. In two years or less they'll all be gone. No one believes the South Vietnamese will be able to hold out against the NVA. Two years after that the north take over the country. When that happens Thailand will be flooded with refugees. The Thai's know this and are trying to prepare for it. They have begun establishing refugee camps along their borders with Laos and Cambodia. The facility being developed here is designated specifically for the Montagnards. The development being established here is more permanent in nature. The Thai's want Montagnards who would be willing to work with them in protecting this remote region against foreign incursion across their borders. In return, they will grant the Montagnards a permanent residency status and give them the land they have always wanted. The area we will tour tomorrow will become, for all intents and purposes, a permanent independent state. This is where you come in Holt. We feel Sergeant Sangh and the group he is with would be agreeable to this arrangement. What are your thoughts?"

"I'd need to see the camp before I comment."

"Karen, do you have those photos.?"

She handed Holt a thick manila envelope.

Holt withdrew the photos after lighting a cigarette and taking a sip of his Jack and Coke. He studied each of the photos carefully. When he was done, he stacked the photos neatly and returned them to Karen.

"Well?" asked Joe.

"Very impressive. I still want to see it in person."

"And you will, tomorrow. We will tour the entire facility. Karen, you'll come with us?"

"Certainly. What is Mr. Holt's function here, exactly?" she asked.

"Holt has a long standing relationship with Sergeant Sangh. Sangh views Holt as someone who can be trusted. We feel Holt can convince Sangh to bring his people over."

"So, he's the Judas goat leading the lambs to slaughter?"

"I'm not going to do anything to betray Sangh's trust in me," Holt said forcibly.

"I've seen many government programs begin with the best intentions. They seldom end that way," Karen said.

"Work on your metaphors. Don't mix goats and sheep," Holt said.

Holt had eaten dinner by himself. Black said he had arrangements to make, whatever that meant. Karen left without saying a word. Holt had several more drinks under the watchful, wary eyes of the wait staff and then went to bed.

The next morning Holt waited for Karen and Black on the veranda. He had finished breakfast and sat drinking coffee.

Karen came out the door and seeing that Holt was alone turned on her heal and headed back to the door.

"For God's sake, Karen, what is your problem? Have I done something to offend you?"

"Your very presence here offends me! This project is a civilian project that now threatens to become militarized. You are a perversion, an obscenity, the very antithesis of everything I've worked for."

"Sticks and stones," Holt said lighting a cigarette.

"What are you, ten-years-old? I've dealt with your type all my life. You see me as some dumb blond to be pushed around. But let me—" Holt interrupted her. "Are you wearing a bra?"

Her face reddened and Holt thought she would leap across the table and claw at his eyes.

Mr. Black joined them, his face brightened. "Ah, this is nice. Glad to see you two kids are getting along."

"Fuck you, Joseph. Let's get going, I have things to do today." Black looked at Holt who spread his hands innocently.

"Our transportation is out front."

They walked towards a pale green, 1965, Toyota Land Cruiser FJ-40.

"This thing is mostly rust! What's holding this piece of shit together?" Holt asked.

"The running gear is top notch. These Toyota's never die," Black replied.

Karen got into the front seat next to Black leaving Holt to squeeze into the miniscule rear bench.

"No guns today, Mr. Holt? Are you sure you'll feel safe?" Karen said without turning her head to look at him.

"I have you to protect me."

"Don't count on it."

"I feel that I may have missed something," said Black.

"Please, Joseph, just drive," Karen said, looking straight ahead.

They drove through town leaving a contrail of dust behind them. They crossed over a bridge with a wide, swirling river beneath them.

"At one point the Burmese government claimed that river was the defining border between Burma and Thailand. I'm pretty sure that dispute has been settled," Joe said. "The development is straight ahead."

They passed through an elaborately carved teak gate. Holt was stunned to see the jungle had been cleared for thousands of feet ahead of them. They traveled down a crushed stone road wide enough for two way traffic. The road was bordered by steel culverts to control water runoff. Small, wooden bridges spanned the culverts at intervals. On either side of the road were traditional Montagnards long houses.

They parked in front of a large stucco building with a bright red tiled roof. The doors of the Land Cruiser squealed in protest as they were opened.

"This is the administrative building," said Joe exiting the Toyota. "So what do you think?" Without waiting for an answer he continued, "we've built over four hundred long houses with more on the way. We've started to clear the jungle for farmland. We've had dozen of engineers and construction experts on site for more than a year. We have a native work crew of over two hundred and they can complete a long house in four days. We started off building five house a day and now we're up to ten a day. All the materials for the homes are harvested from the jungle; nothing is wasted. Karen, do you want to jump in here?"

"When the first phase of construction is completed, we will have a forty-bed hospital and two schools. Sanitation facilities are being worked on as we speak. We're digging wells throughout the village. Everyone will have access to fresh, clean water. We fully expect that there will be shops interspersed among the houses. Until they are self sufficient the USAID will supply them with an ample supply of food and animal feed."

"And Thailand is doing this all out of the goodness of their heart?" Holt asked.

"The Thai government expects the Montagnards to maintain scrutiny of the Laotian border to prevent any communist incursions. As more Montagnards immigrate to Thailand more settlements will be established. They also would require assistance with patrolling the Burmese border to stop the drug traffic into Thailand," said Joe.

"Under whose direction?" Holt asked.

"The United States maintain a significant contingent of Special Forces in Thailand. I imagine they would be involved. That may interest you."

"And this is the militarization of the project that concerns you, Karen?"

"Yes."

Holt walked into the middle of the road. He looked in all directions.

"This is fucking incredible. How much is this all costing?"

"Much less than you would think. As I mentioned, all the materials come from the cleared jungle. We've had to import material for the hospital and the administrative building, other than that the cost is in the labor. I doubt we have four or five hundred thousand in the whole project. Wouldn't you agree, Karen?"

"Give or take," she said reluctantly.

"So what are your feelings, Holt?"

"It's almost too good to be true."

"Not really. Flying here, you saw this area is uninhabited and will remain so. Tourists have no interest here. The only natural resource is the jungle and the Thai's have no plans to exploit it. Thailand isn't some third world, shithole that will allow foreign interests to come in and rape the country. Their concern is border security in these northern regions and the Montagnards will provide that. Let's discuss this over lunch."

"I have some things I need to check on. You two go on ahead. I'll find my own way back," Karen said.

"We'll see you tonight for dinner?" asked Mr. Black.

"Perhaps."

CHAPTER 35

The Kingdom Of Laos

Holt stood on the mountain top and looked out through the wispy clouds to the jungle below. He was on his second cup of coffee and third cigarette since waking. Beneath him, dug into fighting positions, the small encampment was encircled with ethic Chinese Nung mercenaries.

He looked at the assembled team wrapped in their poncho liners sleeping on the ground and decided to let them sleep a little longer.

He ground out his cigarette and walked to where Mr. Black was stirring.

"Wakey, wakey," Holt called out cheerfully.

Black growled an unintelligible greeting and stumbled over to a bush and urinated.

"I've asked you a number of times to stop calling me Mr. Black. Just call me Joe. Jesus, you can be so fucking annoying. Since I met you, a day hasn't passed that I haven't fantasized about killing you in your sleep."

"I find that hard to believe. I've grown very fond of you, Joe." "Don't fuck with me before I've had some coffee. Alright?"

"You're such a guy. Now that you've gotten what you what from me the courtship has ended."

Six days before, when Holt agreed to the mission, plans proceeded rapidly.

The first thing was the patrol itself. Holt was adamant that a ten day trek through the jungle wasn't feasible. They would never be able to carry enough supplies to last.

Black said he had developed an alternate. They would fly into this remote outpost and then would be taken by helicopter to a small clearing. From the clearing it was estimated they would have a four day walk to Sangh's camp. Holt agreed that it was doable. Maps were printed and ready for distribution once the team returned from their R & R.

It was decided that they would travel sterile—no indication to say they were Americans. Belgian rucksacks and French paratrooper boots along with locally manufactured tiger stripe fatigues would be worn. Every piece of gear would be devoid of place of origin. Holt and Black debated on weapons. It was finally decided that the team would carry the Carl Gustav, M 45B, Swedish K, silenced, sub machine gun and twenty, twenty-round stick magazines. A dozen Belgian Mini Grenades would be carried by each man. Black sourced some American radios, Claymore mines, and smoke grenades that were scrubbed free of any identifying markings. The only thing that couldn't be outsourced was Doc's medical gear. There was no suitable foreign source replacement.

When everyone returned from Bangkok, Holt briefed them. Of the seven men, two members of Joe Jenkins' old team declined to participate. They were asked to leave immediately and were returned to normal duty.

Five men remained. He emphasized the pros and cons of the mission. He did his best to dissuade the men from going but they agreed they wanted to go along. The lure of selecting their next assignment was too great to pass up.

When Holt told Black that only six men, including himself, were going, Black seemed unconcerned. He said he would be the seventh man and he would select two others from a pool of men he had access to.

"You can't be serious about you going? How old are you?" he asked. "You gotta be close to forty. You're too fucking old."

"I'm twenty eight, you moron. And I guarantee that I'm in better shape than you and your team of skeletons."

"That was uncalled for," Holt said.

"Awe, did I hurt your feelings? Sack up bitch. It's settled." He lit a cigarette and continued. "Tomorrow we double check all our equipment, and then check it again. The day after we fly in to this small base we have established in Laos and—"

"The USAID has a base in Laos?"

"Yeah, smart ass, we do. We spend one night there and the next day we are dropped into the landing zone we've found. Four days later we hook up with Sangh."

"Enemy activity?"

"Sangh chose a good spot. No enemy activity reported. The Pathet Loa are more concerned in making a push on The Plain of Jars. The North Vietnamese are further east along the border with Vietnam. You good with all of this?"

Holt shrugged. "Sure."

And here they were on some desolate mountain top in central Laos surrounded by Chinese mercenaries for security. There were about a dozen Americans manning a heavily sandbagged bunker bristling with radio gear. The bunker was topped by a variety of long whip antennas. These men kept to themselves, avoiding all contact with Holt's team.

Holt couldn't imagine what type of lunatic would volunteer for their assignment and was happy to keep his distance.

The two men Black had brought along followed him everywhere. They were two ethic Chinese and were hideous. It looked like Joe found two trolls living under a bridge and dressed them in fatigues. Their flat faced, gap tooth, smiles reminded Holt of Halloween pumpkins long past their prime. He had named them Thing One and Thing Two from the Dr. Seuss book, 'The Cat in the Hat'. They, indeed, looked like something a cat had dragged in and mauled for several days. They were courteous to Holt but always wary in his presence.

"Wake your men and get them fed. Have them top off their water and be ready to leave at 0800," Black said.

"Sure thing, boss," Holt said cheerfully.

"And don't call me 'boss'."

"Jesus Christ, what is the bug up your fucking ass this morning?"

"I just want to get started. I don't like being here on top of this mountain."

Holt walked over to Joe and stood in front of him. "Let's get something straight right now. Lose the fucking attitude. When we hit the ground I'm in charge, not you."

Black turned away and started packing his rucksack.

Holt woke the team and they prepared breakfast. As they sat eating, Holt looked around the encampment.

"This place gives me the creeps. Just imagine the type of brain dead zombie that would accept the assignment of sitting up here listening to radio transmissions. Joseph, over there, has been here less than a day and he's already to come apart." Holt shook his head. "There are some weird fucking people in this war."

"How long do you think they'll stay here?" Gino asked.

"From the way they act, too long. I'll tell you a story. When I was back in the Wolfhounds me and this guy got assigned to tower duty. We had to spend three days in this fifty foot tower on the perimeter of the base, standing guard. The tower was maybe eight-by-eight. Now keep in mind we were friends, really good friends. Okay, so day one goes by, no problem." Holt paused to light a cigarette. "Day two and we start to get on each other nerves. By day three I was ready to kill this guy. The very sound of him breathing drove me into a murderous rage. We had this little radio with us and to make matters worse the AFVN kept playing the top ten songs over and over and over. The same fucking songs for three days. There was one, 'Hair' by the Cowsills. Every time it came on this guy would sing along, barking out the words. God, I could have slit his throat and washed in his blood and never blinked an eye. And that was only three days. Can you imagine these mutts after a couple of weeks. They must be close to insane."

They all looked around cautiously.

"You know what would be funny watching Gator and Tuna up here," Doc said. "Watching them slowly descend into madness."

"That would never happen, me and Gator are friends," Tuna said.

"Friends? You can't even spend ten minutes together without arguing over something," Gino said. "You had to see these guys; they got into a fight while discussing the color of girls nipples."

"Darker is better," snapped Gator.

"Asshole redneck, pink is better than dark," countered Tuna.

"Who you calling a redneck, shit for brains."

"Knock it off you two. Get your gear together. We'll be leaving soon," Holt said. "Point taken, Gino."

Two unmarked helicopters arrived at 0800. They circled the mountain top base, and, one by one, they landed. The team piled on board. Holt looked at the door gunner and gave him a thumbs up. The gunner grabbed Holt's hand and pumped it furiously.

"Yeah, baby, here we go into the shit. We're in it now, motherfucker," he shouted over the rotor noise.

Holt recoiled and stared at him. *Yeah, here we go down the rabbit hole,* he thought.

They flew a circuitous route for about forty minutes making several false landings. Finally they came to a landing zone barely fifty feet across. The pilot pulled pitch and flared the helicopter. He cut power and the helicopter dropped from the sky in a wild auto rotation. At the last second the pilot once again pulled pitch to soften the landing. The men jumped from the ship and ran to the trees.

When the second chopper landed they gathered together.

"Those guys work for the USAID too?" Holt asked Black.

"Civilian pilots from Air America," he said bluntly.

"That door gunner was stoned out of his mind."

"They do have some personal issues."

Holt settled the men and organized the order of march. Holt would walk point over the objections of Mr. Black followed by Joe Jenkins at slack. Next was Gino, carrying the radio, then Tuna and Gator. Doc was next, then Black and Thing One and Two would walk drag one hundred feet behind the column. Captain Mason remained in Thailand as the over watch coordinating all communications and air assets. Holt checked his compass heading and moved off into the jungle.

After thirty minutes Holt was gripped by an almost paralyzing fear. This was jungle unlike anything he had ever experienced. He had to will himself to keep walking. This was pure, virgin jungle untouched by man. Holt thought he may be the first white man to ever walk through it. There were no trails or paths worn down by enemy infiltration. There were only small animal trails bored through the bushes and grass. The air was alive with the sounds of insects and birds. Looking up, he could barely see any sunlight through the intertwined leaves competing for sunlight. Vines were everywhere. Vines as thin as wires and others as thick as a man's wrist. They snaked across the ground entangling your feet while others wrapped the trunks of the enormous trees cutting deep into the bark. The humidity was thick amplifying the stench of the rotting vegetation. The ground was spongy and wet. Everything was covered in moss or mold giving the jungle an emerald glow.

A colony of bats hung suspended in the branches of one tree wrapped tight in their wings looking like small vampires. Brightly colored birds and parrots watched over their progress impassively. High up in the trees Holt could hear a troop of monkeys chattering excitedly.

The sounds were good. If predators were present the animals would go silent. Little did they realize that man was the ultimate predator.

Within minutes they were all drenched in sweat. The sweat ran into their eyes and blurred their vision. Holt dabbed at his face with his towel not wanting to remove his camouflage face paint.

After an hour of painfully slow progress Holt called a ten minute break. The word was passed back. Looking over his shoulder, Holt could see Jenkins and barely made out Gino. The rest of the men were invisible, blending into the leaves.

Holt stopped and got out a cigarette.

"Do you think that's okay to do?" Jenkins asked.

"I think we're the only fucking people in hundreds of miles. But yeah, you're right," Holt said replacing the cigarette in the pack. "Have you ever seen anything like this?" Holt asked.

"No! This is one hundred percent pure prehistoric, African bullshit. I wouldn't be surprised to see a dinosaur walk by."

Holt saw Gino swat at a mosquito as big as a bird. "How you doing, Pal? You hanging in there?"

"I'm fine. Christ, I feel like I'm wrapped in a cocoon of leaves. This place is fucking creepy."

"Pass the word back. I want the guys to tighten up the column. I don't want anyone getting separated. Make sure you can see the guy in front of you. If you get lost in this place you'll never be found."

Holt took a long pull of water; it was warm and tasted of iodine. He replaced his canteen into its canvas cover. They were each carrying ten quarts of water. Holt feared it wouldn't be enough.

After three hours and several breaks, they stopped for lunch. The men formed a small tight circular perimeter. Holt opened a can of Turkey loaf and ate it with crackers. He looked back and saw Black talking with the two Thing's. He saw Black nod his head and shrug his shoulders at something Thing One said.

Holt checked his map and his compass heading.

"Are we going the right way?" Jenkins asked.

"Who the fuck knows? We're just guessing at Sangh's location. It's going to be like finding a needle in a dozen different haystacks." Holt, feeling the craving for nicotine, desperately wanted a cigarette. "Hopefully Sangh will find us before we ever find him."

"That is, if he wants to be found,"

As 1800 approached Holt found a suitable spot for their RON, their Remain Overnight position. It was on top of a small grassy knoll about ten feet high with a large tree in the center.

Not wanting to risk a fire they ate their rations cold. This was the problem with the LURP freeze dried rations. They required a fire to boil a pint of water. Eating them without boiled water was like eating a disgusting, dry cereal. Holt had a can of Meatballs and Beans that he opened with his P38. The team had found that by breaking down the C Rations and judicially picking out select components the weight difference was minimal. The cans were stuffed into an old sock, forming a tube, that prevented noise.

At dusk, the Things, Gator, and Tuna ringed their perimeter with Claymore mines and trip flares.

The guard roster was set and Holt leaned back against his rucksack to sleep. At these times, before sleep came, Holt had long imaginary long conversations with Janet. He would compose long letters to her. He would dream of life back home that he knew he would never have. He fell asleep comforted by the jungle sounds.

At 0230 all sounds ceased. It was if a switch had been flicked, turning off all the insects. Holt jolted awake, fear coursing through his body. He was flooded with adrenaline, all senses alert. He sat in the dead silence.

He leaned close to Gino and whispered in his ear. "What's up?"

As his night vision improved, Holt could see the hunched shadows of the team on full alert. Holt clutched his Swedish K to his chest and toyed with the safety. They all sat in silence.

Holt thought he heard some rustling in the jungle but couldn't pin point the location. *It could just be the wind rustling the overhead branches.* He was nauseous with fear.

After thirty agonizing minutes the normal jungle sounds resumed. Gino leaned into him and whispered. "What the fuck?"

Holt put a hand on his leg and squeezed. "Something was out there but it's gone now. I'm going to stay up for a while. Try and get some sleep." "Fat chance of that. I'm shaking like a leaf. This is fucking terrifying," Gino whispered in Holt's ear. Gino's breath was warm and moist.

The night passed without further incident. In the morning, Thing One went to retrieve the Claymore's and the trip flares. He came back and excitably jabbered something to Black. Black followed him back into the jungle, and Holt followed them.

"What is it?" Holt asked.

"Hang found something," Joe said.

Thing One, whose name was Hang, pointed at the ground. "Tiger!"

"What is he talking about?"

"Tiger!" he said again, baring his teeth and holding his hands like claws. "Tiger!"

Holt saw several prints in moist earth. They had to be almost six inches across indicating a full grown male tiger.

"How do you know that?" asked Black.

"How do you not know that?" countered Holt. "You live in the jungle, you know your neighbors."

Holt walked back to his team and reported the prints.

"Great! Just what we need, a fucking tiger," Gino said.

"Maybe he's friendly," Gator said.

"Gator, are you a fucking moron? This ain't Tony from Frosted Flakes! This is a wild fucking tiger. Of course he's not friendly. Jesus, what a shit for brains you are sometimes. Friendly fucking tigers. Unbelievable!"

"I thought maybe he was from a zoo or something," Gator said in his defense.

"What fucking zoo would he had come from? We're in the middle of the Laotian jungle. Do you think he's someone's pet that they let out for the night? Shit! Use your brain, you dickhead."

As Holt walked away Gator whispered to Tuna, "So, now he's a big fucking expert on tigers?"

"Gator, you're as dumb as a bag full of rocks," Tuna said.

"I'm from Florida. What do I know about tigers?"

"You should know they're not fucking friendly, 'They're Great'," he said in Tony's voice.

Gator shoved him hard.

Black was studying his map. He called Holt over. "How far do you think we came?"

"We didn't do ten miles yesterday. I doubt we even did eight," Holt said. "I'm going to tell the men to conserve their food. No more than two meals a day."

"How will that help?"

"Did you pack three a day?"

"Yes."

"So you got twelve meals in total. If we eat just twice a day, that should last for six days. If we don't find Sangh in six days we call it quits."

Black frowned.

"I'm beginning to think you're not cut out for jungle life. You're a house cat, Joe. You should have stayed in Bangkok," Holt said.

At noon they found a small waterfall flowing into a pool of water. The pool lead to a stream flowing south. They saw two, small, red deer drinking from the pool.

Thing Two pointed his rifle at the deer. "We shoot, good chop chop," he said pointing to his mouth.

Holt placed his hand on Thing Two's rifle and lowered the barrel. "We're not shooting any fucking deer. This ain't a hunting expedition."

The men spread out at the edge of the jungle. Three at a time went to the pool and refilled their canteens. The water was clear and cool but they still added their iodine tablets.

Holt rinsed his rancid towel and wiped his face and neck. "We'll break here for thirty minutes."

"We should keep moving," said Black.

"Take your two men and go on if you want. Me and my men are resting here."

Black stormed off to sit with the Things.

"Trouble in paradise?" Jenkins asked.

"He's just being a prissy, little prick."

"Don't we need him to get out of here?"

"Captain Mason is on over watch. He won't let them fuck us."

"What if he goes back on his word about us picking our next assignments?"

"Black ain't that stupid," Holt said. "If he fucks us; he knows that I'll kill him and they won't ever find his body."

"And this is only day two," Joe said wistfully.

CHAPTER 36

Skull People

The second night passed without incident. They woke and found the jungle misted with ground fog. It was like living in a white, cotton cloud.

Holt dug a small hole and risked making a fire for coffee. The other men followed suit. Although security appeared lax the men were tense and on edge.

Holt sat with Joe Jenkins. "Joe, I got a pound cake; do you want to share it?"

"I already opened a Pecan roll. Let's share that."

Holt took a bite of the roll. "This is a poor substitute for a cigarette. Maybe I should quit smoking?"

"What are you planning on doing when we get back? Have you given it any thought?"

"Well Joe, we are jump qualified. Maybe we should go to one of the airborne units. The 101st or 82nd?"

"Fuck no! Those boys are up north in the mountains. They're getting the shit kicked out of them in the A Shau valley. That's not for me. How about we go back to the Wolfhounds?"

"We could do that. Should we stay together?"

"You're kind of nuts… But, sure, why not."

"The Wolfhounds; let's think on it. Maybe they'll offer us something better."

Holt leaned back and sighed. He savored the hot, creamy, sweet coffee. He looked at the sky peeking through the leaves, "Should be a nice day today. Maybe a hundred and four or five degrees. Not more than a hundred and eight."

"Yeah, factor in the ninety percent humidity it should only feel like a hundred and twenty," Joe said. "You know, you might want to consider going home. You're getting to be too much of a jungle boy."

Holt beat his chest weakly. "Me Tarzan, you Cheetah."

"Cheetah was the monkey, right? See, that's your problem… every time I think of you as normal you come out with some crazy off the wall shit. But this is a new low for you. Talking like a crazy, low life, racist redneck."

"Joe don't take offense. We're all descended from the apes. It's just some of us are more along the evolutionary scale than others."

"You should stay in the jungle. You don't belong around regular people."

"Did you ever see that Tarzan movie where Cheetah gets hold of a radio and calls Nazi Germany. Cheetah is squealing and making all these chimp noises and some bigwig Nazi general thinks he's talking to Hitler." Holt shakes his head softy as he remembers. "Classic fucking Cheetah. But what's really strange is no one questions how Cheetah knew how to operate a radio. You don't find that odd?"

"I need normal friends," Joe said.

"You said it, I didn't. You said we're friends. I knew it all along but I just needed to hear you say it."

Jenkins looked away and groaned.

By ten AM the fog began to burn off. The jungle thinned considerably and the trees were widely spaced. They could now see about thirty feet in every direction. They tried to make up for lost time. Overhead a troop of monkeys sat impassively, watching their progress. Holt got Joe's attention and pointed overhead. Joe gave Holt the finger.

"I knew this guy in the Wolfhounds. Him and another guy were sent out on a LP. During the night someone started throwing grenades at them that were all duds. They blew their Claymore's and requested permission to come in. Permission denied. All night they sat there shitting bricks. Turns out it was Rock Apes throwing rocks at them. It was a helluva of story. They never lived it down."

At the noon lunch break Thing One and Two hurried up to Joe Black. They were both highly agitated.

Holt walked over. "What's with them?"

"They got themselves all worked up. They don't like it here. They say this is a bad place," Black explained.

"Yes. This bad place," Thing One said. "Spirits live here, bad spirits. This place number ten."

"We go back and go some other way," Thing Two said.

"I didn't know he could talk," said Holt.

Thing Two looked at Holt and growled.

"They say we're being followed by ghost people," Black said.

"Yes, yes. We followed by people that have no head. Only skull."

"And he saw these skull men?" Holt asked.

"No he didn't actually see them. He says he felt their presence."

"No you can't see them. They move like smoke through the trees," Thing One explained.

"What you're seeing is the fog. It plays tricks on your mind. There are no skull people," Holt said in an effort to calm him down. He could clearly see that both the Nung were terrified. "Tell them they can walk closer to the group and we'll protect them."

Thing One spit on the ground. "You bad man. You demon. You anger the forest spirits by being here." They both walked off and stood a distance away sulking.

"We're not going to change their beliefs. What we believe in seems just as absurd as their beliefs seem to us," said Black.

"I am well aware of that. I respect their customs but we can't go back; we have to keep moving," Holt said.

"Let me talk to them and see if I can calm them down."

"Do what you can, Joe. In the meantime we'll take a break."

"What's going on?" asked Doc.

"The Nung are spooked. Evil spirits live here. They want to turn back."

"Do we really need them?"

"Not really. We can go without them." Holt heard Gino talking on the radio and turned to look at him.

"Is that Covey?"

"Not Covey. No, Call sign Over Watch. Some other plane higher up. Probably some CIA spook plane. They did mark our position for us," Gino said.

Gino showed Holt the coordinates and Holt transferred them to his map.

"This isn't bad. We're only a few miles behind where we should be. We're going too far south. We'll have to make a change. If it stays like this we can make up time," Holt said.

From the forest behind them they heard a long unearthly, ghostly wail. The hair stood up on Holt's neck.

The Nung let out a cry and stood behind Black, peeking around his body into the forest.

"What the fuck was that?" Gino whispered.

"It's got to be some kind of animal," Holt said.

"What kind of animal makes a sound like that?" Gator said.

The moaning continued, first from the right side and then from the left. The eerie sound passed over them and could be felt on their skin. The jungle seemed to take on a phosphorescent, emerald glow casting shadows where shadows shouldn't exist.

"C'mon, let's get moving," Holt said. "Joe, tell the Nung, Tuna and Gator will walk drag. They can walk with us."

"Why us?" Tuna asked, his voice trembling.

"Because the Nung are scared," Holt said.

"You don't think I'm scared too," Tuna said.

They walked until 1730 when Holt found another acceptable RON.

"We'll stop early. Everyone can use a break," Holt said.

Gator walked over to Holt. "The Nung are right. We are being followed."

"You saw someone?"

"I didn't see anyone but I know something is out there. I can feel it."

"Stop it. The Nung got us all on edge. We're not being followed. It's some jungle animal. Maybe we're being stalked by a tiger."

"How is that any better?"

"It's not. I'm not saying it's a tiger but that would explain the spooky presence you're feeling."

"It's no fucking tiger," Gator said walking over to Tuna.

"Maybe Gator is right. We should call for extraction and get the fuck out of here," Doc said to Holt.

"Jesus, Doc. Not you too!" Holt raised his voice, "Everybody gather around. We're staying here tonight. We'll form a tight perimeter. There are no ghosts or spirits out here. We're all tired and on edge. We'll all feel better after we get some sleep."

Holt sat with Gino, the radio on one side and Jenkins on the other. Doc sat with Gator and Tuna. Black sat with the two Nung. Their perimeter was barley six feet in diameter. As the jungle darkened, they put out their Claymore mines and trip flares.

Holt leaned back against his rucksack and started to eat a can of Beans and Baby Dicks. He ate some crackers with it. He took a long drink from his canteen.

It was so dark they couldn't see their hands in front of their faces. Bats fluttered overhead hunting insects. Small creatures moved through the jungle rustling leaves. The night was a time for predators; a time of death. Holt shivered and tried to slow his breathing. His heart beat was so strong he swore he could hear it. He felt his pulse in his ears. He closed his eyes and thought of Janet. *What would she be doing right now?* He forgot the time difference, but assumed it would be daytime in the states. She didn't live in fear of the night. He lowered his head and could smell the sour, greasy sweat on his body. He smeared his face with insect repellant. To his left, he heard Gino make the final radio communication of the night.

Gino leaned into him and whispered. "We're back on track. They have us at thirty miles in, right where we should be."

Holt moved his head. Gino's hot breath tickled his ear. "Good! One more fucking day. If we don't find any sign of Sangh tomorrow I'm telling Joe we're bagging it and calling for extraction."

"Do you believe in ghosts?"

"I don't know. I do believe in an afterlife so why not ghosts too."

"Forest spirits are part of every culture. I know the gooks believe in a lot of primitive shit; who's to say they're wrong."

Holt woke at first light. He stretched and worked the kinks out of his muscles. His fatigues were damp from the morning dew. The forest was once again shrouded in ground fog. He rose quietly, unbuttoned his fly, and urinated in the bushes. *This place really is creepy,* he thought. He turned back and saw the men begin to stir. Doc and Jenkins who had last guard shift were already sorting through their rations. Gino was making the first radio check of the day. Holt looked up and wondered what airplane was up there monitoring their frequency. Holt's stomach was queasy so he decided on a light breakfast of beef jerky and crackers. He made himself a coffee. When he was done he directed Tuna and Gator to retrieve the Claymore's and flares. The Nung were behind him doing the same.

Holt, forgetting where he was, reached for a cigarette. He cleared his head and replaced the pack.

He saw Gator and Tuna return empty handed. Gator was ashen white beneath his camo face paint and shaking.

He said to Holt in a low voice, "The Claymore's are gone. The trip flares too."

Holt swallowed hard, almost too afraid to speak. "What do mean they're 'gone'?"

Gator held up the severed electrical wire. "Gone. Somebody cut the wires and took the mines and the detonator caps. There's no sign of the trip flares."

He looked and saw the Nung return. They were almost hysterical with fear. They were waving the cut wires at Black.

"Go ahead and tell me a tiger did this," Gator said.

Holt turned away and got out a cigarette. He tried lighting it but his hands were shaking.

Gino held out a light. "You okay, Sarge?"

"No, I'm not okay. Fuck, Gino, this is bad. How could someone come and take our shit without making a sound? How could they even find the mines?"

Jenkins came up behind Holt. "I thought we didn't smoke in the field?"

"Jesus, Joe, do you think it fucking matters now?" Holt snapped. "Sorry, Joe. I am really spooked. This is fucking nuts."

"Here comes Black and the Nung," Gino said.

Behind Black Holt saw Gator, Tuna, and Doc huddled together talking excitedly.

"What do you make of this?" said Black.

Holt pinched the bridge of his nose and rubbed his eyes. "We need to calm down. All of us." He took off his boonie hat and rubbed his hand through his hair. "It can't be the NVA or the Pathet Lao; they would have attacked us. It has to be Sangh's men."

"Why would they just take the Claymore's and the flares and not show themselves?" countered Joe.

"Why the fuck are you asking me? You're supposed to be the indigenous expert."

"What are your suggestions?"

Holt pulled out his map from his side pocket. "Here is where we are. This was confirmed by the Over Watch this morning." Holt pointed to red dot. "This is where Sangh should be. It's nine or ten miles due east. I say we head there. If we find a clearing and if Sangh's guys haven't made contact by then we extract and get the hell out of the shit hole. That's my suggestion. Don't worry about your development; when the time comes the Montagnards will find it."

Joe rubbed his chin never taking his eyes off Holt. "Agreed."

"Good. Tell the Nung we're getting out of here. That should calm them down. Get ready, we're moving out in five minutes."

They moved through the jungle for five hours, taking a break every two hours. Their heads were on swivels, always scanning the trees side to side. Adrenaline coursed through their bodies leaving them jittery and short-tempered. Everywhere they looked they saw shadows dancing in the trees.

Holt's fear was so consuming he felt sick. He kept swallowing to keep down the bile that rose in his throat. He heard noises that weren't there.

In the tree tops, monkeys followed them swinging effortlessly from branch to branch, mocking their progress. They slogged along drenched in sweat. Finally, at noon they stopped.

"We'll take a thirty minute break. Gino, get Over Watch on the horn and find out where we are. Ask them if they can see any clearing big enough for a chopper?"

After several attempts, Gino connected with their guardian angel. "They say we made good progress and there might be a sizable clearing two miles ahead. He wants to know if we want to be extracted and if so, why? What do I tell him?"

"Whatever you do, don't tell him we're being chased by ghosts. Tell him we've made no contact with indigenous personal and are running low on supplies."

"Are you going to tell them about the Claymore's?" asked Jenkins.

"Not now, not here. They'll think we're crazy. I'll mention it at the debriefing."

"He says one mile beyond the clearing is an open field that could easily handle an extraction."

"Gino give me the handset." Holt identified himself and said there were no open fields indicated on his map. "Is the field a rice paddy or some other cultivated field?"

Holt handed the handset back to Gino. "Fucking guy doesn't know. If there is a cultivated field there must be people nearby. It could be Sangh's group. This is what he's telling me. What he's not saying is that it could be a Laotian village, or it could be the Pathet Lao, or the NVA. And if it is, and we go blundering in, we're up shits creek. Any comments?"

Mr. Black was first to speak. "We came this far; we should check it out."

Holt dismissed his comment with a wave. "What I should have asked is, who is up to spending another night out here with our spirit friends?"

"Are you fucking kidding me? I say we go in as soon as possible," Gator said.

"For once, I'm in total agreement with Gator. Shit, just saying that sounds crazy. If the first clearing is big enough to land a chopper, we'll call for extraction. Joe you and the Nung are welcome to continue on your own."

"Your mission was to get me to Sangh."

"No mission is worth the lives of my men. This debate is over," Holt said. "Gino when do we check in with Over Watch?"

"Not for another three hours."

"Alright, let's get moving."

They walked through the jungle with the unsettling feeling that they were being watched. All grunts learned to trust their gut. And Holt's gut told him they were being followed.

The Nung stayed within an arms reached of Joe, their eyes as big as saucers. They constantly swiveled their heads scanning the trees. Thing One was visibly shaking. He held his charm bag to his lips and murmured prayers.

The jungle closed in upon them. The thorn vines, once just an annoyance, now seemed like bony fingers tearing at their clothes.

Holt stopped to check his compass. He looked at Gino who just shook his head.

"This sucks," Gino whispered.

"Buck up. We should be there in another hour."

"Wait! Hold up; I saw something. Over there in front and to the left."

"What was it?"

"I don't know. It was like a grey shadow."

"Are you sure?"

"No, I'm not sure. Jesus, get us out of this," Gino whispered.

"Did you say something, Gino?"

"No. I just whispered a prayer."

"Well, don't make any promises you don't intend to keep. In a firefight one time I promised Jesus if he got me out alive I would never masturbate again. I think I jerked off that very evening."

"Hell. We've all done that."

They walked for another thirty minutes when Holt stopped the column. The ground was moist and their boots made sucking sounds in the wet earth.

"There's something up ahead," Holt said. "Jenkins, you come with me. The rest of you guys take five."

Within five steps they lost sight of the team. They walked slowly forward. Nestled in the massive roots of a Banyan tree was a crude stone totem with a human skull on top of it.

Jenkins and Holt stood before it. It was built out of piled stones and stood about four feet high. The skull stared at them with empty sockets. There was some lettering painted across the forehead. There were bare foot prints in the muddy ground.

"Jesus, fucking, Christ! What is this?" Joe whispered.

Holt went to knock it over and Joe grabbed his arm. "Don't."

"If the guys see this they will go berserk."

"Leave it alone. We'll go around it."

"Maybe you're right. Let's get back." They turned to walk back and saw that the jungle had erased all indications of their passage. Holt looked around and couldn't see their boot prints in the mud. He took out his compass and saw the needle spinning wildly. Holt suppressed the urge to vomit. He said nothing to Joe.

They started back.

"Did we come this way?" Holt asked.

"We must have. We can't be far. We only walked a few feet."

They walked in silence. After several minutes, Joe parted some branches. "Thank God. There they are."

As they neared the team Gino reached out and shoved Holt. "What the fuck were you guys doing? We were just about to come looking for you."

"What are you talking about? We've only been gone for a few minutes," Holt said.

"More like thirty minutes. We thought something happened to you. What did you see?"

"Nothing! We saw nothing. Fucking jungle is playing tricks on my eyes." Holt looked at Jenkins. "It's swampy up ahead we need to go around." Holt set a course to avoid the tree and the totem. As they walked Holt glanced to the left. He could see the massive trunk of the Banyan; it seemed to keep pace with their progress.

He stopped and grabbed Gino's arm. "See if you can raise Over Watch. We need to get out of this place."

"You're making me nervous. I know when you're lying. What did you guys really see?"

"Nothing. There was nothing to see."

"Then why were you gone so long?"

"I didn't think we were."

Gino worked the radio. "Can't raise them. They're not due back for another hour."

"When we get to the clearing we'll stay there."

They walked at a slight incline for forty minutes. The clearing was just ahead. They walked up and formed a line around the perimeter of the small clearing.

Holt scratched at his scraggly beard. "Joe, how big do you think this is?"

"Forty, maybe forty five feet across."

"Shit! That would be my guess. The blade span of a Huey is fifty seven feet. No way they can make it in here."

Black came and stood next to Holt. "Looks like we'll have to keep going."

"Don't sound so disappointed," Holt said.

"Look, here's what we do. We find the cleared field. Me and the two Nung will sneak down and take a look. If it's safe, we'll come back and get you. How does that sound?"

"I might agree to the Nung going but so far you haven't impressed with you jungle skills."

"I've done this longer than you. It won't be a problem."

Suddenly all jungle sounds stopped. The hum of insects and the chattering of the birds ceased. it was dead silent.

They turned around. Thing One screamed and fell to his knees covering his face. He began rocking back and forth chanting a prayer.

Behind them, not more than fifty feet, a bone white face appeared in the jungle.

"Keep your guns down," Holt ordered.

A man slowly walked towards them. He was clad only in a loin cloth and was bare footed. His face was painted in a chalky white paint to mimic a skull. His chest was covered in white stripes to simulate ribs. His arms hung to his sides with open palms displayed. His long, black hair was held by a leather headband.

"If I didn't know better I'd say he was an Apache warrior," Holt whispered to Gino.

Thing Two shouted something and raised his rifle. Holt shouted at him to stop.

Six wooden arrows flew from the trees and lodged in the Nung's chest. He dropped to the ground. He stared dumbly at the arrows protruding from his chest, his head sagged down. Blood was drooling from his mouth.

Thing One fell over and scrambled to stand back up again. "No one move!" Holt shouted.

The man advanced. He passed the dead Nung and looked at him. As he neared the team, the men parted to let him through. As he passed, Holt smelt the foul odor of decay. He continued to walk silently across the small clearing and stopped.

Thing One emptied his friends rucksack of all food and water and stuffed it in his own pack. He got up, and without saying a word took off into the jungle. Black shouted at him, but he was gone, Never to be seen again.

The men turned back to the skull man. He waved at them to follow him. As if in a hypnotic trance, they began to follow the skeletal wraith.

Instead of continuing east the man turned north.

They walked for two hours in blind obedience never stopping. The trees overhead began to clear. The man stopped at the rim of a valley and pointed. Then he was gone.

Holt and his team looked into the valley and saw a dozen long houses and some people.

CHAPTER 37

The Lost Village

Holt dropped his rucksack and crawled to the rim of the valley. From where he lay the ground dropped away into a sheer vertical rock wall. Black crawled up next to him. He had a pair of binoculars with him.

"You've been carrying them this entire trip?" asked Holt.

"Yeah, up to now never had a place to use them."

Holt took the binoculars and studied the village below.

"Some of those guys are carrying AK's. Here, see for yourself."

"No one is wearing a uniform. Most are wearing loin clothes," Black said. He put the binoculars down and turned to Holt. "I doubt if they're Pathet Lao or NVA. They would have bunkers ringing the camp. I don't see any signs of fortifications. It looks like a normal village."

"Do you see those three guys standing by the first long house? The middle one looks like Sangh."

Black looked again. "I hate to say it but they all look the same."

"We need to get down there. Regardless of who they are, that field is big enough to land six choppers. That's our extraction point."

Black was looking at his map. "This village isn't on my map. For that matter, neither is the valley."

"That surprises you? These maps are useless. Half of them haven't been updated since the thirties when they were drawn by Michelin Rubber." Holt looked over his shoulder. "Gino, when is Over Watch supposed to be on station?"

Gino looked at his watch. "Five minutes, give or take," he said wiggling his hand.

"When you get them, see if they can spot this valley. Tell them we're about three miles north east of that little clearing." Holt asked Black, "What kind of plane is up there?"

"I wouldn't know."

"Of course not. Look towards the left about eight hundred feet. There appears to a jumble of rocks leading down to the valley floor."

Black leaned out over the edge. Holt held him by his belt. Black scooted back. "You're right. That's our way down."

"As soon as Over Watch confirms the valley sighting we'll start down."

"Are we going to talk about that bone head guy?" Black said softly.

"What's to talk about? He was obviously a guide of some sort."

"What did you and Jenkins see when you went ahead of us?"

"Nothing!"

"Nothing? You were gone for thirty minutes. You must have seen something?"

"I said, we saw nothing. We were scouting ahead." Holt looked at Black who just tilted his head back.

"Alright, you want to know what we saw. We found a stone altar with a skull on top of it. Something happened to us and we lost thirty minutes of time."

Mr. Black exhaled loudly. "Fine. You know, you can really be an asshole sometimes."

Holt shrugged and went back to studying the rock fall. "You asked and I told you."

Ten minutes later Gino established communication with Over Watch. Gino guided him over the valley. "I can see the valley but no long houses. They must be concealed by the trees," Over Watch said. "Standby for coordinates."

With their position marked the team headed for the rock stairway.

Holt was first to step out onto the rocks. He looked down in front of him. The stairway consisted of enormous slabs of rock angled down. Each slab had to weigh in excess of three thousand pounds.

"This has to be a natural formation. There is no way the Montagnards built this. They ain't the Egyptians. The Yards are barely out of the stone age," Holt said making his way from slab to slab.

Halfway down, the ramp switched back and became much narrower. Here it appeared the rocks were carved into steps. The steps were narrow and very steep. Holt put his left hand against the cliff side for balance.

With about two hundred feet to go, Holt noticed three men from the village walking towards them, They all had AK-47's which they carried casually. They did not seem to be aggressive.

Holt continued down the rock staircase which began to narrow; the steps were barely eighteen inches across and no more than five inches deep. He slowed and carefully picked his footing. At the bottom he stood to the side to allow the other men to continue down.

One of the men rushed to greet Holt.

"Trung Si, welcome, welcome," he grabbed Holt's hand in both of his and pumped vigorously. "Do you remember me?"

"Yes, I do. You are Bop."

The Montagnard smiled broadly, "Yes, it is me Bop. And my brother is here, Bong."

"Holt looked at Jenkins, "I gave them those names. There should be another brother I named Bing."

"Asshole," murmured Jenkins.

"Come now, we go to village. You and your friends our guests," Bop said, leading the way to the village.

At the village they were crowded by Montagnards all wanting to touch the Americans. Someone clapped their hands loudly and the crowd parted. There stood Sergeant Sangh. He wore a green fatigue shirt over a brown loin cloth. His hair was now shoulder length and held with a leather headband.

Sangh rushed forward and threw his arms around Holt. "Trung Si Holt, it is good to see you again. It has been too long."

Holt held him at arm's length and looked him over. "Trung Si Sangh, you look good. Strong and healthy."

"I gave myself a promotion, I am now Dou Ta, Sangh said.

"Dou Ta?"

"Yes, I am now Colonel, Dou Ta mean Colonel."

"Good, you deserve it. Do I have to salute you?" Holt asked.

"No we equal like old days. To you I am just Sangh." He looked at Holt's team. "The black man, I think I remember him."

"He is my friend, Trung Si Jenkins. Joe, this is Colonel Sangh." Jenkins stiffened and bowed at the waist. "A pleasure, Colonel."

"Come, we'll get comfortable and you tell me why you have come such a long way to visit."

Mr. Black stepped forward and Holt held up his hand. "Not yet Joe. The time has to be right. We can't rush things."

They walked to a elevated long house and climbed the steps. It was about twenty feet long and ten feet wide. The thatched roof was suspended on massive teak poles. Some of the poles had carvings of jungle creatures.

"This house is yours while you visit." Sangh said.

An old women brought a stone pot of strong green tea. When she neared Holt she wrinkled her nose. The men got their canteen cups and scooped out the tea. They sat in a circle around Sangh and Holt.

Holt sipped the scalding tea. He dug into his rucksack and got two packets of sugar.

"Sugar! I remember sugar. Unfortunately sugar is a luxury that we don't have," Sangh said.

Holt handed him several packets. "If you want sugar, I can get you sugar."

"Americans are always so generous, but they provide things we cannot afford."

"Sangh, your English has improved."

"I always could speak good English but sometimes it is better not to let everyone know."

Holt laughed. "I agree with you." He looked at the Montagnard. "Sangh, my friend, I missed you."

"And I, you,"

Holt could see Tuna and Gator fidgeting.

"Perhaps my men could get settled and we could talk."

"That would be good." Sangh called one of the women over and spoke to her. "She will take your men to the house. Have you brought a change of clothes?"

"If you remember your days with the team you know we carry only the essentials. Clean clothes are a luxury."

"She will bring some clothes to change into and will wash your fatigues."

"Mr. Black, if you would care to stay." When the men left, Holt introduced Joe.

"I've brought Mr. Black all this way to talk to you. He has an interesting proposal for you to consider. I'll leave you two to get acquainted. Sangh, my friend, we'll talk later."

Holt walked back to the long house. Thick woven mats were placed on the floor for the men to sleep on. A young women came up the stairs.

"You come with me. You smell bad. You come and wash. I clean clothes," she said. She held a bundle of native clothing.

The men followed her down behind the house. There they found a large barrel filled with rain water and a smaller plastic bucket.

"You wash here. Give me clothes."

The team stripped down and handed their fatigues to the girl who modestly turned her head away from their naked bodies.

The first thing that had to accepted in the army was the lack of privacy. In the stateside barracks, toilets were placed in a row against one wall with no partitions between them. Showers were communal. Modesty was an illusion.

Each man took his turn washing while a second man rinsed him off using the smaller bucket.

Off to the side a group of young girls stood giggling and talking.

"Why is that girl laughing at us?" Gator asked.

"Not us, you. That baby San says you have the dick of a newborn baby," Holt said.

"Gator grabbed his crotch. "She's laughing at this raging python of love? She's probably in awe."

"More like the worm of affection," said Jenkins blandly.

After washing, the men dressed in the clothing provided. A collection of sarongs and loin cloths. Holt choose a loin cloth for himself and tied it around his waist with a rawhide cord.

"Give me your towels; they are rancid. Maybe she'll wash these too," Holt said.

The girl collected the towels and her and her friends disappeared into the trees.

"There must be a stream or something down there," Gino said.

Back at the long house the men sat on the steps smoking and drinking coffee or Kool Aid.

"How long will we be here, Sarge?" Gator asked.

"A day or two, no more than that. We finished our part, we got Joe to Sangh. We're done here. If Black wants to hang around that's up to him. How is everyone fixed for food?"

They all said they had three meals at most.

"You don't think they'll feed us?" asked Doc.

"That's up to you. Sangh knows I won't eat their gook food. I'll eat rice and vegetables but I won't touch their mysterious, bush meat. It could be anything they catch in the jungle. Fucking snakes, lizards, or monkeys. If you do eat it, don't ask what it is."

"I thought you liked the Montagnards?" Gator said.

"I do. I love them like brothers. But you have to remember they live a simple, very primitive life."

"You know, I just remembered we didn't bury that second Nung.

Where do you think all those arrows came from?" Tuna said.

"We were probably surrounded by those skull fucks. That's why we ain't walking back. I ain't saying those woods are enchanted or anything like that but I ain't in any hurry to go back into them," Holt said. "Sangh once told me there were these primitive tribes that lived in these mountains that were headhunters and cannibals. I thought he was bullshitting me but now I believe him."

"What about Thing One? You think he'll make it back?"

"I doubt he got more than fifty feet before they killed him," Holt said lighting another cigarette.

"Look, here comes Mr. Black," Jenkins said.

Black walked up to them. "What the fuck is going on? Why are you dressed like that?"

"We decided we're going to stay with the Yards. Gator already got himself a girl. How old is she Gator, that girl you were flirting with? Twelve? Thirteen?" Holt said.

"Jesus, Sarge, don't even kid around like that. People will think I'm a podiatrist. I ain't like that."

"Gator, do you even know what a podiatrist is?"

"Yeah, a guy that diddles little kids."

Holt turned to Black "And he's an actual Fort Bragg trained Green Beret. A shining example of the Florida school system. What did Sangh say?"

"So far he agreeable. He wants to speak to his people and to you. When you meet with him don't fuck everything up."

"I ain't going to lie to him. If he asks questions I'm going to tell him the truth."

"I'm alright with that. I didn't lie to him. I gave him the photos of the development; he's impressed. He's going to show them around to the elders. We'll wait and see what he says."

"How long you think we'll be here?"

"Two, three days. I might stay longer," Black said.

"In that case we'll need to get resupplied. We're running low on food. You can go native if you want, but not us."

"Fine, that can be arranged. Sergeant, when's your next scheduled contact with Over Watch?" Black asked Gino.

"1800 hours."

"Put together a supply list and I'll call it in. I'll be staying with Sangh tonight. He wants me to meet with the tribal elders. I'll see you men later."

Holt met with Sangh the next day. They walked down to the river.

"This is a beautiful spot. How long did it take you to build all this?" Holt asked.

"It was started before I got here. it is a very difficult life," Sangh said. There was a sadness to his voice. "The other village you spotted. About one year past, the VC came and the people fled south."

"VC? Do you mean the North Vietnamese or the Pathet Lao?" "Same, same. That's why I was asked to come. I help organize village people. Train to fight. But these people no can fight against VC; I know that. Across river many trails the VC use to go south. One day they will cross the river and we be found. Many of us will die. Many will be taken as slaves. Your friend Mr. Black say to go with and we be safe."

"He's not my friend," Holt said. "I work for him?" "Can he be trusted. Does he say the truth?"

"The village you saw in the pictures is real. I have seen it. There are houses, schools and hospitals. Your people will be safe there. But you need to work for your safety. Thailand wants you to keep out the VC. You will still be fighting."

"I've fought my whole life. I know nothing but war. Here, we cannot grow enough food to feed ourselves. We cannot hunt enough. Animals all gone. We only safe here when we hide. Over time, we will starve and be forced to move again. If this is going to happen, why not go with Joe? He will give my people a better life."

"I see your point. You guys have been screwed over for so many years I am surprised you still trust anyone."

"We have no choice. Sometime, maybe soon, the VC will come here. They want all people under their control."

Holt rubbed his chin and sighed. "Alright, I will tell Mr. Black you agree to move with him. How many people are here?"

"Men, women and children, maybe four hundred and twenty. I tell Black these men are not soldiers. They must be trained to fight."

"Not a problem. He'll be happy to do that."

Holt told Sangh about the skull man who guided them to the valley.

"That jungle to the west contain many spirits. Some good and some bad. Some people go into that jungle and never return. Maybe you meet good spirit who bring you here. Maybe ancestor spirit. Many, many year ago people live there who hunt people and eat them. They believed they could take their strength by killing and eating them. Better we not walk there."

Holt sat with Mr. Black on the steps of the long house. He was smoking a cigarette and drinking coffee.

"I'm glad to see you've come around and support this mission," Joe said.

"My support doesn't matter. Sangh supports it; that's what matters. Now we have to figure out the logistics. Walking out is not an option. They have women, children, and old people. They would never make a thirty day march through that jungle. Is that field big enough for a STOL plane?" "It's big enough but it's not smooth enough. I might be able to get some Chinook helicopters," he said, referring to the large twin rotor cargo helicopters.

"You have access to Chinook's?"

"Not me personally, but Air America has some."

Holt handed Black a piece of paper.

"I've done some calculations figuring you would have to use Chinook's. Four hundred and twenty of the little people weighing an average of one hundred pounds each means you could get seventy five on board. That's seven thousand and five pounds. A Chinook can carry ten thousand pounds; that leaves fifteen hundred pounds of personal shit. It would take six helicopters. Flight time would be around three hours, maybe less."

Black studied the paper. "This is good. If we stagger the flights, have two ships land at a time it shouldn't take more than a thirty minutes to load. We could be out of here in ninety minutes. Could you go another day without resupply?"

"That's not a problem. We can supplement our rations with rice and vegetables."

"Then I'll get started right away. If everything works out we leave the day after tomorrow." Black folded the paper and put it in his breast pocket. "Did you know Sangh sees you as some sort of savior of his people. He says you were destined to be here."

"That's all his voodoo shit. Let him believe what he wants. One other thing, the people here are not fighters. Some are but not many. They will have to trained."

"I figured that. Maybe you'd like to stick around and help with that?" "I'll talk with my team and see what they say. It might be a nice change of pace."

"I'm going to contact Over Watch and have him relay our requirements. Tell Sangh to get his people into six groups and brief them. They are to bring only personal items of value to them. No furniture, no livestock, nothing like that. They will be provided everything they need at Lamphang.

The next day Sangh and his Lieutenants grouped the villagers into six loads. Sangh said he would leave twelve men behind. They would make contact with other Bru tribesmen and tell them about the Lamphang settlement. They would guide those that wished to relocate to the settlement.

A flurry of activity consumed the village as the Montagnards packed up their meager possessions. The atmosphere was charged with excitement. Holt toured the village with Sangh. Old men and women wanted to touch Holt and thank him. The children laughed and played around them as they walked through the village.

"I'm happy for your people Sangh," Holt said.

"Yes. I think this will be good for them. I pray that it will be," Sangh said. "I sent out patrols last night and this morning. No VC anywhere."

"That's good. So, you have everything set here?"

"Yes, all good. We be ready at dawn, tomorrow. What happen here when we gone?"

"I asked Mr. Black that same question. He says he may have use for this place in the future."

"Mr. Black, he is a good man?"

"That's hard to say. He has good intentions, but all men start off with good intentions. We'll have to wait and see."

"You are a good man, Trung Si."

"I'd like to think so, but… America had the best intentions when it came to Vietnam. It didn't work out quite as planned."

At 0630 the first two, flat black, unmarked Chinook's landed. The villagers boarded in an orderly manner. The load master, a burly Thai in civilian clothes directed the old men and women and children to the web seating along the walls of the helicopter. The younger men and women sat on the metal floor in the center of the cargo bay. All sat quietly, wide eyed, clutching bundles of clothes, photos, pots, and pans. The helicopter vibrated violently as it left the ground. It gained altitude and turned west towards Thailand. This was repeated twice more until the village was empty. Holt and his team, Joe, and Sangh were on the last helicopter.

Sangh and Holt looked out the porthole window at the jungle below. Sangh's eyes misted.

Holt put his hand on his friends shoulder.

"No need to be sad. This is a new beginning for you. A new story to written for you and your people."

Made in United States
North Haven, CT
05 January 2024

47110790R00243